Nocturne

Also by the Author

The Beyond the Tales Quartet

The Wanderers

The Storyteller and Her Sisters

The People the Fairies Forget

The Lioness and the Spellspinners

Contributing Author

The Servants and the Beast

After the Sparkles Settled

The Phantom's Story Continues:

Book Two: Accompaniment

Book Three: Dawn Melody

Nocturne

The Guardian of the Opera

Book One

Cheryl Mahoney

Stonehenge Circle Press

Stonehenge Circle Press

ISBN-13: 978-1-68012-636-5

ISBN-10: 1-68012-636-9

First Edition

Cover images courtesy of Master1305/Shutterstock (ballerina) and pio3/Shutterstock (masked man). Cover design by Cheryl Mahoney.

This book is a work of fiction. Resemblance to any persons living or dead is coincidental, with the exception of Charles Garnier, who is used fictitiously. His Opera is a real place in Paris, but it too has been fictionalized. Box Five is real, but the author can make no guarantees about what's located on the other side of the underground lake.

Dedication

For Tim

You are not my Phantom.
You're even better.

Chapter One

S ometimes I believe the course of my life was set because I got
lost one day when I was twelve years old. I got lost often that
year, but only once that mattered.

I had first come to the Opera Garnier only three days before, and
I defy anyone to learn that labyrinth of rooms and passages so quickly.
It didn't help being a girl from a small village, come to Paris with my
mother just a week earlier. The city was bewildering, unimaginably
bigger than my little village of Leclair. And the Opera was the heart
and center of Paris, stranger and wilder and even more confusing.

I was supposed to be on my way to ballet practice. I was a *petit
rat*, the lowest tier of society among the Opera's performers. Madame
Thibault the ballet mistress presided over us, and she did not tolerate
tardiness. I didn't want to be late. I desperately *wanted* to be at ballet
practice—but I was lost.

Some wrong turn mixed me up somewhere, and from there I
could only fly through the maze like a small ghost, unable to find the
way back to my intended path. The Opera held too many similar
corridors, with their polished marble floors, gilt paneled walls, and long
arrays of mirrors. No space in the Opera was plain or generic, until the
dizzying amount of detail, the carvings and the gold designs and the

patterned grates overwhelmed me, so that I couldn't pick out one familiar note in the crashing, thundering symphony of it all.

It felt equally impossible to ask for directions from anyone I passed, the looming scenechangers with gap-toothed grins or the elegant sopranos with their noses in the air. By the time I might have built up enough reckless courage to speak to someone, no one was left. I had got below ground level, probably not very far, but low enough for the halls to be deserted, low enough for it to feel cool despite the summer warmth above. I'd left behind the human smells of the upper corridors, the grease paint, perfume and cigar smoke. Down here the air smelled damp, reminding me of the fabled lake said to be even farther down. In stark and jarring contrast, these walls were plain, white-washed stone, unevenly lit by flickering gas lamps.

When I came to a bleak and empty dead-end, I gave up. I slid down to sit against the cold stone wall, one arm around my ankles and forehead against my knees. With my other hand I held tightly onto my small gold necklace, the barest of comforts in the desolation. My hair fell forward like a golden curtain around my face, blocking out the dismal, silent, baffling corridor. I half-believed that I would never get out, that I would die lost in the depths of the Opera.

Part of me found that the preferable option. To stumble in late to ballet practice would mean facing the ballet mistress' mocking disapproval. She would hate me, the other girls would laugh at me, and my entire life, not to mention dancing career, would be over forever. I'd never earn any money to help Mother afford to stay in Paris, and we'd have to go back to Leclair where nothing would ever happen to me ever again.

So I sat in that dead-end corridor and cried.

"It can't be as bad as all that."

The voice that broke the silence was the most beautiful I had ever heard. Perhaps that was a strange adjective for a male voice, but it was a true one. It was a melodic voice, every syllable flowing smoothly into the next while the pronunciation stayed crisply clear. And it was a kind voice as well, sympathetic with a bracing amount of levity. It was a voice I would have had the courage to ask directions from, just a little earlier.

By now, the situation felt too far gone to be salvaged. Ballet practice would start within minutes; I couldn't imagine getting there in time now even if I knew the way. So I just sobbed out, "I can't find my way to practice and the ballet mistress is going to kill me."

Only then did I lift my head to push my hair back, wipe my eyes and look at the man who had spoken. And then—sob catching in my suddenly tightening throat—*then* I got scared.

The other ballet girls had already taken great delight in telling me about *Le Fantôme*, the Phantom of the Opera, the specter who stalked the corridors, harbinger of death and disaster. I froze, staring at this strange figure so tall above me.

He was wearing the formal, all-black evening clothes the stories had promised. The legend also mentioned hands covered in blood, which his weren't. His eyes weren't the glowing yellow of the tales, but he did wear a molded white mask over the right side of his face in a more mysterious touch, while a broad-brimmed hat cast another layer of shadow.

A mask and evening clothes in the morning were unusual, but we were in an opera house. My instinct that he was the Phantom came from clues harder to define than a mask: a shroud of mystery surrounded him, from the swirling black cloak to the inexplicable way he seemed as much shadow as man, indistinct in the dim light, as though he was so used to blending in that he forgot to stop.

Somehow I thought of the Phantom at once, before he even had time to say, "In that case, I understand why you're upset. There are many people I would rather cross than the ballet mistress."

It was a sympathetic remark, made in that perfect voice, with a faint smile as well. However, my mother had warned me often enough not to trust strange men just because they smiled, and this one was stranger than most. "Who are you?" I gasped out, though I felt horribly sure that I already knew.

He fingered the brim of his hat, and I read thoughtfulness in his stance. "I am a sort of…guardian of the Opera," he said at last, which only confirmed my worst fears. "You seem unfamiliar. Are you new?"

I could think of no answer that felt safe, so I chose the truth and said, "Yes." In a way, everyone was new. The Opera Garnier had opened in January, and this was only June; I couldn't imagine learning every face in six years, let alone a mere six months.

"I see. Old hands have no business getting lost, but when new it is difficult to avoid. I will help you." And he extended one black-gloved hand.

My heart pounded in my chest so loudly he must have heard it, and my fingers tightened, wrapped around my legs. I stared at his hand, unmoving, for so long that he took it back again and said, "Not too new, I see, to have heard of the Phantom."

So it was true, and only more terrifying that he admitted it. I looked up at his green eyes, at that mask, and squeaked, "Are you going to kill me?"

He crouched down, bringing his face nearly to my level, black cloak pooling around him. Closer now, I could see his eyes through the shadows, greener than anyone's I had ever seen. "I will tell you a secret, but you mustn't tell anyone else because it would ruin my reputation. I do not eat girls' hearts. I have never drenched any walls in blood, at least not in this country. I cannot read minds or send nightmares, and—brace yourself, this one will be shocking—I am not actually a skeleton with glowing yellow eyes."

He said it with such perfect solemnity that a giggle escaped me in spite of myself. It may have been slightly hysterical.

He nodded once. "I swear on Mozart, Beethoven, and Stradivari that if you come with me, you will reach ballet practice unharmed."

When he extended his hand again, I took it. Even though I knew it was probably just a trick of voice, I was obscurely reassured by the vow—and I was also acutely conscious that he could kill me whether I went voluntarily or not.

His fingers closed around mine and he rose to his feet, drawing me up. For a supposed ghost, he had a warm and solid hand.

"One story that is true—I walk through walls." He reached out to the wall behind me, and I turned my head in time to see a panel pivot out, revealing a dark space behind it. How many doors like that existed in the Opera, if one had happened to be right next to me all along?

He waved his hand through the air, a candle appearing between his thumb and forefinger. He lifted the candle and blew lightly over it.

I was still noticing that he was a ghost who could breathe when the candle crackled to life with flame.

"How did you do that?" I asked, eyes widening.

His half-smile broadened. "Magic." He stepped through the opening, candle illuminating a narrow tunnel of bare stones and wooden cross beams, more a space between walls than a proper passage.

Following him was either the bravest or most foolish thing I had ever done.

The Phantom guided me through endless turns and up a multitude of tight curved steps, the candle seeming to cast as much shadow as light. At first I walked stiffly, spine tingling with terrors, but slowly my breathing began to steady and my heartbeat to settle down, as we kept walking and he kept up a pleasant, if mostly one-sided, conversation.

He told me that the ballet mistress, though fearsome, had never actually murdered anyone. He advised me to stay away from the cellars, and if I got lost in the future I should keep going upstairs, never down. Some time when I wasn't lost, I should go up to the roof to see the excellent view. He also told me I was not to worry if the ballet girls weren't friendly at first, and I was never to feel that their opinion defined who I was, a statement that at the time seemed absurd and yet became remarkably comforting in later days.

I peeked at him when I dared, though with the shadows around us, the shadows cast by his hat, it was hard to see even his unmasked features. I thought he maintained a friendly expression throughout, rarely looking at me, focusing instead on the path ahead. I couldn't hazard much of a guess at his age. No gray hair or stooped shoulders, definitely not an old man—but also definitely belonging to the foreign realm of mature adults that any people at least ten years older than me seemed to inhabit.

I had little time to contemplate. That dark walk didn't last more than five minutes, though I would spend far more time remembering it. That day, he was soon reaching out to another wall. A movement of his fingers and a panel slid to the left. Beyond it, I could see a brightly-lit hallway, empty of people, full of the Opera's characteristic decorations.

"Turn left, go right at the first intersection, and you should be just in time for ballet practice," he said, handing me over the threshold.

I stepped out into the light, flexing my newly-released fingers. For feeling so reluctant to follow, I now felt strangely adrift to be sent back on my own. I hesitated, looked back at him in the shadows. "Thank you." It felt inadequate.

He touched the brim of his hat in acknowledgement, stepped back a pace and vanished into the darkness. The wall slid shut, looking no different from every other panel in the corridor, as if it had never existed. As if he had never existed.

I tentatively reached out and touched the wall, patterned in pale blue with generous gold molding. Nothing moved, and I couldn't even see a seam amidst the intricate design. I drew my hand back and shook my head, fuzzy, as though I'd just woken out of a remarkably vivid and extraordinary dream.

Here in the waking world, I still had to get to ballet practice, with no minutes to spare. At that thought I dashed off down the hall, spun right at the intersection, and arrived breathless at the mirrored practice room just ahead of my time.

The ballet mistress looked down her narrow nose at me as I came in the door. "Do save some breath for dancing, Mademoiselle Giry."

But that was nothing; that was harmless. I was on time to take my position at the barre and she wasn't angry with me, and besides—I had met the Phantom of the Opera and lived to tell the tale. In the afterglow of that, even Madame Thibault didn't seem so terrifying.

He waited until the rapid beat of her footsteps faded around the corner, then turned to make his way through the narrow passage towards the nearest descending staircase.

He didn't often intervene so directly. It wasn't safe. But he found it hard to consider a crying little girl dangerous. She was small and alone. Before she lifted her head, he had thought she was even younger than she was. Helping her had seemed harmless enough—even amusing, to show off that candle trick. Mere sleight-of-hand, but enough to impress a Persian Sultana, and certainly good enough for a little ballet girl.

Nothing was ever unmixed though, and for all he had found the encounter pleasant, it hadn't been without a pang. He hadn't liked hearing the fear in her voice. Surprising, when it was exactly what he wanted, what he had spent these past months carefully composing.

He needed the fear. He needed the Opera Company to think that *he* was the dangerous one, so it wouldn't occur to them that they, with their numbers and their confidence and their ability to cooperate, were the true dangers, the ones capable of hounding and harrying and hunting down the outcast in their midst.

He ran his fingertips along the rough wall of the passage, mere inches from the busy life on the other side.

Any attack would be more complicated than a raging mob with pikes; France was a civilized country, outside of her sporadic revolutions. But the result would be the same. The guillotine, or even worse—a cage. He was guilty of the crime of being different, the world had convicted him at birth, and he had ample precedent to suggest how they would sentence him.

But not while he possessed the Opera Garnier. Not while he was the Phantom of the Opera, stalking as ruler through its hidden passages, shadowed vaults and lofty catwalks. They would never catch him. They would never cage him.

Not again.

He would do whatever was necessary to ensure that. For all their melodramatic complaints, the Opera Company was happy enough to be occupying a haunted theatre—a high-quality ghost lent a certain prestige—and if Monsieur Poligny the manager was not so happy about paying a salary to a ghost, well…the man should have chosen more wisely than to marry a woman with his wife's background. The Opera Ghost had recently obtained some very interesting information, and a little judicious blackmail should resolve any further issues with the management.

As for the little blonde girl, likely it would turn out for the best with her in the end. The ballet dancers and chorus girls loved telling tales about the Ghost, and they much preferred blood-curdling horror stories to ones about a helpful specter. She would be absorbed back into the anonymous crowd of little dancers, all much alike. It had been merely an educated guess that she was new—he didn't really know every face, at least not yet. By the time she was telling the adventure to a dozen giggling friends, it would be about how the terrifying Phantom had nearly abducted her and she'd barely escaped with her life. He wouldn't waste his time watching that conversation. He knew that was how it would go.

And it was better that way.

When ballet practice ended, I hurried out to meet my mother on the front steps of the Opera. It was always like stepping out of one world and into another, leaving behind the music and the endless elegant intricacy of the Opera, for the bustling chaos of the Parisian street.

I ran down the broad stone steps and jumped the last three. "Mother, you'll never guess! The most amazing thing happened!"

She smiled, calm in the face of my exuberance, eyebrows merely rising in query. "Ballet class was good?"

"Oh, ballet class," I said, dismissing it entirely. "No, it was before that. You'll *never* guess!"

She drew my arm through hers and we started down the Boulevard des Capucines towards home, threading amongst the other walkers and staying well away from the carriages with their stamping horses. Mother had just finished her work too, as one of the Opera's boxkeepers, and neither of us would be needed again until that evening's performance. I had been wide-eyed and eager to look at everything around us for the few days we had been here, all the gleaming carriages and the people in their fine clothes and so many, many shops. Today, I had no eyes for any of it, intent on my story.

"Perhaps you had better just tell me what happened, Little Meg," Mother suggested.

I leaned in closer and in an exhilarated undertone announced, "I met the Phantom! It was the absolutely most thrilling thing that's ever happened to me!" The length of ballet practice had given me plenty of time to disregard how frightening it had been while it was going on.

"Oh yes, I've heard of the local ghost," she said with a half-smile. "Were there strange shadows or billowing curtains?"

I wasn't too excited to notice that I wasn't being taken seriously. I tugged on her arm impatiently. "No, you don't understand, I really *met* him. He's real and I talked to him."

She turned to look at me, smile disappearing and a furrow coming to her brow. "What do you mean he's real? You met someone claiming to be the Phantom?"

I knew that tone. I wanted her to believe me, but not to go off in *that* direction. I rolled my eyes and sighed. "Oh Mother, *really*. Don't be upset. He's nice." He had said not to tell anyone that—but of course he couldn't mean *Mother*. And surely that business about blood on the walls was just a joke. "I got so lost looking for ballet practice, and no one was around to ask for help and I thought I'd be lost forever and die and be dismissed, but then he helped me find the practice room and I wasn't even late after all."

The furrow was only growing deeper. "Wait. You were alone? And you met a strange man—"

"No, that's not—I mean, yes, but he wasn't strange—well, he *was* strange, but not the way the stories say. They're all wrong, he's not frightening, and he's not a skeleton or anything. I don't think he's even a ghost! I mean, his hand was solid just like everyone else."

She had her hand on my arm still and her fingers tightened. "He touched you?"

"My hand." I raised my free hand, waved the fingers. "Honestly, Mother, stop looking so worried. Nothing awful happened."

Her voice was even, but with the tightness that I knew meant she was upset. "I have told you, we are not in Leclair anymore where you know everyone. There is no telling who you might meet and you must be careful and—"

"And I *know* all that." Sometimes she treated me like such a child, not with the respect my twelve years deserved. "Nothing happened, Mother. He wasn't going to hurt me." I hadn't been sure of that myself at the time, something I found more convenient to ignore just then.

She stopped walking, turned me towards her to stare into my eyes. "You're sure that nothing happened?"

I exhaled in a sigh that fluttered my bangs. "Yes, Mother."

"And if anyone ever does hurt you—*anyone*, ever—I want you to tell me. Understand?"

"I *know*." I looked at Mother's face at this newly close-range, seeing the faint lines at the corners of her eyes and between her brows, the threads of gray in her dark hair. I decided the Phantom was probably younger than Mother. Not vastly younger, but some. I wriggled my arm out of her tight grasp, seized her hand, and started off down the boulevard again. We were about to pass a lovely bakery, and a bookseller's stall was just ahead. "You don't have to worry about the Phantom."

"Hmm." The worried lines in her forehead faded but didn't entirely disappear. "So tell me about this man claiming to be the Phantom."

"Not claiming to be," I corrected, sparing just a glance for the pastries on display as we went by the bakery's window. "He *was* the Phantom."

"If he wasn't a skeleton or any of the rest, how do you know?"

Cocking my head to the side, I gave that serious consideration. It hadn't occurred to me to doubt it once he said it, and the question still seemed only faintly relevant. I had just…known. Anyone who met him would know. He had an air about him, mysterious and shadowy and entirely unlike anyone else. Someone like that wouldn't bother pretending to a false identity.

All that was hard to explain, though, and I found an easier answer. "He walked through a wall. And he lit a candle with magic!"

Maybe the very absurdity of it reassured her. All she said was, "Of course he did. Quite the enchanted figure, your Phantom."

I rolled my eyes again. "He's not *my* Phantom, Mother." I gave up the business of explaining as hopeless. Obviously there were some things one couldn't expect a parent to understand. Perhaps my sister—but I put that thought aside quickly.

Excerpt from the Notebook of Jean Mifroid, Lieutenant of Police

14 June, 1875

M. Poligny of the Opera dropped complaints today re: trespasser. Claims all a mix-up. V. disappointing—most interesting case I had. Probably just nonsense to begin with. In absence of victim pressing charges, have closed case.

Chapter Two

T he Phantom of the Opera was a popular topic among the corps de
ballet, and though I was still too new and too shy to bring him up
myself, it didn't take many days before they were on that subject
without my help. The Ghost next came under discussion during a break
in ballet practice. All us younger dancers were sitting about on the
wooden floor, retying slippers and stretching tight muscles. Madame
Thibault had stepped out of the room, but we were watched over by the
mythic dancers in the ceiling mural, flitting about within their borders
of gold, and by our own reflections in the mirrors covering one long
wall.

After a few stories about ghostly music, glowing faces and walls
dripping with blood, I dared to ask how a newly-built Opera had
managed to acquire a ghost.

"I heard he was one of the workers building the Opera," a tiny
girl named Marie announced. "He was helping to set the statue of
Apollo up on the top, fell off the roof and…" She sketched a swooping
arc with one hand, to land palm-down on the floor. "And now he
haunts the place where he died."

"*I* heard he was a victim of the Commune," another girl
contradicted.

My knuckles, kneading my cramped calf, dug deeper into the muscle. This was the first anyone had mentioned the Commune, a revolution beginning with romantic ideals and ending hideously. Some of these girls must have lived through it, and I had wondered what they had seen—but this story couldn't be right. "The Opera wasn't even built then," I pointed out, with more confidence than I might have had on another subject. I knew the Commune had happened when I was only eight.

The girl with that story shot me a look that was deeply pitying. "Of course it wasn't *finished*. But enough walls were up to keep prisoners here." Her name was Jammes, I suddenly remembered. That was her last name, but she always insisted on using it, because most of the older stars went by last names—like Sorelli, the prima ballerina. I already suspected I didn't like Jammes, and it didn't change my opinion when she added merrily enough, "They say scores of people were massacred in one of the basements. We're lucky we're not crawling with ghosts."

A few of the girls shifted and glanced away. My own breath was coming a little tightly, at the thought of dancing on the site of a massacre, perhaps over the graves of a few of the Commune's thousands of victims. Had any of the other girls lost someone in the Commune's violent end? A brother? A father?

"I heard a much better story than that," Adalisa put in, neatly redirecting the conversation. She was my age but so much more at ease. "A handsome young gentleman was desperately in love with one of the lead ballerinas. When she scorned him, he wasted away with love for her. And in his will...well, you know some of the operas have fake skeletons as props? Sometimes the star ballerinas even dance with them?"

Murmurs and nods of assent all around.

"*Well*, in his will, he left his body to the Opera, so that his skeleton could be used in the dances!"

Shrieks of horror suffused the group, but this was the delighted kind of horror, not the throat-tightening dreadful kind. Adalisa's was universally voted the best story. It gave me a thrill, even though I didn't quite see how it fit into the very short timeline of the building's

existence. How quickly could someone waste away with love anyway?
A fever could be fast.

"Maybe the Opera Ghost didn't die horribly," I ventured, after
everyone had calmed a bit. He had told me not to tell them he was
nice—but who could possibly like having all these awful stories told
about them? "Maybe he was just a musician who loved the Opera
and—"

"All ghosts died horribly," Jammes said in squelching tones.
"That's why they end up as vengeful ghosts."

I plucked up courage born of the conviction that I really *knew*
this—not that that had helped with the Commune discussion—and
persisted. "But maybe he's not vengeful, maybe he just—"

"Oh, are you afraid of the Phantom and want to pretend he's
nice?" Jammes asked, voice sarcastically sweet. "Better be careful in
dark corridors."

I was certain I didn't like Jammes. I gritted my teeth. "It's not
like that at all, I only thought—"

"Wait until you're here a bit longer," Adalisa said, not unkindly.
"You'll see."

I saw enough. I saw the confirming nods and the complete
disinterest in the possibility of a pleasant ghost. The conversation went
on with wild tales about walking skeletons, flickering lights and
crashing scenery, with everything from broken ankles to bad weather
laid at the Opera Ghost's feet.

I remained quiet for the rest of the conversation. Clearly if I told
my Phantom story, it would sound dull and pointless if it was even
believed. Likely as not they'd just laugh at me and say I was making it
up. And I wanted these girls to like me. I wanted to belong in this new
circle I'd so recently joined.

My feelings were bruised on the subject of the Phantom for a
while, but I was soon glad I hadn't said anything more. He had told me
not to, after all. And it was my secret—my delicious, magical secret.
It hadn't been dull or pointless to me. It was a shining moment when
something amazing had happened to me, when I had actually met and
talked to the Opera Ghost. I was still the newest girl among the lowest
rank of the Opera Garnier's performers, with not many adventures in

my history, but I knew something no one else did about the Phantom. It was a comfort, when I made a misstep in a dance or in a conversation, when I went home with tired limbs and aching feet.

I didn't tell my mother about every misstep, but I did tell her the ballet girls' stories about the Phantom that evening, just idle conversation. It may have been a mistake to mention the theory that he was a victim of the Commune.

"That's an interesting story, isn't it?" she said, voice in the carefully neutral tone she used when she was worried that I might be worried. We were in our tiny sitting room, Mother in the only armchair, and she kept her eyes on the ripped stocking she was mending.

"Not particularly, no." I stretched my toes out, using the back of the couch like a barre to practice my *plies*, feeling the tension in my sore calves. "The one about the skeleton was far more dramatic, even if it didn't make much sense."

"Perhaps." She set the stocking down and folded her hands over it in her lap. My confident, stern-faced mother was looking unusually tentative. "It's only—we don't talk about your father very often, but if you ever want to—"

I sighed loudly, looking down at my feet as I did a *demi-plié* from third position. "Just because I mentioned the Commune, that doesn't mean we have to talk about Father. I know you don't like talking about him." It made her uncomfortable, and that made me uncomfortable, because my mother was so rarely rattled about anything. We used to talk about him more—but not now.

"I don't find it easy, no. But all you have to do is ask, if you ever want to. About your father, or about—Gabrielle."

She could never get the name out without that pause, that tightening in her voice. We had not often talked about my younger sister, in the six months since the fever had taken her away at the too young age of nine. Maybe I would have mentioned her more, if not for that pause, or the pained look in Mother's eyes that always came with it.

I didn't look at her now. "All right. But I really wasn't trying to start anything by talking about the Commune." Two more *pliés* without lifting my gaze. "I mean, it's something lots of people in Paris lived through. It doesn't have to be significant every time I mention it."

Thousands of people died when the government put down the Commune; just because Father was one of them, that didn't mean we had to talk about him. Just because he wasn't even from Paris, just because he was idealistic enough to come specifically for the revolution, just because my mother had talked to my uncle in hushed tones for a month before we moved to Paris, wondering if it was best for me, if it would be hard because of my father. It had been come here or stay in Leclair, where the memory of Gabi's loss seemed to permeate the very air, so to Paris we had come.

But we didn't have to talk about either of them.

I peeked at Mother in time to see her nod, and to see that she still had a furrow in her brow. "Are you sure that you didn't hear that story about the Phantom and the Commune before you met him?"

I frowned too, confused now. "I told you, the ballet girls were just talking about it today."

"Because you seemed very drawn to the Phantom, and I thought, if you had heard that story and—"

The pieces clicked together and I wobbled right out of fifth position and had to grab the couch with both hands to avoid falling. "Mother! I *don't* think that the Phantom is Father's ghost!"

"I only meant—"

"It's been four years but I *remember* him. I told you I met the Phantom, saw him, talked to him. He wasn't anything at all like Father, he didn't look like him or sound like him, his hair isn't blond like mine and Gabi's, he's not even old enough—I know that he's not Papa." My voice cracked on the last word and I suddenly had to blink rather hard. My hand crept up to wrap around my necklace, tightly. Besides everything else, if it had been Father's ghost, surely Gabi would have been with him.

Mother's smile was sad. "I know you remember him, Little Meg," she said quietly. "Of course I know that."

Chapter Three

B y the time I'd been at the Opera Garnier for two months, I was
tacitly accepted into the circle of the ballet girls. I was still
hopeful of finding just the right friend, the one who'd pick me out of
the circle, who I'd want as a closer companion. For now though, I was
accepted, if still the new girl. No one else was staring at the scenery as
we sat on the cool marble steps of the Grand Staircase one Saturday
afternoon.

Around me the girls were talking about that morning's practice,
about what would happen at that evening's performance, and I *was*
interested. But I couldn't just ignore our surroundings either, much as I
knew I should be casual about it.

We were on one of the branching halves of the stair, its twin
rising up opposite us, the center of the stair plunging down below. Just
behind me stood two elegant statues swathed in robes, flanking the
entrance to the auditorium where all the wealthy subscribers entered.
Pillars soared up and up all around us, supporting the carved railings on
the balconies above, and regal faces looked down from the corners near
the ceiling.   And everywhere, *everywhere*, intricate carvings and
elaborate designs. The stairs were the plainest part, and even they were

in a dozen shades of marble and designed in delicate curves. How could the other girls disregard all this so completely?

A shrill voice snagged my attention more effectively than the girls had, as it rang out from one level above. "Demands! Always demands! I *will not* stand for this!"

The girls' conversation immediately went silent, as all heads turned towards the voice, coming from the direction of the hall leading to the first level boxes. I could just make out a glimpse of Madame Babineux, storming down the hall in a state of high temper.

Madame Babineux was the boxkeeper for Box Five. And Box Five was the Phantom's box.

I hadn't yet encountered any more tangible evidence of the Opera Ghost. In these early weeks as I tried to find my place, I had hugged my secret close and held onto the hope that, any day, the next exciting scene of the Phantom's opera would unfold.

I wanted to see what Madame Babineux was so upset about— maybe it had nothing to do with the Phantom, but *maybe*—and was relieved to see the other girls rising to their feet. I hardly noticed my sore legs as I hauled myself upright using the marble banister behind me, and darted after the rest of the girls up the stair.

Everyone liked drama, not just the ballet. A cluster of people had already gathered around Madame Babineux, as she harangued forth about unreasonable requests. She might have meant any subscriber. Boxkeepers managed multiple boxes, and the Opera's wealthy patrons could make plenty of demands—drinks and programs and extra tidying up. Mother never complained, but I picked ideas up.

But Madame Babineux was pointing towards the carved wooden door of Box Five. A thrill started up deep in my stomach.

"He always wants everything done before the performance," she snapped. "Has a perfect fit if I so much as touch the door of the box while the show is on. And he's never satisfied with anything!" She was waving about a piece of paper with thick black edgings, and now she flung it onto the tiled floor in punctuation, a creamy blot on the mosaic. "Now *this*. An itemized list of requirements! It's bad enough working for a ghost, but I will not work for a demanding ghost! And a cheap one too—never so much as a *sou* in tip!"

"If you want tips, *do your job*!"

My spine prickled and the crowd fell deadly silent as that voice echoed around the marble hall, everywhere and nowhere at once, rolling and reverberating, threatening and thundering.

Somewhere behind all that booming, I recognized the voice of the man in the mask. His pronunciation was perfect even through the echoes, and his voice boomed the way the deepest notes of the orchestra did, still musical in their thunder.

I knew I wouldn't want that voice yelling at me, but I was equally struck that it must take remarkable skill to make his voice thunder like that. I wondered how he did it. The trick of it could make me jump, but it was so easy to see it was a trick, no more terrifying than a baritone villain in an opera.

But of course, I had met him.

Madame Babineux, who presumably had never met him properly, let out one shriek and fled the hall. A few people went after her while the rest of us hung about until the lack of further events made it apparent the excitement was over. I looked for the discarded letter from the Phantom, but it had disappeared beneath too many feet.

By the next day, everyone knew that Madame Babineux had handed in her resignation, effective immediately. No one seemed to miss her, and I couldn't say her complaints about the Phantom had made me think badly of him. She was perpetually bad-tempered and had always made a point of complaining about constantly having to step over ballet girls, just because we were apt to be sitting on the stairs or backstage, usually with legs extended—but we had to stretch, didn't we? I considered that the Phantom had done us all a favor by getting rid of her.

I wondered if Monsieur Poligny the manager would leave Box Five unassigned. Perhaps he wouldn't feel that a ghost really needed someone to dust up after him.

Instead, he went on an absolute campaign to get one of the other boxkeepers to take the Phantom's box on. This went on for a week, as every boxkeeper flatly refused. M. Poligny couldn't fire everyone, but he was looking increasingly harassed. Finally, he called together all the boxkeepers to discuss the matter. I was finished with rehearsal for the day, so I tagged along with Mother. Of course I wanted to see what would happen with the Phantom's box.

I hadn't been in the manager's office before, not even when I was first hired. Managers don't concern themselves with matters like try-outs and interviews for small ballet dancers. It was a simple room compared to the rest of the building, which meant the walls had only a small-print pattern of red and gold diamonds, no murals or gilding. Apart from the impressive wooden carvings on the cabinets and bordering the ceiling, and pillars flanking the wide window looking out on the boulevard, the room bordered on stark. At least compared to the rest of the Opera.

My eyes went naturally to the one portrait hanging on a side wall, a mustached man with a long nose and thick curly hair. I squinted to read the writing at the bottom from across the room: Charles Garnier, Architect.

He didn't *look* like a genius who could construct a magical kingdom, but who could say what kind of a nose someone like that would have, anyway? I was sure I had seen his face before somewhere—and after a moment remembered the silver face in the Grand Foyer, the one tiny spot of that color in a room blazing with gold. Evidently Garnier had left a bit of himself behind in his building.

Monsieur Poligny cleared his throat, drawing my attention back to him where he stood at his enormous wooden desk in front of the group of boxkeepers crowded into the room. He twisted his hands together and smiled unconvincingly. "As you all know, we're having a small bother about Box Five."

"The Phantom's box, you mean," one woman muttered.

M. Poligny's smile turned more sickly. "Well, yes. But really, that's no reason to treat it differently. The Opera Ghost is simply another patron, in a sense. And you're all so very good at handling, er, difficult patrons. I'm sure one of you would be happy to handle our Ghost…"

No one moved, unless you count me. I was trying to be unobtrusive, not really belonging here, but I had to tug on Mother's sleeve at an opening like that. She ignored me.

M. Poligny looked around unhappily. "Come now, surely you're not all afraid of a, um, voice."

I tugged harder, and Mother finally turned to me. I gave her my best big-eyed imploring look. We had already talked about this—repeatedly—and I knew she knew what I wanted. She shook her head.

M. Poligny was growing desperate. "There's an extra hundred francs a year in it for someone!"

This produced a shuffling of feet, but still no volunteers. They had to want the money—a boxkeeper's salary was not luxurious, and most of these women had children. I had picked that information up already too. Did they really think the Ghost was so terrifying? Mother at least had to know better.

"Don't you trust me?" I hissed. It was so obvious, so simple, so clear!

Mother looked at me for a long moment, then sighed. She slipped her hand into mine, squeezed once, and turned back to M. Poligny. "I'll take Box Five."

Every head turned to look at her, and M. Poligny exhaled a gusty breath in relief. "Excellent, excellent! A very wise decision, Madame…ah…"

"Giry," Mother said quietly. "I've been with the Opera two months."

"Of course, of course!" M. Poligny beamed at her. "Excellent, Madame Giry, excellent!"

Mother was solemn as we left the meeting. I was delighted. "You'll see, it'll all be fine!" I promised, skipping along beside her, my footsteps tapping almost like the beat of drums. "Madame Babineux was an awful old hag—"

"Little Meg," she admonished. "Be polite."

"All right, I shouldn't have said it, but she *was*. Anyway, of course the Phantom didn't like her. That's not his fault. So you'll see, it'll be fine having Box Five."

"Perhaps."

"It's all so thrilling," I said breathlessly.

And as if on cue, an envelope dropped down from the ceiling above us, tumbled end over end and landed on the floor at Mother's feet. Perhaps it *was* on cue. I'd come to learn that the Phantom was good at that sort of thing.

We both looked up, toward the elaborately decorated but entirely unrevealing ceiling. No one was crouched among the gilt designs or hidden among the dancing figures. Not that I imagined he would be so unsubtle.

Mother shook her head slightly, then bent down to retrieve the letter. Like Madame Babineux's, it was a heavy cream paper with wide black borders. Mother opened the envelope, and drew out a paper of the same design from within.

I bounced up onto my toes, peered over her shoulder at the brief message. Most of the ballet girls couldn't read, but I had learned in the village school back home in Leclair. It was an invaluable skill for satisfying my frequent curiosity. My eyes swam over the handwriting, full of elaborate swoops in vivid red ink. I blinked and focused on the first words.

Madame –

If you are to take over the handling of my box, it is best that we establish an understanding from the beginning. My requests are simple but absolute, and are as follows:

   ✘ *A new program for each evening performance, every performance without exception.*

   ✘ *A box of chocolates for every opening night.*

   ✘ *The drapes of Box Five are to be closed no less than twenty minutes prior to the opening of the performance.*

   ✘ *Most important of all, no one is to enter Box Five from the opening act to the closing curtain call. I must insist upon this.*

   ✘ *That the box shall be kept clean and in order should go without saying.*

If all is handled as I require, I trust we shall have a long and satisfactory association.

      With kind regards,

O. G.

"Evidently the Opera Ghost has a taste for chocolate," Mother remarked dryly, folding up the letter.

"*Thrilling*," I sighed.

Of course I was hoping that, if my mother was the Phantom's boxkeeper, I'd get to meet him again, that I'd get a special view of his story, or even a part in it.

It didn't work out that way. Once in a while he spoke to Mother, but always as merely a voice in the box, and even that was rare. Mother said that whenever he did speak, he was always a polite voice.

He was also generous. Madame Babineux had accused the Phantom of being cheap, but he had countered that she didn't do her work. He left tips for Mother in Box Five, small at first but rising, steadying off at a generous level. If he missed several performances, he always left a larger tip when he returned. Mother didn't talk much to me about money, but I wasn't blind. We had never gone hungry, but now meat began appearing at our table more often and Mother mended my clothes fewer times before replacing them. I also noticed Mother's forehead furrowed less when she looked at the budget, after she took over the Phantom's box.

She never actually *said* that I was right when I wanted her to take on the job. But clearly I was, and that was some consolation, as I learned that a generous ghost is not the same as a sociable one.

The Phantom sat tucked into a space in the carved molding above the Imperial Box, one knee drawn up and the other foot dangling, and listened to the silence of the empty theater. Silent but for the echoes of music embedded within the walls. Though the Opera had been open only a few months, already he could begin to feel the layers of music blanketing the building, as though wisps of the best performances were captured and held within the Opera's heart. Tonight's performance was only the latest, but it was the one on his mind.

He had reservations about the ballet number in Act Four this evening, but the orchestra had delivered an eminently satisfactory performance. He wouldn't want them to grow too sure of themselves, but perhaps a brief note of approval was in order. Restrained, not too effusive, but approving.

The gentle quiet broke with discordant sounds from the hallway beyond the first-tier boxes. Heavy footsteps, raucous laughter, two male voices pitched too loudly and slurring their words.

He rubbed the unmasked side of his nose, felt his face settle into lines that once upon a time would have made the Opera's construction crew tremble. They had learned not to cross the reclusive, masked foreman.

He liked to think he was as much in favor of a good time as the next man, but when that 'good time' reached the point where one could no longer conduct oneself with decorum, then it was time to conduct oneself out of the Opera Garnier.

This was the third time this week that guests had overstepped the bounds of appropriate behavior. Poligny would have a scathing note on his desk within the hour. If he didn't take action very soon, the Phantom would.

For the moment, he would continue his meditations elsewhere. He rose to his feet, balancing on the narrow platform within the carved decorations, and reached up towards a hidden door above him. Then a new note entered the cacophony outside the auditorium. A woman's voice. Her words were obscured by the noise from the men, but her tone came through. Angry on the surface, and yet—he cocked his head, listened a few seconds more, and nodded. Under the anger, fear. And the men's voices had *that* particular pitch to them, the taunting, laughing tone of the powerful who had found someone to make sport of.

The Phantom slipped down the wide pillar separating the Imperial Box from Box Five, and swung himself into the smaller space. By the time his feet hit the floor, he had identified the woman's voice: Madame Giry, his recently-appointed boxkeeper. He would not generally let himself be seen in a situation like this—wonders could be done with a thundering voice—but her identity changed his options.

She was not a stupid woman, and likely had suspicions about the supernatural quality of a ghost who required a program and ate chocolate. So far, she had made no alarming movements as a result. He had no intention of *trusting* her, of course, but he was willing to take a calculated risk for the sake of his own convenience. He wanted to continue his habits regarding Box Five, and if that meant letting one woman suspect that he wasn't precisely supernatural…no one would listen to her anyway.

By the time he was across the box with his hand on the door, he had chosen amongst the possible courses of action.

He was also motivated by a strong desire to get his hands around the throats of the obnoxious cretins. If all went well, those two would end up with a story they would have no desire to tell to anyone.

He slipped out of the door to Box Five and let it slam behind him. It was the only warning he gave. For gentlemen, he would have issued a challenge. Pigs did not deserve that courtesy.

A few steps across the corridor to seize one man by the collar, yank him back from the cornered boxkeeper, swing him around and connect a fist against his jaw. The Phantom ducked easily beneath a clumsy punch from the other man and kicked out with one boot, hitting just above the knee, likely snapping tendons. Both men howled. Pathetic.

Madame Giry's bootheels clicked against the marble floor, until she backed into the opposite wall with a bump.

The Phantom still had one man by the collar. He hauled the other one up by the same method and shook them both with calm efficiency until they were too rattled to keep drawing breath for more shouts. "You have created enough disturbance for one night," he hissed.

They really had nothing better to do in the evening than harass a boxkeeper? Poligny would certainly be receiving a note about the kind of drunken riffraff he was allowing into the Opera.

"This is an opera house," he went on, with another shake. "Not a brothel. Not an ale house. Not a dance hall. An *opera house*. You will henceforth take your custom to more appropriate places."

One of the men inhaled wheezily. "Y'can't treat m'like this. D'you know who I am?"

Wealthy riffraff, apparently, which mattered to him not at all. "Do you know who I am? *I* am the Phantom. And you are not welcome in *my* Opera!"

With perfect theatric timing the door to Box Five swung open with the slightest of breezes, apparently of its own accord. He hauled both feebly-struggling men through the box, between the rows of seats to the edge, and pitched them out over the balcony. They landed with satisfying thuds on the floor of the auditorium three meters below.

"Count yourselves lucky I didn't throw you from the upper tier. I won't be so restrained if I see you here again."

The only answer was indistinct moaning.

He shook his head in disgust and turned away, back towards the interior of the box.

"Monsieur Phantom," Madame Giry said from the doorway. Two words gave little opportunity for tone, but she sounded—perhaps taken aback, but not afraid. Grateful? That would likely be fooling himself.

He merely nodded once in acknowledgment. "Madame Giry." He turned again to the edge of the box. She might not be hostile, but if she was looking into the box, he would still need to leave by another direction. He stepped onto the low banister, and leapt up to scale the elaborately carved wall. He always knew multiple exits.

It kept him alive.

Chapter Four

W hen I was thirteen, La Carlotta, the famed Italian singer, came to the Opera Garnier for a guest appearance, which turned into an extended visit, which turned into a permanent position as the Company's lead soprano. She was loud and dramatic, on-stage and off. Her demands and her quirks kept the Opera's gossips chattering, and kept anyone who had to deal with her running—but she sold tickets.

The Phantom was never what you might call enthusiastic about Carlotta, and she threw a screaming fit the first time one of his notes described her as "adequate." After that, as far as I could tell they mostly ignored each other. The Phantom gave extensive advice in his letters—to the ballet, to the chorus, to the other solo singers. The absence of recommendations for La Carlotta was noticeable.

We girls of the ballet and the chorus tended to cluster around the stars, and Jammes, who had not grown any pleasanter in the past year, swiftly crossed chorus/ballet lines to defect to the court of Carlotta. I was not sorry to see her go; we still saw each other in our dance work, but I did not miss her sarcastic presence in my circle of friends. Carlotta struck me as too high-strung to be a comfortable queen, and I was happier in my minor position in the court surrounding Sorelli, the prima ballerina.

Sorelli was grand enough for a large dressing room of her own, made cozier by soft peach walls and a comfortable clutter of ballet costumes. A half-dozen of us younger girls often visited before we were needed for a performance. We were *not* welcome after the show, when her gentleman friend, Comte Philippe de Chagny, came to call.

Before performances, we'd crowd onto Sorelli's couch to fix one another's hair and tell tales and beg for ballet advice, while Sorelli's maid helped her with her costume and makeup. It was on one such evening when the pleasant proceedings were interrupted by an intruder.

Sorelli, halfway through her makeup, gave a sudden scream and leapt away from her dressing table. Conversation died as everyone looked up in surprise. Sorelli pointed with a shaking finger, apparently towards her own reflection—until gazes tracked downward and the actual cause became clear.

I doubt an elephant in the room could have created much more consternation than one little spider. Well, big spider, as spiders go, but still pretty small on the grand scale of things. Several girls flew off into the corners of the dressing room with shrieks of horror, Sorelli's maid among them. Three of us stayed huddled on the couch. I pulled my bare feet up and felt none too eager to get close to it myself.

The spider posed on Sorelli's dressing table, skittered this way and that, and seemed to be looking at us.

"Get rid of it!" Sorelli demanded of the room at large.

"Somebody kill it," Francesca said. "Squish it or something!"

"No, don't do that," Sorelli countermanded, "I don't want a smashed spider smeared on my table!"

"We could take it outside," I ventured.

A momentary silence as this was considered.

"But we'd have to *pick it up*," Marie said, as though nothing in the world could be more disgusting.

I regarded the spider. It had a bulbous brown body and eight jointed legs, and while it probably wasn't poisonous, how could I know? I told myself that it was perfectly silly for a girl from a farming village to be scared of a spider. I still didn't move to touch it. "Do you have a glass?" I said at last. "We could trap it."

The spider suddenly made a rapid crawl towards Sorelli's mirror, prompting a renewed chorus of shrieks.

Then the door opened, a man stepped in and the room fell abruptly, deathly silent. He was dark-skinned and thin, tall, with a red fez making his height even more pronounced. I had never seen him this close before, but I knew about him. He was universally called the Persian. Everyone knew him; no one knew why he was always wandering around the Opera Garnier, or why the management permitted it.

The stories about him were almost as sinister as the ones about the Phantom, although they tended more towards curses than pools of blood; I hadn't made up my mind yet whether to believe them. I studied him curiously now, trying to decide if he looked sinister or just intriguing.

Through a thick accent, the Persian said, "I heard cries of distress. Is there a problem?"

No one moved. No one spoke. Everyone just stared, and the girls seemed even more paralyzed with horror now than before.

"There's a spider," Sorelli said at last, pointing one slender finger.

The Persian turned to the dressing table, bent over it to peer at the offending party. "Quite harmless," he pronounced, and scooped the spider up in one palm. I expected him to tighten his hand into a fist, crushing the spider within, but he merely closed his fingers loosely around it.

Without stopping to think I asked, "How can you tell it's harmless?"

His eyes were a liquid brown as he looked at me. I didn't move, froze very still in fact, and could feel the girls on either side of me shrinking away.

"Very few spiders are poisonous," the Persian said at last. "Most have a fearsome appearance, while at heart want only to go about their own business."

I let out a breath, might have let the matter go and ended this fraught exchange—but I wanted to *understand*. "Yes, but how do you tell them apart?" I persisted.

"You must learn about the spider." Then he bowed slightly to the room at large, and retreated out the door, spider still held in one hand.

A collective exhale swept the room.

"Quick, everyone touch iron!" Sorelli said, diving for her dressing table, coming up with an iron key. "We have to ward off the Evil Eye."

"You *talked* to him!" Jeanette and Yvonne said to me in unison, still keeping a distance between us on the couch.

I had made this mistake before. I had let myself be different, and that never helped with finding a comfortable place within the circle of ballet girls. My hand went up to touch my necklace, but I couldn't quite stop myself pointing out, "He didn't seem so terrible." A little unnerving, but not frightening exactly. He was different too. He was from Somewhere Else. And that was fascinating.

"Why do they let him wander loose?" Francesca muttered. "He ought to be in the Anthropological Gardens. I mean, he's a *heathen*. One of those Mohammedans."

"Here," Sorelli said, pushing her iron key into my hand. "Everyone be very careful crossing streets and going down stairs. He may have put a curse on us, and the last thing anyone needs is to break an ankle."

I accepted the key rather than arguing about it. But it seemed to me that all he had done was carry away a spider. And I wondered what Gabi would have made of the mysterious Persian, what stories we might have invented together about him.

Excerpt from the Notebook of Jean Mifroid, Lieutenant of Police

9 May, 1877

Still visiting Opera each nightly round. Not a v. exciting district. Maybe somewhere better with next promotion? Some compensations tho. Shared cigars with a Comte this evening—M. Philippe de Chagny.

Stories still rampant re: Opera Ghost. Have definitely determined mere superstition. No 2 witnesses agree on description, or even on crime. Apparently catch-all explanation for every missed note, lost shoe, minor illness, etc.

The year I was fourteen, I was promoted out of the *petit rats* to be a *premier quadrille*, went to the Anthropological Gardens in the Bois de Boulogne, and had my first kiss. I was excited about all three events, and was only disillusioned by the second.

The promotion was a relief, a little later than the average, though still at a respectable age, and while it was a long, long way from anything like what Sorelli was doing, it did make me eligible to perform in better roles. I knew I had improved as a dancer since I came to the Opera, working hard and growing and reaching for better art, for the ability to make better magic on stage.

The Anthropological Gardens promised to display natives of distant lands and I thought it would be thrilling—but seeing all those people sitting in front of cheap scenery, staring back at the eager crowds, just made me sad instead.

The kiss was in August and wasn't at the Opera, but happened when I was visiting my village of Leclair for a few weeks. I went back to visit our family there every year, for a few weeks in January and in August, when the Opera Company held no performances. It was Mother's idea; she thought I needed to "stay in touch with the real world outside the Opera," or something to that effect. She hadn't proposed it until after she took over the Phantom's box, and I knew his tips were paying for my train tickets. It had been too hard to stay in Leclair after Gabi died, but somehow it was easier going back each time, until I came to enjoy revisiting the place we used to live together.

The boy I kissed was sweet and we both promised to write, but after a couple of letters, we didn't. I shed no tears about it, and I doubted very much that he did either.

When I was fifteen, rumors started floating around the Opera about a mysterious man in a black cloak who hid his face. I hadn't said anything, so evidently someone else, or several someones, had caught glimpses of the man in the mask. I wondered who, and how much they knew and if he had told them anything more than he had told me—but I wasn't truly worried until the stories began connecting the cloaked man to the Opera Ghost. From there it would hardly be a leap to deciding that the Ghost wasn't actually a ghost.

I tried to think of something I could do to help squash the story, help the Phantom keep his proper reputation—but then one afternoon the Phantom handled the matter himself. I was at a full rehearsal in the auditorium, and the huge stage was crowded with the chorus at the back and the ballet in lines closer to the front. All of us stood around waiting, idly practicing pliés and sautés, while La Carlotta discussed her placement in the scene.

That is, if you can use 'discussed' to describe a five minute harangue involving arm-waving and hair-tossing, concluding with the demand, "How can you possibly expect me to stand at the back of the stage where no one will even *see* me?"

Madame Thibault, still reigning dictator of the ballet, was much quieter but no less emphatic. "You cannot stand farther to the front because my girls need room to dance. I see no further point in talking about the matter, Signora."

Carlotta stuck her nose in the air. "It is a very large stage. There would be plenty of space to dance behind me."

"It would have to be a large stage to dance around *her*," a girl near me murmured, and titters ran down our line. Carlotta was what you might call a full-bodied soprano.

Madame Thibault was still staring at Signora Carlotta and now her eyes narrowed, something every ballet girl knew was a dangerous indicator. "No rational person would suggest putting a singer, who is *heard*, in front of dancers who must be *seen*."

"How dare you—"

Every light in the theater, chandelier included, went suddenly out. I'd never seen it that dark; the chandelier normally stayed lit even during performances, casting a glow over the endless rows of red velvet seats, light reflecting back from the gilding on the ceiling and the rows of boxes ranked above the seats. Automatically my hands reached out, searching for something stable in the darkness. My fingertips brushed against a full skirt on one side, a dancer's bare arm on the other, prompting a startled gasp.

"Sorry," I said hastily, drawing my hand back, reaching to hold onto my necklace instead.

Only a second or two ticked by, only a few such exclamations were heard, when a flare of light in the blackness lit up Box Five.

My breath caught in my throat. On the balustrade of the box stood a glowing skeleton. Flames darted like lightning from bone to bone, and dancing fire burned in his eyes. This was no masked man in a cloak, no human in a costume. My brain skittered—an illusion? Or was there a real ghost after all?

Slowly the skeleton raised one hand to point towards Carlotta at center stage, barely visible in the skeleton's light, and then the Phantom's familiar voice rolled and echoed through the darkened auditorium. "Stand at the back, or don't stand on stage at all."

That voice seemed to enter right into my own bones, making me shiver with a kind of delightful creepiness. It could be delightful because clearly it *was* him, surely performing the most magical of illusions. This was better than any opera I'd ever seen.

I took a peek at Carlotta, who stood frozen with terror written across her face, then looked back at the skeleton just in time to see him draw his arm back, curling as though to throw something. He released his hand, sending his fist flying in a ball of flame towards the crowded stage, as all the gas lamps along the front edge flared back to life.

Instantly our lines dissolved into a riot of pushing to get out of the way, and however I felt about the Phantom, I leaped instinctively with the rest. I bumped into one girl, was crashed into by another, and at once a half-dozen of us went down in a tangle of tulle skirts and bare limbs. I rolled away from the worst of the confusion, and looked up in time to see the fireball land on the cleared stage in a burst of smoke that set everyone coughing. When the smoke dissipated, not even a scorch mark remained—and the skeleton had vanished, equally without a trace.

I exhaled. Either the Phantom really was a ghost (unlikely) or the man in the mask was *brilliant*.

Rehearsal was canceled. Carlotta vowed she'd never sing at the Opera Garnier again. She lay prostrate for a week, then returned just when M. Poligny was starting to look at other sopranos. We did eventually put on that production; Carlotta sang from the back without a murmur, and all was well.

Likewise, the stories of the Ghost continued smoothly, once again about skeletons and waves of blood and no more about a cloaked man in a mask, who clearly was far less interesting by comparison.

Most people dated 1878 as the year of the Paris Exposition, the year electric lanterns were installed to light up the Avenue de l'Opera with their near-magical brilliance. I always dated it as the year of the far more magical glowing skeleton.

When I was sixteen, Monsieur Degas the painter sketched me a few times during practice. He was always around the Opera, watching the rehearsals and drawing the girls. I had never known the Phantom to make a comment on him, which meant he had tacit approval. Despite the sketches, he never asked me to come model for a painting, a fact which disappointed more than it surprised me. I wasn't a star, or especially beautiful either. Why should a famous painter single me out?

That same year, I began insisting that people stop calling me *Little* Meg. I'd been called that forever, just because I had the same name as my grandmother. I felt sure I was growing too big for the diminutive now. I never managed to shed it entirely, but for the most part people changed their habits. It took Mother months to adjust. I briefly flirted with the idea of going by my full name, Marguerite, only it seemed such a mouthful.

The year I turned seventeen, Monsieur Poligny departed to be replaced by a new manager, Monsieur Debienne. The Phantom had been quiet for months, hardly more than a story, with no stunts and not even very many letters with recommendations for the performers. Soon after the new manager's arrival the word flew around the Opera Garnier that he had refused to pay the Phantom's salary. And then came letters dropping from catwalks, flickering lights at rehearsals, and renewed stories about faces made of flames.

After nearly a week of hostilities, a new rumor arose—M. Debienne had gone to the police. Everyone else considered this entirely absurd, as the police certainly couldn't do anything about a ghost. I wondered uneasily if they might be able to do something about a man in a mask.

I imagined hordes of police descending on the building. All that actually came was Inspector Mifroid, with his little black notebook, wandering around and asking questions. He wasn't even a new face. I had seen him before, passing through in the evenings. He generally had an expression of amused tolerance, as if we were an entertaining but not very important part of his nightly round.

I watched him covertly as he conducted his examination among the girls after ballet practice, and felt relieved to still see that faint amusement on his face.

After several interviews, he looked around at the crowd, every girl watching him, and asked, "Does anyone else have any particular knowledge of the so-called Phantom of the Opera?"

The room filled with hesitation, a kind of collective drawing in of breath. Everyone wanted to tell blood-curdling stories of the Opera Ghost—but everyone was just a touch wary of a representative of the police. Their institution did not have a history of looking kindly on girls who danced for money, not even at the refined Opera Garnier. I wished I could talk to someone about the Phantom, *really* talk about the Phantom, but that someone was not ever going to be the police inspector. He was the last person I wanted to tell about the man in the mask.

"Meg Giry knows about the Phantom," a voice announced. The words made me start and I turned my head to find the speaker. Jammes, of course. "Her mother is the Phantom's boxkeeper."

Enough gazes were directed towards me that Mifroid had no difficulty identifying me. He paced closer, pencil poised above the notebook's open page. "Your name, mademoiselle?" He looked at me out of cold gray eyes that didn't seem as comfortable and at ease as I had expected. A smirk still lingered in the corner of his mouth, but the eyes were serious. I felt myself go still and grow small under that gaze.

"Marguerite Giry," I said, my voice sounding small too. My hand crept up to touch my necklace.

His gaze followed my hand and he said, "With a G, of course."

I blinked, then realized he was looking at the G engraved on the small gold disk of my necklace. It was not for Giry. It was for Gabrielle. Somewhere my mother had a matching necklace with an M on it, my necklace, but I had worn Gabrielle's ever since—well, for years.

I was as likely to tell the police inspector about Gabi as I was to tell him about the man in the mask. So I only said, "Yes."

"Have you ever seen the Phantom, mademoiselle?"

"Once," I said, and heard girls' breaths all around me, loud in the quieted room.

I don't know what Inspector Mifroid saw on my face, but he leaned closer, seemed to take a new interest. Maybe he read a truth that hadn't been there in the other girls' wild claims. "Can you give me any description? Height, build, eye color?"

At least six feet—broad shoulders but not bulky over all—green eyes. Very green eyes. I widened my own eyes and said instead, voice turning breathless, "He was a glowing skeleton all made out of *fire*!"

Mifroid's shoulders dropped a fraction. "I see." His pencil didn't even move.

"Aren't you going to write that down?" I demanded pertly, lifting my head with my best saucy air.

His lips tightened, and he made a few scratches without looking at the page.

"Of course, Mother's talked to him lots of times," I chattered on. Other people had undoubtedly told him that already. "In Box Five, you know."

"She's seen this glowing skeleton?"

"Oh no, of course not! He only glows in the *dark*." I rolled my eyes dramatically, as though this should have been abundantly obvious to everyone. "You can't see him in the light at all. Then he's just a Voice."

"Of course." He closed the notebook. "Thank you, mademoiselle, that was very helpful."

Perhaps it didn't occur to Mifroid that a ballet dancer could also be an actress. Or maybe it had worked because I had posed as exactly what he expected me to be: a silly, superstitious dancer who loved gossip. I felt both triumphant and a little indignant.

I kept an eye out for Mifroid after that, and contrived to be in the corridor outside the manager's office when he went into it that afternoon. I couldn't hear the conversation inside, but its general content was clear enough from what was said as they came out.

"But you don't understand!" Debienne protested, hands twisting together. "We're being terrorized!"

Mifroid sighed. "For the last time, you do not have a ghost. You have a crowd of superstitious artists who like to tell stories, and that is not a police matter."

"But the letters—the lights—the demands for money!"

"Clearly someone is playing an elaborate joke on you. I advise you to ignore it." He bowed neatly to the manager. "Good day, sir. Remember that I am always available, provided you have a *crime* to report." He turned sharply and walked down the hallway, leaving the manager staring after him in dismay—and leaving me with a satisfied smile.

Try as he might, the Phantom could not find anything to blackmail the new manager with. Matters were becoming simply impossible. Debienne had not managed to convince the police to take an interest, but he still refused to pay a salary. It was a sour note in his carefully constructed symphony, enough to ruin the entire effect. The work of years was going to be destroyed as soon as someone in the Company asked just how fearsome a Ghost could be, if he couldn't make the management pay him anything after all.

Besides, he liked to think he gave good service. Didn't he write endless letters, providing direction on the productions? Hadn't he invested significantly in the construction, and continued anonymous donations? Didn't a ghost add a proper touch of class and subsequent inspiration to a theater's performers? Really, a bit of gratitude didn't seem unreasonable at all.

If only he could find out that Debienne was embezzling funds, or that he had a first wife locked up in an attic somewhere! But no, he seemed to be an honest family man who was far too stubborn for his own good.

Finally, in desperation, the Phantom sat down at his piano with the lid closed and wrote a letter with carefully veiled yet nevertheless clear hints regarding the vulnerability of small children to unfortunate accidents. It was not his preferred option. It was distasteful and lowering and bluffs were always a risk, but the situation had grown extreme.

20,000 francs was thereafter deposited in Box Five with gratifying regularity.

Excerpt from the Notebook of Jean Mifroid, Inspector of Police
17 April, 1880

Old story of Opera Ghost resurfaced this week. Company apparently having joke on new manager sending vague letters, etc. Still no proof of actual foul play, & D. fails to grasp we cannot arrest anyone without *proof* of walls covered in blood.

Interviewed Company about matter, nonsense stories from everyone. Questioned the so-called Persian, but his papers are in order, no information provided and no crime in wandering the Opera. Records show substantial donations in his name to Opera. "Evil Eye" story obviously ridiculous.

Spoke to P. D Chagny as well—also discounts story of "Ghost." Finds Sorelli's belief amusing. Typical artists' superstition.

Chapter Five

B y the time I'd been at the Opera Garnier for five years, I knew everyone there and, perhaps more interestingly, everyone's stories. People didn't pay much attention to a little ballet girl, even one who was seventeen now; while I wouldn't say I eavesdropped intentionally, I generally caught wind of all that went on—and I guess I paid attention.

I had been noticing something strange about Marie for some time, so I wondered one evening when she slipped out before the end of the performance. We were dancing in the same scenes for this opera, so I knew we were both done performing for the night—yet it was unusual for anyone to leave before a production was over.

I frowned as I watched her go. She looked around first, head ducking down, and the movement suggested to me that she wasn't looking *for* something, but rather was hoping *not* to see something. Or someone. It might have been Madame Thibault, but the fear in Marie's eyes didn't look like the right kind.

I had already taken off my dance slippers as I sat in the wings, so when she snuck into the labyrinth backstage I picked up my slippers and followed at a distance. If she was in some kind of trouble, maybe I'd be able to help. No one remarked on my leaving, and I doubted it was me that Marie was trying to avoid, so I didn't make a production of hiding. She never looked back, just hurrying on. She was still tiny, hardly bigger than she'd been when I met her five years before, and looked particularly waif-like in her ragged, much-mended cloak.

Our joint yet separate walk came to an abrupt halt when a dark figure stepped out from between two backdrops. Not tall but burly, in the gloom it took me a moment to recognize him. "Well, well. Good evening, my pretty girl." A familiar voice helped. Joseph Buquet. A scenechanger who liked to tell Phantom of the Opera stories, he was still so personally unpleasant that even I wasn't interested enough to make it worth being around him.

Marie shrank back so quickly and so markedly that I was sure *he* was what she had been hoping not to see. Heart pounding harder, I ducked into the nearest niche between swaying curtains. I was thankful that my old purple cloak, worn for three years now, had faded to the color of shadow and hid my white ballet costume. I pulled the hood over my blond hair, then peeked out between the curtains, digging my nails into my palms. I tried to think, afraid I was unexpectedly far out of my depth. Could I help somehow without drawing the whole Company's attention? That would mean more trouble for Marie than anyone else, if Buquet convinced the right people of the wrong story.

The scenechanger stepped closer to Marie, even as she edged away. "Wasn't that clever of you to come off alone here," he drawled, in a rough voice that sent the unpleasant kind of shivers down my spine. "Nice quiet place for a private meeting."

I could still clearly hear the chorus and the orchestra, so it wasn't really quiet. But it was uncomfortably empty. Back here, in the maze of backdrops and sandbags, there was no one. The people near the stage—and that was everyone—would hear nothing from here.

"Oh…no, Monsieur," Marie said, voice trembling. "I only meant to get home early." And perhaps to leave at a time when he wouldn't see her go, and follow her? "It's very important I get home early. Really. I really must go."

She tried to slip past him, but he caught her upper arm in a grip that looked tight enough to make me flinch in sympathy. "Now, now, pretty girl, you can't be in such a hurry as that. Surely you have time for a little fun with old Buquet, eh?"

He shoved her towards a spiral stair leading to the catwalks. She leaned back over the narrow metal railing as he loomed above her, face descending towards hers, one hand reaching for her dress. I turned to fly for help. She couldn't get into worse trouble than was about to overtake her. I might have rushed forward, but he could overpower both of us as easily as one.

Before I had taken more than a step, a voice echoed through backstage, low and dangerous. "Joseph Buquet."

I felt a knot of fear in my stomach untie. I knew that voice more easily than Buquet's, though I'd heard it less often. Poised to run, I rocked back on my heels instead and kept my hiding place. I didn't need to summon help after all. More powerful help than I could bring had already arrived.

Buquet jerked away from Marie, looking around with a glower. "What the hell...?"

A shadow detached itself from the darkness around us and became a man in a long black cloak and wide-brimmed hat. I could hardly tell where his cloak ended and the other shadows began. My stomach was twisting up again, this time with excitement. It had been so many years since I'd seen him yet he was unmistakable, even with a mask hiding the right side of his face. It wasn't the molded white one I remembered; this one was black metal, glinting in the faint light, cutting a diagonal across his face from the left side of his forehead to the right side of his jaw. "Do you know me, Monsieur Buquet?"

The scenechanger cursed, much stronger than 'hell,' presumably a yes. I could hear Marie's ragged breathing, occasionally breaking with a sob. Did she know too? She probably wouldn't find the Opera's specter as reassuring as I did.

Buquet stepped away from Marie to face the Phantom, gait stiff as though he was undecided whether to fight or to flee.

The Phantom's gaze cut to Marie. "Run, girl," he ordered in curt tones. She remained clinging to the stair's railing, and his voice thundered louder as he repeated, "Run!"

She did, with a cry and a patter of footsteps, and in moments was gone.

I didn't run, though I flinched when he thundered. Maybe I should have fled. But I took a breath and told myself that staying hidden could be the safest option.

In truth, nothing would make me give up my first chance in years to actually see the Opera Ghost. And I wanted to know what would happen.

I had suspected his hand in similar situations in the past. A girl would come to dance practice one day with bruises and a haunted expression; that night her drunken father would meet with a vague accident on the way home from the ale house. One of the dashing young men who frequented the Foyer would try too hard to take liberties with a girl; the next day he would decide to depart for a long trip and never be seen at the Opera Garnier again. No one else seemed to think of the Opera Ghost at those times, but I had wondered. I wanted to *know*.

"You have become a problem, Monsieur Buquet." The Ghost's tone was soft, conversational, yet I could hear an ominous undercurrent as he paced slowly closer to the scenechanger. "It's too bad, really. You've been useful, with your horror stories about the Ghost. Mostly lies, but useful lies. However, you can't expect me to let you get away with *this*."

"Don't see what business it is of yours," Buquet said in surly tones, the shifting of his feet a nervous contradiction to his voice.

"This is *my* Opera," the Ghost snapped out like a pistol shot. "Everything that goes on here is my business."

Buquet took a step backwards, started to turn as though to escape. The Phantom's arm shot out, black sleeve and black glove, and caught him by the throat. He stood perfectly unmoving while Buquet clawed and choked.

I swallowed, pressing back against the dark curtain half-surrounding me, and tugged my hood farther forward over my face. This was no charming guidance to ballet practice, or even a bit of sniping at Carlotta. This was real, raw, so much more disconcerting than the most dramatic scene in the most frightening opera. I still didn't believe the Phantom was dangerous to *me*—but I didn't want to be noticed.

"We are not done, Monsieur." His voice was back to velvet. He shook Buquet once and let go. The scenechanger doubled over, coughing and rubbing at his throat. "I've been watching you," the Phantom went on. "I've had my suspicions for some time."

He wasn't the only one. I had never liked Buquet's lecherous grin, and he had a tendency to stand too close to the girls, or to come suddenly around corners when we weren't expecting him. It could have all been innocent. But it had been enough that, even with the lure of Phantom stories, I had still given him a wide berth for a long time. I wasn't the only girl who had.

"And then there's all that prying about that you like to do," the Phantom continued. "Lurking in shadows, spying and eavesdropping, trying to find out about me, trying to find out what you can use on other people."

Buquet was still bent over, hands on his knees, but he looked up with a glint of defiance in his eyes. "You're not in much of a position to judge. Think I don't know you're skulking around too, doing all kinds of things the police might like to know about."

Even in the darkness I could see the Phantom stiffen. "You and I are not the same. I never trapped a girl backstage."

Buquet straightened up with a sneer. "Why, do they faint on sight of you? That can't be as much fun as when a girl puts up a good struggle."

That sounded like the voice of experience and the implication made me nauseous. I didn't want to think about how many girls there had been before Marie. Had he done his hunting outside the Opera, to avoid the Phantom for so long?

Time had run out. The Phantom's hand lashed out again, but now Buquet was ready. He dodged away, took advantage of the moment to leap over the railing and onto the staircase. His boots pounded up the steps, clanging against the metal.

The Phantom stood still for a moment, and then laughed, sound ringing in the darkness, an odd counterpoint to the continued music of the Opera—and followed up the stairs. I tracked that swirl of cloak around and around the spiral, and heard only Buquet's footsteps.

I forced myself to take a deep breath past the tension pressing on my lungs. Then I crept out of my shadows and stepped cautiously to the foot of the stairs, peering up. It was even darker up there, and I only knew Buquet had reached the catwalk when the clanging ceased. I counted to ten, judged the Phantom ought to be off the steps by then too, and began the ascent myself as quietly as I could, metal cold beneath my stocking feet.

It was foolhardy. Even in the moment I knew that. But I needed to know what would happen; it was like watching an opera, the most intense and terrifying of operas, only to have it halt mid-scene. Amid all the excitement and the tension, I didn't give more than a passing thought to my own danger.

When I was nearly to the top of the stair, I knelt on the icy metal and peered around the curve, my eyes level with the floor of the catwalk. The walk stretched away from the empty backstage over the main stage itself, but too high and too shadowed for anyone in the bright lights of the performance below to realize what was happening here.

The Phantom stood halfway down the walk, his back to me. His silhouette didn't quite hide Buquet beyond him, facing me. With the Phantom between us, I had little fear he'd notice I was crouching here.

Both men had their feet spread, hands loose at their sides but shoulders tight. I imagined they'd be circling if they had room for it. I watched Buquet's glower, watched the way the Phantom stood poised, ready to move. If they had spoken while I was climbing the stairs, I hadn't heard it and they were silent now. I pressed my cheek against the post at the center of the spiral, iron scent sharp, and listened to my heart pound in my ears. I didn't know if it was more from the climb or from the excitement. I thought I might scream if the tension didn't break soon.

When the stand-off ended, it was swift. With a sudden growl, Buquet lowered his head and charged forward as though he meant to barrel into the Phantom, hands outstretched to give what could be a fatal shove on the narrow walk. The Phantom pivoted, turning sideways out of the way as Buquet's momentum carried him on past. I had one hideous, heart-skipping moment of realization that Buquet was heading towards *my* staircase, before he skidded to a halt.

The Phantom's hands had been empty seconds before. Now they held a thin black noose—a noose that had whipped out through the air and settled neatly around Buquet's neck. The scenechanger clutched at the rope, eyes wide, and I felt an involuntary, sympathetic tightening in my own throat. I didn't *want* to be sympathetic to Buquet.

The Phantom paced closer until he was directly behind the scenechanger, still holding the rope taut, leaning over his shoulder from behind. "I want you to remember this," he growled in a low tone I had to strain to hear. "The next time you think it might be *fun* to threaten some poor girl, remember what it feels like to be trapped, helpless, horrors unimaginable staring you in the face. And remember what happens to people who make the Phantom angry."

I knew the Phantom was dangerous. That was part of the mystique. I knew something had happened to those men before, the ones who had hurt girls and then quietly disappeared. But I had never imagined this, this darkness in his voice that sounded *real*, not like the thunder he put in to shout at Carlotta. That was theatrics. This wasn't.

But wasn't he *right*, to be angry? I had been horrified for Marie too, and if it had been me—I'd want someone like this to step out of the shadows, to do the distasteful task of dealing with someone like Buquet.

The thoughts raced through my mind in only a second, and it was barely more than that before the scene changed. Buquet twisted in an abrupt lunge. The Phantom stepped back a pace and Buquet took advantage of the greater freedom to turn and throw a punch. The Phantom dodged in an easy, fluid movement and, off-balance, Buquet lurched against the rail of the catwalk.

The rail was only a thread of metal at thigh-height, connected to the walk at intervals by narrow posts, but otherwise open. Buquet crashed against it, off-balance, propelled by his own forward movement, and tipped over the edge.

The Phantom reached out for Buquet's shirtfront.

I saw that. I *know* I saw that.

He missed by inches. Buquet fell from the catwalk, shriek choked off barely an instant after it began, and the Phantom slammed down to his knees, shoulder catching against the rail, still holding the rope, reaching down.

I didn't look down. I didn't want to see. I knew Buquet was dead when the Phantom's shoulders sagged and his eyes closed. I hadn't been conscious of putting my hand over my mouth, but now I pressed down, hard, pushing back a scream, trying to push back the cold crawl of horror rising from my stomach.

I knew that Buquet had fallen far enough to be visible from below when the singers faltered and the music screeched and died away. I had stopped noticing the sound of the opera, but now the quiet pressed on my ears instead. A second or two ticked by in heavy, silent dread. Then the screams began.

The Phantom threw a few loops of rope over the railing, and though it was hard to see what his black-gloved hand did, he must have tied knots. When he let go of the rope, it remained hanging from the railing. I tried not to think about what was at the opposite end.

He rose to his feet and my breath caught again as it seemed inevitable that he would come towards the stairs, towards me. Instead, he never even glanced my way. He turned to the back of the auditorium, away from the audience in their tiered rows of seats, shaking out his right arm in a suddenly vulnerable gesture, just a second before he leapt from the catwalk, black cloak like wings behind him.

I came closest to screaming then. He barely dropped at all before catching hold of one of the innumerable ropes above the stage. He flew from that first rope to another and then a third, and then I couldn't see him in the deeper darkness.

For a heartbeat or two I was frozen, not moving, not breathing. Then my lungs clenched at the lack of air, making me inhale in a gasp. My thoughts picked up again and I knew I had better fly too. It was obvious Buquet had dropped from above the stage. Even with shock slowing them down, men would be on this catwalk very soon.

I plunged down the spiral stairs at a reckless pace, one hand on the railing, the other still ridiculously, absurdly clutching my dance slippers. A dancer doesn't drop her slippers.

I reached the bottom breathless and dizzy and only seconds before the first few men rushed up to climb the stairs. I was mere feet from the spiral but they charged right past me, paying no regard at all to one small ballet girl. I scurried back, back into the shadows, farther away, until I was too far from that stair to be suspected of having anything to do with all this.

I stopped in a dark nook between canvases, sank down to sit with my knees drawn up, and locked shaking hands around my ankles. I breathed as steadily as I could, trying to get some kind of balance back. As soon as I had my breath, as soon as I felt I could navigate the Opera again, I wanted badly to find my mother.

He slammed the door with a bang behind him when he reached his rooms across the underground lake, flung his hat and cloak at an armchair and threw himself into the corner of one couch. He snapped his fingers, and a dozen candles lit.

Stupid, meddling, clumsy, damned, wretched imbecile! The man was a scenechanger, his *job* was to clamber around the catwalks. He couldn't keep his balance the one time it really mattered?

This could cause serious trouble. No one called the police over fantastic tales about rooms covered in blood when there was no indication of who the blood had come from. But a body, an identifiable, indisputable body, hanged above the stage in the middle of a performance with hundreds of witnesses—that was something no one could ignore.

He breathed deeply, trying to calm his racing mind, trying to assess this reasonably. He steepled his hands before him, let the silence fill him with its soothing melody, with the distant echoes of the Opera's many years of music.

He knew every inch of the Opera Garnier and no one in the Company knew the way to the far side of the lake. They couldn't catch him, not if he was careful. He'd stay below in the darkness where it was safe for as long as necessary—weeks, maybe, until the initial furor died down, until any extra scrutiny had relaxed.

Perhaps he could find some way to plant the idea that it was suicide. It had been a good instinct to tie the rope over the railing. The lasso wasn't unique enough to identify him, and it would have been difficult to explain how a rope could disappear after a suicide victim was dead. The only witness was the girl Buquet had threatened, and considering the position she had been in—no, she wouldn't be telling any stories. He had no illusions she would try to protect him, but she would stay quiet for her own reputation.

If the police decided it was suicide, ending serious danger…it might, *might* work out in the end. It wouldn't hurt his reputation with the Opera Company. Most of them believed he had murdered hundreds anyway, and tangible proof…no, that wouldn't hurt anything at all. It would likely be more effective than years of flickering lights and booming commands.

So that was all right. It would all be all right.

Except for Buquet, of course. He pressed his palms against his forehead. From Buquet's misstep on, it had all played out with the inevitability of an opera libretto. He couldn't reach to catch him. Letting go of the rope—a forty-foot drop would not have been a more merciful end. As it was, Buquet had barely even kicked, so his neck must have broken at once.

He brought his hands down to his lap, stared at them for a moment, then slowly peeled away his gloves. He held up first one hand, then the other, studying them in the candlelight. No blood. There wouldn't be, with a hanging.

He surged up to his feet and went to wash his hands anyway.

Chapter Six

A fter a lot of deep breaths, I thought I had an outward calm by the time I located Mother in the ballet's dressing room, where she had gone in search of me. She still took one look at my face and announced we were going home, immediately. That had been her plan anyway, considering the chaos after Buquet's body appeared, but her hand on my arm was tighter than usual as we left. I didn't altogether mind.

It had all happened so fast, so easily. One misstep and a man's life was over. Not a good man, a man I would frankly be glad to not see around the Opera anymore, but still a person. I knew someone could, for example, go off to Paris in the midst of a revolution and never come back. Or grow ill with a fever and never get better. But death *here* in the Opera, so fast, so simple, was like a cold wind blowing across my world.

I saw the police arrive just as Mother and I were leaving, some half-dozen policemen with Commissaire Mifroid leading the pack. Back when Debienne made his complaint, I had imagined hordes of policemen descending on the Opera, and no such force had materialized. Apparently the police took matters more seriously with a body.

Mother's expression was enough to tell me it was pointless to suggest we stay to see what would happen. I didn't entirely want to anyway, caught between twin forces of horror and curiosity.

So we went home, and Mother had the whole story out of me by the time we got there. Then she made me drink two soothing cups of tea and go to bed. Part of me resented being treated like a child—and part of me was glad enough to pull a quilt over my head and block out everything else.

The thoughts didn't go away, but warm in my bed I felt safer, more able to take the whole event in. I could think about the Phantom, about his voice as he threatened Buquet. I had never imagined that before.

I knew it wasn't an opera. And yet—wasn't it something like one? In a hazy half-sleep, the casting seemed to make it all easier to understand. Buquet was the baritone, the threat, the hulking danger. His death had been an accident, in one way, but like any villain he had sowed the seeds himself—threatening Marie, fleeing up to the catwalks where he must have expected to have an advantage, trying to attack the Phantom despite his own precarious situation.

And the Phantom. Dangerous, yes. Not to be trifled with. But still in the tenor role, still the one who was defending against the true villain. He was simply powerful enough to be an effective guardian, to protect everyone else from the harm Buquet could have gone on doing to girls at the Opera.

I liked that way of thinking about it. It made it easier to turn over, pull my quilt tighter, and get to sleep.

I returned to the Opera Garnier at the usual time the next morning, only to find rehearsals were canceled, on M. Debienne's slightly hysterical order. I stayed anyway, and so did many of the Company. Some people must have taken advantage of the unexpected holiday, but for me, the Opera was the center of things and nothing else in Paris was going to be half so interesting.

Besides, Mother felt she had been kind and soothing long enough, and had spent all of breakfast upbraiding me for being so "foolish, hare-brained and reckless" by following two dangerous men onto a catwalk. Going home again for more wasn't an appealing option.

I wandered around the Opera, picking up stories. I kept an eye out for Marie, but didn't see her. Most of the Company was sure that the Phantom had killed Buquet, although no note or other indication had appeared of the Phantom claiming responsibility. A dozen or more people were prepared to swear that they had seen the deed done, or at least seen the Phantom nearby at the time. Most of these also believed the Phantom was a glowing skeleton.

I debated whether I ought to say something to the police myself. Surely it was bad for the Phantom if the police became convinced on false testimony that he had intentionally murdered Buquet, instead of the accident (or was it self-defense?) I had seen happen.

And yet…I saw Commissaire Mifroid around the Opera too, with three or four officers with him. For all his efficient, serious demeanor, Mifroid still had an amused smile at the corner of his mouth whenever the Phantom came up. I felt reasonably sure that whatever Mifroid believed had happened to Buquet, he didn't think a ghost had killed him. If I spoke up and convinced him that a mysterious man in black had accidentally hanged Buquet, that would probably just make things worse.

So I kept my mouth shut, because it seemed sensible and because not mentioning the Phantom's secrets had been ingrained for years as the best policy. It wasn't because Mother had very firmly told me to guard my own well-being first and stay out of the whole affair.

The heroes of operas don't generally need substantive help from anyone, certainly not from a dancer at the back of the stage. But if I could help guard the man who was guarding my friends and the magical world we danced through, at least by staying silent, I had no reservations about doing that.

The alarm bells in the Phantom's apartments began ringing the day after Buquet's death. This was followed almost at once by a rapping on the door in *allegro agitato*. He slapped the controls for the bells to silence the chiming, and went to see if a strangely polite mob had descended on him. It was some comfort that his door was very strong and that his apartments had a half-dozen other exits.

By the time he reached the door, he had already recognized the pattern of knocks, knew who they indicated. Not a mob, though the visitor's identity still made him grimace. He should have expected this. Every tragic opera had to have a reckoning at the end, a summation where blame was cast and a moral told.

Two taps to release the lock, and he swung open the door, half-bowing to his visitor. "Good morning, Daroga." Everyone else at the Opera Garnier called him the Persian, but Daroga, translating loosely to 'police chief,' was a better if outdated title.

The Daroga did not bother with formalities such as greetings or an invitation to come in. "What happened yesterday?" he demanded, footfalls loud as he strode into the room.

He kept his head firmly erect and refused to look abashed. "The ballet was quite good but the chorus made an absolute muddle of the Act Three finish."

"You know that's not what I mean!" The Daroga's words had lapsed into Farsi. Always a sign he was upset, if the tone hadn't been enough.

"It was an accident," the Phantom said, remaining stubbornly in French.

"How can a man be accidentally *hanged?*"

"All right! I confess!" He let the door swing shut with a bang and crossed his arms defiantly. "I missed the delights of the rosy days of Mazendaran, so in a fit of nostalgia I killed an irritating scenechanger. Is that what you came to hear?"

The couch cushions gave a sigh as the Daroga sank onto them. "You *promised* me—when I saved your life, when the shah ordered your death and I protected you and helped you leave Persia, you promised—"

"—no more killing, yes, yes. How can I forget, with you hanging around to make sure I don't break that vow?" He sat on the other couch and smoothed the legs of his pants, palms lingering against the fabric. "I don't enjoy death the way you worry I do."

"Do you know you rub your palms when you feel guilty?" the Daroga snapped out.

His hands froze. "That is ridiculous," he said with an icy dignity, and very slowly and carefully folded his arms. "And I did not murder Joseph Buquet." He briefly sketched over the events of the previous evening.

"You swear that is exactly what happened?" The Daroga's tone was still intense and interrogative, still like the police chief he had once been, but at least he was speaking in French again.

"Shall I swear it by Allah and Mohammed?"

"Do not make jokes!"

"I am not. I will swear it by Allah or Christ or Apollo, whoever you like." He took a breath, and in a more conciliatory tone said, "Joseph Buquet's death was an accident. I swear to it on Mozart, Beethoven, and Stradivari." And just for good measure, he repeated the words in Farsi.

"Very well," the Daroga said slowly, not happily but in tones of acceptance.

The Phantom sighed and leaned back on the couch. "You know, Daroga, next time someone offers to save my life, I intend to refuse. It is far too taxing being indebted to someone, especially an overly moral, upright and uptight individual who feels painfully responsible for all my subsequent actions. Aren't you exhausted trying to keep track of me? I find it exhausting watching you."

He knew it was a token complaint. If he ever truly wanted to get rid of the Persian, it would hardly take any effort at all to encourage the Opera Company to stop permitting his presence. Far from doing that, he'd even smoothed the other man's path. Any management looked more forgivingly on a stranger who made large donations; the Persian did not have that kind of money, but the Phantom did.

"Every man has to be accountable to someone," the Daroga said, but his voice softened as he added, "So behave, or I'll put the Evil Eye on you."

The Phantom laughed. "If you do, I'll haunt you."

Excerpt from the Notebook of Jean Mifroid, Commissaire of Police

6 September, 1880

Investigation of death of J. Buquet proceeding. As expected, Opera Company blames all on "ghost." Still no tangible evidence of so-called Phantom's existence, or of crime relating to Buquet. Probable cause of death suicide. Assigning two men to watch at Opera Garnier for present, in case of hysteria from crowd—or management.

Chapter Seven

I slumped into one of the front row seats in Box Five. "Still nothing." For a week there had been no tip from the Phantom, and even though Mother left a program at each performance, none had been touched.

"I don't see why you're surprised," Mother said, dropping that night's unmoved program into her bag. "You know he left 40 francs just after Buquet's death."

The two ideas might have seemed unrelated, but the Phantom had a habit of leaving extra money if he had missed several performances. I guessed at the time that leaving extra money beforehand meant he was planning to be gone. 40 francs was equivalent to about seven weeks of normal tips, so after only one week I shouldn't be expecting him back. Not really.

"I'm not surprised, I'm just..." I wrinkled my nose, toyed with my necklace as I hunted for how to explain what I felt. Disappointed wasn't quite the right word. Close, though, even if I could understand why he'd want to disappear for a while, with Mifroid's men at the Opera.

I twisted around to lean on the back of the red velvet seat, my blue-striped skirt bunching beneath my legs, and watched as Mother opened the curtain over the door's small window. "What do you think he does, when he isn't here?"

"I haven't the slightest idea. Hopefully something more sensible than moping around an empty box." She pushed open the heavy wooden door. "Come along. This is perfectly silly. You know months often go by with no excitement from the Phantom anyway."

"But there's always the *possibility*!" Life felt flat, as though a certain sparkle I'd almost stopped noticing had disappeared. I slid out of the seat and moved across the carpet to the door. "Nothing interesting happens when the Phantom's gone."

I felt a twinge of guilt a moment too late. I probably shouldn't have said that, considering the last thing that had happened around the Phantom had been Buquet's death. But I didn't mean *that*, of course. That hadn't been something he intended to do—and he'd stopped a different horrible thing from happening to Marie. And I meant everything else, more than five years of other things—advice for the dancers and caustic comments for Carlotta and no one ever knew when a glowing skeleton might appear, or unexplained thunder crash through a rehearsal. It kept life exciting. Magical, even. Anything could happen—at the Opera or in my life.

Mother held the door open and I stepped out, nearly bumping directly into a girl about my age in the busy corridor outside. We exchanged quick, apologetic smiles. I watched her walk away while Mother locked Box Five behind me. The girl's pink dress was nice but not expensive enough for a guest. I didn't recognize her as part of the Company and I was sure I would remember her dramatic cluster of brown curls, so she had to be new.

"Lots of interesting things go on that have nothing to do with the Phantom," Mother said firmly, reclaiming my wandering attention. "And you know that. Now go on to the Dance Foyer. Get to know some pleasant young man and stay out of trouble."

I smiled wickedly. "I can't do *both*."

"I would be worried if I thought you were serious." She quickly tidied my bangs, just as though I was still a child and not seventeen years old, turned me around and gave me a light push towards the end of the corridor. "Go ahead. I'll meet you to walk home after I finish with the other boxes."

In the Dance Foyer, portraits of ballerinas smiled down on their living counterparts, while gold shone on the walls and on the girls' jewelry. It was mostly gilt, in both cases. The room was crowded with clusters of admiring men gathered around smiling dancers, standing about the room or claiming the green velvet banquettes along the walls. A wall of mirrors doubled the apparent size of the already-large room, one of the Opera's many tricks of illusion. A hum of voices and laughter rose from the crowd, a familiar hum that I enjoyed for its energy, its intrigue, its many stories unfolding all throughout the room.

I smiled at Francesca when she caught my eye, raised a hand when Adalisa waved to me from another group. Maybe I'd go join them. But first I peered into the mirror, frowning at my smoothed bangs. I could not convince Mother that rumpled hair was the fashion. I ran my fingertips through the strands, but my hair was just too straight to accomplish much. You needed curls for the right look—like that girl right over there, just behind me and plainly visible in the mirror. It was the one from the corridor, with her artful brown curls piled on her head, loose strands wisping about her neck.

Our glances met in the mirror almost at once and I turned to face the real girl with a smile. "Good evening. I'm sorry for nearly running you down before." I could go talk to any number of friends around the room, but I was curious about this probable new arrival.

"Oh, that's all right." Her long lashes made her brown eyes look even bigger as they widened. "It was really my fault, hovering in front of the door. I couldn't decide which direction I ought to be going. This place is so confusing!"

"I thought you might be new. I'm Meg Giry."

"Christine Daaé. But how did you know I was new?" With a light laugh, she indicated the crowded room around us. "You can't recognize everyone. Or did I just look particularly lost?"

"I know most people around here." And she wasn't the type to blend into the crowd. I had already noticed male glances turning our way, and I didn't bother telling myself that they were looking at me. "I've been here for years. Don't worry, you'll get used to the place."

She sighed, twisting her fingers together. "I hope so."

I remembered my own new days, all those years ago, and it felt nice being the one who belonged, who understood the world around us. Some girls arrived more confident than others, and this one seemed like she would need more help. Her posture, her anxious glances around the room, all suggested a lost uncertainty. Maybe I could give her some guidance, if I knew more about her role here. "What level of the ballet are you with?" She was old enough for a leading position, but I didn't think she had one; though she walked gracefully, she didn't move like Sorelli or the other premiere ballerinas.

"The ballet?" A tiny crease formed between her perfectly arched eyebrows as she frowned. "Oh no, I'm in the chorus. I'm a soprano." A certain pride betrayed itself in her voice as she said it. And why not? Not many people could hit the notes sopranos did.

All the same, she was far too tentative and hesitant for me to feel overawed by her singing status. "If you're from the chorus, you're in the wrong foyer," I told her, trying not to laugh. "The singers have a different reception room than the ballet."

"Really?" She threw her hands in the air, a gesture that should have seemed theatrical yet looked natural from her. "You see? Hopelessly confused!"

I did laugh then, because it felt more like a shared joke than like I was mocking her. "Don't worry, I won't tell anyone you don't belong. No one's likely to notice, and nothing too awful will happen even if they do." I pointed toward an empty banquette. "Let's snatch that before some duke sits down, and you can tell me when you got here."

Christine had been at the Opera Garnier for four days. The very next thing I learned was that her father was a wonderful violinist who had died three years ago, leaving her alone in the world. He had always dreamed she could be a great singer, so she had studied at the Paris Conservatoire and now she was here.

I told her that I was originally from Leclair, a village in the south of France, but I had been at the Opera for five years with my mother, one of the boxkeepers.

"I thought your name sounded familiar…" Christine said, and that tiny crease appeared between her brows again. Suddenly her forehead cleared and she said, "Isn't your mother the Phantom's boxkeeper?"

"For several years now," I said with a nod. That was mostly how Mother was known at the Opera these days. Sometimes I enjoyed the association. Sometimes it annoyed me that no one seemed to care much for anything else about us. But that wasn't Christine's fault, if she had happened to hear the story.

Christine shivered. "Don't you find it alarming? I've heard so many horrible stories about the Phantom since I came here!"

Walls dripping with blood and disembodied heads, no doubt. "You sort of get used to him. It's exciting, really." It was bad enough that he had apparently gone away for a while; I couldn't imagine the Opera Garnier permanently without its resident ghost. He was the Opera's spirit, in more ways than one.

She shook her head decisively, brown curls swaying. "I'm sure I'll never get used to a ghost. Some of the stories are so upsetting. If I was ever to meet him in a dark corridor, I just know I'd faint right away."

Definitely not one of our more confident new arrivals. "You're not likely to bump into him. He doesn't show himself often." A part of me was still disappointed that Mother's position as his boxkeeper had never, not even once, given me an opportunity to meet him. "Besides, most of the stories aren't true. He's not as bad as people say."

I didn't know why I was telling her that. I had known for years that it was pointless trying to dissuade the other girls on the subject of the Phantom's sinister nature. They didn't want to hear it, and I didn't think he'd want it told either. He worked at that reputation. Christine, though...when she shivered and looked so alarmed, there was something childlike about it, and I instinctively wanted to reassure her. Anyone would have. And perhaps I wanted to see if, unlike the other girls, she would listen.

"Have you met the Phantom?" she asked in hushed tones, leaning in as though even the question was a private secret between us.

The answer was certainly a secret, and not one I was going to tell. I shrugged, tried to relax the atmosphere a little. "He talks to

Mother sometimes, from Box Five. He's always very polite, and gives the highest tips of any subscriber."

She frowned slightly. "But they say he can be terribly angry."

Buquet, the moment on the catwalk, flashed through my mind. Yes. He could. Another story I wasn't going to tell, and not truly representative anyway. "He's mostly only angry if there's a bad performance, and even then he usually just writes something scathing to the management. Or Signora Carlotta. And he gets upset if there's trouble about Box Five or his salary." Or if a true villain is committing far worse atrocities than a bit of thunder and theatrics.

"His salary?" Christine said, eyebrows rising as she tipped her head slightly in query.

I wondered how she had heard about the Phantom and not heard about his salary. "Yes, 20,000 francs."

Her fingers tightened, curled on the green velvet of the banquette. "He's a very well-paid ghost! 20,000 francs a year is very—"

"20,000 francs a month," I corrected.

Her mouth dropped open in almost childish awe. "But that's almost a quarter of a million francs a year—a million and a half since the Opera opened! What does he spend it all on?"

"I've no idea," I admitted. People didn't usually ask why a ghost needed money at all; it was just part of the legend. I had personally surmised that the man in the mask had something he was using it for. Beyond that, I hadn't given the matter much thought either. Other things about the Phantom were more interesting, like why he wore a mask, what his name was and why he was here to begin with.

I'd been accepting the fact of his salary without asking many questions since I was twelve, and had less conception of just how much money that really was. The solo dancers, the highest level I could aspire to in my most wild dreams, were lucky to earn 600 francs a month. Sorelli surely earned more, but I was never going to be that good, even in my imagination.

Christine folded her hands on her lap, fingers white against the pink cloth of her skirt. "Oh well, I don't suppose we can understand why a ghost cares about certain things—money and Box Five and performances."

"He's passionate about art—and he's brilliant." None of my friends in the ballet ever wanted to talk about this. I hadn't wanted to talk about the horrors of the Phantom, but this was different. This was a chance to tell a receptive audience my own unorthodox views about the Opera Ghost. "He often makes suggestions for the Company. Musical arrangements, or ways singers can improve their voices. Usually by letter, of course, though once in a great while he'll thunder something aloud at a rehearsal. Everyone grumbles when they get a direction from the Phantom, but they always follow it, and what nobody ever admits is that he's always *right*. When he gives a suggestion, it really does make a performance better."

Christine laughed lightly, a laugh full of innocence. "My, he's quite the intriguing figure, your Phantom!"

Receptive, but she didn't really understand after all. I had been leaning forward in my enthusiasm, and now I pulled away, reached up to touch my necklace. "He's not my Phantom. He's just...the Phantom." He couldn't be my Phantom. I'd only met him once.

The conversation turned to other subjects after that, and Christine was an eager and interested audience to every other topic about the Opera, asking all the right questions. She seemed interested in me too. It was nice to talk to someone I hadn't known for years, who hadn't heard every story already, and was willing to listen even to the ones most people wouldn't.

By the time Mother came to find me, Christine and I had agreed to meet after the next day's rehearsals for a tour of the building.

I had had years to learn all about the Opera, and I loved the opportunity to show it off to someone new. The next day, Christine was full of questions and admiration. We walked through the Grand Foyer with its shining gold and shimmering chandeliers, ventured down to the stables to see the Opera's horses, and rambled through innumerable passages, past dressing rooms and into practice spaces.

I liked many of the ballet girls, some very much, but they never seemed the least bit interested in anything outside of the areas utilized specifically by the corps de ballet—geographically and otherwise. Even though we danced in the middle of operas, most of our work went on separately from the singers and the musicians, just inserted into place at the right moment. They seemed to look at the world around us the same way, just a backdrop that had little to do with us. I had never understood how they could take such a narrow view. I enjoyed dancing, sometimes very much if I had a particularly good role, and I worked hard at it—but it was never the entire focus of my life, and certainly not the only part of the Opera that interested me.

To me, the Opera Garnier was full of dozens of fascinations, hundreds of stories, and I wanted to know them all. It was a magical kingdom where fantasies were performed on stage and a ghost reigned from the shadows. Why would anyone limit their attention only to what went on at the ballet barre?

The kingdom had borders, though, as I had to admit when Christine halted on a curving stair and asked about going lower.

"It's just the cellars down there," I said, though that was a vast oversimplifying of five cavernous vaults. "Some people have work there, but the Phantom doesn't like anyone else poking about." I had gleaned information, but hadn't ventured down myself in years. The place held some eerie fascination, but I had never felt compelled to explore—not enough to overcome the memory of getting so hideously lost, only a level or two down.

"Do you suppose the Phantom lives below?" Christine asked, still looking down.

"What makes you think a ghost lives anywhere?" I asked as lightly as I could, and hurried on up the steps. I didn't think the man in the mask lived down there, even though that was where I had met him. Who would choose a dark cellar to live in, with the glittering Opera Garnier above ground?

I had saved the rooftop for last, but that turned out to be a mistake. Christine balked at the ten flights of stairs, after we'd already walked so much. So the roof was saved for another day. Somehow, by that point, it was already established that there would be other days— that Christine and I would be friends.

Chapter Eight

I listened to the chorus practice from backstage, stretching my toes, tight from my own recent rehearsal. La Carlotta was going over a solo after this, and I would be able to talk to Christine while all the rest of the Company waited around for the soprano to finish. When I started looking for moments like this, I'd found many over the last few weeks, chances to intersect with the chorus and catch Christine. I had had to wander off from the ballet today, but that was all right.

Soon enough Carlotta strode majestically past en route to her solo, the chorus dispersed, and Christine joined me sitting backstage. "How was your Sunday?" I asked as she arranged her skirts. Somehow she looked elegant sitting on the clutter and boxes of backstage. I crossed my legs at the ankles and smoothed my tulle skirts, though they would never look like the graceful long skirts of the chorus.

"Oh, Sunday was lovely!" Christine said with a far-off smile. I hoped for an interesting story, but the first comment was followed by, "Madame Valérius and I spent the whole afternoon just sitting together at home. So cozy."

Madame Valérius was the widow Christine lived with. I had met her once; she was nice and thought Christine perfection itself, but was not terribly exciting. Sort of like porridge with the salt left out—sweet, nourishing, not much flavor.

"I thought you might have done something more exciting," I hinted, and when Christine looked blank I was forced to be more direct. "That young gentleman in the Singers Foyer Saturday night seemed quite ardent…"

I had begun attending the Singers Foyer with Christine on a semi-regular basis. I could blend in well enough there, and it had quickly become impossible to sneak Christine into the Dance Foyer. She was always noticed. The rest of the ballet might have tolerated a quiet visitor, but she attracted too much male attention for the girls to welcome her.

"Now really, Meg," she protested, "M. Allam was merely being friendly! And it hardly matters. You *know* I only care about my career. Many men have been very pleasant, of course, since I came here, but none of it is serious."

Not many girls could have made that remark about "many men" without sounding like a flirt, but I knew that was a ridiculous idea for Christine. Some of the most popular girls at the Opera so obviously *tried* to be popular, always with the low-cut dresses and the arch looks and the teasing with the men. Christine was always demure, always innocent. A circle of men gathered around her even when she hadn't really done anything to encourage it. It was merely the way things fell out. Her beauty and soft smile brought them over to her couch in the foyer, and she seemed more surprised by that than anyone.

All the same, it was just as well she hadn't made that remark where the other ballet girls could hear. No one seemed to precisely dislike her. She was so wide-eyed and sweet that it would have been like hating a kitten. Still, I didn't think they were terribly fond of her. I would have liked to bring her into my circle of friends among the ballet, but the reception was too frosty, and I could see Christine looked pained the time or two I'd tried. It was much easier to spend time with Christine just the two of us, and I didn't altogether mind that myself.

I liked the ballet girls, of course, but I had never quite found the closer friend I had imagined when I first came to the Opera. Someone to share confidences with, to choose first to spend an afternoon with, to talk to about a whole range of subjects and wishes and thoughts that had little to do with ballet. I had told myself for years that a group of friends was enough. But now suddenly Christine seemed to be neatly filling a hole I'd been ignoring.

"But suppose you ever met some young man you really liked..." I ventured, retying the lacings of my ballet slippers as I spoke. I hoped I would meet someone some time, so I supposed I ought to hope Christine would too. But I did sort of like that we were both unattached, that I was the first person she'd seek out to spend time with too.

She shook her head, light catching in her curls. "I just don't have any interest in all that. I buried my heart when Papa died."

From anyone else, that would have sounded like melodrama, but from Christine, it was just sweetly sincere.

"I suppose so," I said, and part of me was glad. Though I had some doubts. I mean, I missed my father too, sometimes very much, but that didn't seem to me to have much to do with whether I fell in love. Maybe she just wasn't interested in romance, but the reason she always gave confused me. I crossed two ribbons, drawing the lacings tighter around my ankle. "But what if some man takes the flirting more seriously some time?"

"Oh, well, that's why it's much safer to have a group of them around," Christine said with an airy wave of her fingers. "No one can get too carried away with sentimental speeches when they're all together. And of course it's much easier to dissuade any man who does get too caught up."

I frowned down at the bow I'd just tied. "But if you always have a whole group around, when do you have an opportunity to dissuade anyone?" I couldn't imagine trying to kindly let a suitor down while all of his rivals were listening.

She laughed like a child, all bubbles and no edge. "I just show a preference for another one, and whichever one is getting too serious gets the message well enough."

"It seems to me a jealous one might find that to be an encouragement," I countered.

"Well, yes, I guess that's possible. I suppose I've been lucky so far." She sighed, head drooping, suddenly looking weary. "It really is all so very complicated, isn't it?"

Sometimes. But turning down an unwanted suitor didn't seem that complicated. Difficult and uncomfortable, perhaps, but not complicated. "I don't know…in the operas, they never just *talk* to each other. In life, it seems like it would be so much simpler to just be honest and clearly say—"

"Oh no, I couldn't stand *rejecting* a man openly." She looked at me with her brown eyes wide and stricken. "You know I hate confrontations. It could so easily become an unpleasant scene and I just can't bear ugliness."

"Yes. I know." Anyone who had seen Christine react to a spider knew *that* (and she never listened when I said that the spider was more afraid than she was). "But it wouldn't have to be ugly. And wouldn't it be kinder to—"

"No, no, I couldn't." She shook her head again, more vigorously this time. "It would be so awkward. Have you ever tried to tell a man who loves you that you just don't care for him?"

That halted me rather. The situation had never come up. A reasonable number of pleasant young men wanted to talk to me after a performance, thank you very much, but declarations of love…well, it had never come to that yet for me. I hadn't met the right one, I supposed, the one who would see me amongst the crowd of beautiful, talented girls at the Opera and think that *I* was the one he wanted to know. "No," I managed. "I suppose it would be awkward."

"Quite," she agreed, and I was glad by then to let the subject drop.

We finally made the climb up to the roof a month or so later, one sunny afternoon when the sky was a gorgeous blue and a light breeze ran through the strings of Apollo's lyre, held by the statue at the highest point of the shining copper dome.

The roof was empty, as usual. Hardly anyone seemed inclined to take advantage of the air or the view, which had always baffled me. Christine and I walked around the edge to look at the expanse of Parisian rooftops stretching away from us. Light glinted off of windows and the Seine was a ribbon of reflected sunshine, curling across the city to the south. Notre Dame Cathedral rose up from its island in the river, seeming tall despite being shrunk by the distance, much too far away to see its famous gargoyles. I had always liked to imagine the Opera Garnier's statues and Notre Dame's gargoyles nodding to one another from across the city.

After I had pointed out the Louvre and the Church of the Madeleine and the Arc de Triomphe and every other identifiable landmark, Christine and I stretched out on a convenient patch of sun-warmed tile to talk. The October air was just beginning to cool, but the sunlight made a perfect balance. Our conversation ranged from hair ribbons to gossip to our deepest dreams.

"I just want to be a great singer," Christine said, cheek resting on her folded forearms. "Like Papa wanted."

I was lying on my back, watching the faint streamers of clouds above, with a lazy sort of feeling that all was well in my world. "You're in the right place then. He'd be proud of you."

A long pause. "Maybe. The chorus isn't quite…"

"But it's a starting point," I encouraged. I had learned that Christine needed encouragement, now and then. "A first step. If you're good, someone's sure to notice and give you more opportunities."

"*If* I'm good," she said, voice dropping to a lower, dejected tone.

I winced, regretting my poor phrasing. "Oh no, I didn't mean—"

"I know, I shouldn't have taken it that way." She sighed, then made an apparent effort to be more cheerful. "Anyway, enough about *me*. I suppose you'll be a star ballerina in a few more years."

"It's not very likely." I was able to smile as I said it. "I'm good, but I'm not that good. It's all right, though. I enjoy dancing and I want to do well—and the money helps Mother. But it's not my *life* like some of the girls."

I had only begun dancing because of Gabrielle. We had shared dancing at first, and I had grown to love it, for the joy of dancing itself and because, even now, it still reminded me of her. *She* had dreamed of becoming an *etoile*, a star ballerina, and perhaps, if things had been different… But I didn't have the talent she had had, something I'd never resented, and I didn't have the same degree of passion either. I had too many other dreams to pour my whole life into just the one.

"There's *so much* I want to do." I stretched my arms above my head, tiles warm against the backs of my fingers and through the sleeves of my blue and white striped dress. If only it was possible to reach out and seize wishes. "I want to dance, but I want to learn all about opera and music too, and then sometimes I think I don't want to be at the Opera Garnier forever because I'd like to get married and have children—but I want to travel too."

"Where would you go?"

Dreams floated by, nearly as tangible as the clouds above us. "*Everywhere.* I want to climb pyramids in Egypt and explore the Taj Mahal in India. And I want to listen to music in Vienna and fall in love in Venice and visit the Colosseum in Rome." I rolled over, propped up on one elbow, caught in my visions. "I want to see everything, and maybe after I've been everywhere and done everything, maybe then I'll get married and go home to Leclair and raise up a lot of children. And visit Paris to go to the opera."

Christine giggled. "You don't believe in dreaming small, do you?"

"Dreams aren't proper dreams if they're small," I said swiftly. "Mother says I dream too much, but my father was a dreamer too. He used to talk about all the things he wanted to do too…" Until he died, of course. While he was chasing a dream. But I had reconciled that long ago, and I knew Father would tell me that it was more important to keep having dreams, whatever the risk, whatever the consequence, than to live small and safe. If only I knew which one dream I wanted most.

"Dreams can be painful though," Christine said, mouth drooping as her face turned somber again. "Especially when they don't happen."

On a sunny day with visions dancing in my mind, I refused to let my spirits be crushed. "But why shouldn't they all come true? Why shouldn't you become a great singer, and why shouldn't I travel all the way to India?"

"Because I'm buried in the chorus, and most people never even leave the city they were born in. Not unless they're very rich."

That did flatten me rather. I rolled onto my back again, looked at Apollo looming up above at the top of the copper dome. Were the clouds growing darker? Or maybe I just felt a shadow on my spirits, a shadow reflected by the frown on my face.

"I'm sorry, *chérie*," Christine said after a moment. "It's just—I get so discouraged, singing with so many other girls who are so very good and...I didn't mean to...you're not angry with me, are you?"

"No." A bird was sitting on Apollo's head; even the God of Music only got so much respect. I sat up, wrapping my arms around my knees, skirts bunching. "They're not impossible, you know. Dreams." I believed that. I needed to, because what would life be without dreams? Or magic. If dreams didn't matter, then why had my father given his life for one? "And besides, even impossible things can happen, sometimes."

Christine frowned at me, brow wrinkling. "They can't. That's why they're impossible."

"Seemingly impossible things," I clarified, since she was technically right. But seemingly impossible things happened at the Opera Garnier all the time. "Things like...walking through walls or taking flight from a catwalk."

Her voice sounded amused. "You know someone who can do that?"

I looked down at my hands, clasped around my knees, feeling a flutter of mingled excitement and nerves in my stomach. My glance edged sideways to look at her. "I'll tell you a secret, if you promise not to tell anyone else, ever." I had never even been tempted to tell any of the other girls this secret. But Christine was different. She was my closest friend, someone who might finally listen to me and believe me. Christine wouldn't be dismissive the way Jammes and the other ballet girls so often were. She might understand, why the Phantom and everything he stood for was so important to me.

Her eyes widened. "Of course I promise."

I took a deep breath. "When I first came to Paris..." And I told her about meeting the Phantom, about how he had helped me find ballet practice and given me advice about life at the Opera Garnier, like seeing the view from the roof. "So that's why I don't believe most of the stories about him. He's definitely not a glowing skeleton, and even though he puts on a terrifying show sometimes, I don't think he's really dangerous."

"And he's not really a ghost," Christine said slowly, gaze fixed in the distance, as though she wasn't seeing anything in front of her at all.

"I don't *know* that." It wasn't as though I had met another ghost to make a comparison. Maybe all ghosts were solid. "But I don't think so. And don't you see, if the Phantom is really a man, and he can still do such incredible things—it means *anything's* possible. If he can light candles by breathing on them and make the management let him keep Box Five, I don't see why you can't be a great singer."

Maybe it wasn't a perfect analogy, but for years the Phantom had been my proof of a wide world of possibility. Not proof of something supernatural, but proof of what a *person*, one not truly different from me or anyone else, could do. If he could do all that he did—then surely I should be able to do all that *I* dreamed.

She sat up and twined one shining brown curl around her finger. "And I suppose I won't have to worry about the Phantom being angry if I miss a note in my debut performance, if he's so harmless after all."

That wasn't the point, nor quite the impression I had meant to give. I bit my lower lip, arms tightening around my legs. "I'm not saying he's harmless. I just don't think he's vicious the way the stories say."

It was hard to explain the Phantom. He was…complicated. Not someone to be dismissed or to be crossed lightly; I'd always thought that, and the incident with Buquet had proved it. And yet, he wasn't someone to fear either, not for people like Christine and me. "He can be dangerous," I went on, "but it's not the mindless mayhem the ballet girls talk about. And they really don't need to be afraid of him, because I think he watches out for the girls at the Opera, even if they don't realize it."

Then I wound up telling her about Marie and Buquet, so she got two secrets instead of one. Marie had left the Opera just a few days after the incident. I had still been trying to work up a way to talk to her about it, and then it was too late.

It was hard to tell Christine's opinion of it all. She listened attentively and made the appropriate horrified exclamations and remarked at the end that it was a relief to know the Opera wasn't really haunted by a murderous ghost. But something in her eyes, not quite meeting mine, made me feel she wasn't saying all she thought.

For an afternoon that had started so well, I walked back down the stairs with a peculiar twist of disappointment, of dissatisfaction. I couldn't put my finger on exactly why, on what was missing in Christine's response. She hadn't laughed at me. She had believed me.

Maybe I just wanted too much. After never telling anyone all I knew about the Phantom, I was bound to have unrealistic expectations about how that conversation would finally go.

It was a very long eight weeks below the Opera Garnier. The first two were passable. He composed three concertos and an entire symphony, and read a stack of books, including *The New Paris Opera* by Charles Garnier. It was still excellent on a fourth read, though of course it left some crucial details of the construction out. Such as a certain masked foreman who had brought significant innovations to the design, and may have quietly arranged secret doors and passages as well.

By the third week, he was growing bored by his own thoughts. By the fourth week, he was aching to go up above and see what was happening in his Opera. More than that, he longed to hear voices that weren't his own, longed for the parade of humanity in its endless variety and infinite capacity for interest. He had given up asking for meaningful engagement years ago, but he hadn't realized how much he valued his role as an observer.

At that point he considered abandoning his self-imposed exile. It was possible that the Buquet business had completely faded. Could he risk it?

No. If the Opera was still alert, if the police were still taking a particular interest, he could throw away the refuge of years through a momentary impatience. He would wait.

By the fifth week, when he found himself flirting with the mad idea of leaving Paris and going out into the country for a bit, he knew he had to do something different before he wound up succumbing to dangerous temptation.

Examining that country visit idea, it occurred to him that the desire was as much about open space as it was about people. Normally he felt safest in close spaces, in darkness, in the refuge of cellars and tunnels. You can have too much of a good thing, however, and just now he was longing for a horizon, for some distance. Considering that open spaces made him highly uncomfortable when he actually encountered them, this seemed like an insurmountable paradox. Until he thought of the mirrors.

As soon as the idea occurred to him, he donned a cloak and went up to the second cellar. This was a minor risk at most. It was a little-visited place, and one that was easy to slip away from. The cellar stored an endless assortment of presently-unneeded props and set-pieces, everything from fake swords to a nearly full-sized sailing ship. Even he didn't know everything that was down here, though he probably had a better working knowledge than anyone else.

Today he went directly to the mirrors, a large stack in one corner that might have been part of a past set or even come from the Opera's construction days. Without frames, they could easily be leftovers from the endless mirrors that lined rooms and halls all over the building.

He ran his fingertips along the smooth surface of one mirror, automatically averting his eyes from his own reflection, examining the dimensions and the quality. Excellent.

It wasn't easy to bring the mirrors down to his rooms, but he welcomed the interest of the challenge. Once he had them down there, he went to work converting a small storage chamber off of his parlor. He blocked off the corners to turn the square space into an octagon, put lights in the ceiling and covered each wall with mirrors. He valued the project as much for the diversion of the work as for the intended result. When he was finished, every wall was lined with mirrors and he retreated hurriedly before his own endlessly repeating reflections. He went back up to the prop vault to requisition an iron tree with spreading branches, to put in one corner of the mirrored chamber.

When the tree was in place, he stretched out on the floor of the chamber and looked up at the reflected reflections of branches, spreading into eternity. It wasn't quite a horizon, certainly not a living forest, but it would do. It took some pressure off for the remaining days, until he felt safe returning to the only slightly less artificial world of the Opera Garnier above.

Exactly eight weeks after Joseph Buquet took a tragic fall from a catwalk, a black-edged envelope with red writing came tumbling down onto the stage in the middle of the day's final ballet practice. We had been performing *pirouettes*, and I came out of my turns just in time to see the envelope land, surprise and delight making me dizzier than all my spins. Groans rose around me, and I was careful to match my expression to the dismayed looks on the other girls' faces. Inside I was doing *jetés*.

I had guessed the Phantom would be gone for seven weeks, based on the money left in Box Five. I had spent the last few days since we'd passed that point wondering with increasing worry whether he might have left for good.

Madame Thibault signaled a halt to the rehearsal, even though we'd all stopped anyway, and pointed at Francesca, who was nearest the envelope, to bring it over to her. Francesca picked it up by one corner, using just two fingers, and the ballet mistress gave it a cursory glance. I wished it had landed closer to me, or that I was close enough to Madame Thibault to get a peek. I smiled slightly at the unlikely picture that conjured, of trying to peer over her imposing, ramrod-straight shoulders.

She snapped her fingers at a stagehand loitering nearby. "You, take this to the manager's office." She handed off the envelope, and sighed loudly. "If the Phantom *must* send notes to the manager, I wish he'd deliver them there and not disrupt my rehearsals. Now, girls, from the beginning again and try to make respectable *ronde de jambes* this time."

Mother found ten francs and no program in Box Five that night. I was giddy with delight, and even my solemn mother smiled.

He was back.

Chapter Nine

T he Phantom had scarcely returned before Christine started teasing me about him. Kindly, of course, not with the sting some of the ballet girls would have put in, but she kept on joking that perhaps she'd sing off-key at the next performance to provoke him.

"I told you, he takes the performances seriously," I said, as she sat on one wide step of the grand marble stairs, and I used the carved railing to practice my *grande battements*. It was a quiet afternoon, the stairs otherwise empty of all but statues. "You don't want to make him angry."

I wished the Phantom would do something truly impressive, something so that Christine would see he wasn't someone to be trifled with. Not a monster. But someone *serious*. As serious as all this elegance around us. I didn't seem able to explain it to her. The Phantom's return had so far made little perceptible change at the Opera, save for a new energy in the Company—or maybe it just felt that way to me.

"But perhaps then he'd give me advice on my singing!" Christine suggested merrily.

"What good would advice be if you deliberately sang badly?" We weren't getting anywhere, talking about the Phantom, and I cast about for a new topic as I kicked one leg out to the side. Or perhaps a related topic. She was always willing to talk about singing. "Do you know I've never actually heard you sing?"

She shook her head, brown curls flying. "That's silly, I sing every performance."

"Always in the chorus." I stretched my leg higher, genuinely intrigued myself by the new line of thought. "The voices all blend together. I've never really heard *you* sing." What a strange thing, for a friend as close as Christine.

"Oh well, I suppose I'll have to some time," Christine said, leaning back against the smooth marble balustrade and closing her eyes.

I grinned, bringing my leg down into third position. "Why not now?" In this time between rehearsals and the evening performance, no one else was around.

"Oh no, I couldn't, *chérie*," Christine protested, blushing a delicate pink. "I'd feel so silly and self-conscious. I can't just sing an aria on a staircase."

I could see her point if we were on some back steps somewhere, but you could hardly call the Grand Stair, with its marble steps and soaring pillars and high, high ceiling, a mere staircase. "Surely the setting is fine enough," I teased.

"It's not *that,* I need a music room or a stage or—"

"Good," I said, stepping away from the railing, seeing an obvious solution. "Nothing is happening in the auditorium right now. You couldn't ask for a better stage than *that*. It's only the biggest in all of Europe."

"No, really, I can't..." she said faintly, but followed me up the stairs and past the marble statues standing vigil before the entrance. And while I didn't think we'd bump into the Phantom—well, you never could tell.

Girls' voices broke in on the Phantom's meditations, echoing in the empty auditorium. His first instinct was to leave. He could easily slip out of Box Five without being seen. But after all those weeks of silence belowground, he didn't mind a pair of voices so much. He settled in his seat, prepared to let them be a background melody to his own thoughts, birdsong hardly impacting the quiet of the afternoon. Certain members of the chorus, and most especially a certain lead soprano, had grown decidedly lax recently. He turned his back for a few weeks, and the grand symphony of the Opera lost its perfect synchronicity and developed sour notes besides.

"Unless the Phantom's listening, no one will hear you—and you can't tell me this isn't the right setting."

His own title caught his attention to the conversation. So they thought he might be lurking about. All to the good if they thought he was omnipresent.

"Do you think he might be here?" a second girl asked, and he was both satisfied and resigned to hear the quaver in her voice.

"No one ever knows." The first girl sounded far more matter-of-fact about the idea. "He told Mother to keep Box Five's curtains closed all the time, so that probably means he's there sometimes between performances."

Ah. So this must be Madame Giry's daughter. Little Meg, if he recalled correctly. Her voice did sound vaguely familiar, undoubtedly from times he'd heard her speaking with her mother. The other's voice rang no bells of recognition, though she had the inflections of a singer. Chorus member, presumably.

"You'd think people would try to find him in Box Five, then. Keep a watch, or something."

"I don't spread the theory around!" Little Meg protested. "And you can't mention it to anyone either."

For a moment, he indulged in the thought that she was anxious about him. He knew it was mere pretense, though. No doubt she was worrying about her mother's income.

The other girl promised silence, and Little Meg resumed, "Anyway, what are you going to sing?"

He released a nearly inaudible sigh. If chatter wasn't distracting enough, they had to sing. Wasn't Giry's daughter in the ballet? Couldn't she do a nice quiet dance so he could return to his musings on how he was going to get Carlotta back in the proper key?

"I don't know. You mustn't be disappointed if I'm not very good. Father thought I was, but…" Faintly he heard the swish of skirts, the scuff of shoes against the wooden stage as she moved her feet. "I just don't know anymore, after all this time buried in the chorus."

"Nonsense, I'm sure you're wonderful!" Little Meg said with bright enthusiasm.

He wasn't sure. He'd heard far too many girls with dreadful voices who were convinced they were gifted. If a girl doubted she was any good, he was inclined to believe her. There could be no point trying to continue any real contemplation here now. He rose to his feet to go.

"Of course, it would all be different if the Angel of Music ever came like Father described," the singer continued.

"If he does, have him put in a word for me with the Angel of Dance. I could use a bit more talent myself."

"Don't joke, Meg! It's very serious. Father always told me about an Angel who inspired all the great singers—"

"—and he promised some day the Angel would come to teach you, I know. I wasn't laughing, and you're just stalling now."

An Angel of Music. Almost to the marble pillar hiding his exit, he paused instead, mildly interested in spite of himself. It wasn't a bad idea, as far as superstitions went, though he couldn't fit it to any particular theology. A blending of pagan Apollo and Christian Gabriel, perhaps.

On stage, the reluctant singer finally began to run through a few scales. He was pleasantly surprised to find that she could at least hit the right notes—and quite high ones too. Very nice soprano range, a bit more extended than average.

Then she began an aria from *Faust* and, without making any conscious decision, he drifted back towards his seat, listening intently.

Angelic visitations or not, she was a very fine singer. Oh, her high notes were a bit harsh, her low notes were undeveloped, her technique and execution could be improved any number of ways. But he had never heard anyone with such enormous *potential*. She had a fine basic control and an impressive range. She was achieving notes that Carlotta couldn't hit on her best days. And there was more, something harder to quantify or even describe. A depth he wouldn't have expected from such a young voice, a nuance of tone most singers never achieved, and with it all a certain heart-rending beauty in the sound…

Likely as not all that potential would never come to anything, mishandled by teachers who didn't have the subtlety to see it. One of the small tragedies of a harsh world.

He would remember this voice if he had heard it before, so she must have come to the Opera Garnier recently. Likely while he was absent. Best to have a look now and see who this girl was, in case he ever wanted to send her a suggestion in the future. Perhaps he could give her some hints on what to do with that voice.

He rose from his seat and stepped up to the front of the box. With long practice he reached for the divide in the thick velvet curtains, parting them exactly two centimeters.

The singer was standing in the middle of the stage, tiny in the vast emptiness. She was slender, too young for the ability her voice demonstrated, the light glinting off her thick brown curls and full red lips.

She finished her aria with one last dizzying soar of notes, leaving behind a silence filled with the ghost of the song. In that silence, she lifted her face and looked up towards Box Five. She couldn't possibly see him, and yet he felt as though their gazes were meeting. Something stirred in the pit of his stomach, and his hands tightened on the rail before him, suddenly feeling a need for the support.

Her dark eyes were limpid and full, with a sadness and vulnerability that made the most eloquent of appeals. All at once the emptiness of the stage seemed not like a mere fact, but like an elaborate metaphor for a vast, cold, uncaring world, surrounding and threatening this beautiful girl with her beautiful voice.

The silence broke with a patter of applause from a figure in white he hadn't even noticed off on the edge of the wings. "That was lovely!" Little Meg Giry exclaimed. "See, I knew you'd be wonderful, Christine!"

Christine.

Far from the Phantom cursing us for using the empty auditorium for Christine to sing, good luck followed the very next day. Christine received a promotion, and I was the first one she went to tell after choral practice let out. We did a proper flurry of delighted exclaiming, and then I accepted the invitation to come with her as she handled the logistics. So I followed Christine as she followed Monsieur Brodeur, the stage manager, through a corridor lined with doors. We were in the singers' portion of the building, a less familiar but not wholly strange landscape for me. I glanced at the portraits of elegant sopranos as we passed them, bright against the pale green of the walls.

"I wish the vocal director would consult me before he makes these decisions," Brodeur complained to the world at large. "It's as if he thinks I'm building dressing rooms at will! Does he have any appreciation for how crowded we are? Where he thinks I'm going to put you, I have no idea."

The promotion was a long way from making Christine a star, but it did entitle her to a dressing room. It was much easier to get your own room in the chorus than in the ballet. But that made sense, of course. Chorus members needed private space to practice, and the ballet all worked together. I understood that. Though *sometimes*, when our dressing room was particularly loud and busy and crowded, I was envious.

"Isn't that one at the end empty?" Christine asked, pointing to a room at the farthest reach of the corridor, the only door without a name.

Brodeur's eyebrows scrunched in aggravation. "You don't want that one. It's haunted."

My interest immediately rose, while Christine merely laughed. "I thought the whole building was."

"Yes, but that room is problematic." He sighed deeply, invoking all the troubles of the earth. "All the girls moan about disembodied hands and strange voices, but that's the only one where they actually refuse to keep the room."

I had heard of a haunted dressing room, but couldn't recall the details. So many ghost stories floated through the Opera, and this one was too much the property of the singers for me to have focused on it.

Christine glanced at me, and said to Brodeur, "I think I could risk it." I coughed, a fake cough, a pointed cough. She didn't look at me again, going on with a warm smile, "After all, that would settle the matter, and I would hate to inconvenience you if you had to find me somewhere else."

"Mark my words, I'll be finding you somewhere else in a week anyway," Brodeur muttered. "Still, if you want to try it, very well. It's on your head. I'll send someone to put a name on the door."

He disappeared muttering down the hall, and Christine and I went the other direction to see her new dressing room.

"Oh, this is lovely," she said, turning up the gas lamps to reveal a small but comfortable room with a low couch, an elegant dressing table, and an enormous mirror with a gilt frame covering most of one wall.

"I'm not sure this is a good idea," I said, perching uneasily on the cream-colored couch and smoothing my lavender skirts. "It sounds like the Phantom doesn't want anyone in here." He had been absent from the last performance (a little surprising, though he had always come and gone) but I felt sure he would be back soon enough, and take notice of this change in room assignment.

"Oh well, I hardly think he's going to kill me over a dressing room." She ran one fingertip along the top of the carved wooden vanity table. "Hmm. Needs a good dusting."

"I know I said he's not as dangerous as the stories say, but that doesn't mean you can just ignore him." I twisted my necklace on its chain, wondering if I never should have told Christine about meeting the Phantom at all. I couldn't seem to explain him right, so that she could understand. "He does get angry and he is serious when he makes demands and—"

"—and I promise, *chérie*, I'll run screaming to Monsieur Brodeur for a new room at the very first disembodied hand. Happy?" She bounced over to the mirror and did a twirl, watching her reflection. It wasn't the kind of twirl a ballerina would do, but she still looked charming. "I hope the Phantom will let me stay. Where else am I going to find a mirror like this?"

He paced for hours through the lower depths of the Opera, wrapped amongst the shadows and the brooding silence, remonstrating with himself. This girl was no different than the hundreds of other girls who passed through the Opera Garnier, all more or less talented, all more or less beautiful. She was hardly the first one to be alone and in need of a champion.

After so many years of singers and ballet girls in their wisps of costumes, he had all but convinced himself he was immune to their attractions. Well—not *immune,* precisely. But capable of controlling unwise impulses, as well as avoiding the maudlin, sentimental notion that one girl's eyes were any more special than the eyes of a dozen others.

Ghosts did not fall in love.

Ghosts did not want things they could not have.

Ghosts did not wish and ache and long for life—not life among the shadows and buried in the catacombs, only observing, but actual *life,* full of passion and joy and pain.

And as Hamlet would say, there was the rub. Because how could this end in anything but pain? What possible ending did he imagine this would lead to?

Oh, he could imagine all sorts of ecstasies involving pale skin and limpid brown eyes and that exquisite voice—but what kind of ending could he *realistically* imagine?

Death. His own, if he was lucky. And rejection and heartbreak and fear and pain. What else was there for him? What else had there ever been?

So many operas ended tragically. Why should his story be any different? The happy ones, the comedies and the romances, ended with a marriage. He had always known that was not in his fate, that no woman would ever—no, this changed nothing, that was still far, far out of his reach. And only a fool would start playing a symphony that could only finish in a discordant crash of heartbreak.

He should go home, pour all this absurd emotion into an actual symphony, into notes instead of deeds, and let that be the end of it. He could write it all into a *nocturne*, a pensive piece suitable for the endless night of his world beneath the earth, and then lock the piece and the emotions away together.

He tried it, put the finished pages away, and discovered that the emotions didn't disappear with the papers. Music didn't seem to be able to help him in this particular struggle.

He might still have resisted longer, if he wasn't so sick of being underground, alone in the silence that held no voices, not even the memory of anyone else's music. As it was, it was only a few days before he slunk back up to the Opera above, telling himself it had nothing to do with *her*, he wasn't going because of *her* at all. And if he did chance to hear her voice among the crowd, well, that could do no harm, he could merely listen. He had always listened to the Opera Company's business, that was quite normal, nothing extraordinary, no need to become involved.

Although she did have that remarkable voice, and it really would be such a shame, a crime against music, if no one took an interest and helped her to develop that voice. For the music's sake. For the sake of the Opera.

All he wanted to do, after all, was to help her. Nothing was wrong with that, that was even a noble impulse. She needed help. She had spoken about her father in the past tense, and she had seemed so alone, so helpless. If she was languishing in the chorus, then plainly she had no one to take her part.

He wasn't going to ask her for anything. He wasn't even going to think of that. He was only thinking of giving her something, something she wanted, and that was an act of generosity, wasn't it?

It would be so easy, so simple. He had scrawled a quick letter to M. Montagne the vocal director before fleeing belowground, and already that had produced results. Unexpected ones, as well; it was so convenient that she had been placed in the dressing room at the end of the hall. That one had a hidden door and he had always preferred to keep it empty, lest some blathering chorus girl come across his secret, inconveniencing one of his routes through the Opera. Really it seemed like an act of Fate that Christine had been placed there now—not that Fate had ever done him any favors before, but perhaps just this once, just this *one* time…

And so, somehow he found himself on the back side of the full-length mirror in Christine's dressing room, hidden in the shadowed tunnel, watching her comb her long curls in front of the much smaller mirror on the vanity.

It wasn't too late yet to walk silently away. Instead, he watched that comb work slowly through her shining hair again and again. Finally he projected his voice into the room beyond.

"Christine."

The comb stilled and she looked around the small dressing room, a puzzled frown appearing on her face. "Who's there?"

"Do not be afraid." That put him on script, didn't it? If he really planned to play this all the way through.

She dropped the comb with a click as it hit the table, her gaze darting more quickly around the room. "…where are you, Monsieur?"

"You cannot see me, but know that I am a friend." She *might* believe that, if he stayed just a Voice. A man in a cloak and a mask would be far more alarming.

"I don't understand." Her voice wavered with the inevitable fear. "Who are you?"

He hesitated. He had a plan, an answer for this question. It was only because he had that answer that he had dared to speak to her at all. Now, when the moment arose, he wasn't so sure. Could he tell her such a preposterous, absurd, impossible lie? She would never believe it. She would know it wasn't true, would suspect something sinister.

Christine's eyes brightened, face lighting with a glowing hope. "Are you the Angel of Music? The one Father promised would come to me?"

Well. If she was going to give the answer *for* him… "Yes, Christine. I am the Angel of Music, and I've come to help you sing."

Chapter Ten

C hristine grew quieter in the weeks after her promotion, and
busier too. I tried to pretend, both to myself and to her, that I
didn't notice the change, that I didn't feel as though I was being set
aside as she focused on some unknown, more important thing. I knew
Christine wouldn't do that. And yet it made me inordinately pleased
when she suggested sneaking with me into the Dance Foyer after an
evening's performance. At least, it did until I spent several minutes
sitting around as she gave minimal responses to my near-monologue
about the most recent opera.

I gave up talking finally and leaned back on the green banquette.
At least I was sitting down. My feet hurt from the dancing today, and
just at the moment being at home soaking them sounded like a much
better way to spend the evening. I tried to stifle that wish, and instead
watched Christine in the mirror as she watched the crowd. The tall
mirrors reflected the whole room, doubling the throng. Nothing
seemed remarkable about it, just the usual crush of ballet girls and their
admirers.

After a moment or two of silence, she brought her gaze back to
me. "I'm sorry, Meg, what were you saying?"

"It wasn't important."

"No, I'm sure it was, *chérie*," she protested, with a smile. "Something about Carlotta, wasn't it?"

"Just that she wasn't at her best tonight. She really should think about retiring, or at least give up trying to play ingénue roles." Not an original observation, but it was hard to carry on a one-sided conversation for very long. The Phantom remarked on Carlotta often in his notes. It was even the sort of thing the ballet girls liked to gossip over, that I always professed boredom in. I hadn't been in one of those conversations for some time, I realized.

"I don't think Carlotta is ever going to give anything up," Christine said, still smiling—and then her gaze drifted away from me, out towards the rest of the room again.

I stifled a sigh, and when my right foot throbbed I thought again of giving up and going home. Why suggest coming if she didn't want to talk to me?

Was she looking for someone in the crowd, someone she'd rather talk to? But surely I'd know if she had another intimate friend at the Opera, and she hadn't seemed interested in a closer relationship with anyone else. Maybe it was one of the gentlemen. Maybe she had a romance or an attraction she wasn't sharing with me. But that didn't make sense either. She had sworn she wasn't interested, of course. I still went with her to the Singers Foyer sometimes, and I hadn't seen her favoring any particular admirer. She never entertained anyone in her dressing room.

I was about to ask her directly if she was looking for someone, when her hand closed around my arm and I saw that her gaze had settled on the far end of the Dance Foyer. "Do you know that man? The one talking to Sorelli?"

This could be the answer to the question I hadn't asked. I looked for Sorelli in the direction of Christine's gaze. The lead ballerina was easy to spot in her vivid red gown, talking to two men dressed in somber grays. The older one was a usual visitor to the Foyer, and with a little thought I recalled the younger man's name too. "That's Philippe, the Comte de Chagny, and his younger brother the vicomte, Raoul. The comte and Sorelli have been, you know, keeping company for years." Surely Christine couldn't have been looking for *him*.

"But Raoul," she said in a low voice, "what do you think about him?"

"I don't, usually. I guess he's nice enough." I looked at him appraisingly across the room. He was slim and handsome, with pale brown hair and a barely-visible mustache. He had little resemblance to his brother, who had to be at least forty with a thick brown mustache, the beginnings of a paunch, and a laugh that could routinely be heard from across the Foyer. I wondered if Raoul had grown his facial hair in an effort to look more mature; if so, it was failing. No one would mistake him for over twenty. "He's good-looking, if a bit boyish. And he's a gentleman, which is more than can be said of many young men in this room."

"Then you like him?"

I shrugged. If we were going to gossip, surely we could find someone more interesting to do it about. "I don't dislike him. It's only…"

"What?" she asked, and I was surprised by the intensity contained in that single word, by the way her hand tightened on my arm and her gaze stared right into me.

"Nothing, really," I said uncertainly, suddenly feeling I was dancing across treacherous ground. "Only that the first time I talked to him, I felt sure I knew everything about him after ten minutes. Maybe I'm wrong, only that was months ago and he hasn't shown unexpected depths yet. Why so interested?"

She looked away, suddenly relaxing her hold on my arm, her tone turning casual. "Oh, just curious. I used to know him. Years ago, when we were children. He was vacationing in the same village Papa and I lived in, and we were…sort of friends. I was surprised to see him. That's all."

If she was truly surprised, why did it seem like she'd been looking for him? Or someone, at least. Maybe she was embarrassed to admit her interest? "He's a regular subscriber, though I guess I haven't seen him lately." I couldn't be sure; it wasn't as if I paid attention to him. "I think Sorelli mentioned once that he's in the Navy. Maybe he was away."

"I had heard he was living in Paris, but after all this time not seeing him, I didn't think he'd ever be at the Opera."

"Well, he's here now," I said, and slipped my arm through hers. "Come on, we should go say hello." Raoul wasn't who I would choose to spend an evening with, but it seemed clear enough he was important to Christine somehow.

"No, I couldn't!" she protested, not moving in response to my tug. "It was such a long time ago—I'm sure he won't remember me at all."

He might have forgotten me from a year ago, but I had no doubt that he remembered Christine. No one would ever forget her. "Of course he'll remember you. Not that it matters either way if he never gets to see you. So let's go."

I got to my feet (a sacrifice, as my toes reminded me how much I'd danced on them today), then pulled her off the banquette and over to the trio. Sorelli knew me, Philippe didn't care about knowing me, and Raoul looked slightly troubled, as though he was trying—and failing—to place me.

"We spoke a few times before, several months ago," I prompted, extending one hand to Raoul. "Meg Giry."

"Ah. Of course." He gave my fingers a polite and perfunctory kiss, barely brushing the skin.

"I think you also know my friend Christine," I said, indicating her with a tilt of my head.

"Monsieur," she said, dipping a slight but elegant curtsy. Sorelli looked her over and put a proprietary hand on Philippe's arm.

"Christine...surely not Christine Daaé?" Raoul said, eyes and smile widening. "I haven't seen you since you were..." He gestured vaguely around waist-height.

Christine blossomed into the most brilliant of smiles. I knew from that moment that Raoul had no hope of escaping with heart intact. I didn't imagine she meant to make him fall in love, but how could he resist? "You remember me, Monsieur!"

"Of course, and your father the violinist!" Raoul turned to Philippe and Sorelli. "Christine and I used to play together as children, when the family was visiting Lannion."

"Ah yes, the halcyon days of youth," Philippe remarked. "Long behind us all now."

"Speak for yourself," Sorelli said with a decided nudge.

"I meant *childhood*, my dear." He winked at her and elbowed Raoul. "Can you believe my little brother is now in the Navy? He just completed a trip around the world."

Suddenly the Vicomte de Chagny was granted a glow of interest he had never before possessed. "Really?" I said. "That must have been so exciting! Where did you go? What did you see?"

"A lot of water, I'm afraid," Raoul said with a laugh.

I waved my hands. "Never mind that, you must have gone ashore some time!"

"Well, you see one port, you've seen them all."

"Remember the port in Lannion?" Christine said, voice eager with excitement. "And the little beach by that inlet. What was it called?"

"Trestraou," he supplied, turning towards her as he spoke. "Where we met, the day I rescued your scarf from the ocean!"

And then they were off on childhood reminiscences that were perfectly sweet but couldn't be *half* as interesting as stories about a trip around the world—provided one had the eyes to see and the tongue to tell. First I tried to get the conversation back to Raoul's trip, and then I tried to enjoy the childhood stories, but I didn't succeed very well with either effort.

When we finally parted company, Raoul kissed Christine's hand with significantly more enthusiasm than he had kissed mine. She only smiled, but her cheeks turned a shade pinker.

"Still only interested in your career?" I asked in a low voice as we walked away.

"Of course," Christine said in puzzled tones.

"Mm-hmm. If you say so," I said with a smile. It had been a dull conversation, but I could still be happy about this if it made Christine happy. And besides, so much teasing would be possible.

"Meg! Raoul and I are just old friends, that's all."

That was her story and she stuck to it, even after word got around the Opera that the Vicomte de Chagny had abandoned his brother in the

Dance Foyer and taken to attending the Singers Foyer instead. Even after the rest of Christine's admirers quietly faded away into other circles around other girls, evidently not willing to contend with her old childhood sweetheart the vicomte.

I wouldn't have picked Raoul if it was me, but at least he was nice, and what mattered was that Christine liked him. So on the whole I was pleased. Raoul was such a simple, understandable explanation for any time Christine was distracted.

He was not pleased by the arrival of Raoul de Chagny in Christine's life. The boy was a discordant note in what up until then had been the beautiful symphony of Christine's presence at the Opera. It was a symphony in minor key, perhaps, composed as it was of mingled pleasure and pain, delightful singing and hopeless longing, dreams and self-reproaches. Beautiful, all the same. Until Raoul.

He had always known young men chased her in the Singers Foyer. He hadn't liked that either, but had gritted his teeth and accepted it as unavoidable, meaningless, and essentially harmless—as long as she didn't do any chasing back. Raoul, though. From the beginning he was different.

It was obvious Christine had gone to the Dance Foyer with her little friend in order to look for him. And once they met, they went on meeting. All at the Opera, all perfectly proper, all simply as "old friends." It was charming, in a way, the picture of a childhood friendship renewed—if only that old friend hadn't grown older!

He consoled himself with the thought that nothing could come of it. Christine might talk over long-ago stories in the Foyer with Raoul, but she knew what was truly important. Her art, her singing, her career. Her father's dream. Her angel's lessons.

And then, of course, it wasn't as though the Vicomte de Chagny could ever consider marrying a girl from the Opera. He wasn't fit to touch Christine's shoe, but society wouldn't view it that way. Noblemen didn't marry chorus girls; that was how the world would put it. If Raoul himself was naïve enough to think that dictate could be flouted, his older brother certainly wasn't.

Besides, Christine's voice had made glorious advancements in little over a month of proper training. Within perhaps that much time again, she would be ready to step out of the chorus and show the world what real singing sounded like. Her recent promotion had given her better standing at the Opera, given her the odd line of dialogue here or there in performances, but it didn't provide her the opportunity to truly show her ability. He would arrange for just that opportunity, launch her on a breath-taking career, and the Vicomte de Chagny would dwindle to utter insignificance in the process.

More days slipped by. Christine and her guardian, Madame Valérius, came to visit Mother and me on Christmas. Quite a lot of the afternoon was spent talking about the future glories of Christine's career, though of course she modestly protested.

January was always quiet at the Opera, and so it was the time for one of my twice annual trips to Leclair. Most years I was happy to visit my cousins and step out of the typical routine. It wasn't the kind of traveling I dreamed of doing, but at least it was a change of scenery— even if Leclair's scenery was just as familiar to me as Paris.

This year I was reluctant to go. Even if I could explain Christine's distraction by the presence of Raoul, I still couldn't entirely shake uneasy qualms. It seemed like a bad idea to go away for three weeks just when I wasn't sure what was happening with my best friend.

These worries were far too vague and unsubstantiated to hold any weight with Mother.

They seemed vaguer and more meaningless to me too, once we got away from the Opera. Leclair was like a different world, a small village of mostly farmers where everyone knew everyone. Opera

Ghosts and even overpowering sopranos seemed like they must be mythical. So I worried less than I had expected while we were gone, and then when we came back, Christine seemed so pleased to see me that my concerns felt just silly. She remembered my 18th birthday too, at the beginning of February; we went to a bakery near the Opera that afternoon, then sat near the Seine giggling over Opera gossip and eating far too many beignets and madeleines.

And it was always harder to worry about anything in February, when the daffodils started blooming in corners and window boxes all around Paris, like little scraps of sunshine.

The Wednesday after my birthday I went to the Singers Foyer after the performance to meet Christine, a daffodil tucked into my hair, feeling happy with the world. It was harder to *stay* happy once I had arrived and spent fifteen minutes listening to Christine and Raoul talk about childhood memories. They never seemed to tire of them.

"I remember Nurse was so angry with me for getting soaked," Raoul said brightly, just as though they hadn't talked about this story at least three times in my hearing. Even half-listening, I knew exactly which story it was.

"But it was so noble of you to rescue my scarf from the ocean!" Christine said, smiling warmly. "And just think—if you hadn't, we never would have met."

And wouldn't that have been a terrible loss. I tried to push that thought down. Raoul wasn't so bad, and Christine liked him, so what business was it of mine? Even if Christine had had more time for me before, more attention for me in conversations. Perhaps I should have gone to the Dance Foyer tonight. I hadn't been there since before I went to Leclair. And the Singers Foyer was much less interesting, smaller and emptier, still gilded but with no mirrors to give even the illusion of space and crowds.

"Chance encounters make me believe in Fate," Christine burbled on. "Don't you think so, Meg?"

"Perhaps," I said. I should have seized the opportunity to change the subject, but this was the first comment that actually caught my interest. Was it Fate that I encountered the Phantom when I first came to the Opera? Fate that Christine and I bumped into each other outside

Box Five? It was strange to think that if any of us had taken a different turn in a corridor, it all might have changed. Was it just random or was nothing really chance after all?

It was probably only coincidence, though, that I was musing on meeting people just as Christine caught Raoul's arm and said, "Oh look, there's Léon. You simply must introduce him to Meg."

"Léon?" I repeated, shaking away philosophical thoughts.

"Yes, he's one of Raoul's very good friends. I've been wanting you two to meet!"

The excited tone in Christine's voice suddenly made me wary. "Christine, what are you—"

But by then Léon was joining our group. He exchanged easy greetings with Raoul first, giving me a chance to look him over. He was tall, with thick blond hair that shone in the light from the candles in the chandelier above us. He seemed vaguely familiar so I'd probably seen him around the Opera, but I couldn't remember ever speaking to him. I guessed he was about the same age as Raoul, around twenty. He carried his age more comfortably, unlike Raoul who seemed narrowly able to convince people he wasn't younger. Maybe it was the jaw. Léon had a good firm jaw, nice features overall, really, and I was ready to judge him as reasonably handsome—until Raoul was introducing us and I got a better look at his eyes.

Léon's eyes were an absolutely startling, captivating shade of blue. They were almost as striking as the Phantom's green eyes.

"Léon de Troyes, Meg Giry," Raoul said, and Léon lightly kissed the hand I extended, with a murmured, "*Enchanté*, Mademoiselle Giry."

"The pleasure is mine," I replied, feeling a little tingle from where his lips had brushed my fingers. He was a welcome alternative to Christine and Raoul's stories—and not only because the stories were boring.

"Are you in the chorus with Christine?" Léon asked, still holding my hand.

"No, I'm in the ballet." I flashed a smile. "Don't tell anyone. I'm not really supposed to be here."

He grinned broadly and winked. "I wouldn't breathe a word."

I extracted my hand; he needn't presume he had a right to it. Although I did keep smiling.

The conversation meandered on in a general way, and I learned that Léon had lived all his life in Paris, had only recently begun attending the Opera, and moved in the same social circles as Raoul. That last told me that he had to be wealthy, and his clothing suggested it too; the style was understated enough, but the fit was tailored and the fabric expensive.

I learned he owned an expensive carriage when he and Raoul spent five minutes talking about horses and carriage maintenance. I doubted either of them had ever fixed a carriage in their lives; they had people to do that. That didn't stop them from talking about it, and the conversation only turned interesting again when Léon proposed we should all plan a ride together.

Raoul seconded the idea immediately. "That would be wonderful! I never get to see you outside of this place, Christine." He waved a hand, encompassing the room and the Opera beyond. The gesture was a shade dismissive for my taste.

"I don't know..." Christine said, head tilted as she twisted one stray curl. "You *know* I have to concentrate on my singing."

"No one can sing all the time," Raoul said briskly, brushing that objection right away. "This Saturday afternoon. It would be perfect!"

"I can have the carriage ready to pick you up at noon," Léon said at once, and grinned at me, those blue eyes shining. And it was definitely at *me*, not at Christine. "We could make a picnic of it."

An afternoon picnic with a charming young man did sound decidedly tempting. So I was genuinely regretful when I said, "We can't on Saturday. We have to attend a rehearsal."

"You *knew* that, Raoul," Christine said, forehead puckering in distress. "I've told you we have rehearsals on Saturday."

"Perhaps another day," Léon suggested, enthusiasm unabashed.

"Or skip one rehearsal," Raoul said, shoving his hands into his pockets with a shrug. "It's just one. What's the harm?"

I was so used to Raoul saying ridiculous things that this didn't upset me. I had never expected him to properly appreciate the Opera.

That may not have been so for Christine. "I thought you understood that my singing is very important to me." Her chin wobbled as she blinked rapidly. "I thought you *understood* how important it is to dedicate myself and fulfill Papa's dream."

Raoul began to look alarmed, hands rising as though he thought he ought to do something but didn't know what. "Now don't overreact, I didn't mean anything—"

"How can you say that caring about my art is an *overreaction*?" she asked in wavering tones.

I frowned, wondering if I had a handkerchief. Though really, if she was going to let a little thing like this distress her—maybe she cared more about Raoul than I thought.

"I didn't mean—"

"I think I want to leave." Christine crossed her arms and looked away. "Meg, are you coming?"

She turned towards the door without waiting to see if I was coming or not. I might have liked to talk to Léon longer, but what I could do? I gave an apologetic shrug to both men, though Raoul probably didn't deserve it and was too busy looking at Christine to notice. Léon gave a smile and a slight bow in response. I smiled too, said a quick, "It was so nice to meet you," and hurried after Christine to offer her my handkerchief.

We went back to her dressing room, where she went on for several minutes about how she couldn't fathom why Raoul couldn't grasp the importance of her singing, and how she just didn't have time for other things, and after all they were only old friends and he shouldn't think it could be more. I said "mm-hmm" a lot. I was sorry she was upset, but it all seemed like she was reading a great deal into one comment about one rehearsal. It hardly made Raoul a monster, or required reassessing their entire relationship.

Finally I ventured, "I really think he just meant to suggest one day—"

"Oh, never mind, *chérie,* I don't want to talk about it anymore," Christine concluded, picking up her comb and skimming it through her curls. "And what did you think of Léon?"

"Oh—I don't know," I said, thrown by the abrupt topic change. "He seems nice. We barely spoke."

"I've been hoping for a chance to introduce you two! He's one of Raoul's very good friends, you know."

"So you said." I wasn't sure that was a recommendation. On the other side of the scale, well, Léon did have striking blue eyes and seemed friendly—and I hadn't really minded that he held onto my hand longer than necessary. I found myself smiling without entirely intending to.

"You must come with me to the Singers Foyer again Saturday evening," Christine decided. "I know you'll like him when you get to know him better!"

I didn't *know* that…but I wasn't averse to finding out.

Chapter Eleven

T he following Saturday dawned sunny, surprisingly warm for February, and absolutely perfect weather for a carriage ride and a picnic. I noted this glumly, then went on to the afternoon rehearsal. All the ballet girls were discussing the latest news: M. Debienne wanted the entire Company in the auditorium for 'an announcement of the highest importance.'

Madame Thibault herded us to the auditorium among the first arrivals. Most of the girls sat together near the back, but Christine was already sitting in the third row. I walked up the long aisle and took a seat next to her, to watch the rest of the Company trickle in and find places on the stage and among the red velvet seats. We didn't come near to filling the long rows.

I saw Mother across the auditorium, deep in discussion with one of the other boxkeepers, and Carlotta came in with a crowd of devotees—mostly singers though I saw Jammes in their midst. I even saw the Persian, in his distinctive red fez, sitting at the end of one of the back rows with a wide swathe of empty seats around him. I couldn't imagine what right he had to be there, and yet I knew no one would dare approach him to order him out.

I leaned back in my seat and looked up at the glittering chandelier, high enough to be shrunk by distance and yet still breathtaking in size. I had never seen it unlit—except when the flaming skeleton appeared and all the lights went out—and it was as steady as the sun. More so, since the sun disappeared over the horizon every night. The chandelier was always there, casting its light over the scarlet seats and the gold carvings decorating the stage and the first few boxes. The imperial boxes were the grandest, but Box Five came close—and it was the most secluded.

Finally Monsieur Debienne came to the center of the stage, twisting his hands and looking out at us with an uneven smile.

"He looks nervous," I remarked to Christine, as Debienne glanced up towards the catwalks, then stepped closer to the front of the stage. But then, he usually looked nervous, so it didn't tell me much about how important his news was.

"I have a very significant announcement," he said, struggling to project his voice in the cavernous space. He wasn't an actor. "I am leaving my position as manager of the Opera Garnier. In fact, today is my final day."

A murmur of surprise ran through the crowd, and I commented to Christine, "That's so soon—he wasn't here nearly as long as Poligny." But he had never seemed to like it here very much, so maybe it made sense. I didn't know him well enough to regret his leaving, feeling mostly a pleasant buzz of curiosity about who might replace him.

Debienne glanced upward again, then hurried on to say, "I am delighted to announce that the Opera's new managers are here with us." He waved a hand towards two men who had evidently been waiting in the wings and now approached. "Monsieurs Armand Moncharmin and Firmin Ricard. I trust you will welcome them among you."

They came forward with bows and beaming delight. I wondered which was which, studying them with interest. New managers could be a significant change in casting, in the story of the Opera. One man was tall and had a wide smile, a shock of reddish hair, and the very latest style in evening coats. The other had gray hair and last year's suit, but with every crease pressed to a sharp point and buttons gleaming.

"Do you suppose new management will change things much?" Christine asked.

"Maybe." They were a significant role, but this was still an ensemble story. "It depends on how much they *want* to change things. In the end, managers come and go. The Company goes on." As did the Phantom, though this was too public a space for me to say that out loud. Was he here somewhere? Most likely. Everyone else was.

Carlotta came sweeping forward at that point, ascending the steps to the right of the orchestra pit, and Debienne was quick to introduce her to the new managers. Since he did it one at a time, I learned that Ricard had the red hair and Moncharmin the sharp creases. Ricard bowed deeply over Carlotta's hand and began an enthusiastic appreciation of the many performances where he had heard her sing. Carlotta, naturally, preened and accepted it all as her due.

"If he can make Carlotta happy, he'll do all right as manager," I observed. I wondered if he was sincere or just charismatic. "Provided he makes you-know-who happy too."

"Who?" Christine asked, eyes wide and innocent.

I stared at her pointedly for a moment, and when she continued to look blank, I nodded towards Box Five.

"Oh! Well, yes, of course."

"We are planning a small reception after tonight's performance," Moncharmin announced to the crowd at large. "An opportunity to get to know our new Company better, we hope, so you are all invited. We would be simply delighted if Madame Carlotta would—"

"Signora Carlotta," she interjected, nose in the air at a dangerous tilt.

"Er, yes. If Signora Carlotta would sing something for us at the event."

"Delighted," Ricard reiterated.

Carlotta was plainly *not* delighted, nose staying up and eyebrows rising too. "I am sorry—let me be sure I understand—you wish me to sing. This evening. After the performance."

A sigh swept through the Company, including from me. The new managers had made a tactical error. We all could see when a Carlotta-tantrum was coming on.

Not so the new managers. "Just a little something," Moncharmin said with a wave of his hand. "Whatever's easy for you."

I leaned back in my seat, resigned to the melodramatic explosion on the way. It was too bad for the managers. I was sorry they hadn't got through at least a day without encountering Carlotta's temper. Or even an hour.

Carlotta snatched her hand away from the attentive Ricard. "I do not sing *little somethings*. And I do *not* sing on six hours notice, *after* a full performance."

"It was only an idea," Ricard said hastily. "If you'd rather not—"

"It is not a question of what I would *rather*." She pressed a hand to her forehead. "It is what my art *allows*. I am, you understand, an *artist*. It is a demanding role, a constant effort. I am *not* a trained canary to perform here, there and everywhere at the drop of a whim!" She put her nose in the air again, shoulders flung back. "It is so deeply distressing to be so *badly* misunderstood!"

Both new managers were protesting apologies by now, which we all knew would be useless, while Debienne had completely turned his attention to the shadowy reaches above. What was he looking for? I looked up myself, but could see nothing in the darkness above. Was the Phantom there? Was that what Debienne was thinking of?

"No, I cannot stand this strain!" Carlotta at last proclaimed. "The insult—the emotional agony—I must go lie down."

At once she was the center of an adoring cluster of girls, eager to help her along to her dressing room. They could have gone out directly through backstage; Carlotta took the more dramatic route down from the stage, around the orchestra pit and out through the seats. As they all went past Christine and me, I heard Carlotta remark to her devotees, "Best to put one's managers in their place immediately, no?"

I wondered what Carlotta was *really* like, under her poses and her manipulations. Did anyone know, even her?

"Signora Carlotta will be back for tonight's performance…won't she?" Ricard asked, watching her go with a strained expression.

Debienne dragged his eyes down from the ceiling. "I wouldn't count on it. Probably best if you start arranging to cancel now."

"Just because we asked her to sing?" Ricard protested.

"But we'll have to give refunds!" Moncharmin said in gasping horror. I tried to hold back a smirk, because he was suddenly just as dramatic as Carlotta.

"Yes," Debienne said, evidently to both of them. "Now if you don't mind, there's one or two things I'd like to cover in my—your office, and then I have a train to catch. I already have tickets booked on a ship to Australia."

The three men departed and proper rehearsals got underway. They began with the dancers but not a group I was in, so Christine and I both remained where we were.

"Did you know they have something called a kangaroo in Australia?" I commented. "They're big creatures with enormous feet and they can do these incredible leaps."

Christine laughed merrily. "Oh *chérie*, you think everywhere is fascinating!"

"Not everywhere. But lots of places are."

"Well, I hope Monsieur Debienne will enjoy your giant leaping rabbits, or whatever they are."

"Kangaroos," I said under my breath.

The other dancers had gone through their routine twice and I had not brought up any other details about Australia when M. Montagne, the vocal director, came up to us. "Mademoiselle Daaé, if I might have a word?" he said, tucking a piece of paper into his jacket pocket as he spoke.

"Of course, Monsieur," Christine said, rising to her feet.

"This way, please," he said, and turned to go.

Christine shrugged at me, and followed him. I watched them go, curious what that was about. Likely Christine would tell me later. I returned my thoughts to the new managers. They hadn't begun very well, but after all, I didn't know *anyone* who was good at keeping Carlotta calm. Even the Phantom sent her into fits on a regular basis— though I suspected he meant to do it. With that thought, my gaze drifted back up overhead. Was he in the catwalks? Or Box Five? Surely he'd want to know about something like a change of management. It would have been nice to know what he thought of the new managers too. I didn't know quite what good the opinion would be, but I would have liked to know it.

With that I got up to my feet, thinking I'd join the ballet girls at the back of the theater. I could find out what they thought, anyway. But when I turned, the group had evidently dispersed while I wasn't looking. Some were onstage, and the rest must have gone off somewhere else until they were needed. I could go look for them.

The idea gave me a queer, awkward feeling as I imagined it. They could have asked me to come with them. Of course that surely wasn't a deliberate oversight. I was just off with Christine and they hadn't thought—but all the same, I sank back down in my seat. I could wait here, until it was my turn to dance.

The evening performance was not canceled. I hung about the Opera after rehearsal, didn't successfully cross paths with Christine again, and finally headed to the ballet girls' dressing room. The room was in its usual state of crowd and chaos, with girls in various states of dress spread everywhere, against a backdrop of bags and cloaks and stray costumes and props sprawled all over the lines of dressing tables and scattered chairs. I wound through the crowd to my own dressing table.

I noticed Jammes was holding forth to an audience of other dancers nearby, as we all stretched and dressed and made final checks on the lacings of our slippers. "I think it's simply disgusting," Jammes said. "The very idea is absurd; it must have come from those new managers, who plainly don't know what they're doing."

I was curious about what she found so disgusting—but I didn't talk to Jammes if I could avoid it. I continued my warm-up run through the basic positions and hoped someone would say something illuminating.

Jammes did, though I would have preferred that she do it without addressing me. She fastened her gaze on me and said, "Have you heard? Your precious friend Christine has been chosen to sing the lead tonight."

I stopped with my feet in fifth position, arms extended in second, and stared at Jammes, my breath growing shorter. "Not really?"

"Oh yes, they decided she can sing Carlotta's part." She made a derisive noise. "I suppose next they'll ask *you* to dance for Sorelli."

Frustration simmered in my stomach, but I made myself smile sweetly, bring my arms in smoothly. "Probably not—but it *is* more likely than that they'll ever ask *you* to sing for Carlotta."

A red blush spread up from Jammes' neck to her cheeks, and her eyebrows lowered in anger. I bobbed the quickest of curtsies and slipped away and out of the changing room before she could formulate a comeback. It was not often that I got the last word.

Also I wanted to find Christine, of course. I went to the backstage area, but didn't see her anywhere. It didn't take much asking to find out she was still in her dressing room, and by then it was too close to the performance for me to go there, not without risking the towering wrath of Madame Thibault. So I found myself a place off Stage Right, sufficiently far from where Jammes and her cluster of girls had taken up positions, and with a good view for the performance. I went back to my warm-up exercises as I kept my eye on the stage. If I wouldn't have a chance to talk to Christine, I could at least watch her debut.

Christine had a solo in Act One, and she sang it—well enough. She was too tentative, and though she hit all the right notes, her stage presence was lacking. It had me clenching my hands and holding my breath, silently willing her towards success. Things improved with her duet in Act Two. She played well off the tenor, M. Gascoigne, and I felt better. No significant song for Christine in Act Three, and then as usual Act Four was mostly given over to the ballet.

I got back to my place in the wings for Act Five, where Mother joined me midway through.

"She's doing very well," Mother said.

"Yes," I agreed, trying to believe it against the worried flutters of my stomach. "Especially considering she wasn't even an understudy." Carlotta never had understudies. I reached out and closed my hand around Mother's. "Is it silly that I'm nervous?"

"Of course not. She's your friend."

I bit my lip. "The final number is the hardest one."

It was a long solo, difficult to sustain, and with a high-C near the end that even Carlotta missed at times.

Christine came to center stage for that last song—and it was like a different girl from the one who had sung at the beginning. The audience had been restless, plainly expecting very little. Christine lifted her head and opened her mouth, and notes came out that were pure and clear and filled with emotion. Within a single line the audience fell completely silent. She sang towards the farthest row, and filled the enormous theater with the sound.

She hit the high-C perfectly, giving me goosebumps all down my arms.

The last note died away to a lingering moment of silent appreciation. Then the auditorium erupted with applause.

I joined in the clapping that was spreading backstage as well, a grin stretching across my face. "Did you ever hear anyone sing like that?" I asked Mother.

She shook her head. "Never."

"I knew she was good, but—I didn't realize she was *that* good!" In that moment it felt like a privilege and a source of pride to be friends with an artist so extraordinary.

Among the seats, the Vicomte de Chagny was the first one to his feet, but soon the whole audience was with him. Christine curtsied again and again, and even when the rest of the cast came out for their bows, the crowd called for Christine. Ducking her head, she tried to retreat back amongst the others, prompting them to laugh and push her forward again.

She started to sink into another curtsy—swayed—and was narrowly caught by M. Gascoigne before she fell across the stage in a faint. My stomach clenched and I took an unconscious step towards her, then stopped. I was pulled between conflicting needs, between hurrying to my friend and the ingrained knowledge that I must never, *never* step on stage when it wasn't my part.

The ovation from the house, meanwhile, only grew, because obviously applause was appropriate when a singer had collapsed. I frowned, started forward, stopped again when it became obvious the cast was bringing Christine off anyway.

They carried Christine backstage and I ran forward as soon as it was clear which direction they were going, managing to wriggle through the still-laughing, exuberant crowd surrounding her. Did *no one* realize or care that she might be hurt or ill?

I caught Christine's hand as her head lolled against M. Gascoigne's shoulder. "Christine! Can you hear me?"

"Give her space," Mother ordered, somewhere farther back in the crowd.

Christine's eyes half-opened. "It's all so...overwhelming..." I felt a rush of relief—it couldn't be too bad if she was talking.

"You'd better carry her to her dressing room," I told Gascoigne. No one else seemed to be taking control of the situation, so why not me?

We got Christine back to her room and laid on her couch, and Mother managed to herd everyone else out. She had a Look that people didn't like to argue with. Just one person got past her: the Vicomte de Chagny, and I think that was because she knew of recent events and let him by. He had somewhere managed to acquire a truly enormous armful of roses, and he stood half-hidden by it in the center of the room, gazing at Christine with a stricken expression.

"Is she all right?" he demanded. "Is she ill?"

At that moment Christine's eyelashes fluttered, her eyes opened and without even looking around the room she said, "Raoul?"

In spite of my worry, I smiled. Just old friends, was it? Clearly.

The Opera Ghost paced behind Christine's mirror, fuming. It had been magnificent, a triumph of the highest order, and now that silly boy was going to push his way in and spoil things, bringing a discordant strain to his perfectly composed evening. It was all right for Madame Giry and her daughter to be there, someone had to help Christine off-stage, but he objected vehemently to the presence of that vicomte in Christine's dressing room.

It had been glorious to finally hear Christine's voice as it was meant to be. Two months of careful teaching had worked wonders, and all that latent potential had achieved a success he had hardly dared hope for. He had sat back in Box Five with his eyes closed, soaring and uplifted by her voice. Clearly the emotions had overwhelmed her as well; the mark of a true artist, carried away by one's art.

He gazed at her as she lay across the couch, the pale gold setting off her creamy skin and shining chestnut hair. She was a shining presence in his drab, dark surroundings, brighter than even the most gilded feature of the Opera Garnier.

Beyond the mirror, Raoul rustled about with his mound of roses, finally pushing it off on Meg before dropping to his knees with a thud beside Christine.

"Christine, you were amazing! I've never heard singing like that!"

As if that foolish boy was any judge of music.

Christine cast her eyes down. "You're very kind…"

"No, truly, it was as if an angel was singing!"

He had no idea.

"You know, we don't have any vases in here."

Christine, Raoul and the man behind the mirror all turned to look at Meg. She raised the vicomte's pile of flowers. "For the roses. We don't have any…"

"Oh, just put them anywhere," Christine said with a vague gesture. "They're very beautiful, Raoul."

"Not as beautiful as…your singing."

The Phantom seethed anew. That was plainly not how the vicomte had meant to end that sentence when he began it. And what right did he have to think she was beautiful? What right did he have to be here at all? It was monstrously unfair that that boy could be in there, holding her hand if he wanted to, here at her moment of success, while he, her teacher, was confined to the shadows.

"You must let me take you to dinner. To celebrate your debut!"

"Oh no, I couldn't."

No, she couldn't. Conversations in the Singers Foyer were one thing, but an intimate dinner, a moonlit carriage ride—oh, he did not approve of this at all. He had found it so reassuring the other night, listening in on Christine's conversation about how she simply didn't have time for anything but her singing, about how Raoul could never be anything but an old friend. Just now, all that reassurance was crumbling away beneath his feet.

"But we must go out to celebrate!" Raoul persisted, bounding up to stand in front of the mirror.

The silly fool was *straightening his cravat*. The Phantom glared at him, resenting that he blocked the view of Christine, resenting his entire existence.

"Don't be ridiculous," Meg said sharply. "Can't you see Christine is exhausted?"

Yes, precisely, well-done.

"And a pleasant dinner will be just the thing." The boy's footsteps were loud as he loped towards the door. "I'll go make all the arrangements, you needn't worry about any of it. I'll be back in a few minutes!"

Regrettably, the door did not hit him on his way out.

"Well!" Meg said, tulle skirt rustling as she sat down next to Christine. "Who knew the Vicomte de Chagny could be that persistent?"

She was right; it was a new and disturbing strain of his character.

Christine clutched at Meg's hand. "*Chérie*, let's leave before he comes back. He'll insist about dinner and I really can't, not tonight."

"Of course not, but if you just tell him—"

"Oh no, it could be so unpleasant trying to convince him. If he argues I might end up upsetting him and—no, I'm sure it's better if we leave. I'll write him a note of apology and that will be much simpler."

He had hoped to speak to Christine himself tonight, and if she left, there would be no opportunity. He struggled with the disappointment, tried to balance it against the knowledge that at least she was going to lengths to avoid the vicomte. But this should have been *their* night, their triumph… Impossible, with that foolish boy hanging about.

Out in the dressing room, Meg Giry sounded worried about far more banal questions. "I'm not sure you should write to him, Christine, that's not quite—"

"Now don't tell me it isn't proper, I'm just talking about a very short, very formal note. You needn't be scandalized about it."

"That isn't what I was thinking—though it isn't really proper. I was just thinking it would be simpler to—"

"No, nothing could be simpler than a brief note." Christine rose to her feet. "Do you suppose your mother would mind if you came home with me tonight? I feel quite dizzy from all the excitement and the company would be nice."

Very soon Christine was gone, and the world felt darker for it. He leaned against the back of the mirror, pressing his forehead to the cold glass. He had so hoped…still, it had been a triumph, nothing could entirely ruin that. The first of many. Surely there would be many more nights to listen to Christine sing, and he'd be able to speak to her about it soon enough.

And she hadn't gone off with the vicomte.

For the moment, he should take a look at this reception the new managers were holding. He had to find out more about them too. He'd need to write them a letter, do some research into their pasts, determine the quickest way to come to a proper understanding. He was really quite annoyed with Debienne for choosing such a time to leave. What with Christine's career to be launched, that vicomte to keep an eye on, and, oh, a dozen other things, now was a deeply inconvenient time to break in a new management.

Well, let the poor fellow scurry off to Australia if he wanted. Acting on his annoyance with Debienne would just be one more task he didn't have time for. And he *had* been hoping the man would leave soon. He had never felt that they had a really effective working relationship.

It might be for the best, a new management team. With any luck, they'd have a suitable appreciation for rising sopranos, and a healthy superstition regarding ghosts.

Excerpt from the Private Notebook of Jean Mifroid, Commissaire of Police

4 Feb 1881

Attended reception held by Opera Garnier's new management, Moncharmin and Ricard. Very dull event. Seem sensible business men, respectable. No criminal history. Opera always sensitive locale but management seems to have all in hand.

Chapter Twelve

"I wish you'd tell me how you learned to sing like that," I said, sitting on the edge of Christine's spare bed as I wound my hair into a braid. We had retired to her tiny room, to go about the business of preparing for sleep. She lived in a small flat in the Rue-Notre-Dame-des-Victoires with Madame Valérius, who was pleased about Christine's success but didn't quite see why anyone was surprised by it.

In front of her mirror, Christine was arranging her brown curls. "I told you, I studied at the conservatory." The mirror was the most prominent feature of the room, closely followed by an ink portrait of her father hanging on one wall. He had nice eyes.

"I know, I mean more recently. I heard you sing a couple months ago, remember, and you didn't sound like you did tonight. Your voice was always lovely, but tonight was extraordinary." I wasn't a singer, but I could hear the difference.

"The excitement of the performance, I suppose," she said, with a light laugh.

I had only been half-serious when I began the line of conversation. It seemed to make more sense—or perhaps less—the more I thought about it. "It was beyond that." I frowned slightly, not annoyed, just trying to think it through. "I didn't think your range was that extensive, and some of those long notes..."

"I had a good teacher," Christine said, comb moving more slowly.

Likely that was all it was—that and natural talent, of course. I smiled, intending to lighten the oddly serious mood that had descended. I picked up a ribbon to tie off my braid and remarked, "Perhaps I should go ask M. Montagne to teach me. If he can improve voices that much, I ought to be able to get a second career in the chorus after all."

"Oh no, you can't do that!" Christine's comb dropped onto her dressing table and she looked at me with alarmed eyes.

"I was only kidding," I said, confused by the intensity of her reaction. I hadn't really thought anything strange was going on, but now? "I don't understand, Christine...what's so mysterious about your singing? It *is* M. Montagne who taught you, isn't it? If you do have a teacher outside the Opera, there's no rule against it." Surely she would have told me about a special teacher. Though that would explain why she had been so busy lately.

She picked up her comb, ran her fingertips across the tines. "It's a bit...complicated."

I let my half-tied ribbon drop, as stories about singing instructors taking advantage of their pupils suddenly ran through my mind. My mother had warned me about things like that. I leaned forward, trying to look supportive and not as alarmed as I felt. "Christine, if you're in some kind of trouble—you know you can tell me, right? If there's anything I can do to help, or Mother too—"

"It's nothing like that," she said with a slight smile.

"Are you sure?" She was obviously getting real singing lessons, but that didn't mean other things couldn't be going on too. I pushed my unraveling braid back over my shoulder, tried and failed to meet Christine's eyes as she went on studying her comb.

"Goodness, *chérie*," she said with a less genuine laugh, "you sound quite capable of knocking on doors of singing instructors until you find my teacher!"

"Maybe I will," I said promptly, though I didn't see how I'd manage the practicalities of that. "Or at least ask around at the Opera."

She looked troubled again. "Meg, can you keep a secret?"

She was my *best friend*; didn't she trust me? "Of course!" I had kept the Phantom's secret all these years. Mostly.

"Well—it's not at all what you're thinking." She looked at me now, leaned forward towards me with a smile lighting her face. "You see, I've been visited by the Angel of Music."

She was right. That wasn't at all what I had been thinking. "The Angel of Music," I repeated blankly. If she didn't want to tell me about a teacher, she could have just said so. We both knew the Angel of Music was only a fairy tale—or did she really think I would believe any whimsy, just because I believed there was a man living under the Opera who could do wondrous things?

"Yes, just like Papa always promised," Christine said, nodding too vigorously. "The Angel of Music has been teaching me to sing."

"Oh, I see," I said, smiling tightly. Christine wouldn't make up a story to be mean; that was nonsense. Perhaps it was a joke? "With breathing techniques and advice on how to extend your range, I suppose?"

"Exactly," Christine said, clasping her hands together, face still alight. "He's been so very helpful about improving my voice."

"You said he. So the Angel of Music is male?" At the back of my mind, a small suspicion began to form. I pushed it away.

"Yes. That is, I don't know if angels have gender, and of course I've never seen him, but his voice is male."

"Mm-hmm." The next question was obvious, if you knew singers. "Tenor or baritone?"

"Tenor, although his range is really very—" She stopped, a troubled frown crossing her face. "You're laughing at me."

"No, I'm not," I protested. All I was doing was going along with the joke *she* had started. Because surely it was a joke. "But you can't really be serious about the Angel of Music giving you lessons…" That seemed the most unlikely possibility of all.

"You don't believe me! You wanted me to tell you the secret and now you don't even believe me!" She flung herself on the bed and hid her face on the pillow.

"I do, of course I do." I didn't, but what else could I say? I felt all at sea with this sudden outburst. It hadn't been a very funny joke, but this insistence was far more disconcerting. And I hadn't meant to upset her, had forgotten for a moment how sensitive Christine could be. I hunted for reassurances to offer, for signs of belief. "Tell me more about him. When does the Angel give you lessons?"

I hunted for an explanation too. Maybe someone was playing a trick on her. That scared me slightly less than the idea that Christine was actually hearing voices.

"He gives me lessons after rehearsals." Her voice was half-muffled by the pillow. "In my dressing room."

"In your...dressing room," I said slowly. That suspicion I had pushed away returned, more insistent this time, and I didn't know how to feel about it.

"Yes." She rolled over, looked up at me. "You do believe me, don't you, *chérie*? And you won't tell anyone else?"

I said I believed her and that I wouldn't tell anyone, and let her prattle cheerfully on about how wonderful her lessons were. Eventually we turned down the gaslights and her breathing went quiet, presumably asleep. I lay awake longer despite my tiredness from the performance, trying to reason through this extraordinary revelation.

I was a good Catholic girl and I believed in angels in the abstract—but to believe that an angel was speaking audibly to Christine in her dressing room, and giving her advice about how to improve her singing? I was more likely to believe that the Ghost was really a ghost, and I didn't even believe that.

Besides, when there's a man lurking around an opera house, possessing an amazing voice, an ability to walk through walls and strong opinions about music, you don't have to look far to find an explanation for an angelic visitation involving singing lessons.

It was that likely conclusion that was keeping me awake more than the uncertainty. Should I suggest the idea to Christine? But the thought of telling her made my stomach hurt. And besides, I was only guessing that the Angel was the Phantom. Perhaps I shouldn't upset Christine if I wasn't *sure*. Even at the time I knew I was trying to convince myself of a way to avoid an uncomfortable conversation, but the half-decision still let me fall asleep.

We didn't speak of the Angel the next morning, parting on the most cheerful of terms, and the whole idea seemed no more plausible while I was sitting in Sunday morning mass. Angelic visitations had precedent, true, but angels had had more important things to say to Joan of Arc than recommendations on singing techniques.

Clearly the right thing to do, as Christine's friend, was to try to get to the bottom of this. The Angel spoke to her in her dressing room after rehearsals. Christine's debut had been on Saturday, and the next rehearsals were on Monday. After ballet practice finished, I slipped over to the singers' area, to the dressing rooms.

We had fortunately ended earlier than the chorus, so the hall was empty and it was easy to duck unseen into the storeroom at the end. Heart pounding, I pulled the door shut tight behind me. Christine's was the last dressing room, sharing a wall with the storeroom. I hoped I'd be able to overhear something from here. I was not going to try to hide in her wardrobe; that was certain to end in disaster, and was really only suitable for the more ridiculous operas.

The storeroom was little more than a large closet, lit only by light around the edges of the door. I climbed over boxes and pushed past old costumes to sit down in a back corner, knees drawn up to fit. It was a tiny space against the adjoining wall, with silk and tulle hanging around me from a rack overhead. I brushed a stray skirt aside, so it wouldn't tickle my nose. The thought made me smile a little despite my nerves; people *always* sneezed at inopportune moments in operas.

I soon heard noise from the corridor outside, and knew the chorus was out. A bustle of steps and voices filled the space briefly, and it was an effort not to hold my breath, hoping no one would come in here. No one did, and soon the sounds faded away again as most people left. More minutes ticked by, enough that I had to figure out how to stretch one foot that had fallen asleep, without knocking stray boxes about. I was rubbing my numb toes when I heard a voice, as clearly as if the speaker was in the room with me.

"Christine."

A tingle ran down my spine and my kneading fingers went still.

"I'm here, Maestro." Her voice sounded farther away. It was as if the voice of the 'Angel' was in the wall itself. A secret passage?

"You did very well Saturday night."

Christine sighed. "It won't do any good. Were you listening at rehearsal today? Carlotta got so upset, and now I'm back in the chorus. She's *never* going to let me sing a real part again."

"It is inevitable that Carlotta will have her volatile moments. Do not concern yourself."

"But I want *so much* to sing and make Papa proud. And you, of course."

A pause, then, "We shall see what we might do about La Carlotta. Have patience, my dear. In the meantime—have you practiced those breathing exercises I mentioned?"

My sleeping foot twinged with a sudden needle of pain, and I mechanically began massaging the muscles again. I already had my answer to the mystery. Just a few sentences, just Christine's name, had been enough. No one but the Phantom had that perfect pronunciation, that melodic intonation.

Answer in hand, I half-wanted to leave; I felt sure that I *should* want to leave, to not eavesdrop more than strictly necessary. But I didn't entirely mind that I couldn't possibly climb out of my position without noisily knocking into all this clutter. I was trapped, so I listened while an apparently rational singing lesson went on in the room next to me.

It was more than I'd heard from the Phantom in all the years I'd been here. But somehow I didn't enjoy listening the way I would have expected. Disappointment was rising in me, an anxious, dissatisfied feeling as though something important to me had been damaged, though I couldn't explain exactly what.

I pulled my knees up a little closer, wrapped my arms tighter around my ankles and rested my cheek on one knee. Now that I knew I was right about the Angel, I also knew I had wanted to be wrong. I wasn't sure I wanted Christine to really be hearing an angel—I didn't want someone else to be maliciously tricking her—I certainly didn't want her to be hallucinating—but I hadn't wanted the Phantom to be the Angel.

This would be disappointing for Christine, of course. But that didn't account for why I felt so bruised, so like something magical had lost its shine.

I always said he wasn't my Phantom. He helped me to ballet practice once and I kept his secret. That was all, and that didn't give me any claim on him. It had been so many years ago and he probably didn't even remember doing it. Just because I was fascinated by him, that didn't obligate him to have any interest in me. I had never thought he did. Only, I suppose I had thought, if he was ever going to decide to be interested in anyone...

I blinked hard, tipped my head back against the wall and wrapped one hand around my necklace. Of course he picked Christine. He was training a singer, and I wasn't a singer. And she was beautiful, but it was more than that, she had...something, charm, innocence, some quality, that attracted people to her. It wasn't quite romance, though many men had been attracted. And the Phantom was a man. But Christine seemed to draw *everyone*. Even the apparent exceptions, the ones who didn't like her, still noticed her and felt strongly about her.

Those ones were mostly jealous. As I thought that, I felt a pang of shame. Surely I wasn't like *that*, jealous because Christine had attracted the attention of someone I wanted to notice me.

I didn't want to be like that, to be so petty about my best friend. I should admire the Phantom's taste. I had chosen Christine too, in a sense, so why shouldn't he? He could have taken an interest in any of the hundreds of girls flocking through the Opera. Maybe he had, in plenty, and I'd never known. Maybe it wasn't special at all, knowing the truth about our local ghost.

Though presumably it was only Christine who believed in an Angel of Music. If he wanted to take an interest without revealing his own secret, that made it convenient for him. He must have heard her talking about the idea some time, and seen the opportunity.

Next door, Christine had been through the scales and a piece from *Carmen*. I was so used to hearing singing in the background at the Opera that this had been little distraction to my thoughts—until the Phantom spoke again.

"No, no. You are reaching the correct notes, but you are not putting any emotion into your voice."

"I tried," Christine protested. "If you'd explain what you want me to do—"

"That would be pointless. It cannot be explained. You cannot think music, you must *feel* it."

A moment's silence, then the Phantom began to sing a love song I couldn't identify. After a few words, I stopped trying. After a few lines, I was finding it vastly more plausible that Christine really believed she was talking to an angel.

I had used words like melodic and perfect to describe his speaking voice. It was nothing compared to when he sang. Goosebumps rose on my forearms even as my cheeks warmed. He had a voice made to carry the listener away, soaring dizzyingly up to the high notes, descending down to the low ones. Within just a few notes he could span a range I didn't think was possible, and the raw beauty and emotion made my breath catch.

It made jealousy seem even more small-minded than it had before. The Phantom had always been a sign for me that the impossible could be achieved. That single song opened up vistas of art and beauty that were far beyond what I had ever imagined. Of course a man with a voice like that would choose to talk to a singer.

When he finished, silence lingered for a moment. I closed my eyes, took a long breath, luxuriating in the mental echoes of that song, reveling in that charged moment that comes after a truly amazing performance.

A patter of applause sounded from the next room. "I see now!" Christine exclaimed. "Let me try the piece again."

She was quite good too. It wasn't fair to compare—though I no longer wondered why the Phantom could be so impatient with the chorus.

The lesson went on long enough that I was aching to stretch my legs when it finally began to wrap up.

"There is one other matter," the Phantom said, and the words came slower, a new hesitation in his voice. "The Vicomte de Chagny."

It actually took me a second to think who he meant. Raoul seemed like such an utterly uninteresting topic, it was astonishing that the Phantom would spend any time thinking about him, let alone discussing him.

"You mean Raoul?" Christine said with a laugh. "What about him?"

"He is…important to you?" Again the hesitation in the words. I had never thought the Phantom could be uncertain about anything.

"Oh, Raoul's an old friend. We were children together. Father used to tell us both stories about the Angel of Music. When I mentioned my lessons to him—"

"You told him about me?"

I flinched at the sudden sharpness in his tone. Surely she heard that new undercurrent of danger too.

I had flinched instinctively—but he was right. Why would she possibly trust a secret like that to *Raoul*? She had barely trusted it to me. I wondered uneasily if he had had to pry it out of her too, or if she had been happy to share it with him.

I had told her *my* most important secret, about meeting the Phantom—the secret I'd never told anyone. Except Mother, of course.

"Yes, we went for a carriage ride yesterday afternoon, and he asked about my singing. Like I said, Father used to tell us both—"

"He *is* important to you, if you reveal secrets to him!"

Christine laughed lightly again, as though oblivious to the growing tension in the Phantom's still-perfect voice. "Raoul wouldn't tell anyone, I'm sure of it."

"That is not the point," he said in clipped tones. "You must not see him again."

That…seemed extreme. I frowned, pressing back against the wall, trying to hear every nuance. Though I wouldn't mind Raoul quietly disappearing, what gave the Phantom the right to demand it?

"What?" Christine gasped, at last sounding alarmed. "But he's an old friend. How could I possibly explain it?"

The Phantom's voice had grown cold, so different from the passion of his singing. "Tell him you must concentrate on your art. You cannot afford distractions."

"He'll be offended. He'll think I'm angry with him." Christine's voice was rising, the way it always did when she felt hurt or grieved. "I'm *sure* there's no harm in—"

"*I will not give singing lessons to a foolish girl who will throw it all away over a handsome face!*"

I jumped at that thunder, bumping my head against the wall and setting the clothes around me swinging. I rubbed the back of my head, listening to Christine call "Maestro?" twice, as I thought of catwalks and the darker side of the Ghost.

No response, not to Christine or to whatever noise I'd made. Christine's retreating footsteps made a flurry of sound and the door of her dressing room banged.

I took a deep breath, trying to recover my former calm, and set about to extricate myself from the storeroom. I could think all this through later, when I wasn't in this compromising position.

I was reversing my judgment on whether the Phantom's angelic act was plausible. The singing voice was most convincing. But he was also demonstrating a very un-angelic quality of jealousy.

Evidently someone with the voice of an angel could still have the heart of a man.

Chapter Thirteen

I spent the rest of the day in a fog, and was still deep in it when I met Mother to walk home in the evening. I didn't know what to do. If it had been anyone else lying to Christine, it would be obvious that I couldn't let a friend be deceived like that.

Only it wasn't anyone else, and how could I betray the Phantom's secret? Surely he couldn't mean any harm. He was helping Christine and she was happy thinking an angel was talking to her. That was all good.

I glanced at Mother as we walked down the Boulevard de Capucines. Maybe I should tell her about this. Maybe she'd agree with me that it was best to stay silent and uninvolved.

Except the Phantom was forbidding Christine to meet with Raoul. Much as I wanted to believe otherwise, I knew that wasn't a disinterested, well-intentioned request with Christine's well-being in mind. Especially when I remembered that thunder in his voice. No matter how I described it to Mother, I knew she'd get a worried crease in her forehead and then I'd worry even more myself.

What if the Phantom had some darker motive? What if telling Christine the truth was the only way to avert a disaster? But...surely not. Not the *Phantom*.

I didn't want to tell Christine. I dreaded every aspect of that conversation, of how upset she'd be. Of how upset he'd be. So I didn't want to tell Mother either, in case she said I had to tell Christine and then I'd feel even more cowardly for not wanting to do it.

But I *should* tell Mother, and then I should tell Christine. I knew that. I stared at the day's leftover loaves in the bakery as we passed it, barely seeing them. I could try to evade that truth, but I did know that.

I should tell Mother now, and find a chance to visit Christine at home tomorrow. We couldn't have a serious discussion about angelic visitations in between rehearsals. It would be the height of foolishness to discuss the Phantom's private business then. You never know who's listening at the Opera Garnier.

I glanced at Mother again, noticed that she already had her worried crease in her forehead, and it occurred to me that she had been as silent as I had been so far on this walk.

I took a deep breath, intending to tell her the truth. Mostly. By the time I exhaled, what I said instead was, "Is something wrong?"

"Likely not," she said after a moment. "I had a note from the new managers. They want to speak with me tomorrow morning."

It was rarely a good thing when the management wanted a private meeting, and I added a new worry to the swirl in my mind. "About what?" I asked, as lightly as I could.

Her lips pressed together in disapproval. "They did not mention a topic, but I imagine it is about the guest in Box Five."

He loomed so large in my thoughts, it didn't even surprise me that the Phantom would come up in this other arena of conversation. Besides, it made sense. Debienne had wanted to talk to Mother too, at the beginning; he had given up after a few rounds, when she insisted she didn't know anything important about the Phantom—which was mostly true.

"I suppose they'll complain for a while, then settle down," I said. This at least was nothing new, nothing unaccountable. Just the management being the management. Uncomfortable maybe, for a little while, but it would be all right in the end. "Monsieur Debienne did."

"Yes," Mother agreed, with a frown. "It was much simpler in the days of Monsieur Poligny. This changing of managers makes things very uncertain. Eventually we're bound to have a manager who doesn't believe in ghosts."

"Oh well, the Phantom will make them believe," I said, and though I might doubt everything else, I did have confidence still in the Phantom's haunting abilities. I slipped my arm through Mother's. "Maybe the glowing skeleton will be back."

"More likely Commissaire Mifroid will be back."

"And he believes absolutely and without reservation that the Opera Ghost doesn't exist and it's all just a prank or superstition." It was funny, how comforting that certainty felt. "So that's all right."

I believed that, truly. And it was easy to also believe that I shouldn't worry Mother about this Christine business after all, when she was worrying about the management. So maybe I should wait to tell her. I could still talk to Christine, if I had a chance. I'd tell Mother eventually. Surely that could wait until the management calmed down again.

Mother's meeting was early the next morning, before dance practice began, so of course I came along. I knew the meeting was unlikely to be pleasant, so I had the virtuous reason of coming to support Mother. And the more voyeuristic one of curiosity.

I had only been in the manager's office once or twice over all the years. Opera managers do not generally have an interest in dealing with small ballet girls. Now I looked around, soaking in the scene. It hadn't changed much from my hazy memories. A big window looked out on the Avenue de l'Opera, casting morning sunshine over the scene within. One big wooden desk dominated the center of the room, with chairs in front of it and ranks of cabinets in formation all along the sides. Desk, chairs and cabinets were elegant with carvings, mostly vines though I spotted at least one satyr's face peering out. Garnier's portrait was still on one wall, and production posters hung above the cabinets. I had danced in three of them, something that made me feel warm with pride. It offset the effect of a terrifyingly large poster of La Carlotta staring down from the opposite wall. I wondered if Debienne had left it, if the new managers had put it up, or if Carlotta had somehow contrived to slip in and hang it herself, in between managerial reigns.

Moncharmin was seated behind the desk, head bent over a stack of papers while Ricard greeted us, pumping Mother's hand enthusiastically. He ushered her to a chair opposite the desk, then turned to me. "And this is…?"

"My daughter, Meg. She is with the ballet."

I bobbed a slight curtsy while Ricard beamed at me. "I might have guessed! I always know a dancer's body when I see it."

I tried not to laugh, lest he take it the wrong way, while Mother raised her chin an inch and leveled him with her sternest Stare. "Do you?"

In her own way, Mother could be as terrifying as Madame Thibault. I wished it was a quality I had inherited. No one was ever afraid of me.

Ricard blanched. "That is—what I meant, of course, was to say…"

"Yes, I'm sure it was quite clear, Ricard," Moncharmin interrupted. "Shall we get to the business at hand?"

I hid a smirk and took the chair next to Mother, even though it hadn't been offered. I knew the managers were people I should be nervous around, people with power at the Opera, but it was harder to feel that way than I had expected.

Moncharmin smiled in what seemed to be an attempt at geniality, though it looked a great deal like acting I'd seen on the stage—and not the highest quality either. "Now, Madame Giry, I understand you've been with the Opera for over six years. And you have had the care of Box Five all this time?"

So they did want to know about the Phantom. I settled more firmly in my chair, crossing my ankles and relaxing a fraction further. At least it wasn't something worse, and while this might not be good, it was something we'd always weathered.

"All but the first few months," Mother answered.

"And you don't find it a bit, well, taxing, to take care of a box for a, ahem…ghost?" A broader smile was visibly tugging at M. Moncharmin's mouth.

"Not at all," Mother said with perfect solemnity. "The Phantom has been consistently generous in tips and respectful in manner, which is more than can be said of many of our subscribers."

"Oh, then you interact with this ghost?" Moncharmin asked, and I didn't like his mocking tone. If he could refer to the *Ghost* in that voice, he didn't understand about the Phantom at all.

"We rarely interact directly," Mother said evenly. "I leave programs; he leaves franc notes. Occasionally he has a particular request, in which case he leaves a note or a voice speaks from Box Five."

"Oh, really!" The lurking smile had emerged to take over Moncharmin's face. He shot the grin towards Ricard. "Did you hear that, Ricard? A disembodied voice makes requests!"

"For chocolate and fresh flowers, I imagine," Ricard remarked.

I dug my fingernails into my palms, growing warm in a way that had nothing to do with pride. What right did these two have, to come waltzing into the Opera Garnier and start laughing behind their sleeves at Mother and the Phantom both?

Mother's face was impassive, but I could see from her posture that she was no more pleased than I. When she rose to her feet, I quickly did the same. "It is obvious that you gentlemen find this all highly amusing," she said. "If you are not intending to take the matter of the Phantom seriously, I can see no point in further discussion."

"Now, now, there's no need to grow upset," Ricard said, with a patronizing tone that had the exact opposite effect of the reassurance he no doubt intended. "It was all a grand joke, and we'll vouch for you to Debienne that you played your part beautifully."

Mother raised one eyebrow. "I have no idea what you mean."

"Debienne's joke about the Phantom," Moncharmin said. "It's all very amusing, but enough's enough."

"I have never known Monsieur Debienne to be a man given to jokes," Mother said. I could think of practically no one *less* likely to make a joke about the Phantom, considering how anxious the subject had always made him. "He did not take the matter of the Phantom seriously when he first came either, but he soon changed his opinion."

Ricard laughed outright then. "You can't really expect us to believe that Debienne was catering to a ghost?" He picked up two envelopes from the desk, and I recognized the Phantom's distinctive handwriting. I leaned forward a little, read the managers' names across the front of the envelopes. Too bad the letters themselves weren't visible. "Especially not this business of paying him 20,000 francs every month?"

"That has always been the Phantom's salary," Mother said, without so much as blinking. Though that salary probably did seem very strange, to anyone not familiar with it.

Ricard went on smirking. "Seems a bit high, don't you think? That's practically the salary of the entire corps de ballet combined."

I jumped in with, "He's a very high quality ghost," because I couldn't resist. It was half a joke—and yet I meant it too.

Both managers stared at me as though they had forgotten I was there. I wished that surprised me. In the momentary silence, Mother said, "It is clear you gentlemen have no serious interest in learning about the Phantom, which you will find is a mistake. I recommend you follow the Phantom's requests, or like Monsieur Debienne, you will regret it."

Moncharmin rose to his feet behind the desk. "Is that a threat, Madame Giry?" he asked, a new and unpleasant edge in his voice. My back straightened and I wished I was taller, stronger, braver. I wished I was like the Phantom, who could make managers stay in line.

Or like Mother, who Stared at him and with perfect, intimidating precision said, "A warning. One you should heed."

In an opera we would have swept out at that moment, dramatically. Maybe we would have in life too, but the office door swung open before we could, and Comte Philippe de Chagny came strolling in as though he belonged there.

"Pardon me, gentlemen, am I interrupting anything important?" he asked in cheerful tones, and didn't wait for an answer. "I'll just need a minute. It's about this chorus girl my brother's gone and lost his head over."

Christine. A new qualm joined my tangle of emotions. I didn't altogether think the comte should be getting into Christine's business, though I couldn't quite say why. Comtes had power. They could help singers and dancers. At a price, usually, though everyone knew this particular comte belonged to Sorelli.

"Ah, young love!" Ricard said, hands thrust into his pockets.

The Comte de Chagny barked a laugh. "Don't be absurd! Love's got nothing to do with it, it's just a bit of—" He broke off, glancing at Mother and me. "Ahem, well. You know." He squinted suddenly, looking at me more closely, and I was abruptly conscious of every mended place in my lavender dress. I should have worn the blue stripes—it was newer. "I know you…you're Christine's friend, aren't you?"

Actually, I'd introduced *her* to him, which ought to make her *my* friend. But I just nodded and said, "Yes, Monsieur." She was Christine. Naturally he saw it that way.

"Excellent!" he said, although it was hard to tell exactly why, and turned back to the managers. "Anyway, Raoul wants his Christine to get a promotion or sing solos or some such business. I said I'd sort it for him."

"I believe we were just going," Mother interjected—and we went, even though I would have liked to know more, to find out whether the managers were inclined to take Christine or the de Chagnys more seriously than they took the Opera Ghost, and what cost there might be to Christine in all of it.

I cast one backward glance, hoped I could find out more later somehow, and turned my attention back to my mother. "You were splendid," I said, once we were out in the hall and walking toward ballet practice.

She looked solemn, not quite frowning, and didn't accept the compliment. "It doesn't appear the managers are about to put 20,000 francs in Box Five. Your Phantom may have to bring back his glowing skeleton after all."

"He's not *my* Phantom!" I said without thinking, without attempting at all to moderate the sudden tension in my voice.

Mother stopped walking to look at me, not sternly but very searchingly. "Is something wrong?"

Could all mothers turn in an instant from thinking about completely other business to worrying about their daughters, or was it only mine? "No. Of course not. I'd best get to ballet practice. See you later!" And I hurried down the hall, ducking around a cluster of chorus girls and nearly bumping into the Persian where he stood leaning against a pillar. I went on without meeting his gaze, quickly putting a corner between myself, the Persian, my mother, and any questions she could choose to ask.

I might have been able to explain to Mother about the Phantom and Christine, only I didn't want to now. Not yet, at least. It had occurred to me that Mother would expect me to also explain how I felt about it—and that would be much harder.

The Opera Ghost leaned his head back, sitting against the rough scaffolding of a hidden space alongside the managers' office, and felt thoroughly displeased with the state of his world.

The managers were going to be troublesome. He had investigated. Monsieur Moncharmin was the difficult one, the *businessman*. What was a businessman doing in the arts? Monsieur Ricard at least had a great affection for music and dancing (and, apparently, dancers). He had very little taste, but he liked music and could probably have been pushed quite easily into the proper directions, shaped into playing the role of manager as the Phantom directed. It was Moncharmin who was going to be a challenge.

And neither man believed in ghosts.

Most inconvenient!

He had listened to their conversation with Madame Giry, and did not like what he'd heard. That bit from her daughter about a high-quality ghost was amusing (he did take a certain pride in his haunting abilities) but most of the conversation was not at all satisfactory. He was just wondering how long it would be before the matter grew serious enough to warrant threats or bribes when the Comte de Chagny came blustering in. That drove the managers' beliefs, and Madame Giry, quite out of his attention.

The chair in front of the managers' desk creaked discordantly as the rotund comte lowered himself into it with a loud laugh. "Surely you can do something about this little singer, yes? The oldest law in theatre, isn't it, there's always a part for the subscriber's woman?"

The phrasing, the dismissive tone—they made the Phantom's hands clench into fists. Equally disturbing was the import. It was no great shock that the wretched vicomte wanted his brother to help Christine's career, but the fact that the comte had agreed felt strangely like a betrayal. He had been counting on Philippe to be as much against Christine and Raoul's romantic entanglement as he was himself. But of course the comte didn't see it as anything *serious*, not even as love, it was just a bit of—you know.

It was lucky for the nobleman he hadn't finished that sentence, or the Phantom might have done something drastic.

"I'm sure we can manage something," Ricard said in hearty tones. "Pretty girl, is she? Always nice to have those front and center in our performances."

Yes, of course, never mind whether they could *sing*.

"She's very beautiful," the comte affirmed. "I'll not have my brother's taste impugned!"

"Well, I'm sure we can do something for her then," Ricard said, contradicted at once by Moncharmin's, "Though of course our budget may not allow for a significant promotion. Running an opera house has many expenses, you know."

Leave it to the businessman to care more about his budget than the potential of a new artist. The Phantom was disgusted.

"But perhaps a new donation would help?" the comte said, and the Phantom could practically hear the accompanying wink. "As if I don't spend enough on Sorelli…but I'm sure we can work something out."

Moncharmin's voice sounded especially slimy as he said, "Then I'm *sure* we can do something for your brother's little Christine."

If a couple of bumbling managers and even more bumbling noblemen thought they could do what an Opera Ghost might have done for Christine's career, they would find themselves sadly mistaken. They had no respect for her ability, no finesse, no sense of what roles Christine was best suited for, no idea how to manage the problem of Carlotta, no concept of launching a career in just the right steps to secure an audience's passionate adoration. *He* had it all thought out, a careful progression of roles, exactly which operas to move through, a timeline and a plan and—

But of course he wasn't going to do any of that.

He rested his forehead against one fist. Had it only been yesterday that he'd ended the singing lesson so abruptly, vowed that the entire, ill-advised business was done? Already it felt like eons. Already he ached to see Christine again. To hear her sing again.

She would be expecting to hear from her Angel, just a few hours from now.

He wouldn't do it. She had made her priorities clear. He was going to go down to the very lowest cellar and *stay* there. This Angel business had only ever been another mask, and a very foolish one to don. It was time to give up the Angel and crawl back into the darkness where he belonged.

Christine proved remarkably elusive over the next few days. Maybe I didn't try as hard to find her as I could have. I knew I had to tell her the truth about the Angel—I just didn't want to. Finally, a week after Christine's debut, I managed to catch her at home. I plunked down on the end of the bed while she stuffed handkerchiefs and other sundries into her bag, getting ready to go back to the Opera Garnier for that night's performance, and we whiled away a few minutes on meaningless pleasantries.

Christine closed up her bag and remarked, "We'd better be going, if we don't want to be late."

"We still have plenty of time," I said, and took a firm grip on my wavering courage. I glanced at the portrait of her father, who surely would want someone to be watching out for his daughter. "Sit down for a minute; I want to talk to you about something."

She perched on the edge of the bed. "My, *chérie*, you look so terribly serious!"

I twisted a fold of my lavender skirt between my fingers, nerves fluttering in my stomach. "It's about your Angel of Music."

She stood up abruptly, moved in front of the mirror. "I don't want to talk about that." She leaned in to look at her reflection and straightened a curl.

I didn't want to talk about it either, but that was beside the point. "I think there's something you need to know."

"If you're going to tell me angels don't exist, don't bother. Raoul already did."

"No, it's not that." Should I pretend to be surprised that Raoul knew? No, that would only be a delay and a distraction. "It's just, well, this *particular* angel. Who speaks to you at the Opera. And who's so interested in your singing career…"

"He isn't anymore!" Christine moaned, and collapsed into a chair with a tragic air.

The horrifying possibility flashed through my mind that this could be more like my initial suspicion, that maybe it wasn't about singing lessons anymore, and Christine's interactions with the Phantom had taken a different direction. He wouldn't. Would he? No, of course not. And yet—

"The angel left me!" Christine announced in anguished tones.

I exhaled. "Oh." I wasn't supposed to be happy about that, was I? I tried for a sympathetic expression. "I'm so sorry."

"It was all my fault. I made him angry." She buried her face in her hands. "He got upset because I told Raoul about him, and he hasn't spoken to me since. And it's been days and *days*!"

Yes, a whole five, since I'd listened to that lesson. I'd been waiting years to encounter the Phantom again…not that I had any real expectation I ever would. And if the Angel had been speaking to her daily, I supposed that was a long time. Sort of.

I still hadn't told her what I needed to say. I did still need to say it, didn't I? Maybe I could pose it as a comforting silver lining. It was better to be abandoned by a man than an angel. Better on a spiritual level, at least. "Maybe I have good news, then. I've been thinking about your Angel and—" Could I really say this? Did I dare? At the last moment I prevaricated. "—remember how the stories said your dressing room was haunted?"

She lifted her head and stared at me. It was not a friendly expression. "What are you suggesting?"

Now I wanted even less to say it. If she'd just figure this out herself, then I wouldn't have to tell her I had eavesdropped on her lesson. I threw another hint. "And the Phantom knows so much about music. So maybe…"

"Are you saying," she said in a low voice, "that you think my Angel of Music is the Phantom of the Opera? That's supposed to be good news?"

I probably shouldn't have put it that way. But *spiritually*… "I only meant, compared to offending an angel—"

"How can you say that my Angel is some horrid prankster who goes around frightening people for fun!"

That stung and I drew back. "The Phantom is not like that!"

"I've heard plenty of stories about your Phantom, and he's nothing at all like *my* Angel."

Not if she was going to distort the Phantom so badly. "Surely you can see for yourself—the similarities are obvious, especially considering everything I told you about the Phantom—"

"I think you had better go." Christine turned her back to me.

I stared at her back, stunned into silence by this sudden dismissal, by the unexpected hostility. I hadn't expected this to go well—but Christine, angry? I hadn't expected that. I willed her to turn around with a smile, to turn back into the sweet and kind friend I'd always known. My own anger was already fading, confronted with her hunched shoulders, with this refusal to even look at me. I should have kept my mouth shut. Why spoil her pretty imaginings?

She didn't move, and finally I stood up from the bed, fingers twisting my gold necklace. "All right, I'll go. But…I did just want to help. If things weren't what you thought."

No response.

I went to the door and paused on the threshold, some little spark of remaining frustration causing me to throw back, "And he's not my Phantom anyway."

Chapter Fourteen

A t the Opera, I found my place backstage among the ballet girls warming-up before the performance began. I sat down on the floor and tried to concentrate on stretching, not on my argument with Christine. Of course I thought of nothing else, the words running through my head again and again. If I had been more careful, if I had found a better way to say it…if she hadn't overreacted!

I saw Christine arrive shortly after I did. She went immediately towards the cluster of singers gathered backstage and I did not follow her. I had been trying to *help*. I wasn't going to go apologize for that. Certainly not in front of the entire chorus.

I wasn't the only one to notice Christine arrive. Carlotta was sitting at the center of an adoring crowd, who seemed to be consoling her on some point. This happened so frequently that I'd paid it no attention—until she suddenly reared up to her feet and stalked towards Christine. Her court followed her, and I noted Jammes right at the front of the pack.

"There she is, the little brat!" Carlotta hissed. "How *dare* you!"

Christine's eyes widened and she fell back a pace. "Signora Carlotta, I've no idea—"

Automatically I rose to my feet. I'd seen Carlotta tear into people before; what defenses could Christine possibly have against it? I'd only gone a step when I felt a tug on my arm. I glanced back to see Adalisa shake her head and say softly, "Better not."

Carlotta had by now launched into a string of Italian that I could only assume was profanity. By the time she returned to French, the entire auditorium had gone deadly silent. She had everyone's attention as she shrieked, "I made it clear to the managers and I will make it clear to you. No chorus girl will ever replace *me*, certainly not at the request of the Vicomte de Chagny! *I* am lead soprano of the Opera Garnier. Audiences come to see *me*. I will never step aside for a bit of trash who thinks she can advance her career from on her back!"

A collective intake of breath whooshed around the auditorium and my cheeks grew hot. How dare Carlotta say that to Christine, of all people—and what hypocrisy, coming from Carlotta! I pulled free of Adalisa, tried to get through the rest of the crowd of ballet girls.

Christine stammered, "How can you—I never—"

Carlotta jabbed with one forefinger. "What you will *never* do is sing a solo in my opera house. Remember that!"

With a flounce and a flourish, she swept out with all the majesty of an advancing army. All her girls followed suit, leaving Christine standing deserted and alone on the stage.

I was still only partway there when Sorelli spoke up from among the dancers. She didn't shriek like Carlotta, but her voice carried just as clearly.

"Hey, Daaé. Do whatever you want with whoever you like and advance your career however you choose—but don't use Philippe."

Christine gaped at her, hands visibly shaking. "It was only— Raoul suggested—"

Sorelli waved a hand, almost a bored gesture. "Sure he did. And I couldn't care less what you do with the pretty vicomte. But stay away from his brother, or you will find out that Carlotta's not the only one with influence around here."

Christine's face crumpled, and she fled the stage, with absolutely none of the majesty Carlotta had commanded.

Around me, the buzz of gossip rose, mostly in tones of awe and delight.

I tried to follow Christine. It seemed like I had to dodge and maneuver and push through *everyone*, not just the ballet girls; backstage was packed with scenechangers and stagehands. I even glimpsed the Persian, his red fez the only spot of color as he stood among the shadows. I avoided eye contact with anyone, head down as I maneuvered through the throng. They had parted for Christine, but not for me.

By the time I reached Christine's dressing room, she had disappeared inside. "Christine?" I rapped my knuckles against the hard wood. "It's Meg, let me in."

"Go *away*."

I knocked again. "If I can help—"

"Leave me alone, I don't want to see anyone!"

I stared at the wooden panel in front of my nose, even less communicative and inviting than Christine's back had been so recently. Short of sitting outside her door, I didn't see anything I could do. I rattled the door handle, only confirming that it was locked and generating no reply. Finally I walked slowly back to the auditorium.

Nanette, a ballet girl I only knew slightly, bounced up to me the moment I returned to backstage. "You're Christine Daaé's friend, aren't you?" she said, then in hushed tones continued, "Do you think it was true? What Carlotta said about Christine and the vicomte?"

Around us, a good dozen heads turned to hear my answer.

I leveled my best imitation of my mother's Stare at Nanette. "I think Carlotta is a vindictive liar," I said flatly, "so there's nothing else to discuss."

The Stare must have worked. She didn't ask any follow-up questions.

He sat behind Christine's wall, listening to her sob, fighting opposing desires to step through the mirror and comfort her, or to go find Carlotta and strangle her. A last shred of self-control told him that either action would be extremely unwise.

He could see Christine through the mirror, where she had flung herself on the couch, face among the pillows, shoulders shaking. Without giving it much conscious thought, he pulled off his gloves and began twisting them between his hands.

He would act, certainly. But he *would* act calmly. He would assess the situation, and then he would respond.

And the situation was not entirely bad. Frustrated and furious as he was, he still found a small satisfaction in watching the vicomte's ill-begotten plans go horribly, magnificently awry. Surely Christine would have to see now that the nobleman was useless in any real way.

He crumpled his gloves between his palms. Clearly the vicomte had shown the absolute height of his capabilities on his first meeting with Christine. He had overheard that little story, and what idiot ran into the ocean after a scarf? How charming could the boy possibly have been, offering her a soggy scarf? Bad luck that he didn't catch pneumonia and die on the spot. And what did she even need a scarf for on the beach?

But enough of that. If scarf-rescuing had seemed charming before, surely *now* Christine had to see Raoul's essential uselessness. Therefore it was the ideal time to demonstrate what a man of subtlety and intelligence could accomplish. Raoul might be a charming folk melody for children, but the Phantom was a thundering symphony by comparison. If one in minor key.

He rose to his feet, shoving his mutilated gloves into his inside jacket pocket, and projected his voice into the dressing room. Quiet. Calm. Iron with resolve. "Do not concern yourself, my dear. I will deal with Carlotta."

Christine moved as though to lift her head, and he turned his back. He couldn't risk the sight of tears threatening his precarious self-control. He started down the dark tunnel, away from the lit dressing room behind him. He didn't halt even when he heard Christine call, "Maestro?" behind him.

He had work to do.

Among a line of dancers backstage, I went through the ballet positions by rote too fast, impatient and anxious as I watched for any sign of Christine. The evening performance began before I finally saw her in the distance backstage. She was going towards the chorus and did not look my direction. I started to move anyway, barely more than shifting my weight to take a step, before the long-standing habit shared with every ballet girl made me glance towards Madame Thibault.

She was looking directly at me, intercepted my glance and coolly raised one eyebrow. If I had been deathly ill I could have requested permission to leave, but needing to talk to my scandal-scarred friend? I subsided back into my place.

Madame Thibault looked away, probably to stare at some other poor girl, and I bit my lip and kept one eye on Christine. She was, more or less, in among the singers, but a distinct empty space stood out around her. No one spoke to her. Carlotta had marked her.

I wondered if Raoul or his brother had heard about the results of their efforts. I wondered if they would do anything about it.

Mostly, I wondered if the Phantom had heard, and what he might do.

I wished I had some idea, some ability to predict, but after this Angel business, I no longer felt I had any accurate insight into the Phantom's actions.

As I looked at Christine, I suddenly noticed a pillar of black, not far from the more brightly-dressed chorus. Not the Phantom—he wouldn't be seen so easily—but the Persian was standing backstage again, a wide space around him, quite out of the way but still in a place guests certainly didn't belong. What *was* the answer to his mystery?

A ridiculous over-the-top stage laugh brought my attention to the opera, just in time to see Carlotta throwing her head back dramatically.

It made me wince, and yet she did have a certain magnetism, drawing everyone's eyes to her. Like watching a carriage as it careened out of control and you waited to see if it would right itself or crash.

Usually I cared enough about the good of the performance—and I didn't *really* want to wish ill on other people anyway—to hope Carlotta would be successful even in her absurd ingénue roles. Today, I unashamedly hoped she would crash.

She sparkled and glittered all the way through to Act Five, covering any less-perfect note with enormous stage presence and confidence. She had an aria in the final act, her character's lament over a lost love; Carlotta considered it appropriate stage directions at that moment to step to the front of the stage, raise her head and beam out at the audience. I sighed again, but it was just Carlotta all over.

Head high and shoulders back, she opened her mouth wide for the first notes—and a hideous croak emerged. The sound seemed impossible, even as it echoed and reverberated through the auditorium.

I sat up straighter, doubting I could have heard right, staring at Carlotta while every faint rustle and whisper backstage ceased completely. Carlotta had been singing without accompaniment, sparing us any screeching discords of surprise from the orchestra, and for a moment perfect silence reigned. Everyone I could see, behind the stage or before us, was staring in silent, motionless shock at La Carlotta at centerstage.

Carlotta looked as stunned as anyone else, eyes wide with one hand pressing to her throat. I felt a reluctant admiration at how quickly she recovered, at how quickly she put on a reassuring smile; it only looked nervous around the edges. She took a deep breath, chest swelling, and opened her mouth to sing again.

This time the croak was even louder, and long enough for varied tones. This time the first shock was past, and titters and murmurs spread through the audience.

We weren't laughing backstage. I was thinking of twisted ankles, sloppy *jetés* with stumbled landings, collisions and lack of synchronicity—all the ways a dancer might fail humiliatingly before an audience. Though none seemed quite as colorful as sudden, inexplicable croaking.

I had hoped Carlotta would crash—I still didn't like her, I still resented what she had done to Christine—and yet a crash of this scope took my breath away, sent a creepy sensation down my spine. I felt like I'd wished death on someone and had it happen.

But Carlotta was still Carlotta, and she wasn't succumbing easily. She had given up smiles and reassurances to glare at the increasingly merry audience. Hands on hips, fury etched in every feature, she opened her mouth—and croaked again.

And again and again.

Laughter was growing among the audience, and even backstage among some of the Company. Not Carlotta's devotees, of course— Jammes looked appalled where she was sitting not far from me.

Carlotta gave up at last and stalked off the stage, even now striding with angry majesty.

The drama continued onstage, though, as a positively green M. Moncharmin came stumbling out to make profuse apologies to the laughing audience—and then close the curtains.

This was almost as disturbing as anything else. True, there had only been two scenes left, one final dance number. But to end a show uncompleted—I'd never seen it happen, not in all the years I'd been here.

I tried to blame it on M. Moncharmin not knowing the theater. It would be ridiculous to take it as a violation of the natural order of the world, a harbinger of disasters still to come.

Show ended, Carlotta's followers abandoned their places backstage to hasten after her, while everyone else seemed to go into motion at once as well, in search of the best people to discuss the evening's incredible events with. I looked around for Christine. I could see her across the way, her gaze still focused in the direction Carlotta had gone. She wasn't laughing and she didn't look horrified. She had an odd, unfamiliar look in her eyes, like she was deeper in thought than I'd ever seen her. I wished I knew what she was thinking.

I also wished I knew how the Phantom had orchestrated this. It was clearly beyond the abilities of the Vicomte de Chagny.

His revenge on Carlotta was a finely crafted artistic achievement, and when she found the black-edged envelope he had delivered to her dressing room, she would understand exactly what she had done to provoke this richly-deserved disaster. With luck, she'd leave the Opera Garnier entirely, and at the least she should be thoroughly cowed for a long time to come. True, she had maintained what shreds of dignity she could onstage, but she was certain to collapse after. No artist could cope with thousands of mocking gazes.

He hadn't felt this good in *years*. He was feeling practically— gleeful! How extraordinary.

While most of the Company ran about in clattering, chattering confusion after Carlotta's precipitous exit, Christine made directly for her own dressing room. He slightly regretted leaving the aftermath of his success, but no real contest existed between the choices; he followed Christine, was behind her mirror when she entered the room and called to him.

"I am here," he answered, carefully restricting himself to a short phrase that wouldn't reveal too much unangelic mirth.

She clasped her hands together, eyes shining in delight. "Out there—Carlotta—oh, that was—it was—" She spun around, flung her arms out wide. "It was *miraculous*!"

A low chuckle escaped his control. "That is somewhat my area." It wasn't really a miracle, of course, only a bit of ventriloquism, but applied in the correct way…just the effect he wanted.

She spun around again, stepped lightly up to the mirror and pressed her palms against the glass. He swallowed as he looked into her brown eyes, seemingly looking back at him—but of course she saw only a mirror, it was only her own dancing reflection that had drawn her to the glass.

"I was so afraid you had left me for good!" Christine exclaimed, face flushed pink with excitement.

Slowly he reached out a hand, laid his palm against hers—only cold glass separating them. "I never went far." If she only knew how true that was.

She exhaled deeply, sank down to sit with her back against the mirror, turning her head so her cheek touched the glass. "Do you know how much that means to me? Ever since Father died, I've just felt horribly *alone*. I'm so sorry I upset you by seeing Raoul; I think he just reminded me of the old days, of when Father was alive. But this past week when you refused to speak to me, I've been so lonely. I know now, nothing is more important than my singing, than my lessons."

It took all his extensive vocal abilities to keep a revealing tremor out of his voice. "I'm glad you understand now." The importance of her voice, what a gift it could be to the musical world. And she understood loneliness. His hand slowly trailed down the glass, down towards her cheek, so close and so much out of his reach.

"Only...I do wish..." Her voice turned wistful. "...couldn't I see you? Not merely a voice, but actually see you? I wouldn't want or need anything else then!"

His fingers curled, instinctively pulled away from the glass, as the question knocked him back a step in automatic retreat. A curt no was the only answer required, the only answer possible. It caught in his throat, as impossible to sound as notes from a pipe with no holes. "What if," he said instead, reaching out to touch the smooth glass again with just his fingertips, "I am not what you expect? What if...I am not who you think I am?"

"Oh, but I know you! I know the *real* you!"

He slowly knelt down on one knee, the better to see her profile, still turned to the mirror, long dark lashes nearly brushing the surface. She didn't know the real him, she knew nothing about him—but what if, given the chance, she could accept him as he truly was? What if she didn't want an angel anymore—but a man?

Could he? Dared he?

A mad surge of excitement flooded through him and he rose again to his feet, cloak rippling around him. *Why not?* He was the Phantom— he could make an entire Opera Company dance to his melody, could deliver justice on Carlotta and perform feats unequaled by mortal men. Why not this too?

"Do not be afraid," he said softly, and with a flick of a switch the mirror began to shift, to slide sideways into the wall.

She must have felt the movement, getting quickly to her feet. By the time she had risen and turned to the mirror again, it was done. He stood within the frame, black cloak no doubt making him look, not angelic, but supernatural in some form. He had donned a full-face mask today, unfortunate as a half one might have been less alarming. At least it wasn't the skeleton mask.

He held his breath as she looked at him, her eyes widening. He saw surprise, interest—would she feel fear?

"You're...not an angel," she whispered, voice wavering uncertainly.

"I am your teacher. And, I hope, your friend." The calm words stood at odds to his still-roiling excitement, mingled with the terror that this was all about to go horribly wrong. It was strange how those feelings could coexist, even feel similar in the tautness in his body, the shallow catch of his breath. He fell back on manners, executed a perfect bow, lifted his eyes cautiously in case her expression had turned frightened.

It had not. Slowly, she dipped down into a curtsy, came up again and extended one hand in just the graceful move he'd watched her perform in the Foyer dozens of times.

He reached out his own hand, lightly took her fingers between his. The touch sent a jolt through him, like hearing a singer hit the most exquisite of notes in the most finely written canticle.

He had had no clear plan when he revealed himself, no conscious one at least, but now—*now*...

"Do you trust me?"

"Yes," she breathed, and he led her through the mirror into the darkness.

Chapter Fifteen

Excerpt from the Private Notebook of Jean Mifroid, Commissaire of Police

11 Feb 1881

Signora Carlotta of Opera Garnier attempted to file complaint against "Opera Ghost" for ruining performance. Company still adamant about every ill-luck being fault of so-called ghost. So far has not proved too time-consuming a nuisance for department.

Christine expressed no surprise at the tunnel he took her through, not at the descending staircases, the archways and branching corridors, or even the dimlit, deep black underground lake they walked beside; maybe anything would seem reasonable, once someone has accepted an angel who turns out to be a man. She asked only one question, not about the tunnels or where they were going—but about the mask.

"The mask must always stay on," he said, voice even, stomach twisting. "That must be a rule. An inviolable one."

And she simply nodded, no questions or demands or uncomfortable cajoling making light of the situation. It was a relief that he didn't have to explain, didn't have to convince her. It was enough, she understood, and they walked on in silence.

Revealing as much as he had already was madness. To take the mask off—to let her see his face—unthinkable.

But she understood, and this obstacle that could have ruined everything was passed in a single step, freeing him to set those worries aside.

Carlotta's croaking had been only a parlor trick; *this* was truly miraculous, that the twisting path of his life, of recent events, had brought him here. Brought him to this beautiful girl, willing to walk through a mirror and trustingly follow him below the Opera, despite the mask, despite everything. The dark caverns felt so different with her beside him, as though illuminated by her light.

The path below the Opera was nearly as twisting as his life, full of branches and turns leading from the Opera's basements into the catacombs that ran throughout Paris. It was a maze that had always given him a sense of security, knowing that the complicated path to his home was another layer of protection.

This was the first time it had ever felt short, too brief with Christine's hand in his. He was conscious at every moment of the faint warmth of her fingers through his glove, of every slight movement she made.

He couldn't remember the last time he had touched someone.

Well, he had roughed up Buquet a bit, but that wasn't what he meant. The last time he had touched anyone as a—friend. The Daroga was much more the fold-hands-and-bow type. He had shaken hands with Garnier, on the final inspection of the completed Opera, Garnier's farewell before he left Paris.

And there had been that little blond girl, not long after the Opera opened, who had got lost on the way to practice. He'd held her hand.

He hadn't thought about that in years. He had never found out who she was, never wanted to. There had been a moment, just after she had stepped back into the light, and looked back to thank him. She had looked—awed. Not frightened. Her face had gone vague over the years, but he remembered the expression. He had never wanted to ruin the memory of that moment by finding her again, and watching her tell her friends about the terrifying Phantom.

Very likely she had left the Opera long ago; many ballet girls had come and gone in the intervening years. If she was still here, she could be any of a dozen light-haired dancers in the corps de ballet, all equally unremarkable, all equally prone to shrieks of horror over the Opera Ghost.

That brief moment so long ago had been the pleasantest interaction he'd had with a member of the Company, and he had never wanted to spoil it by encountering her again.

The pleasantest until now, that is, until Christine.

She averted her gaze from the gargoyles guarding his front door, and halted on the dark threshold when it opened. Unlit, the room beyond was black and impenetrable, easy to populate with any horror. It had never looked so to him, but suddenly seeing it through her eyes... He needed light, light would help—a quick snap of his fingers, and candles all around the room flared up and cast their glow through the space.

"Oh, that's much better," she said, and stepped into the parlor.

At once he thought of a hundred things in the room he wished he could change. There still weren't enough candles and would she find the gargoyles on this side of the door alarming and was it obvious those curtains in the corner were hiding a secret door? He shoved those thoughts away, tried to reassure himself that this must be better than anything she might have expected after the dark passages and the gloomy lake—which didn't greatly help.

Christine, meanwhile, had wandered across the room to the pipe organ on the far wall. She ran a hand across the carved back, and he was suddenly possessed with the conviction that he hadn't dusted it recently enough. When she looked back towards him, it was with a smile and the world-tilting words, "Would you sing something for me?"

Well. That was an idea.

He dropped his long cloak on his armchair and crossed over to the pipe organ, to Christine as she stood beside it, still smiling up at him. He looked away from her face, focused on the ivory keys as he seated himself at the bench. His fingers didn't tremble as he placed them on the central keys, but it took all his control to hold them steady.

This was incredible, unreal. For her to step through the mirror to him had seemed impossible, the walk had been a kind of dream, but now in his familiar room, sitting here where he had spent countless hours before—he had to be awake. And yet Christine was still here, still smiling, still willing to be a part of this strange world he had drawn her into.

In some ways it felt as if he was awake for the first time, the candle-lit room brighter than any daylight he'd ever known, the colors more brilliant than ever before. Had the wood of the organ always gleamed so, the couches always been such a deep maroon? Not until she came.

Music. He was supposed to be playing music for her. He snuck a glance and saw that she was still undisturbed. He took a deep breath and tried to think what song. He knew thousands of songs, endless melodies, but in this moment, to bring the *right* one to mind…

Perhaps "The Bird Song" from Bizet's *Carmen*. It was a daring choice and he began the opening strains before thinking too carefully about it. Using his own words was unthinkable, so he would use Bizet's, as Don Jose confessed his love for the beautiful, willful Carmen.

"The flower that you had thrown me, I kept with me in prison… For you had only to appear, only to toss a glance towards me, to take hold of all my being."

Bizet knew of what he wrote. It had been exactly that way, that moment when she had sung on stage then looked his direction. Yes. Bizet knew.

He reached the end of the song, Don Jose's final declaration of love, before he risked looking at Christine again.

She was still smiling on him, eyes still alight with lively interest. No trace of fear. He had sung her a love song, and she was still unafraid.

He cleared his throat, carefully. "Carmen has a very lovely aria in Act One. It has a descending chromatic scale, varying a repeated phrase. I believe it would be quite good for your voice…"

She willingly assented to attempt the song, a song about the wayward, uncontrollable nature of love. Her voice was glorious and though of course she wasn't singing this love song *to* him, she was, still, singing it *for* him. His fingers moved over the ivory keys, providing the melody almost without thinking, as he remained entranced by her voice.

It was all going so well, so much better than he could have hoped. She was happy here, in his world of music. They spoke of the aria, of the opera, of the variations in the melody. Carried away on the music and her voice, a dream-like quality had returned, a kind of hazy rapture as he carried on a fine outward calm and inwardly thrilled and exulted.

After a few times through Carmen's aria, he cautiously suggested a duet.

"Why not?" she said, leaning a little closer where she stood beside the pipe organ.

He looked down at his hands again. How much would his eyes betray, if she looked into them for too long? What would she see there? "Act Four," he said, clinging to this opera that had been serving him so well. "Carmen and Escamillo sing a duet together…"

They had sung duets before, but not like this. Before there had always been a mirror between them. Before he had always chosen songs with an eye towards teaching. Not towards feelings. It had always been—well, at least mostly professional.

But tonight—tonight their voices intertwined in a romantic duet, singing declarations of love, inhabiting the words, inhabiting the characters. A single step from Don Jose the solitary prisoner to Escamillo the glamorous matador, but tonight he could do anything. He could be anyone. Because she was here, accepting his world, accepting his mask, accepting all he had to offer of music and wonder.

The song came to a lingering end, the echoes playing in his mind, and he wanted to offer his heart too, make a true declaration not hidden within the words of another man's song.

No—no, too much, too soon.

He grappled for his control. He had done enough mad things for one night. To move too fast could ruin everything.

And yet if they kept singing, if he kept gazing on her smile, listening to her voice…

He pushed away from the pipe organ, rose to his feet. "Perhaps that is enough for one night." His voice had been steady, hadn't it?

"I don't mind singing something else," she said, taking a few steps nearer to him, coming around to the front of the pipe organ and in another second she would be within arm's length.

He backed hurriedly away. Too soon! "No—no, I wouldn't want to strain your voice. I really think that was enough tonight."

"Doesn't Carmen have any other songs?" she murmured.

It was tempting, so tempting to go on singing with her long, long into the night. But at the same time, fear was rising—not in her, perhaps, but in him. He was going to get this wrong somehow. End it, end it now while the night was still good and beautiful.

"Perhaps another time," he managed.

"Perhaps tomorrow?" she suggested.

He should take her home. To *her* home. That was the only sensible thing to do, the only reasonable thing to do. Yet somehow, inexplicably, he found himself saying, "I have a guest bedroom. If you would…consider staying."

That room had always been a rather silly indulgence, a nod to taste and proper ways of doing things, since he had never anticipated having a guest. But she smiled, nodded, assented to staying.

"Well, I'll…show you the way, then," he said, feeling more unsure with every word.

"Of course," she agreed, and moved closer to him again.

He turned quickly, moved away towards the side door. He wanted to take her hand, wanted it too much, so much that he was afraid to do it. If he moved too fast—if he did the wrong thing, said the wrong thing…

He led the way through the side door, up the spiral staircase, trying to keep a proper, appropriate distance between them though she kept moving as though she meant to walk beside him.

Such a small thing, and something he had never, ever had. Someone to walk beside him.

He left her at the door of the bedroom with a faint, "Good night." How long had it been since he had wished anyone good night?

He retreated to his pipe organ again, sat down in that so familiar place and tried to steady himself. Had so much happened in only a few hours? So many impossible things?

For a few moments he struggled for calm—then surrendered. If so many impossible things could happen, why couldn't *anything*? He gave way completely to the wild hopes that had been fighting to come forward, past his control, past his caution.

Tonight was too soon, but some day, on the right day—if she could accept his world, accept his mask, accept *him*… Was it so mad after all, for a Ghost to fall in love, if it was with the right woman?

Maybe the world could offer him something more than loneliness and rejection after all. Something more than merely watching life's opera, but an actual role to play.

She loved music. Maybe, just maybe, she could love him too.

He stayed up all night, stayed at the pipe organ. Music was welling up inside of him, born of this wild, impossible hope, needing to be put into sound, put down in notes on paper. He wasn't tired, couldn't think of sleeping, not now, not on this night when light was shining into his darkness.

Sunlight never reached him here, but he knew when it was morning. He should wake Christine soon. After he finished this new concerto, a melody full of life and joy, and it wasn't quite right yet. When it was done, he'd wake Christine, and play it for her, and then—

And then there was a scraping against his face, an unfamiliar touch of air on his cheek, and he turned instinctively to face this unexpected attack, realizing properly what had happened only after he had risen to his feet from his seat at the organ.

By then it was far too late. In that single instant, it was all over.

Christine stared up at him, his mask clutched in one hand.

He saw her eyes change.

Her whole face transformed from eager interest, to shock, to dismay. To stunned horror.

It was the expression he had seen so many times in so many gazes, the fear that had stalked him from birth, looking out at him through all the eyes that had ever looked on his twisted, deformed face.

She was supposed to be *different*.

He thought she *understood*, that she accepted his life and his world, that the mask must remain, part of the magic necessary to keep this delicate dream between them intact. Perhaps then she might have someday come to know the true him, not the monster's face or the angel's voice but *him*, the man somewhere in between the two.

He had dared to dream of love and instead—betrayal. And terror.

The man retreated, and it was the Phantom who asked, "How could you?" voice low and soft. Then, a thundering roar: "*How could you?*"

She screamed, a high note piercing the silent depths, and stumbled backwards to one of his couches where she collapsed amid loud, wrenching sobs.

He stalked after her, fists tight at his sides, shaking with fury and the death of dreams. "I only gave you *one* rule, was that asking so much? I thought you *understood* and now—now you've ruined everything! We could have been happy, but no, you had to look, you had to know. Are you satisfied?"

She shrank back into the corner of the couch, covering her face with her hands as he loomed above her, like every dark villain in every opera.

He reached out, caught her wrist and yanked her hand down. "You wanted to see, so *look at me*! Look at the horror that's haunted my life, ruined my every step."

She turned her face into the pillows, went on sobbing. He released her hand, turned his back and clenched his fingers in his hair. "What did you expect?" he demanded. "That the mask was just an eccentricity, just a whim? That really I was like other men? I am not. Now you know the truth. I am a monster. A poor, foolish monster who was mad enough to fall in love with an angel."

A sharp inhalation, followed by the jerky, sob-punctuated sentence, "You're—in love—with me?"

"You must have known that." The burning heat of his fury was already dissipating, dying down as fast as it had flared up, leaving the cold and lonely ashes of despair behind it.

In a sudden hopeless impulse he knelt down before her where she huddled among the cushions. "When we sang together—you *must* have known. And…you cared about me a bit, didn't you? About your Angel of Music? You might have loved me too, one day, if only…but can't you try to see, that's still me, I'm not really any different. This face isn't me, it's just another kind of mask, and if you could only…"

He started to reach out, and she shrank away.

He drew his hand back. Why was he even trying? How could she possibly understand? How could he ask her to believe something he didn't believe himself? He rose to his feet, backed away a few steps, fingers curling into his palms so tightly they ached. "Go." When she didn't move, he shouted it. "*Go!*"

She scrambled off the couch and fled the room, footsteps audible on the spiral stair towards the bedroom. She left his mask behind, creamy against the rich maroon of the couch cushion. So much more attractive than the horror it had failed to hide.

He stared at the mask, at his so inadequate protection, until he heard the sound of the bedroom door closing with a bang. It was the plagal cadence to this symphony that had veered so sharply into minor key, from love song into tragedy.

Then he picked up the mask, put it numbly back into place. He walked with leaden feet to the pipe organ and sank down onto the bench. He reached out to the instrument, for some support, emotional or simply to keep him upright, and his hands encountered papers. Musical scores. His newly-written concerto, full of hope and love and impossible aspirations. The ink hadn't even dried, and already the dream was blighted, already harsh reality had reasserted itself. As it always must. He tore the score from its place, swept the pages down to the floor in a rustling cascade.

He lowered his head onto the keyboard and wept silently against the smooth ivory keys.

Chapter Sixteen

S unday morning saw Mother and me back in the managers' office.
A note had arrived, demanding to see Mother immediately. Of
course I went along to find out what they wanted. The atmosphere was
so uncomfortable when we arrived that I almost regretted it. No
beaming smiles this time; Moncharmin looked stern, looming behind
the desk, while Ricard hovered about with a nervous expression. M.
Garnier's portrait on the wall, gazing into the distance, was the
friendliest face in sight. The poster of Carlotta seemed to be gloating.

We sat down as before, and after an absolute minimum of
pleasantries we got to the matter at hand. "What can you tell me about
this?" Moncharmin demanded, standing behind his desk and waving a
black-edged envelope in punctuation.

Mother's eyebrows rose. "It appears to be a letter."

"From the Phantom," I put in without thinking, my attention
mostly on trying to read the glimpses I was getting of red writing on the
front.

Moncharmin verbally pounced. "How did you know that?"

My stomach tightened in sudden nerves as he stared at me, but I
kept alarm out of my voice. "Anyone at the Opera would have known
that. The Phantom's stationary is distinctive."

Moncharmin frowned but didn't pursue the point—though that may have been because Mother interrupted with, "I fail to see why you brought me here to discuss the Phantom's correspondence. Surely the matter could have waited until Monday."

"This letter," Moncharmin said, tapping it against the edge of the desk, "takes full responsibility for Carlotta's...incident yesterday evening, and recommends that we give Mademoiselle Daaé a leading role in the future. He also reminds us that his salary is due at the end of the month!"

Nothing in that message surprised me, except possibly the Phantom's sheer gall in sending it. Though really, that was true to character too.

"We both feel this prank has gone quite far enough," Ricard said, clasping his hands behind his back and trying to look stern. He wasn't as good at it as Moncharmin.

"This has gone beyond the realm of a *prank*!" Moncharmin snapped. "We had to give *refunds* yesterday!" He sank down into his chair, overcome, and pulled out a handkerchief to mop at his brow.

It was so easy to see them both as comical, to want to laugh and enjoy the Phantom's joke on them. I tried to restrain the smile tugging at my mouth, tried to look properly serious. I reminded myself that they did, after all, manage the Opera Garnier, that they could levy fines or suspensions or change job assignments. That Mother and I both depended on their goodwill to a significant degree.

That thought effectively stopped me wanting to smile.

"I still do not see why you wish to discuss this matter with me," Mother said, voice cool and professional. "You are surely not suggesting that I had anything to do with Signora Carlotta's indisposition?"

"We think you know something about what this so-called Phantom is doing," Ricard said, face earnest as he apparently made a genuine effort to explain.

Mother's eyebrow rose in silent, subtle disbelief. "I know no more than anyone else about the Phantom's motives, methods or intentions."

I felt an irrational, regretful pang. Of course it was better to *not* be involved. To not be guilty of collusion, or whatever the managers or Commissaire Mifroid would call this. But I had always wanted to be part of the Phantom's story.

"This is nonsense!" Moncharmin broke in. "The Phantom doesn't exist! This is all some prank Debienne came up with, and disrupting a performance is taking matters far too far! I want this stopped!"

"We have already discussed that matter, gentlemen," Mother said frostily, "and I see no advantage for anyone in going over it again. If you have nothing further to address?"

"Very well," Moncharmin said, inhaling deeply. "You may go, Madame Giry. And you needn't bother coming back."

The words hung in the air between us. We had already risen to our feet, and I wished now I hadn't, as my knees went wobbly and my stomach dropped. Surely he didn't mean…? He meant for the day—maybe the week, but not…

Moncharmin's knuckles were white where he gripped the edge of the desk. "We cannot have employees who are dishonest, or who disrupt performances."

My face felt hot, my hands curling into fists. "My mother is not—"

"*Meg*," Mother said sharply and I fell silent, a lifetime's instinct responding to *that* tone, *that* look. Mother had her most terrifying expression on, the one that had taught me the absolute futility of trying to hide transgressions all through my childhood. She looked at me only for a second or two, then turned that same expression on M. Moncharmin. "*I* do not wish to have an employer who is insulting," she announced, and swept out with back straight and head up.

I could do nothing but follow, and I didn't manage the same majesty—or even think to worry about that until it was too late and we were already gone.

Mother kept up the regal walk as we exited the Opera, while I frankly bounced anxiously, hands clutching and bunching in my blue-striped skirt. "I am not a child; you should have let me say—"

"What good would it do?" Mother asked, voice too iron-controlled to betray any but the barest hint of weariness.

"But they can't *do* that!" I protested, then swallowed uneasily. "Can they?"

"Of course they can; I hardly had a life contract. The managers have the authority to dismiss whoever they choose."

"But it's—it's…" Having just claimed not to be a child, I couldn't revert to the universal plaint that it wasn't fair. "But what are we going to *do*?"

We were on the front steps of the Opera by now. Mother took my arm and threaded it firmly through hers, giving my hand one light pat. "We are not going to starve, for a first point. This city is filled with opportunities and I am sure there will be other employment. In the meantime, they haven't fired you, so we still have some income. Many people get by on less than we had."

I had been looking at it more from an injustice principle than from an economic view, more from the shock of a fundamental state of the world suddenly changing. Not starving was good in the abstract, but it didn't signify much in the moment. It was all the fault of the new managers, disrupting our comfortable world. "Why did Debienne have to go to Australia anyway?"

"Even you must admit he was helped along in that decision," Mother pointed out.

"We don't *know* that he was trying to escape the Phantom," I said, though the swiftness with which I said it probably only revealed how sure of it I was. And then, against all odds, I thought of something that made me feel more hopeful. "You know—the Phantom is not going to like this at all."

Hours passed, and Christine did not reemerge from the bedroom. He could hardly blame her. He also couldn't ignore the situation indefinitely. Finally, reluctantly, checking twice that his mask was securely in place, he climbed the spiral stairs to the second floor and knocked lightly on the door.

"Christine? I'm sorry I upset you." Conciliatory was good, yes? And reassurances. "I won't hurt you. Can we discuss this...unfortunate situation?"

Silence from inside.

"For better or worse, we cannot avoid each other forever and..." And that was not as reassuring as he had meant to sound. "...and I really think it would be better if we attempted some sort of understanding."

Nothing. He might as well have been talking to the pipe organ downstairs.

Maybe he should just walk away, leave her alone until she chose to come out. Let this intermission in their story last as long as she chose. What was the worst that could happen?

At that question, a too creative imagination supplied him with too many hideous possibilities. A prickle of fear crawled up his spine as he focused in on the most awful. No one could hurt her in there, but she could hurt herself. Surely she wouldn't have done anything rash, she couldn't be that desperate? For the first time he tried the door handle—and it wouldn't turn.

Of course it was locked. Of course she'd lock the monster out.

In less than a day all his fragile hopes had collapsed into *this*.

For a long moment he stared at the locked door handle, dying dreams building up around him like a slowly rising crescendo. Then, with a jolt, he remembered again the worry that had made him try the handle to begin with. Might she have locked it before trying to kill herself? The ultimate, final escape?

He rapped his knuckles against the wooden panel again, called, "If you don't say something so I at least know you're alive in there, I'm going to have to—break the door down."

In actual fact, he had a key to the door. And he hadn't found a lock he couldn't pick since he was ten years old. And the room had a second, hidden door. Those observations would only be likely to frighten her more, nor did they do anything to lessen the symbolic impact of that locked door.

"I'm fine, I want to be alone!"

It was an answer, and that was at least a mild relief. He tried to analyze the brief sentence, the sound of her voice in the handful of words. She sounded upset. Not hysterical, though. Should he insist on going in, just in case? Only that would upset her more, make desperate action more likely.

He retreated, to pace around his parlor, hit random keys on the pipe organ, and try to work out what he could possibly do now. If he had just kept his temper and his pain hidden when his mask came off—but what did that matter, really?

She had seen his face. That would be enough.

Still, they *were* trapped with each other. She couldn't find her way back to the surface without his help, and she must realize that. Somehow, he had transformed from a guiding angel to a captor.

It had to be possible to reassure her, to start repairing some of this disaster. If she wouldn't talk to him, perhaps a letter? He'd had far more experience in recent years with letters than with conversations. He opened cabinets and shuffled through piles of musical scores until he found blank paper—his black-edged stationary wouldn't send quite the right message—and black ink, instead of his customary lurid red.

He began: "My dear Christine, I am very" and then stopped. Was that the right salutation? He began letters to the management that way, it was a perfectly acceptable means of address. Would it be too formal? Or would she read it all the wrong way, read too much into *dear*—or worse, into *my*!

He crumpled the paper, threw it over his shoulder into the fire. Perhaps just "Dear Christine." Perhaps just "Christine." That was probably safest.

Now for the body of the letter...

He burned six drafts and finally wound up with a brief, stiff, apologetic note. He told her he had been wrong, he had reacted badly, he never wanted to frighten her or to hurt her, he hoped she would forgive him and he would do anything she asked to make amends.

He still didn't like the wording, but it was the best he could manage.

He hesitated anew at the bottom. No real necessity existed for signing it; there could be no doubt who it was from. And yet...he *could* put his name. His real name. It would be a gesture of trust, an offering of vulnerability. Names had immense power in almost every mythology.

On a practical level, at present precisely one person knew the Phantom's name, a possible second suspected, only those two in all the world had any ability to connect the Opera Ghost to a complicated past life. Granting Christine that information was placing a very real weapon into her hands. It was a far more profound apology than a stilted letter.

Would she see any of that subtlety behind a simple word on a page? Probably not. He signed the note anyway, folded it in thirds, and slid it beneath her door.

Chapter Seventeen

He sat down at the pipe organ, tried to lose himself in music. He was plainly in no frame of mind to compose anything worthwhile, so he let his hands wander at random. A few bars of one of his own compositions merged into a bit of Mozart that shifted into Gounod and then Wagner, became an old French lullaby before circling back into his own music again. He was hardly even listening, his thoughts far more tangled than the notes, circling and branching and spinning just as haphazardly.

There was a delicate cough behind him.

Instinctively his fingers flattened on the keys, producing a discordant clash of sound. He flinched, lifted his hands, tried to stand up and turn around at the same time and came perilously close to falling backwards into the pipe organ. He kept his balance, barely.

Christine was standing several feet away, brown eyes wide, hands clasped behind her back. "I didn't mean to startle you..."

"No, no, I'm fine." How had he let her sneak up on him *twice*? "Perfectly fine. Ahem. You look...well." It was the first thought he could summon, immediately regretted it. Bringing up appearances, that would *certainly* help the situation.

"I feel better after a bit of a rest, thank you." Her chin drooped. "And I am so *very* sorry about—before. It was quite unforgivable of me and you must think I'm the most horrible of traitors."

This was not remotely anything he had expected her to say. He had no idea what his half of the script was meant to be . "I wouldn't say—"

"Oh no, it's true! I just feel *awful*, and you must think I'm horrid and wicked and absolutely *hate* me—"

"No, really, I don't!" he interjected, appalled by her forlorn expression and self-recrimination. He had been too angry before; he had frightened and upset her.

"Really you don't?" she said, and her face lit in a smile. "That makes me so glad! I was hoping we could try to still be—friends." She extended one white hand.

He stared at it. This was what he *wanted*, wasn't it? Except it was too impossible, too much to expect from any woman; she couldn't be thinking straight. "But how can we be?" he whispered. "How can you want to be? You saw my face."

Her hand drifted back to her side, her gaze slid away. "It was a bit of a shock, of course. It was not quite what I had been expecting."

"I wouldn't think so," he said grimly.

"Your voice is so beautiful, I was so sure—and I just didn't want there to be any secrets between us, you see. I can't abide secrets."

He breathed secrets every day. Secrets were in his blood. "Some secrets are better left unrevealed."

Christine nodded once. "Perhaps it would be best if we simply never spoke of the matter again."

He never wanted to even *think* about it ever again. "I agree," he said, holding his voice carefully steady.

She clasped her hands together, in front of her this time. "Very well, then we won't discuss what occurred or—what was said."

With the pause before the final phrase, with the particular emphasis given those words, he had no doubt that she meant his confession of loving her. Clearly it had been a stupid, reckless, mad thing to say. Of course it was true, but he shouldn't have *said* it. He didn't trust his voice now, and merely nodded.

She sighed, lowering her gaze to her still-clasped hands. "I only wish—if only there was some way to go back to how things used to be."

"If only," he agreed, fervently.

"You think so too? But that's all right then!" Christine exclaimed, looking up with an absolutely dazzling smile.

His heart did flips over the smile even while his head tried to figure out why on earth it was there. "It is?"

"Of course! Now where were we?" She tripped lightly over to the end of the pipe organ, picking up the top sheet from the stack of music there. "Oh, I remember, Marguerite's aria in *Faust*. You had some ideas about how I could reach that high-C more naturally."

He had? That conversation had been several hours and at least three lifetimes ago. "Yes. Of course." He turned slowly back to the pipe organ, sat down, mechanically reached out for the smooth ivory keys.

Afterwards, he could never remember quite what they said in regards to *Faust* or high-Cs. But it was definitely a singing lesson. And while he didn't quite dare to mention the subject, it would appear that Christine was staying.

It would also appear that they had locked the monster away, were pretending the man didn't exist, and he had gone back to being the Angel of Music. He just wished he knew exactly how that had happened.

As soon as Mother and I got home from the Opera, she pulled out all her account books and budgets and sat down at the round table in our tiny kitchen to pore over them. I perched on a chair opposite her, fiddled with a fountain pen and watched her from under my lashes. My stomach, my shoulders, my jaw were tight with tension. All my worries and fears and feelings of outraged justice wanted to come bubbling up, but I recognized Mother's expression and knew this was not a time to talk.

The concerned furrow was in her forehead. It was fine to say we still had my salary, but we had needed both of ours to get by, to keep food on the table and stay decently clothed. Maybe we should have saved the money the Phantom gave Mother just after Buquet's death, instead of buying me a new cloak. I could have made do with the old one for a fourth winter.

I kept my teeth locked together, holding all words back, and stayed silent for as long as I possibly could. When it was finally too much, I managed to direct all my nervous energy into just asking, "Can I help somehow?"

"I don't know yet," Mother said, gaze running down a column of figures in the book open before her. "We have some money saved, though not as much as I'd wish. We still have your income too, although I don't think we can consider that secure, under the circumstances."

I lost my grip on the pen and it clattered onto the table. I slapped my hand over it so it wouldn't roll away. "But they wouldn't fire me!"

Mother sighed. "I would like to tell you that's true, but we must be realistic."

"I *am* being realistic," I muttered, slumping back in my chair. "They won't remember I exist long enough to fire me."

She just narrowed her eyes disapprovingly. "Besides which," she continued, "we can't live indefinitely on your income alone. I'll have to look into some options on finding a new position, although there could be, shall we say, challenges, when I was just fired from the Opera Garnier..." She tapped one finger against her chin, brow wrinkling in thought. "Although that might matter less away from Paris."

I straightened up. "Where would we go?" I didn't want to leave Paris for all sorts of reasons—but I wanted to go all sorts of places too, magical, exciting places that people wrote operas about.

"I was thinking of my friend Amelie. You remember her; she used to work at the Opera."

"I remember," I said, hopes already sinking.

"She and her husband moved to Bordeaux a few years ago to start a theater. I might write to her, see if she has any positions available."

I gripped the edges of the chair seat beneath me, fingers tight. "Right. Maybe." Amelie was nice, and probably Bordeaux was too—but I wanted to go to Italy, Egypt, India. Not to a smaller version of Paris, one without Christine, with none of my friends, none of my favorite places, certainly nothing to equal the Opera Garnier. And I doubted Amelie's theater was haunted.

Mother looked at me sharply, and it did no good trying to keep my face blank. Her tone was more curt than apologetic when she spoke. "I'm sorry if this is not what you've dreamed of, but—"

"I didn't say anything!" I protested. It wasn't fair to reprimand me when I wasn't even complaining. "I'm sure Bordeaux is lovely." My best efforts made the sentence half-hearted at most.

Her expression softened, and she reached out to squeeze my hand. "It's just one idea. We'll see." She looked down at her books again, turned a page. "We can always go back to Leclair. You like it there."

"Yes." It was true. I liked visiting. I even wanted to go back and live in Leclair, someday. But I wanted to have adventures first, to play a part that mattered in a story that mattered. If I went back to Leclair *now*, I'd end up working in a shop until I married some nice farmer, and never do anything.

I pushed away from the table and stood up. "If there's nothing I can do, maybe I'll take a walk. Get some air."

Mother didn't look up. "Fine, we'll talk more later. Try not to worry. We'll manage."

I nodded, went to my room for my bag, then leaned into the kitchen again. "Maybe the Phantom will fix things."

Mother glanced up. "Maybe."

I smiled, a wide smile, and tried to pretend to both of us that I believed it. He might. If he wasn't too busy being an Angel of Music.

Maybe it wouldn't be the worst thing in the world if Amelie's theater wasn't haunted. You can't be disappointed by a ghost if there isn't one. But would any magic exist in a theater with no phantom in the shadows?

I stood on our doorstep, took a deep breath, and tried to focus on what I was going to do *now*, this afternoon, never mind the future.

I walked two blocks toward Christine's apartment before thinking better of that idea. If she was still going to be upset, I didn't want to find out. Now not, when I'd lost my footing on this suddenly tilted world, when I felt like one more disappointment would completely undo me. We'd both be at the Opera on Monday for rehearsals. Better to talk to her then.

The walk toward Christine's had taken me toward the Opera Garnier too. I could see its copper dome rising over the buildings between us, the statue of Apollo shining on the top. A sudden stab of nostalgia hit me, missing a place I hadn't even left yet. Or maybe I was missing the days when going up to the roof of the Opera to dream had been enough to leave all my worries behind.

I blinked, breaking off my staring at the rooftop, and shook my head, irritated with myself. Those halcyon days I was thinking of had been hardly more than a month ago, and for all I knew, they could come back by Tuesday. Everything could sort itself out. And I could go up to the rooftop right now, if I wanted to.

I *could.* Except I could only get there by going through the Opera, and enormous and labyrinthine though it was, it would be just my luck to bump into the managers, and if I reminded them that I existed while they were in the wrong mood about the Phantom... My shoulders, momentarily squared in defiance, slumped again. Maybe I had better stay away from the Opera Garnier today.

I drifted farther down the street, through patches of sunlight and shadow, maneuvering unthinkingly through the crowd out walking Sunday afternoon. I was disturbed by my inability to think of something else I wanted to do. There had to be someone I could go visit, though just at the moment no one was coming to mind. It was a sudden shock to realize I couldn't remember the last time I had spent a Sunday afternoon with the ballet girls. It had surely happened some time since Christine had come to the Opera...but not recently.

I reached up to touch my necklace. If only Gabi was here. I had thought that often, in the early days, and now in this sudden crisis I missed my sister with a renewed sharpness. She had always been excited by any adventure I proposed, had seen the adventure even in ordinary things and always looked on the world with bright eyes. She would have been sure that we'd be able to stay in Paris, and equally sure that Bordeaux would be wonderful if we ended up going there.

Alone, it was not so easy to feel hopeful. That was the real trouble this afternoon. Anything I might do, I knew I'd start wondering if it was the last time I would do it. About whether anything would be as good in Bordeaux.

I kept walking forward because it was the easiest direction, gazing into the distance without paying attention to the view. I had been staring at Notre Dame's towers for at least a block before I properly realized it.

I could go *there*. I didn't know anywhere more serene, stable and unmoving than Notre Dame Cathedral. Where better to go when my world had fallen out of balance? And it couldn't be anything worse than the last time *for now*. Beignets and booksellers' stalls were fleeting, the Opera Garnier might close its doors to me, but I could always go back to Notre Dame. Maybe not soon, not if we moved away, but Notre Dame would never be gone. I'd be back someday.

I walked east along the Seine, took the Pont Neuf bridge across to the Isle de la Cité. The Seine sparkled below in the sunlight, so much more cheerful than I was feeling. I made my way through the narrow streets on the island, and as I approached across the last square those looming stone towers seemed to cut into the sky. It wasn't the friendliest of buildings, but at this moment that solid sternness felt reassuring. I knew where the door to the towers was, and the priest sitting by it barely glanced up from his hymn book to give me a nod, acknowledging that visitors were allowed this afternoon. I stepped over the threshold, lifted my long skirts a few inches so I wouldn't trip, and began the climb.

It was hundreds of steps up, most of them in a tight, circular stone stair. The stones were smooth from centuries of footsteps, shallow depressions worn into the center of each step. At intervals, narrow windows pierced the wall, each one showing a little more of the city as I went higher and higher. I could see the Opera's roof before I was even halfway up. My legs were strong and my breathing good from years of ballet, but I was still glad to see the top.

The stairs finally ended at a ledge wrapped around the towers, only a few feet wide, making me grateful for the waist-high stone banister. I ran my hand along the rough stone as I walked, searching for an empty corner. Since only a few people had made the climb this afternoon, it wasn't a long search.

I fit into a niche on the front of the cathedral, leaned my head against the stone, warm in the afternoon sunlight. A whisper of breeze curled past my cheek, carrying the cawing of birds with it, as I looked out over the distant spread of the city. The streets full of life felt much farther away than they did from the Opera's roof, everything small and quiet. If the Opera Garnier was small from here, shouldn't that make all my problems around the Opera small too?

I ran through them in my head, testing. Christine? No, flutters of nerves about the possibility that she would still be angry. Or that singing lessons weren't her only secret. The Phantom? Definite confusion and worry about what it meant, that he had been pretending to be an angel. And that he was *so* angry with Carlotta, just because she was nasty to Christine. Leaving Paris? No, still a sinking feeling at that thought.

It was much easier to climb 400 steps than it was to get above my problems.

Eventually I sighed, and turned my head to focus closer by, on the nearest gargoyle. He had horns, and was sticking his tongue out at Paris below him.

With all those steps to climb, I hadn't come up to the towers often. Still, I had been fascinated by them and their gargoyles ever since I read Monsieur Hugo's popular novel about a hunchback living up here. It took me six months to wade through it (skimming most of the architecture), and I thought Esmeralda was rather an idiot (not so much for not loving Quasimodo, but for the way she handled it), but I enjoyed the read despite that.

I left my niche to walk the few paces to the gargoyle. "You're lucky in some ways, you know," I told him, lightly tapping one curved wing. "You've been up here guarding the cathedral from demons for centuries, and you can go on doing it for centuries more. Nothing important in your world ever changes. No one's ever going to make you leave."

The gargoyle did not reply. I leaned on the weathered stone barrier next to him, propping my chin on my hands in a similar pose. "It's not exactly that I don't want things to change," I remarked, turning my head toward the gargoyle. "I just want things to change...well, the way I want them to." I wrinkled my forehead, certain I was stating the obvious. It wasn't my fault he wasn't holding up his end of the conversation.

"What do I expect from a conversation with a *gargoyle*?" I said under my breath. Maybe Notre Dame hadn't been a good choice in the end. All this clear air just gave me a clearer picture of everything that was wrong in my life. Like how I could find myself having a problem, with no one better to talk to about it than a statue.

I frowned, tried to shake self-pitying thoughts away. It wasn't *really* that I didn't have anyone to talk to. I'd had a fight with my best friend, and my mother didn't need my worries on top of her own thoughts. Those were temporary situations. And I had friends in Leclair, they just weren't *here*. And I had other friends at the Opera.

My mind flipped through mental pictures of the other girls— Adalisa, Francesca, Mignonette, Clarisse, Odette, Martine… Nice girls, but none felt like someone I could share worries with, or join for the afternoon on an impromptu whim. The way I would have with Gabi. The way I could with Christine, if things were different right now. I had had no particular friend before her at the Opera; that was part of why it had meant so much when she chose me. I had always been part of the circle of ballet girls, but in recent months I had joined them less and less, occupied with Christine instead. It occurred to me for the first time that no one had seemed to care much about my absence.

Maybe that meant I could have fit seamlessly back into the circle again, but somehow it was no comfort. It would have been nicer to think I was missed. Somehow I felt sure that if I descended on any of the girls with my problems now, the reception would be cool or disinterested at best, and I couldn't blame them. Gargoyles, unlike people, don't grow offended if you show up on their doorstep with a crisis after not being around much for a few months.

Gargoyles also don't offer advice or sympathy.

"You're not helping at all," I informed the statue, feeling lonelier than before I had come here. I pushed away from the balustrade, and walked on. A second staircase led down, around the other side of the cathedral. It was much faster than climbing up and if I wasn't a dancer used to spins, the tight curve would have made me dizzy.

The stairs opened back onto the plaza in front of the cathedral, letting me out into a rush of light and noise and bustle of people. The sudden change made me dizzier than the stairs.

My eyes had barely adjusted to the sunlight by the time I got to the heavy wooden doors of the cathedral and stepped back into the shadows. I could, after all, talk to someone else at Notre Dame besides gargoyles.

The cathedral inside was cavernous and dim, the ceiling feeling barely lower than the sky outside. Colored light streamed in through the rose windows, cutting pink and orange rainbows through the shadows. The silence had a heaviness that was different from the silence of the stairwell. That had merely been the absence of noise. This silence had a presence, made up of solemnity, dignity and tradition. The incense smelled different here than it did in other churches, a smokier scent. Or maybe it wasn't the incense that was different, just that there were so many candles, around every statue and in every niche. Something in me relaxed, just a little, as I inhaled that familiar scent.

I had been coming here for Easter morning mass for six years, and I knew the way to my favorite statue. It was of the Madonna and Child, much friendlier than some of the sad martyrs in other niches. There were two statues of the Madonna and Child near each other, but one looked bad-tempered to me. I always went to the other one, the kind-looking one. I fished a centime out of my bag, dropped the coin into the small metal box nearby, and picked up a taper to light a candle in the racks around the statue.

After I lit the candle, and while I was watching the flame dance, I realized I wasn't entirely sure what I was praying *for*. Mother, the disaster at the Opera this morning, and everything that might come from it, certainly. But also Christine and our stupid fight that still worried me, and I couldn't help wondering if the abrupt disappearance of the "Angel of Music" meant the Phantom needed a prayer too, and I was so used to lighting candles for my father and sister that suddenly I was thinking of them now, and... Finally I decided I'd better just cast all of it heavenward and let God sort it out.

Chapter Eighteen

C hristine hadn't come out of the bedroom until late morning on Sunday, and seemed to be repeating the pattern Monday morning too. He was awake long before dawn and paced impatiently until sunrise—not that it was visible, from his chambers. Finally he decided it would be best to go up to the Opera, just briefly, to check on a few matters there. He didn't *need* to—he had enough stores of food, water and candles to last a month, and no other supplies ran out as quickly. But still, venturing out, that was better than climbing the walls belowground or waking up Christine long before she'd want him to. It would be easier to resist doing that, if he went above. He scrawled a quick note to Christine, in case she rose early, donned his most enveloping cloak, and set out through the cellars.

The Opera wasn't stirring yet either, the rooms still quiet with emptiness, the quiet before the day's overture began. He liked this time at the Opera, with all the people away and only the Ghost and the ghosts of past melodies prowling the halls. He delivered a letter for the vocal director, informing him that Christine would be away for some time, but would be returning. Now was not the time to jeopardize her position at the Opera, although maybe…well, best to keep options open and not think too far ahead.

Next he went to the managers' office, using his master key for access, to find out what he could learn of the effects of Carlotta's unfortunate incident. He quickly located a letter from Carlotta herself, announcing she had taken to her bed, etc. etc. It was her usual reaction to any distress. With luck, she'd *stay* there. He couldn't find any indications on how they planned to fill her roles, which was less satisfactory. Even if Christine wasn't immediately available, they ought to be looking at her as a replacement.

With a frown, he hunted out the notes on ticket sales. His frown deepened when he saw that Box Five had been sold for the next week. Evidently the managers really were going to be difficult. They couldn't have had worse timing.

He almost missed even more irritating news. He was doing a final sort through the piled-up correspondence—he always read the management's correspondence—and discovered a letter pertaining to Madame Giry. A few checks through records confirmed what had happened.

He turned his back for one day and the whole place went mad! Even Debienne had never gone this far.

He dropped into the chair behind the desk, clenched a hand around the armrest. This required a response. A warning first, so they understood the situation, then a swift reprisal if the warning wasn't heeded. That should do.

The managers' desk was piled high with papers and books. He swept it all off onto the floor with rustles and thuds, seized pen and ink from a drawer, and wrote a message across the smooth top of the wooden desk.

Reinstate Madame Giry at once, keep Box Five empty, and deliver 20,000 francs on the first of the month—or you will regret the consequences.

O. G.

He surveyed the effect, and was satisfied. He considered drawing a grinning skull in one corner, but that seemed a touch too theatrical.

He left the office by the conventional door, a small risk so early in the morning—or so it seemed, until footfalls announced a presence approaching from the opposite doorway.

His hands tightened instinctively into fists, heart racing, running through a half-dozen methods of escape or defense in the brief moment it took for him to realize this intruder's identity.

He exhaled, heart rate beginning to calm. "Do not sneak up on me, Daroga. You may not like the consequences one day."

"I was not intending to sneak up on you," the Daroga said, the usual impassive note in his voice. "Merely testing a theory that you might come visit the managers' office one of these early mornings."

"I congratulate you on your intuition," he said, and sketched a slight bow. "Now if you will excuse me, I am very busy this morning." He had no time for an amiable conversation today, not with Christine below the Opera.

As if the other man could read his mind, the Daroga softly said, "You've taken an interest in Christine Daaé."

His right hand slowly clenched into a fist again. "What of it?" he asked, striving for a light tone. "She is an excellent singer, could be a wonderful asset to the Company if they had the wit to notice it. Did you see her debut the other day? Quite the triumph."

"I saw her sing," the Daroga said slowly. "I also saw that Carlotta had a bit of…trouble on Saturday. And that Christine Daaé did not leave the Opera Garnier that night. Nor has she been seen by anyone since."

His fingernails dug into his palm. "In the vast crowd, you noticed the absence of one singer? Aren't you taking your faith in your powers of observation a bit far?"

"You took an interest in her. Therefore so must I."

Far too many people thought they had a right to be interested in Christine. "No one asked you to get involved," the Phantom growled.

"Tell me the truth," the Daroga said, and now more steel had entered his voice. Steel—and a touch of concern? "Where is Mademoiselle Daaé? What have you done?"

"I have not *done* anything. I have not committed any crime; no harm has come to her." He realized suddenly that he was rubbing his left palm against his coat, a sign the Daroga would surely take as guilt, and quickly dropped it to his side again. He turned, strode down the corridor. "Stop worrying, Daroga, she's fine."

"If you abducted that girl—"

"She wanted to come!" he snapped, wheeling around again.

The Daroga's tone shifted into sadness, all too close to pity, as he said, "You know this cannot work."

"Do not ruin this! It can, it will—she saw my face, and she's still willing to stay. She's different, she's not like everyone else." When had a note of pleading entered his voice? He took a breath, squared his shoulders. "It will be fine."

"Listen to me—"

"It *will be fine*, Daroga." He turned to the wall, hit a hidden lever to trigger a secret door, stepped through and let it swing silently shut again on whatever protest the Daroga cared to make.

She was different.

And it would be fine.

I knocked on the door of Christine's dressing room after Monday's ballet practice. The girls were all abuzz about Carlotta still—at least, when I was there. When I had first come in, and once or twice when a conversation had gone on at the other side of the room, I had thought the topic might be different...but perhaps spending all night worrying about Mother's dismissal was making me hear ghosts of it everywhere. No one was talking to *me* about it, and I didn't want them to. I just wanted to talk to Christine.

I knocked again when I got no initial response. The world had grown unstable and I badly needed to patch up this fight with my best friend. If I could talk to Christine, everything would feel better. Surely she was done being upset about the Phantom-as-Angel accusation by now.

My second knock met disappointing silence too, and the door was locked when I tried the handle. I glanced up and down the hall, and stepped in the path of an approaching singer. I thought her name was Lisette or Cosette or something like that. She was a tall girl who took advantage of her height to look down her nose at me.

I persevered anyway. Dancers are just as good as sopranos, thank you very much. "Excuse me—I'm looking for my friend, Christine Daaé. Do you know where I might find her?"

"Oh, you're *Christine's* friend," Lisette-or-Cosette said, suddenly relaxing her haughtiness. I wasn't sure I appreciated it, considering the apparent cause. "She wasn't at practice today." The girl shrugged. "She might be coming for a special practice or something. Everyone is saying that the Phantom has sent orders about giving her better parts."

My mind whirled with new questions. Did that mean the 'Angel of Music' was teaching Christine again? If he was helping her as the Phantom, did she know the truth now? Surely that meant she couldn't be mad at me anymore for suggesting he was behind it all. But why would he have given up the Angel pretense? And, oddly, contradictorily, I felt a stab of dismay that she might know he was the Phantom. That she might have an acknowledged, understood connection.

I badly missed the days when the Phantom's actions had seemed, well, comparatively reasonable. When I had believed that I had a special understanding of all that went on.

More important than whatever was happening with the Angel, if the Phantom was delivering orders relating to Christine, had he done anything about Mother's job?

I didn't know how to find that answer, much as I might want to, so I stayed on the Christine track instead and went to the chorus' rehearsal rooms. I found Monsieur Montagne the vocal director alone in a practice room where he was sorting musical scores. I recognized him but we had never spoken. I took a deep breath for courage and put my question about Christine to him.

M. Montagne was as haughty as Lisette-or-Cosette, with more weight behind it, and his haughtiness never relaxed. "If you are Christine's friend, surely you should have heard already. I had a message she has gone away for a few days. Some sudden trip, and she neglected to mention when she would be back so do not bother asking. It is all extremely inconsiderate." I was then treated to a five-minute monologue on the irresponsibility of the average chorus girl, before I managed to escape back into the corridor.

I put a corner between myself and the chorus room, then leaned against an ornate pillar and tried to regain my balance. I closed my eyes, closed my hand around my necklace, took a few slow breaths and tried to be rational. Surely our fight hadn't been *that* serious, that she'd leave town for a trip and not even tell me. Maybe it had been sudden and she hadn't had a chance to tell me. Maybe she had sent me a letter, and I'd get it when I went home.

I was startled out of my thoughts and back to my surroundings when my name was called. "Mademoiselle Giry!"

Monsieur Moncharmin came stalking up in a state of high outrage, Monsieur Ricard trailing a few steps behind him with a worried expression. "Mademoiselle Giry," Moncharmin repeated, face red with fury, "you can tell your mother and your Phantom that we will not be intimidated!"

My anxiety, only slightly calmed, tripled at once, my palms damp and my breath tight. I stared at him, every possible response flying out of my head, and finally fell back on the automatic, "He's not my Phantom."

"I don't care *whose* Phantom he is," Moncharmin said, with a wild gesture of one hand, "he vandalized our office this morning and I will not tolerate it!"

"Are you sure it was him?" I ventured, in some uncertain effort to deflect whatever inexplicable blame was coming to me over this. Though it certainly sounded like the Phantom.

"Of course we're sure, he signed the blasted message! Unless there's another O. G. besides the Opera Ghost mucking around—" Suddenly he looked at me very hard. "What is your first name?"

"Marguerite," I said with the slightest relaxing in my breath, profoundly grateful that it wasn't Olivia or Ophelia.

His scowl did not diminish. "Hmph. Well, whoever is behind all this nonsense, you can tell them that their threats are not amusing and will not be effective."

"I can't tell the Phantom anything," I protested, "I don't—"

"Why can no one in your family cooperate?" Moncharmin roared. "I suggest you keep in mind that ballet dancers can be dismissed as easily as boxkeepers!"

My stomach dropped and my cheeks flamed suddenly hot. I had lain awake over being fired, but somehow I hadn't really *believed* in the possibility until that moment. Now all I could feel was that I *couldn't* leave the Opera; how could I walk away from the world I knew best, the kingdom of magic and mystery that kept me constantly intrigued? From Christine, from the Phantom, from practically everyone I knew?

Ricard made a strangled sound, seized Moncharmin by the arm and half-turned him away. "We *talked* about this," Ricard hissed, his next whispered words dropping too low for me to hear.

I stared at them, mind spinning, as they carried on their argument in undertones. If I had to leave…Mother would insist on going to Bordeaux. And even if we stayed in Paris, I wouldn't be *here* anymore. I didn't have the money to come back as a guest, even in the cheapest of seats, so if I was fired that meant—no more dancing, no more magic on stage, no more of the hundred stories all around the Opera. I might meet Christine outside the Opera, but there would be no more Phantom.

Finally Ricard's voice rose to an intelligible volume, to snap, "Then *you* can explain it to Madame Thibault!"

Moncharmin winced, and when he looked back at me at last, his tone was more restrained. "Fine. Stay in the corps de ballet. But watch your step!"

"Yes, Monsieur." I managed a curtsy that only wobbled a little, despite the shaking of my legs, and the managers went on their way.

Chapter Nineteen

A fter the management's threats, my life felt as delicately balanced
as a dancer en pointe, but by Wednesday night nothing had
toppled yet. I tucked myself into a space between two cold pillars in
the hall outside the boxes, studied the intricate mosaic of the tile floor,
and hoped no one would notice me. The performance was due to begin
soon, but I couldn't stand to go backstage just yet. The gossipers had
begun talking about Mother's dismissal—or they had just grown
bolder, and begun talking where I could hear them.

Everywhere I went today people were shooting me glances as
though I'd had a death in the family. It was disheartening how few
people said anything sympathetic, and how many just looked at me like
I might be carrying the plague, as though a dismissal could be
contagious. Jammes had actually asked me, in front of most of the
ballet, if I expected the managers to fire me soon too. I had said no, but
not as gracefully as I wished.

Out here, near the boxes, most people were guests who ignored
me, or people with business in this area who were going about it. I kept
my head down and listened to snatches of conversation. Chatter about
hats and shoes and what they were wearing these days in Milan. Some
gentleman planning a shooting party next week. Several other young
men planning a rousing Mardi Gras celebration. Not much discussion

about the upcoming show, but of course the point of attending the Opera was to see and be seen. It was oddly comforting, the ongoing, background music of the Opera Garnier in the voices of everyone who came here.

Then I heard a conversation in low tones between two women about the unreasonable demands of subscribers, and of course they all had to want something all at once, and the timing couldn't be more inconvenient. I looked up to see who was having that conversation, just in time to meet glances with Madame Travere, who practically pounced on me.

"Meg! You know all your mother's boxes, don't you?" she said, hurrying forward and seizing my arm. "Won't you be a dear and help me? Box 15 wants a new cushion and Box 19 wants to know when Act Three will finish and I have all these programs still to deliver—"

"I can take care of these," I said, deftly tugging a bundle of programs out of her hand. An excuse to avoid backstage was welcome—though I would have helped anyway.

"How the management expects us to just keep going with one less boxkeeper I'm sure *I* don't know—especially Marie, she was so good at making sure everything went smoothly for everyone—I got all of her boxes on the upper tier, if you can just deliver programs to the ones on this level…?"

"Yes, of course." I balanced the stack of programs in the crook of my arm. "Wonderful, I so appreciate it," Madame Travere said, turning to go. She got four steps away before she stopped and looked back with a guilty expression. "And I am *so* sorry about Marie."

"Thank you, I'll tell Mother you said so," I said quickly. That sounded like she had *died.* Expressions of condolence like that weren't much better than being looked at like a plague-carrier, even if they were better intended.

She hurried off. I took a deep breath and began the rounds. I delivered programs to the first three boxes without incident, or nearly. One man made a slightly inappropriate comment about the change in boxkeeper (he approved), but since his wife smacked his arm with a fan, that didn't escalate.

I was approaching Box 11 when I remembered whose it was: the Comte de Chagny. Would Raoul be there, had Christine told *him* she was leaving town, and could I manage to ask without admitting she hadn't told me?

Those questions dropped out of my mind as I approached the door. I could hear the noise inside from three steps away.

Philippe's voice was a deep rumble. "I brought you to the Opera to give you some experience with women, but for God's sake, you can't start taking the matter seriously!"

I hesitated, torn between conflicting worries. This would be a terrible time to knock on the door. But I had to get backstage soon, and if no one came at all, they might complain to the management.

Raoul's voice seemed thin compared to his brother's. "The situation is my affair—"

"Yes, and by all means, *have* an affair. You've always been too pure by half. Buy the girl flowers, jewelry, make her your mistress. But it's out of the question to give the wench your name and you know it."

Raoul's voice went shrill with indignation. "I will not have you speak of Christine in that manner!"

No, best not to knock on the door. I started to retreat but got only a step before a roar came of, "No de Chagny is ever marrying an upstart, gutter-trash *chorus girl!*" and the door of the Box burst open. I froze, staring at the towering figure of Philippe de Chagny, halted in the doorway.

I held up the two programs as though they were a shield, trying and failing not to shrink behind them. "Your program, Monsieur?"

He glowered at me. "You're not the boxkeeper."

I edged one foot farther back, heart pounding even though I knew I wasn't in the wrong. "I was only helping—"

He grabbed me by the arm, grip tight enough to hurt, and my breath caught in my throat. He couldn't *do* anything, we were in the middle of a busy corridor, so why was I afraid? "Don't even think about spreading my family's business around to your chattering friends." He released me, stormed past and was gone down the corridor.

I exhaled, rubbed my upper arm as I watched him go, confirming he wasn't coming back. Then I looked back at the doorway to find Raoul standing there. "Programs?" I said, reaching for normalcy, and held them out.

He took both without looking at them, eyes worried. For just a moment I entertained the comforting idea that he might offer some expression of concern, or an apology for his brother. When he spoke, it was to say instead, "You won't tell Christine about this, will you, Meg?"

Of course. Because that was all he cared about. "That depends," I said slowly. I hadn't given any thought yet to what to say to Christine. Assuming we were speaking. "Your brother made his feelings about marriage clear. What are yours?"

He looked at the ceiling, the programs, the far end of the corridor. "You must understand—my options are very limited—it's all nonsense about the aristocracy having more freedom, we're really very constrained in many ways—"

"I understand perfectly, Monsieur," I said in my politest tones, because why waste any more time on this nonsense?

"Oh good," he said, shoulders visibly relaxing, which just went to show that he had no idea what I meant.

I understood that he genuinely cared about Christine, that he thought well of her and, maybe, wanted to do the right thing by her. I also understood that none of that weighed as heavily as the pressure of Philippe, or of societal opinion. Nothing was surprising in that. Everyone knew that men like Raoul didn't marry girls like Christine. Or like me. Though with a sudden, uncomfortable feeling, I realized I wasn't sure that *Christine* knew it. But did I dare try to point it out to her?

I felt a surprising pang of disappointment too. I didn't even like Raoul, it wasn't exactly that. But it didn't seem fair, that even Christine, beautiful, talented, magnetic Christine, wasn't good enough for a silly vicomte.

Raoul may have said something else, some pleasantry about the performance, but I wasn't listening. The door of the box closing behind him jolted me back to the present. Sort of. Enough to remind me that I still had to deliver programs to three more boxes, though I was in such a fog of thought while I delivered them that I had my hand on the door to Box Five before I even remembered which it was.

At that, I couldn't help smiling in spite of myself.

I knocked once, waited a breath, then pushed the door open. I didn't expect my knock to receive a response.

I also didn't expect the couple who were sitting in Box Five. And if I was any judge of the rumpled state of his cravat and of her hair, they had gotten out of a compromising position half a second before I opened the door.

I halted on the threshold, hot with embarrassment and outrage. This was *Box Five*—this was no place for romantic carrying-on!

"Don't you know it's rude to barge in on people?" the woman snapped.

"I knocked," I said, reaching desperately for that flimsy defense. Though they were more in the wrong.

"But we didn't answer, did we?" she countered. In a calmer back corner of my mind I observed that from the flashiness of her jewelry and the heaviness of her rouge, she was probably his mistress, not his wife. "And what's a ballet girl doing here anyway?"

I smoothed a hand over my practice skirt, visible between the edges of my blue cloak. "I just—"

"Or can *you* explain why the little blonde's here?" she demanded of the man, who had been concentrating on his cravat.

"Darling, I have no idea—"

"I'm just delivering programs!" I held them out, all too aware of how red my cheeks were surely growing. "One of the boxkeepers asked for help."

"A likely enough story," she said, snatching them out of my hand. "Don't expect a tip."

I bobbed a curtsy as quickly as possible and ducked back out the door. I pressed my back and my palms against the cool wood and tried to calm my newly racing heart. Box Five, who would have the audacity to sit in *Box Five*... Or was I so distracted that I went into the wrong box?

I took a step away from the door to turn and check the number. No, I'd been right. Apparently the new managers really were foolish enough to sell the Phantom's Box. I let out a breath, murmured, "He is not going to like this."

And Madame Thibault was not going to like it if I wasn't backstage in the next three minutes. Right now, the stern and terrifying ballet mistress felt like one stable element in a wildly shifting sea.

No candles were available to light for prayers, but with a mental effort I cast the problems of Mother, Christine, and Box Five out into the universe, towards God and the Phantom both, and hurried off towards backstage.

Excerpt from the Private Notebook of Jean Mifroid, Commissaire of Police

16 Feb 1881

PDC visited station, v. worried re: brother—mixed up with chorus girl. Told PDC no official recourse at present, but will personally investigate.

Notes

Name: Christine Daaé

Family: Johannes Daaé, Father (deceased); Mother?

Birthplace: Uppsala, Sweden

Education: Paris Conservatoire, graduated May, 1880

Explore: Conduct at conservatoire, present connections, history in Sweden, past romantic liaisons?

It was Thursday morning before Christine brought up the subject of leaving. It was a casual, almost off-hand remark about how the chorus master would forgive her absence from Wednesday's performance, but she had best be back for the next one.

The Phantom's fingers tensed where they rested on the ivory keys of his pipe organ, and he tried to aim for the calmest tone possible. "I do not think leaving would be wise at this juncture."

A long, *long* silence from where she sat on the couch behind him. Finally, her voice tremulous, she asked, "Are you saying I'm a prisoner?"

"No, not at all!" he said hurriedly, looking over at her and regretting it, because her eyes looked as worried as her voice sounded. He was alarmed by the trembling of her chin, distracted by the corresponding trembling of her lips, and betrayed that she had even asked the question.

Of *course* she was a prisoner, at least insofar as that she couldn't leave without his help. The route was far too complicated for a single journey through to teach her the way back to the surface. The situation had surely been obvious for days, but how could she break their unspoken pact by pointing it out? They had been pretending so nicely together!

He looked down at his hands, black gloves stark against the ivory keys. "I only mean—I need more time." Time for her to trust him, to love him, to realize that surely she didn't need sunlight when she could have music. "For your *voice*. For the training."

"I just…don't see what good all the vocal training is if I don't sing for anyone."

You can sing for *me*. The thought was so loud in his head that it was a wonder she didn't hear it.

"I mean," she went on, "if I can never leave…"

Her voice was wavering more and more, and he was going to have a full-scale catastrophe on his hands in a moment. "No, I didn't say *never*." He had thought it, he had dreamed it, that she might someday choose to stay forever, but he hadn't said it. "I simply don't think it would be wise right now. At this juncture. In your training."

"I see." She sniffed once, the kind of sniff that meant tears could be mere seconds away. A disdainful sniff would have been easier to handle.

His fingers flexed, tips moving against the smooth keys, while he counted up operas where someone held a girl captive and she eventually fell in love with her captor. It *did* happen. Often, even. Not that that was precisely what he was doing. Not really.

"Well!" he said after a long silence, with a heartiness he didn't feel. "Didn't I promise to play the violin for you this afternoon?" She liked it when he played the violin. It reminded her of her father. Father figure wasn't the role he was hoping for, but it was better than captor. He stood up from the piano bench. He'd play the violin, that would smooth things over.

"I don't think I'm in the mood, thank you," she said, voice tight as she stared into the distance, pointedly not in his direction.

He sat down again, back to the pipe organ this time. He rubbed his palms against his pant legs uneasily. Why couldn't she *understand*? "You agreed to come with me."

"I know."

"You wanted singing lessons."

"Yes."

"Consistent training is very important."

"Of course."

"You have a remarkable gift in your voice, and I am merely trying to help you achieve the potential I know you're capable of. They won't appreciate you up there. They'll just—they'll ruin your voice with poor training if they take any notice at all, which, considering they keep someone like Carlotta in a starring role, is extremely doubtful. They don't appreciate true art up there, it's all about the glamour and the money. I can help your voice to be what it should be, what it's *meant* to be."

"I understand perfectly," she said, in just the tone that indicated she didn't understand at all.

His fingers clenched where they rested against his knees and it was a conscious effort to straighten them, pressing his palms against his legs. Why couldn't she *want* what he was offering? "You really want to throw your voice away just to see that idiot boy?" Because of course that's what this was all about.

Her back stiffened. "I don't know who you mean."

He knew and accepted that she was not intellectual, but she wasn't nearly that foolish. "Do not play stupid. It isn't becoming."

She frowned. "I don't see how it affects my voice at all if I'm friends with Raoul."

"Of course. *Friends*," he said with heavy sarcasm.

"A man and a woman can be just friends!"

Could they? He had exactly zero personal experience on this subject, it didn't come up much in operas, and the cross-gender relationships he was able to observe at the Opera tended to be romantic or business. He supposed it was possible. But not in this case. He had watched them together enough to be sure of it. "We are not discussing abstract philosophy; we are discussing you and that vicomte—"

"Raoul understands that singing is important to me!"

"He understands that you'll leave it all behind if he beckons," he said, a new harshness entering his voice unintentionally.

"That's not true!" Her eyes crinkled and her face crumpled. "You just don't trust me!"

Of course he didn't trust her. He didn't trust anyone.

"I *promise* I would never give up my career for Raoul, but you don't believe me! You think you have to keep me here to protect my voice, but that's just not *true*." The last word dissolved into a sob. With a dramatic gesture that would play well in any opera house, she flung herself down amongst the cushions on his couch, shoulders shaking.

He winced, pressed two fingers to the bridge of his nose. "Please don't do that."

No response.

"There is no need to become upset…" What was he supposed to do now? What did one *do* about a crying woman? His breath was beginning to come more shallowly, as he felt his unstable ground dissolving below him. How could he fix this? How could he make this better for her, how could he possibly come back from this with the slightest hope that she might look at him with any favor?

She thought he didn't trust her. So he had to show he trusted her. Even if he didn't. "Give me one week," he said, not giving himself time to think too carefully.

A moment, and then she half-turned her head on the cushion, profile coming into view. "A week?" she repeated, gulping another sob.

"That would be enough time. For your voice." It was not nearly enough time. The Fairy Queen had held Tam Lin for seven years. In other stories, a year and a day was a quite normal length for sojourns into magical realms—but suggest a figure like that and she'd probably make herself sick with hysterics.

"A week," she said again, rubbing her eyes. She pulled a handkerchief out from inside one cuff, wiped at her face as she slowly sat up again. "I suppose that's…reasonable. Yes. I think that will be fine."

He let out a breath. "Excellent."

"If I leave in the morning—yes, then I'll be in time for the rehearsal and the performance on Saturday."

Saturday? How had she landed on…with a sickening drop in his stomach, he realized she wasn't counting from today, but from the first day she came here—the previous Saturday night. He opened his mouth to correct her, then closed it again. She had stopped crying, she had sat up. He couldn't risk it.

So he had two days. What could he possibly do with two days, when he had got nowhere in the past five? Four days since the disastrous removal of his mask, which they had never spoken of again. Four days during which he hadn't dared approach the subject of love. Four days and she hadn't even once called him by name.

Two days more was nothing. Two days to a finale scene and she would leave him and… "But you must promise to come back," he said, trying not to let his panic sound in his voice. "To continue your training." It couldn't be the end of their opera, only a transition from one act to the next.

She flashed the most dazzling of smiles, a flare of sunshine after a thunderstorm—and he *wanted* that light, even as it surprised him. "Yes, of course. What would I do without my Angel?" She clasped her hands over her knees. "Now…perhaps some violin music would be nice after all."

He wanted to bask in that sunshine, even as he wondered if it could really come so quickly after a rain. So he just nodded, stood up and went to retrieve his violin from its cabinet. He lingered over the tuning of the strings longer than they needed, trying to quiet the voices in his head enough to play. Trying to tell himself that she would come back, that nothing need be rushed, that everything would be fine.

It shouldn't surprise him that she had collapsed in tears at the thought of staying here. Of staying with him. His own self-doubt accepted that idea all too readily—but his paranoia was almost as strong, and it asked, if the idea was so horrible, was it strange that she had been reassured so quickly?

He stomped that thought down, as entirely counter-productive towards trusting her. Trying to trust her. Trying to act as though he trusted her.

The change of mood just meant that she was volatile. That was perfectly normal for an artistic temperament. Nothing to worry about.

Maybe he could even take it as a good sign, that she calmed down quickly. Maybe she hadn't been as upset as he had thought. Maybe she really would come back.

Chapter Twenty

I was preparing for Saturday's rehearsal when someone knocked on our door. Mother answered, and from my bedroom I heard Christine asking to see me. I stopped midway through tightening the bow in my hair. Considering our last conversation, fighting about the Angel and the Phantom, and the week's silence since, I didn't know if I should be relieved or worried. I took a deep breath, gave a quick tug to settle my bow, and stepped out of my room.

Relief prevailed when I saw Christine standing in the doorway and she flashed me a brilliant smile. "Hello, *chérie*," she said, just as though we'd never argued. "I was hoping to catch you before you left for rehearsal, so we could walk together."

"Yes, of course," I said, smiling back, feeling lighter than I had in days. At least *something* was looking better, even if Box Five had been sold again at Friday night's performance, even if the Phantom had done nothing at all about Mother, even if Mother had written to Amelie about work in Bordeaux.

Very soon Christine and I were out on the crowded boulevard, and she slipped her arm through mine. "Now, you have to tell me all the news from the Opera, *chérie*!"

"It's been…a busy week." All I had was bad news, and I would have liked to enjoy our renewed friendship longer before I got into it all. And I was suddenly, belatedly worried about Christine's reaction. Half the Opera was still treating me like an omen of bad luck, when they bothered to notice me, but surely Christine wouldn't do that.

I almost didn't catch the significance when she laughed and said, "I *would* have to get sick just when things are happening! Such terrible luck."

"Yes, that's—" I stopped. "Sick? But the vocal director said you were on a trip."

Christine blinked once. "That's strange. Maybe you misunderstood him."

I frowned slightly, trying to recall exactly how the conversation had gone. "I don't think so. He said he had a letter telling him you were traveling."

Another blink, and then she shrugged, unconcerned again. "Well, maybe *he* misunderstood. Or he mixed me up with someone else."

"Maybe." No one would mix Christine up with anyone else. But I let that oddness go, in favor of a new relief. "It makes more sense that you were sick. I wondered why you didn't tell me you were leaving town." I hesitated, concluded, "I thought you were still upset with me about that argument."

"Oh, that?" She shook her head. "That wasn't important, *chérie*, I overreacted. But tell me what happened this week! How did Carlotta react to that awful croaking?"

"She took to her bed, of course," I said, and answered a barrage of questions about how the chorus had been managing without their lead soprano before I could bring up the real news. "So the managers wanted to talk to Mother recently…" and I told her as briefly as I could about her firing.

"Oh, *chérie*, that's terrible!" Christine said, with all the sympathetic distress I might have hoped for. "But why?"

"They think she was somehow involved with Carlotta's croaking." I shook my head, disgusted by the very idea. "The Phantom took credit for it, and they think Mother had something to do with it too."

"Did she?" Christine asked, so pleasantly it took me a beat to be shocked.

"No, of course not!" I protested. I couldn't *imagine* Mother involved in anything like that. If nothing else, it was too undignified. Not that it was undignified for the Phantom—but somehow it would be for Mother.

"I'm sorry, that was silly." Christine smiled brightly. "I just meant—I mean, she does know more about the Phantom than most people."

"A little." Not as much as I wished we knew.

"Did she tell them anything?" Christine asked swiftly, looking at me with surprising intentness. "Of what she knows about him?"

"No... Since when do you worry about the Phantom, anyway?" It came out more sharply than I meant it to, as I remembered her referring to him as a troublemaker who scared people for fun. Or something like that.

"I wasn't worrying," she said with a shrug, gaze relaxed again. "But never mind the Phantom, what are you going to do now?"

That discussion took us two blocks closer to the Opera Garnier. We were almost there when Christine changed the subject again, to ask if I could do something for her.

"Probably," I said. "What do you need?"

"It's practically nothing, really. I was just hoping you could deliver a letter to Raoul for me."

It wasn't a hard thing to do. But it was a strange thing. "Why? I mean, I can, but he'll probably be at tonight's performance and you can just talk to him."

"I didn't expect an interrogation for one small favor," she said with a slight laugh.

One question was hardly an interrogation. I looked at her face more closely, trying to decide if something had been off about that laugh. "Is anything wrong, between you and Raoul? Did you see him this past week?"

"No, of course not. I told you, I was sick. I didn't see anyone."

She didn't *look* like she'd been sick for the past week, eyes alight, cheeks pink, step as easy and energetic as ever. And it was strange that the vocal director had a different story. This was silly—and yet suspicions were growing in me. "Christine, what are you not telling me?" I asked carefully, knowing I could be making her upset again.

"Nothing, *chérie!*"

"Does it have something to do with the Phantom?" I asked, watching for a reaction.

It wasn't a big reaction, but I could see her face and her shoulders tense. "No, I—that is…" She exhaled. "I guess I'd better tell you. But we can't talk about it at the Opera." She pointed ahead to a little corner garden with a couple of benches. "Let's sit there."

"We'll be late for rehearsal…" It was merely a token resistance. My heart was already beating faster and I'd have missed a performance to learn what Christine had to say about the Phantom. I wouldn't even care about the fines for dancers who missed rehearsals or performances, or about Madame Thibault's inevitable lecture.

"It's just one rehearsal," Christine said, and the concern was dropped.

We sat down on an empty bench, and Christine leaned toward me, voice hushed. "I wasn't sick last week, or traveling. I'm so sorry about lying to you, but I didn't think he'd want me to tell anyone."

"He?" I repeated, thrilling deep inside. Surely there was only one person she could mean.

"The Phantom. That's where I was, with the Phantom."

"For an entire *week?*" The idea made my head spin. I had spent six years fixated on one five-minute conversation, and she had spent a week with him. The things she must have found out!

She pulled back, chin rising and eyes growing hooded. "It was perfectly proper," she said crisply. "All we did was sing."

It took me a second to catch up to the fact that presumably no chaperone had been present, and spending an entire week alone with a man would do irreparable things to a girl's reputation, would imply things that I didn't want to think about in the context of the Phantom and Christine—but anyway, she said they had only been singing, so what did it matter? "Of course," I said quickly, shoving other ideas away. "I wasn't thinking that anyway. So the Phantom really was the Angel?"

"Yes, he was after all," she said complacently, as though the idea hadn't made her outraged a week ago. "And he asked me to come below the Opera with him—"

"Is that where he lives?" I interrupted. I had wanted to know for so long.

She nodded. "Yes, way, way deep down under the cellars, across the underground lake."

"I always thought he'd live up high somewhere in the Opera, in secret rooms maybe." That was where I'd pick, up in the light and the air.

"No, he lives way down in the dark through this perfect labyrinth of tunnels. Anyway, he wanted to give me more lessons on my singing and—"

"So he has musical instruments? I mean, if you were practicing singing—is it an apartment or—"

"Yes, it's an apartment, he has a pipe organ and a violin. But the point is that—"

"So he is a musician." He knew so much about music I had always thought he must be. "He's good, right?"

"Excellent. But the *point* is that he wanted me to focus on my singing. My voice is very important to him, you see. And he thinks Raoul is a distraction."

He was probably right, but who cared what he thought about *Raoul*? I clasped my hands around my knees, leaned forward. "What did you talk about? I mean, with a whole week—"

"We talked about singing!" Christine straightened up, a frown on her face. "Meg, are you even listening to me?"

"Of course," I said, baffled. "I want to know everything, I—"

"I'm *trying* to explain why I need you to deliver a letter to Raoul." She paused, looking at me with narrowed eyes, and I swallowed back the dozens of questions I wanted to ask. None of them were about Raoul. Finally she nodded and went on. "The Phantom thinks Raoul is a distraction and that I shouldn't see him anymore. So I can't talk to him at the Opera because it might upset the Phantom, and even mailing a letter—well, he just seems to know things. But I have to explain to Raoul why we have to be careful where we meet, and the Phantom won't notice if *you* give him a letter."

Her very reasonable tone couldn't quite stop the uncomfortable twist in my stomach. "So…you want me to help you lie. To the Phantom." Who obviously wouldn't notice anything I did.

Her chin rose, even more affronted than she had been earlier. "Meg, whose side are you on?"

I shook my head, confused by this sudden demand. "How is this about sides?" I hadn't thought about it that way, and I didn't want to. We were all friends, weren't we? Christine and the Phantom, Christine and me. "I just—you always said Raoul was only a friend, and your singing was more important. Surely the Phantom can be reasonable about—"

"You know, he's not who you think he is." She folded her arms across her chest, head held stiffly up. "He has a terrible temper."

That wasn't news. I had watched him with Buquet, seen plenty of angry letters. But it implied something new. My hands, still on my knees, tightened into something more like worry than excitement. "He was angry with you?" I ventured, hoping I was wrong.

Christine looked off into the distance. "He got very upset over practically nothing. I am sure he would react equally badly if—"

"Practically nothing?" I interrupted, because I couldn't just let that go by, not if I was going to understand what happened. *Why* the Phantom was angry was surely important.

She shrugged. "I just took his mask off, and he—"

"*You took the Phantom's mask off?*" This time I pulled back, staring at her in utter horror. How could she—that wasn't—my skin positively crawled at the utter wrongness of that idea, coupled with her complete calm about it all.

Her eyebrows rose, apparently surprised by the vehemence of my reaction. "I just wanted to know who he was."

I was speechless. She clearly had no idea of the sheer magnitude of—I couldn't have been more shocked if she'd told me she had stripped naked in the middle of the Place de la Concorde.

There are things you *just don't do*, and ripping the mask off a mysterious masked man was one of them. Did she ever even watch the operas we performed?

"Anyway," Christine resumed, as though the mask removal was merely an unimportant side-note, "he was so angry. He started yelling and ranting—"

"Because you ripped his mask off!" *Of course* he was angry. In my memory, that perfectly molded white half-mask had seemed as much a part of his face as the skin on the other side. If all he had done in response was yell, that seemed to me to say more about his restraint than about his temper.

Christine's face crumpled, one hand rising to half-cover her trembling mouth. "Now you're angry with me too! And I didn't mean any harm, I just wanted to find out who he really is!" She sniffed, swallowed visibly. "I didn't *mean* any harm," she repeated, and I felt sure I was supposed to say that I understood, and it was all right. Only it wasn't, not quite. When I didn't speak, she continued, "Aren't *you* curious about what's under the mask?"

No. Not very. Not until she *said* that. I took a deep breath, briefly struggled between curiosity and the fear of hypocrisy, and finally asked, "Is something? I mean, something unusual?" The half of his face I had seen was ordinary enough; I had usually presumed the other half was much the same.

"He was hideous!" Christine announced, voice positively ringing, tears apparently fought back to provide this information.

That only gave me more confusion than answers. "But he wasn't. I saw him."

Christine made an exasperated sound. "Under the mask, Meg! The right half of his face—he's so horribly deformed, all misshapen— he hardly has a face at all. It was a miracle I didn't faint."

"He can't be that ugly," I protested automatically over that piece of melodrama. I'd never seen anything hideous enough to make me literally faint, couldn't even imagine what that might be.

But the idea that he was ugly…I tried to fit this into my head, into my image of the Phantom. A facial deformity, hidden under that elegant mask. A hideous facial deformity. It didn't seem to fit that charming, impeccably-dressed gentleman I remembered. But he had been wearing a mask. And masks hide things.

"*You've* never seen his face. I did, and it was simply awful," Christine said with a delicate shudder.

I had had years to wonder why the Phantom wore a mask. When I was thirteen, I firmly believed he must once have been a highway robber. In later years I mostly attributed it to a fondness for spectacle, or a desire for a symbol. But a deformity—that wasn't a completely new concept. It wasn't the top of my list of guesses, but it had occurred to me before, at least in passing, that maybe he was hiding something more than an identity under that mask.

If he was hiding a deformity—did it follow that he was hiding in a larger sense, that the choice to live under the Opera Garnier was a kind of hiding too? I hadn't often asked *why* he was there. When I was twelve it had seemed like a delightful and exciting thing to do, to live in an opera house posing as a ghost; I had accepted it then, and done little wondering since. He had always seemed so confident, so powerful in his position as the Phantom. But what if it was more tragic than I had ever considered; maybe he hadn't chosen the Opera as a place for adventure but as a refuge. The world was not usually kind to the ugly, the deformed or the different.

"That's so sad," I murmured, half to myself.

"So you see now why I can't let him know that I'm continuing to see Raoul."

I had all but forgotten that strand of the conversation, and didn't see the connection now. "What does his face have to do with…"

"He's jealous of Raoul, of course," Christine said, as though it was patently obvious. "Because Raoul is handsome, and the Phantom is in love with me."

The Phantom was in love with Christine.

The sentence arrived with no fanfare, no special emphasis, yet it knocked the breath from my lungs and scattered every other thought right out of my mind. The Phantom…and Christine.

I turned the idea over, repeated it a few times, testing it rather the way I might turn a sore ankle to see how badly it was going to hurt.

The Phantom was in love with Christine. I held my breath, checking myself for a clenching stomach or a tight throat. No—nothing.

I took a deep breath, and the normal progression of thoughts and connections and ideas resumed. Really this news was less unexpected than learning about the Phantom's face. Some part of me had known it ever since I heard him react to her relationship with Raoul.

The Phantom was in love with Christine. It stung a little, not much. It wasn't as though I had ever looked at him as a romantic prospect myself. In some ways I still saw him through the eyes of a twelve-year-old. Even to my adult gaze, when I considered that aloof man in the dark cloak...he could hardly seem more remote, or more different from the handsome subscribers who flirted with me in the Dance Foyer.

It had hurt realizing he had chosen her at all. This didn't add much.

"Maybe you should stop seeing him," I said.

"But I can't stop seeing Raoul just because the Phantom doesn't like it. He doesn't control me and—"

"I meant maybe you should stop seeing the Phantom," I interrupted. "It might be kinder, if he's in love with you—and you're not in love with him...?" Not that I really cared about the answer. Not much.

"No, of course not. He's, well..." She let the sentence trail away, as though it was too obvious for words. "But I can't just stop seeing the Phantom either, certainly not while I'm still singing at the Opera Garnier. He'd be devastated if I didn't allow him to continue training my voice. It's very important to him."

I kept turning ideas over in my head, and the more I thought about it the more it seemed to make sense that Christine should just end any involvement with the Phantom entirely. "But you were worried about his temper. And if you start lying to him, he could be angry again. It could be dangerous."

Christine's forehead wrinkled, and she shook her head slightly. "No, I don't think—I mean, yes, he has a temper, but he apologized afterwards."

I felt simultaneously reassured and disappointed, and didn't try to analyze why. "Still. Singing lessons aren't more important than protecting yourself." Not that I had ever known the Phantom to threaten a woman; he was very gentlemanly in that way, but *still*.

"My singing lessons *are* important and—he wrote me a letter apologizing." She reached into her bag and yanked out a folded sheet of paper. "Here, see for yourself." She opened it up and thrust it into my hand.

I took it automatically, but looked down at it almost reluctantly. Even though she gave it to me, I felt like I was prying. He hadn't meant for me to read this. "I shouldn't..." The sentence trailed away as my gaze slipped down to the last line, to the swirling signature.

Erik.

Not O. G., not the Phantom. *Erik.* He had signed a name. I turned the word over in my mind. The Phantom had a name. No one is born being called the Phantom, but I'd never found the least, slightest hint of what his name might be. Until now.

Erik. An answer to that most basic question about this most mysterious person. And I had more questions. How would it sound if he said it, in that perfect voice? What did it mean, that utterly un-French last letter? Did anyone else know it, did he ever use it, did he have a second name?

"Erik," I said, trying to pronounce the K, fitting the sound of the word into my understanding of the Phantom. Of Erik.

"What?"

I raised the note, tipped it towards her. "He signed it. His name, it's—"

"Oh, never mind *that*," Christine said with a quick dismissive gesture of one hand, "that doesn't matter. But you see now that this is the only option, right?"

It was too many revelations for one conversation, every new one sending me off in a direction quite different from whatever thread Christine was still trying to follow. "The only option is...?"

"I *have* to keep seeing both the Phantom and Raoul, but I can't let the Phantom know I'm seeing Raoul because it would hurt him too badly. You understand, don't you, that I just want to protect him. And

I need your help to keep it all secret, to help me communicate with Raoul." She reached out and seized my hand, looking straight into my eyes. "You will help, won't you? You're the only one I can trust!"

I didn't really think she was in danger from the Phantom. And it sort of made sense that it would be better to keep a secret, if the reason was to not hurt him. And while I wouldn't see a significant problem in just not seeing Raoul anymore, Christine obviously did. And she was my friend. My best friend. And so... "Yes, all right. I'll help you get a message to Raoul."

"I *knew* you would, *chérie!*" Christine said, hugging me. "Of course, it might not be just the one letter. I mean, we'll see...but I feel so much better knowing I can depend on you to help me!"

I didn't feel any better about it all, now that I was committed and the question decided. Although...it was all rather exciting. Unrequited love and secret messages. It was like an opera. I always knew life would be more thrilling wherever the Phantom (Erik) was involved. Even if I was a bit, well, periphery to the story...this was the best chance I'd ever had to find out more about the Phantom.

I had already found out more in the past few minutes than I'd been able to learn in years previously. His face, his name, where he lived...and it just made me want to know more. I leaned forward, hands clasped on my knee. "So. Tell me more about the Phantom. He lives underground and he plays a violin and—"

"Oh, later!" Christine said, rising to her feet. "We're already so late for rehearsal!"

"It's just one rehearsal," I pointed out. It seemed quite dwindled in importance compared to the possibilities of more conversation.

"Meg! It's important," she said in scolding tones. "Come on."

I reluctantly got up, reluctantly followed Christine. Later, I promised myself. Later I'd find out everything. And maybe—if Christine was going to go on being friends with the Phantom, and I was *her* friend...well, people with mutual friends very often met each other.

Chapter Twenty-One

E verything was fine. And maybe if he kept telling himself that, it would be true. Or he would believe it was true.

He leaned against the interior of the pillar in the corner of Box Five, and wished the production would hurry up and start. He always hid in the pillar until the opera began, and it had never felt claustrophobic before today. There was enough room, barely, for one man. It was his thoughts that were taking up all the space.

It wasn't as though he had believed Christine would come below the Opera once and stay forever. He hadn't *really* believed that. Maybe for a few heady moments, but not otherwise. So she went, but she would come back. Close of Act One only, not of their opera. So everything was fine.

She hadn't fled the city yet. That was promising.

She had been late to rehearsal, giving him more than a few bad moments and enough time to formulate a complete plan for infiltrating the de Chagny residence—but then she had come rushing into the Opera with Little Meg Giry and so, after all, everything was…fine.

She surely hadn't gone anywhere in the fifteen minutes since he had listened to her talking with a friend backstage. And soon the opera would begin, and he could go take the far more comfortable seat at the front of the box, and Christine would sing, and everything would be *fine*.

The door to Box Five opened, a familiar sound that he always noted but had stopped being disturbed by years ago. It was all part of the familiar rhythm, the familiar pre-performance melody.

The giggle that followed, though. He should not be hearing a woman's giggle. In six years he had *never* heard Madame Giry giggle. Had those imbecile managers still not reinstated his boxkeeper?

A male voice following the giggle confirmed an even more inconvenient reality. Clearly the management had sold Box Five.

They could not *possibly* have missed a message written in six-inch letters on the top of their desk! He would have to do something serious, just when he had no time for such things.

Beyond the pillar, the giggler left off giggling to remark, "Why do you suppose all those curtains are closed? Who can watch an opera like that?"

He knocked his forehead against the marble, exasperated with himself. He had closed the curtains when he arrived; if he was thinking clearly, he would have realized that open curtains meant trouble. Madame Giry knew to close them.

"Closed curtains do make this little spot private," the giggler's companion said, "and I can think of better things to do than watch a screeching opera."

Of all the—this was the *last* thing he needed right now! Throwing his voice out into the box, the Phantom growled, "Why don't you find a hotel?"

A female shriek, a male curse, and then a moment of silence that even through marble felt charged with confusion.

In a whisper laced with alarm, the giggler said, "Luc, no one's here!"

"A ghost is here," the Phantom said. "Did no one tell you this box is haunted?"

"I will not be intimidated by a silly trick," Luc snapped.

"I am not a trick, I am a ghost. Get out of my box."

"If you're a ghost, why don't you find a graveyard to haunt?"

If he was less irritated by the man, he might have been impressed. As it was, though, he was forced to be flashy. A few taps in the right places inside the pillar, and the curtains of Box Five billowed in a sudden wind, the gas lamps lighting the space went dark, and flames shot up in each corner.

More shrieking, more curses, and he judged the moment right to tap once more and swing the door of the box open. He waited for the footsteps to fade, then swung the door shut and stepped out of the pillar. He straightened his shirt, relit the gas lamps, and locked the door. The boxes weren't intended to have locks, but Box Five had long been customized. And it would do no good leaving it unlocked for Madame Giry anymore.

Someone else would probably come to investigate, but he was sure of his locks, and with any luck, it wouldn't be during a significant part of the opera.

He dusted off his favorite seat in the front row, sat down and parted the curtains two precise centimeters, then leaned back to wait for the performance to begin.

Half an hour before the opening curtain, I knocked on the door to Box 11. I hadn't managed to corner Christine for a good conversation about the Phantom, though she gave me a letter for Raoul as she flew by on the way to something with the chorus. So here I was, wondering uneasily what to do if the comte answered. Run, possibly.

Luckily, the voice that said, "Come in," didn't sound nearly deep enough—or confident enough—to be the older de Chagny brother.

I pushed the door open, and stepped across the threshold onto the red carpet of the box. Raoul was facing the doorway, shoulders hunched, but he relaxed as soon as he saw me, turning towards the stage.

"Oh. Hello, Meg," he said absently over his shoulder. "I thought it was Philippe."

"He wouldn't knock," I pointed out. If his initial tension was any sign, they had not resolved Wednesday's argument.

Raoul shrugged slightly without glancing at me. "I suppose not. Do you have the programs again?"

"No. I have a letter," I said, held out the envelope, and added what would surely be the magic words: "From Christine."

"You do?" Sure enough, he turned back around, to snatch the envelope from my hand. "I haven't heard from her in a week!"

"She's been—" I stopped. Would Christine tell him that she had been sick, or that she'd been on a trip? Or maybe she'd even tell him the truth, and in that case, I definitely didn't want to be the one trying to explain it to him. "—away from the Opera," I concluded.

He didn't acknowledge the awkwardness, barely seemed to notice that I was still in the room. He was already pulling the letter from the envelope.

I crossed my arms, waited a moment to see if he would remember my existence on his own. No sign of it. "So...enjoy the production."

"Mm-hmm. Right." His eyes never wavered from the page.

I let myself out. It wasn't like I wanted to linger until the comte arrived anyway.

I started to thread through the pre-opera crowd, needing to get backstage to warm-up, when a disturbance at one end of the hall drew my gaze. A couple came running out of Box Five, the door slamming behind them.

"A ghost! A *ghost* is in there!" the woman shrieked.

The nearby guests looked baffled, while the half-dozen people present from the Company started telling them about the Phantom, in tones that ranged from resigned to alarmed.

As for me, it put a smile on my face. At least *something* was normal. My gaze lingered on the closed door of Box Five. If only I could open it, step in, tell the Phantom—no, *Erik* that I knew he was teaching Christine and since I was her best friend...surely I could be involved somehow? We ought to get to know each other too?

The mere idea of trying to articulate what exactly I wanted, much less articulating it *to* the Phantom, made my cheeks grow hot.

Even if I'd had a clearer idea of how to explain what I was looking for, it would break what was practically the first rule regarding the Phantom: never disturb him in Box Five.

Maybe that was the second rule. Surely the first rule, the rule so obvious that it shouldn't need to be a rule, was *never touch the Phantom's mask*. I wondered again, not for the first time this afternoon, how Christine could have done it. And, more guiltily, just what she had seen. A hideous, distorted face. What did that *mean*? What was the most horrible face I could imagine?

I studied the smooth wood of Box Five's door and wondered about open sores or hollow cheeks or bulging mounds of flesh. Though that last couldn't be too extreme—he got a mask on, after all. Maybe flaking skin or pulsing veins. Something horrible behind that elegant, refined mask and impeccable clothes.

No—best not to surprise a man like that in the place he was so adamant about keeping undisturbed. I tore my gaze reluctantly away, shook myself out of my distraction and hurried on towards the auditorium.

I reached backstage before the performance began. La Carlotta was still prostrate over her latest indignity. Rumor said the management was talking about promoting one of the other sopranos, as a permanent position instead of the temporary fill-in they were doing now, which meant Carlotta should be back any day. Christine had returned to the chorus, and my ear wasn't nearly good enough to pick her out of the crowd of voices and detect whether a week with the Phantom had done anything for her voice.

I spent the entire time on the nervous edge of anticipation, thinking that afterwards I'd finally be able to talk to Christine—to *really* talk to her and find out more about that week.

I found her after the performance, just as she was about to leave the backstage. But when I suggested finding somewhere quiet to talk, she looked rather blank. "Oh, but *chérie*, I have to go to my dressing room because, well…" She glanced upward, significantly.

Even knowing he lived below the Opera, it still seemed to make sense to think of the Phantom as always lurking overhead somewhere.

"Oh, of course," I said quickly. I should have thought of that, and I shouldn't intrude. "Maybe afterwards—"

"And I thought you'd be going to the Dance Foyer," Christine continued with a bright smile. "I wrote Raoul you'd be there if he had a message for me. I didn't mean to presume of course, but I thought you would be anyway—you'll go see if he has a letter for me, won't you?"

What could I say but yes?

"I knew you would," Christine said, giving me a quick hug. "I don't know what I'd do without you!"

And that at least was some consolation, as she tripped off to see the Phantom and I went to see the Vicomte de Chagny.

The Dance Foyer was its usual flurry of animated dancers and amorous suitors, romances and negotiations and stories playing out in little knots of people all around the room. Just tonight it didn't feel nearly as interesting as what was surely going on elsewhere. I tried to appreciate my surroundings; if we went to Bordeaux, this could be one of my last times here.

That thought didn't make me feel more cheerful.

Nor did the sound of Jammes' voice, calling across the room, far too honey-sweet to be genuine. "Oh, Meg, I've been wanting to talk to you!" She came gliding up, with four other girls clustered behind her. Jammes was hardly a reigning queen like Carlotta or Sorelli, but she had her attendees. One dancer and three singers, who really had no business being here—though considering I had brought Christine, I was in no position to comment.

"Good evening," I said cautiously, already trying to think of how I could get out of this conversation when—if it went badly.

Jammes put on an elaborate expression of sorrow. "I was so sorry to hear about your mother."

As if I believed that. "Thank you," I said, in my politest, least emotional tone.

She stepped closer and in a lower voice said, "Although, of course, *certain* people feel that with all that time she spent…consorting with the Phantom, it was inevitable."

My eyes narrowed. Suggestive remarks about Mother (*Mother!*) and the Phantom were as absurd as they were infuriating. "*Certain* people are mistaken. Mother has never done anything but her job."

"Of course not." She leaned even closer, eyes hard. "But if I were you, I would watch my step. Carlotta is very displeased with your Phantom."

That was a much less barbed remark. "He's not my Phantom." Looking past Jammes, I caught a glimpse of Raoul across the room. "And I could not possibly care less about Carlotta's moods. Now excuse me, I need to see the Vicomte de Chagny."

"How interesting," Jammes drawled as I brushed past her. "Does Christine know?"

"I don't need her permission," I said, trying to make it sound calm and unconcerned but probably sounding more snappish than not. I quickened my pace forward through the crowd, relieved once a screen of people stood between myself and Jammes.

I worked my way through the masses to get closer to Raoul, abruptly thinking better of my relief when I realized that he was in a tight knot with Sorelli and the comte.

Sorelli waved her hands in the air. "But if she won't be your mistress, why waste any more time? I know so many lovely dancers. Let me pick one out for you!"

Raoul glowered at her. "I don't want you to—"

"Oh really now, boy," Philippe interrupted, "you know you're being unreasonable about this!"

I was hesitating a few paces away when Raoul caught sight of me. His eyes brightened in a way they never had before on seeing me. "Excuse me." He turned his back rather pointedly towards his brother and Sorelli. "Meg, I was hoping to see you."

"Good evening," I said with a slight dip of a curtsy, wishing I was anywhere else.

"Isn't that Daaé's friend?" Philippe demanded. I supposed that was better than being thought of as the nosy dancer who lurked outside his box.

Raoul grimaced, squared his shoulders, and took my arm a little too tightly to lead me away from his brother. "Léon says hello," he said, too loudly.

"He does?" I said, wondering if it was true, or if Raoul was just making it up to fool his brother into thinking we had other business besides Christine. It would be kind of nice, if it was true.

"Yes. I forgot to tell you earlier."

"Did he say anything else?" I asked, and hoped it wouldn't make me look too eager. Not that Raoul was likely to notice if it did.

"No, just hello."

It probably was true. I liked thinking it was. And if Raoul was any good at making stories up, he'd have done better than that. "Well...tell him hello for me too, then."

"Of course." He looked over his shoulder towards Philippe. By now there were three or four clusters of people between us. Raoul reached into his jacket pocket and handed me a letter. "Here, this is for Christine. You'll make sure she gets it?"

"Yes." I slipped the letter into a pocket of my cloak.

Raoul was already peering over his shoulder again. "Do you think we fooled my brother, or should we pretend to keep talking for a while longer? I think he'll believe I wanted to talk to you, for at least a few minutes."

I gritted my teeth, tried to brush the mental sting away. He probably didn't realize he was being rude and...somehow that ought to make it better, right? "I believe I need to be going," I said tightly. I didn't have anywhere to go, but that didn't mean I had to stand around and be ignored by a silly nobleman I didn't even like. "Good evening, monsieur."

I couldn't stay in the Foyer after that, but what would be the point anyway? I headed for the door, wondering just what I had thought would be so awful about moving to Bordeaux.

Excerpt from the Private Notebook of Jean Mifroid, Commissaire of Police

18 Feb 1881

More Opera trouble—Phantom prank again. A & F complained of man barricading a box. Sent officer to investigate, found door open and box empty.

Little progress on investigation of C. Daaé for PdC. All reports positive from Conservatoire. Daaé described as "beautiful, sweet, innocent," ad nauseum.

Chapter Twenty-Two

I left Raoul's letter at Christine's apartment Sunday morning. She wasn't home, not then or when I came back in the afternoon. I finally got to talk to her Monday, walking home from rehearsals. Christine lived only a few blocks from the Opera, but it was long enough for me to find out that she didn't know the Phantom's history, had no idea why he was haunting the Opera Garnier, could not describe his rooms beyond "dark," and barely remembered that his eyes were green. I could have screamed.

Somehow, I didn't quite like to ask what he looked like under that mask. Besides, after so many other fruitless questions I doubted she'd offer much detail on that either.

She may have had very little to say about the Phantom, but she had plenty to say to Raoul. I carried a half dozen letters back and forth over the following week. I was growing irritated by the third, and when she handed me the fourth backstage at Wednesday's performance, I couldn't stop myself saying, "If this goes on, people are going to start thinking *I'm* involved with Raoul."

"Oh, don't be silly, *chérie*," Christine laughed, "no one would think that!"

I said nothing, and after a moment Christine, with a more troubled expression, said, "Of course, I don't mean…it's just…"

"I know," I said, cutting off an explanation that could only make things more awkward. Anyway, it was true. Everyone knew that Raoul was in love with Christine; they were hardly likely to believe that he'd turn around and fall in love with *me*.

Saturday became much better after he had dealt with the amorous couple in Box Five. The opera was excellent: Christine sang, only in the chorus, but her voice lent a shine to the entire production. Someone came to pound on the locked door during Act One but they went away again. If anyone summoned the police, they didn't arrive until after the opera was over, the door was unlocked, and the Phantom was gone.

Sunday was a good day. Christine came to the Opera even without any rehearsal or performance, and let him lead her below again for another singing lesson. She only stayed a little over two hours (two hours, nine minutes), but the point was that she came.

Monday was completely empty until three in the afternoon, when Christine arrived for rehearsal and then the evening's performance. He took the precaution of locking Box Five an hour before the opera began, and was undisturbed apart from some knocking. Madame Giry had still not been reinstated, so no one had any business coming in. He enjoyed the performance and watched Christine carefully afterwards. Even though that wretched vicomte was still hanging about, she didn't go near him.

Tuesday was a bad day. Christine didn't come to the Opera Garnier at all. He passed much of the time shadowing the managers, slamming doors and flickering lights, but it wasn't as amusing as it should have been. Or as effective—Ricard seemed spooked, at least somewhat, but Moncharmin just gave orders for someone to check the gas lines.

Wednesday should have been better, with another rehearsal and performance. But it wasn't enough. It didn't satisfy the ache of longing that had built up over the long void of Tuesday. Being her Angel was something, but he wanted so much more—and being an adoring audience member was so much less.

Thursday was good. Not Thursday morning, but Christine arrived early for the afternoon rehearsal, and spent an hour in her dressing room for a private lesson with her Angel of Music. It wasn't even close to all he dreamed of, but it was something, enough to cast a glow over the rest of the day, even when Carlotta made her return appearance, and the managers got new ideas into their heads.

I arrived early when the management summoned the entire Company for a special announcement Thursday evening. I walked down the wide center aisle of the auditorium, sat down in the fourth row, and speculated. The last "special announcement" had been Debienne's departure. It was probably too much to hope that this would announce the imminent departure of his unsatisfactory replacements. Maybe it would be the imminent departure of Carlotta back to Italy.

Probably not that either. The best I could reasonably wish for was that it would be something exciting within the next week or two. Leaving Paris still loomed; if it was farther out than that, it probably wouldn't matter to me anyway.

I waved to Christine when she entered the auditorium. She smiled and came over to sit next to me. She leaned back in her seat and closed her eyes. "It was *such* a long rehearsal today. I wish I could just stop going to them. It's not as though they're very helpful anymore. You know, comparatively."

I knew, and despite all the multitude of things Christine *didn't* know about the Phantom, I still felt a flutter of excitement. "How is your—" I glanced upwards, and lowered my voice. "—private instructor?" Several dozen people were in the auditorium by now, with more arriving, and there was no point in being stupidly transparent.

"Oh, fine. So helpful about that problem I've been having with vibrato in my upper range."

Not quite the kind of information I was looking for. Could I risk more questions right now? I let my gaze wander around the auditorium, trying to judge the likelihood of anyone listening to our conversation. A scattering of people, none too nearby and most talking to each other anyway. My gaze swept on towards the back corners and stopped, my attention caught by the mysterious Persian, sitting as usual in a remote corner. He was certainly too far away to be eavesdropping on Christine and me—yet as I looked, his gaze lifted, met mine and held.

I blinked first and looked away, a prickle running down my spine. I wished I knew how the Persian fit into the Opera Garnier. His very reason for being here was a complete enigma. And was it improbable to think that two mysterious men in one opera house might have some connection to each other?

Another mystery I'd probably never learn the answer to. Not if things went the way I feared in the near future.

Christine, meanwhile, straightened up in her chair and asked cheerfully, "So what do you think the announcement will be about? Maybe the plans for the next season?"

"Maybe." I stared at the red curtains over the stage. "I don't expect I'll be here for next season anyway."

"Oh no, did your mother decide something?" Christine asked, voice rich with concern.

"No," I admitted, "but she hasn't found a new job yet either, and she wrote to Amelie about working in her theater and…I don't know, Mother has just had this look lately. I think she's going to decide soon." She wasn't one to put things off. And we couldn't afford to anyway. Meals had already grown simpler as Mother looked for ways to economize.

Maybe I should ask Christine to ask the Phantom to help us. I'd carried enough messages for her, surely she could return the favor. And yet…something about the idea made me profoundly uncomfortable, made me twist and sink a little lower in my seat. To ask Christine to be an intermediary for me to the Phantom—who was

not my Phantom, had never been my Phantom, obviously, and yet—
maybe I'd keep the idea as a last resort for now.

Christine didn't appear to notice my discomfort, just waved one
hand airily. "Well, if nothing about leaving is definite yet, why worry?
Maybe it won't happen."

I was surprised she didn't have something more sympathetic to
say, or more distress at the prospect. I frowned. "And maybe it—"

"Oh, there's Carlotta," Christine interrupted, looking towards the
double doors at the back of the auditorium, then quickly turning away.
"She's glaring at me, isn't she?"

I looked past Christine, to where Carlotta posed in the double-
doors at the end of the center aisle, flanked by her usual admirers.
"Yes."

Christine sighed. "I don't think she likes me."

Was there any doubt? "She doesn't like anyone who's
competition."

Carlotta swept down the center aisle with her nose in the air, just
as though she had never fled the stage and hid for over a week. If she
heard the low croak that rose from somewhere in the audience, or the
nervous titters it set off, she didn't give any sign. I didn't feel that
much like smiling, envying her ability to command a situation. She sat
down in the front row with as much majesty as if she owned the Opera
Garnier. Jammes claimed the seat to her right, and all her other
followers filled in the seats around.

Carlotta's timing was perfect, taking her place not more than
thirty seconds before the managers came striding out on stage. They
both looked wonderfully pleased with the world as they found it. I
resented that.

"Thank you all very much for being here today," M. Ricard
began, projecting his voice better than Debienne had managed. "And I
think I speak for us all in saying how very glad we are to see our
soprano return to us. Signora Carlotta, our warmest welcome back."
He clapped loudly.

Enthusiastic applause sprang up around Carlotta, much more
scattered clapping from the rest of the theater. She rose and made a
deep curtsy anyway.

"Now, Moncharmin and I have very exciting news!" Ricard continued. "We have been making plans ever since we arrived at the Opera, and with the last pieces in place, we can finally reveal them. For Mardi Gras next week, we have arranged to hold a special gala performance!" He beamed at us as though he expected another round of applause.

Mostly he got confused murmurs. It wasn't the fact of a special performance—those happened now and then. It was the timing.

Carlotta rose to her feet again, and I could see that her back had gone stiff, meaning she was two breaths away from full-blown indignation. "I hesitate even to mention this because I am sure it has occurred to the management—but what effect will this have on the Masquerade?"

"Ah! Yes, yes, of course!" Ricard said with vigorous nods and one hand pressed to his chest. "I would never forget about the annual masked Mardi Gras Ball. Why, I was here for last year's, and I never had such an evening! It was at that very time that I decided I must become more involved, possibly after a few—"

Moncharmin coughed loudly, and took two steps to move half in front of Ricard. "We decided the Masquerade will be moved to Sunday."

Murmurs continued, but they were starting to sound more interested. *I* was feeling more interested. I'd have been as upset as anyone if they canceled the ball, but I didn't much care if it was on Sunday or Tuesday. It might be better on Sunday—no dragging out of bed the next morning for Ash Wednesday services.

"As M. Ricard said," Moncharmin continued, "we will be celebrating with a gala performance next Tuesday evening, to present our Opera to a number of very select friends and business acquaintances."

"With bonus pay for all the performers, of course," Ricard put in, and the interested murmurs grew much more excited.

"We'll also be selling any extra seats," Moncharmin quickly added, "at a special price for this special performance, so be sure to tell anyone you know who might be interested in attending!"

That clarified something. If I was any judge of M. Moncharmin's character, that 'special price' was higher, not lower, and if he sold enough higher-priced tickets to cover the cost of paying the performers…yes, that sounded just like M. Moncharmin, and that suggestion to tell our friends was surely not directed at someone like me, but rather at someone like, say, Sorelli, with her dear friend the Comte de Chagny who could surely afford a higher price for a *special* performance.

I may have reveled in the magic of the Opera, but that didn't mean I was entirely blind to the more practical machinations going on too.

While the managers continued describing plans, Christine clutched my arm and whispered, "The rumors say that M. Ricard knows everyone important in the arts, and M. Moncharmin knows everyone important in business! And they'll probably *all* be at this event. Can you imagine, Meg? It's fine to sing at a normal performance, but to sing lead soprano at something like *that*…" She sighed. "But of course they'll have Carlotta sing."

"Maybe. Or maybe not," I said, casting a glance towards Box Five, towards the closed curtains above the gilded decorations. One person, firmly rooted in the magic of it all, might have something to say about this.

This was *it*. It was what he had been waiting for, the one opportunity that could change everything. This kind of performance could change a singer's career, could launch a talented ingénue to a completely different level. No vicomte could give her this, but the Phantom could. And then, surely then, she would finally see. If he could give her what she wanted, prove that he could be what she wanted—then maybe she would see him for who he wanted to be. Not an angel, not a ghost. Just a man. Just Erik.

And *then...*

He sat back in Box Five, listening with only a fraction of his attention to the continued discussions in the auditorium about plans for the gala performance. He didn't care what the plans were, and he could steal the notes later if he did need to know anything. Some other time he would have cared intensely. All that mattered now was who would sing lead soprano, and it was obvious enough who would be chosen.

So he had to get rid of Carlotta. But how? She had come back from the croaking debacle with her head up, and what could he do that was worse than that? He'd admire her courage if he didn't find her so aggravating.

He *could* do worse things to her, of course, but... He flexed his hands, rubbed his palms uneasily against his thighs. He had rules for himself, a code of honor of sorts. Physically attacking a woman, even one like Carlotta—no, that would class him with the Buquets of the world.

He had to have a line he would not cross. Something to say that he was a man, and not a monster.

Besides, the death, serious injury or sudden disappearance of Signora Carlotta, star of the Opera Garnier for five seasons, would not be hushed up and swept away as easily as one scenechanger.

He tapped his fingers on the arm of the chair. Much better if she could be...persuaded to bow out of the event. Perhaps a well-placed message, delivered in just the right way?

It was really too bad he'd never been able to find any effective blackmail material on Carlotta. She had some less than savory parts in her past, but nothing that wasn't true of half the Company, and nothing that would be effective enough to bring down a reigning soprano. All her scandals were public knowledge, long since stared down and now ignored.

He stood up from his seat. Carlotta and her devotees would be busy in the auditorium for at least the next twenty minutes. Best to begin work at once.

A few hidden doors and secret stairwells later, he stepped out of Carlotta's closet, into her opulent dressing room. He was immediately attacked by the cloying scent of her perfume, permeating the space. He coughed and tried to breathe shallowly. What would be both effective and efficient?

He picked up a letter-opener from the vanity and slashed through the posters of Carlotta in her various roles blanketing the walls. His sense of the artistic felt that a blazing bonfire would have been more dramatic than shreds of paper left behind, but with no fireplace in the room he didn't want to risk structural damage.

And if he couldn't burn the posters, he could still add another artistic touch. He stopped in front of Carlotta's mirror, studying its dimensions and trying to ignore his reflection, running one hand lightly along its edges. It was a full-length mirror in an oval shape, set in an ornate frame away from the wall; no hidden passage behind this mirror.

He reversed the direction of the letter-opener and used the handle for one strike in the appropriate spot on the mirror, for a very effective shatter pattern.

He turned quickly away from his splintered reflection and dropped the letter-opener on the dressing table. He picked up the ink bottle to add a flourishing *O. G.* on the wall above the mirror and the job was done.

Hopefully Carlotta would take to her bed through the gala performance, if he had any luck at all. He smiled mirthlessly at that thought. He had nothing to fear from superstition here. If the fates wanted to give him seven years of bad luck, it would be only what he was used to.

Chapter Twenty-Three

B y Friday, Erik decided that perhaps something existed in that bad luck superstition after all. Carlotta didn't even go to her dressing room after Thursday's special announcement, so he had to wait until the next day for a reaction. He paced impatiently in the passage behind her closet in the morning, until she finally deigned to arrive. The door opened to a chatter of female voices, all falling abruptly silent. Carlotta and her entourage, clearly, and he waited for the anticipated shriek or string of furious Italian.

Seconds ticked by. A murmur of worried voices grew, but only silence from La Carlotta herself. He rubbed his palms impatiently against his thighs. Just scream and collapse. Get it over with.

When she finally spoke, it was only a sharp Italian command, "*Andare ora!*" followed by a swift patter of many footsteps.

Go now? Go where? Or did she just mean she wanted them to go out and leave her alone so she could shriek in solitude? But that didn't fit, Carlotta always liked having plenty of people around to catch her when she crumpled. He listened intently, and when the door closed again only silence remained. If Carlotta had left too, that put him back on the question of going to *where* and…

He smacked the wall with one clenched fist. Of course, she needed a better audience for a proper collapse, and the best audience could only be fawning M. Ricard. There was a stair at the end of this passage, if he cut across the Opera on the third level…yes, that should do.

His route was more circuitous than Carlotta's, but he reached the managers' office in time to hear her still in full-scale rage. She had evidently already explained what had happened, and was on to the lamenting and accusing stage.

"I will not tolerate this anymore! You are the managers, you will stop this *ingerenza* ghost!"

Clearly he had not done enough to her if *meddling* was the worst she was calling him. It was slightly insulting, really, to not have provoked anything stronger.

"But there *is* no ghost," Moncharmin protested, unwisely. "This is all merely a prank and—"

There came the string of Italian, with far more inventive insults regarding M. Moncharmin's intelligence, perception and ancestry. When she ran out of breath, Ricard rushed into the gap with profuse apologies. He might have succeeded better if he hadn't tried to point out that they had already done what they could by firing Madame Giry.

"That does not matter," Carlotta snapped. "The old woman is not important. So she dusts Box Five, so what? She is not the one you must deal with!"

"Surely you're not proposing we fire a ghost?" Moncharmin said drily.

A hacking cough came from Ricard, and from Carlotta, "No, *maccabeo*, I am saying you must stop this disturbance in the Opera. You do not believe in ghosts, you believe it is only a prank, then find the man behind the prank! And until you can ensure my safety, you will give me double pay."

Double pay?

"Double pay?" Moncharmin choked.

No, that was all wrong, she was supposed to refuse to perform at all! She wasn't supposed to *benefit* from the situation with a higher salary. She wasn't supposed to actually stand her ground about this.

"We'd be only too happy to," Ricard said swiftly, and probably kicked his associate, based on Moncharmin's abruptly cut-off, "But that's—"

A few more angry remarks from Carlotta, a few more reassurances from Ricard and strained comments from Moncharmin, but by the time Carlotta swept out, nothing important had changed. She wasn't backing out of the gala.

The Phantom was sorely tempted to follow her when she left. Maybe he could drop a sandbag on her.

No, that was no good, that would just make them cancel the gala entirely. He remained sitting in the passage by the managers' office, head in his hands, trying to think how he could get rid of the blasted woman.

He only slowly realized that perhaps he had better listen to the managers' conversation too. When he started paying attention again, Moncharmin was saying, "I don't care what it will do for morale, it won't help to *pretend* to catch a ghost! They'll see through it anyway as soon as some new disaster occurs."

"It was just an idea," Ricard muttered.

Too bad it hadn't carried; he could have ignored that plan entirely.

"Our angry soprano is right, we need to find whoever is behind this absurd prank," Moncharmin snapped. "Broken mirrors are expensive, and double pay for the lead soprano is even more so!"

"Debienne is in Australia by now, and Madame Giry is already gone. Who else could be behind it?"

"Obviously that's what we have to find out. I still think we should fire Giry's daughter; she might be involved."

"Only if *you* explain it to the ballet mistress," Ricard said swiftly. "Besides, I doubt she's important in all this. I know ballet girls, and they're not clever enough or good enough at keeping secrets to carry off this kind of prank. If that girl had any information about the Phantom, the whole Opera would know it."

He felt a twinge of guilt about Madame Giry. If not for him, she wouldn't have been fired. He rubbed one palm idly against his jacket, tried to think if there was something he ought to do. Maybe write her a letter, or say something to her daughter...but either option would be risky and what would he say? My apologies, I haven't dealt with this yet, I've been distracted by more important things? Yes, that would go over well. The best thing would be to finally get the managers in line, have her reinstated, and then there would be nothing to worry about.

"If Giry's daughter isn't part of this nonsense," Moncharmin continued, "someone else at the Opera must be. But we don't have the first idea who it could be!"

"Maybe," Ricard said with hesitation in his voice, "we could lure whoever it is out."

"A lure implies we have something he wants, and the man is too unpredictable—"

"We *do* have something he wants. 20,000 francs at the end of the month."

Erik actually leaned away from the wall in response to the infuriated tirade at high volume produced by M. Moncharmin, who was not, under any circumstances, for any reason, with any provocation, risking 20,000 of *his* francs.

"But we aren't going to *lose* the 20,000 francs," Ricard insisted when Moncharmin paused for breath. "We'll just bait Box Five with them, and be ready with the police on hand to catch whoever picks them up."

"And won't we look ridiculous to the police when no one comes!"

"The last day of the month is the night of the gala performance. We'll tell the police we want them here because of the special event. And I have an idea to make sure the Phantom won't suspect it's a trap."

"I wish you'd stop calling him 'the Phantom' as though there is such a person!"

The Phantom wished Moncharmin would stop interrupting Ricard so he could find out the rest of the plan.

"All right, the prankster, then. We'll get Madame Giry back for the evening, and convince *her* to deliver the money. He'll think it's perfectly safe. *And* we'll have the woman on hand for questioning too. Neat as you please!"

It wasn't a terrible plan. Aside from the fact that they were talking about it here where he could listen, and that no one knew how he got in and out of Box Five so the police were unlikely to catch him there, and that he would have found Madame Giry's one evening reappearance suspicious even without overhearing this. Other than *that* it wasn't a terrible plan. He had seen any number of operas with more ridiculous plots.

As it was, he approved. It should be easy enough to foil, and if he could divest tight-fisted Moncharmin of 20,000 francs, likely the man would take the Opera Ghost more seriously in the future. Really it was an excellent opportunity to finally deal with them. The only aspect he didn't like was the timing. He was *hoping* to listen to Christine's triumph as lead soprano the night of the gala performance, and he did not appreciate the possibility of a distraction.

Which reminded him that he still had the Carlotta problem.

He was positive that a time had existed, only a scene or two back in his life's story, when everything had been so much *simpler.*

Both of the managers smiled when they intercepted me in the corridor on the way out of Friday's rehearsal. It made me deeply suspicious.

I dipped a shallow curtsy and watched them warily.

"Mademoiselle Giry, if we might have just a moment of your time," Ricard said, positively oozing good cheer. "We were hoping we might trouble you to deliver a letter to your mother for us."

Had no one in Paris heard of couriers? Should I get a uniform and start selling stamps? "No trouble at all," I said through gritted teeth, trodding down my irritation. I lived with my mother, it really wasn't any trouble, and it wasn't an irrational request. It was the dozen letters I had carted around for Christine that bothered me.

"Marvelous!" Ricard said, handing me a sealed envelope. "And we do hope there are no, ahem, bad feelings after…recent events."

Those would be the recent events when they accused my mother of a conspiracy and fired her, after six years of working at the Opera, probably forcing the both of us to leave Paris as a consequence? I kept my gaze on the envelope as I tucked it into my bag. "I am sure there are no feelings in any way out of proportion to what the situation merits," I said and smiled as sweetly as I could.

Moncharmin coughed. Ricard looked confused and said, "Er, yes. Well then. Excellent."

It wasn't, but I wouldn't argue with him.

I was so bothered that I walked almost two blocks before it occurred to me to wonder about the letter. I tried to spin a theory about what the managers could want to communicate, and came up blank. I inspected the envelope but it had a seal, so I reluctantly put it away again unopened. I was reasonably sure Mother would let me see it anyway.

"Mother?" I called as I came in our front door. "I have a letter…" I trailed off as I caught sight of her sitting at the kitchen table. She looked serious, even for my usually solemn mother. "What is it?"

"I had a letter too. Sit down for a minute." She gestured towards the opposite chair.

I slid into the seat, stomach churning. "Bad news?" Maybe one of our relatives in Leclair was ill? Mother had already lost her job and the managers would have told me if I had lost mine, so it wasn't something like that.

"Good news, actually," she said, with an unconvincing smile. "A letter from Amelie in Bordeaux. She's offered work to both of us."

"Oh." I looked down at the wooden tabletop, traced a grain of wood with one fingertip. "All right."

"You know none of my inquiries about employment in Paris have led anywhere."

"I know."

"It would be a significant change for both of us, and I'm not taking the matter of leaving lightly but—"

"Why don't you just say we're going and be done with it?" I curled my fingers, knuckles white against the dark wood.

"Frankly, because you're too old for me to unilaterally announce plans like leaving the city."

I glared at the tabletop, because I didn't dare glare at Mother herself. "So instead you'll just tell me about how there aren't any other options!"

"There *aren't* any other options."

I leaned back in my chair, rubbed my forehead. "Then what are we even discussing? We're going to Bordeaux. The end, curtain closed." The end, no more Christine, no more Phantom, no more

handsome subscribers in the Dance Foyer, no more magic, no more...
"This position Amelie has for me, is it dancing?"

The pause told me the answer before Mother said, "No."

No more dancing either, then. No more becoming lost in the music, in the movements, creating beauty and magic myself. No more stretching and reaching and growing to attain new abilities, new heights of ballet. "Oh well, it's not like I was ever a great dancer anyway," I muttered. I was good, that was all, just like dozens of other girls. I would be no great loss to art—though the art would be a loss to *me*.

And it had been my entry point, my doorway into all the other magic of the Opera Garnier.

"Meg..." Mother said, reaching for my hand across the table.

I pulled my hand back. "How soon do we leave? Do you have the train tickets already?"

"No, of course not," she said, withdrawing her own hand. "I'll need to write back to Amelie. It will probably take some time to sell the apartment as well."

That idea gave me a new twist of sadness. It wasn't an ancestral home or anything, but we had lived here for six years. Mother sold our farm in Leclair to buy the apartment when we moved here; acres and acres in Leclair to buy a small apartment in Paris, but still much better than renting rooms somewhere.

When we came to Paris I had been so sure that we were going towards something wonderful. Now I could only think about all the things we were leaving. Christine and my friends in the ballet and Notre Dame and my favorite bakery and of course the Opera...

I straightened suddenly, recent Opera events coming back to mind. "I just remembered—the managers gave me a letter for you." I reached into my bag, and tossed the letter onto the table between us.

Mother took it with a perplexed expression and broke the wax seal. Her expression only grew more confused as she read.

"What?" I asked, mingled nerves and hopes fluttering in my stomach. "What does it say?"

"They want me to come to the Opera to speak with them Tuesday evening."

"The night of the gala?"

"Yes, but they don't say why."

"Maybe they feel bad and want to rehire you!" And that would mean we didn't have to leave after all. That would solve *everything*.

Mother raised an eyebrow and didn't succumb to my enthusiasm. "I think we both know that's unlikely."

"Maybe the Phantom pressured them." I wanted so much to believe that. And it did make sense, I was sure it did, with a sureness that bubbled up like champagne, delightful if not very substantial. "I kept saying he was sure to do something soon—"

"We know the Phantom has always been unpredictable. I never thought you should depend too much on—"

"But he's always been so polite and left tips in Box Five and always insisted for years that you stay his boxkeeper. It makes sense, it really does." I wanted her to agree. If she would agree, then I could be truly sure, with a steadier sort of surety.

My hopeful gaze was met only by a frown. "If they were going to rehire me, they would say so."

"We don't know that, maybe they're just being dramatic about it. And M. Ricard said he hoped there were no bad feelings!"

Mother reached for my hand again, and this time I let her take it. "I know you want this to work, Meg," she said gently, "but I really don't think this is likely to change anything."

"But it *might*." I squeezed her hand. "At least don't make any final decisions until you talk to them, please? It's only a few days away!"

She sighed. "All right, we'll wait a few days. But after the gala—"

"We'll figure that out then." I bounced up to my feet, gave her a quick hug. "Now I have to go to Notre Dame. I'll be back soon."

"Why are you going to Notre Dame?"

"I have to light a candle!"

Chapter Twenty-Four

T he Phantom waited behind the wall of Carlotta's dressing room after Saturday's performance. Three letters with explicit instructions regarding Tuesday's gala performance had still not produced the results he wanted from her. Not even the one that was left on her dressing table at her home, accompanied by a pile of dead rats. Distasteful, and he regretted lowering himself without it even proving effective. Now, he was running out of time.

Carlotta entered with her usual flock around her. He gritted his teeth, leaned back against the wall and endured several minutes of mindless chatter, almost as grating as a badly-played violin. The chair before her dressing table creaked as she lowered herself into it, and he hoped she was finally picking up the note he had left (prominently!) on her dressing table. He felt encouraged when her shrill voice dropped out of the cacophony.

The note was only a brief line.

If you would speak with the Phantom, dismiss your attendants.

Listening intently, he heard her inhale, and then give an imperious order for everyone to leave the room.

He smiled slightly. An invitation like that could have caused her to flee—arguably the sensible option—but this woman had come back after he had chased her offstage with croaking, had refused to be cowed by a broken mirror or dead rats. He had gambled that she would be more curious, or perhaps angry, than afraid.

Once the door had banged closed behind the last confused, worshiping fan, Carlotta addressed the room at large in the same imperious tone, "Well, Phantom? You wanted to speak with La Carlotta?"

Why waste time on pleasantries anyway? He projected his voice into the room, giving it all the cold solemnity he could. "You will not sing at the managers' special performance."

This was greeted with an unmelodic snort. "That again? You think I will back out because you say so? Oh no, I do not take orders from you."

Life would be so much easier for him if she did. But so many things would make his life easier, most of them even less attainable than Carlotta's obedience. He set those thoughts aside, maintained his stern tone. "This is a warning. You know I can stop you any time I choose."

"I would like to see you try—" She broke off as a loud croak filled the room. It wasn't good for his vocal muscles, but it wasn't beyond his ventriloquism abilities either. After a moment she coughed, very faintly, then said, "Your tricks are not amusing and are frankly embarrassing for anyone claiming to care about art."

"I was not attempting to amuse," he said, all the more coldly because he had no good defense to her second accusation. Maybe that was also why he took the frankly theatrical step of knocking her newly-replaced mirror over. It fell forward with a satisfying crash, an even more satisfying gasp from Carlotta following. He had estimated it would fall mere inches from her seat when he arranged the mechanism. "Some of my tricks are even less amusing," he said. "Do we understand each other now?"

The pause that followed seemed promising. Then she spoke, and not with the kind of repentance and acceptance he wanted to hear. "We both understand that you can threaten me, and you can create a disaster at the performance..." Her voice turned mocking. "...but that won't help your pretty Christine, will it?"

He grimaced and managed to keep his curses silent.

Carlotta's laugh still echoed the fine soprano voice she had possessed several years ago. "Did you really think I would not put the pieces together? Monsieur Montagne the Vocal Director so kindly told me about your recent directions—and then you try to order me away from an evening that would be a perfect opportunity for your little ingénue. Ruining the gala will not get you what you want."

He pitched his voice into an even lower, threatening tone. "I could get you out of the way before the performance." It would be so *easy*. Strangle her, break a leg—there were ways and means aplenty to ensure she would be thoroughly, even permanently, out of the way.

He took a deep breath, carefully unclenched his hands. He had *rules*.

He did not inflict violence on women. He had done many things in his life, but he would not do that.

"If I disappear, they will cancel," Carlotta snapped. From her defiant tone, she had no idea how close she was to provoking him into something drastic. "Or they will put on an evening of exclusively ballet. La Carlotta is not replaced. Your brat will continue to languish in the chorus."

"Are you sure you want to risk disappearing?" he growled, triggering the lights in her room to flicker, the bottles of perfume lining her vanity to fall over one by one, crashing against the tabletop.

"Opera is my life!" Carlotta shouted, with a kind of sincerity he did not usually hear in her tantrums. "Killing my career will not help you. Killing me is no worse a threat."

Erik felt a creeping sense of…respect? Absurd. Nonsense. Not for *Carlotta*. But she was calling his bluff, and he could see only one option. He took a deep breath, steadied his voice. "We appear to be at an impasse, Signora. I suggest we negotiate."

Laughter again. "I do not need help from you."

"Debatable." She could certainly use his singing advice, but he had no interest in lost causes. "You do not want my enmity, and if you do not cooperate, I will ruin every performance you attempt in this opera house. Not merely the special one. *Every* performance."

It was gratifying, the new level of alarm in her voice. It was still a subtle alarm, but he could hear it there below her more defiant words.

"You are bluffing. You would ruin the Opera that way, and you would never do that."

That was true enough. She understood him better than he liked. But he still had cards to play. "Do not worry about the Opera. Grinning Ricard and Centime-Counting Moncharmin will take you off the stage long before they let the Opera Garnier fall. And you will end an illustrious career in hideous humiliation." He let that hang for a moment, filling the space. "Or...we negotiate. You step aside for the gala performance. You tell the vocal director, the managers, anyone else necessary that you recommend Mademoiselle Daaé to sing. And I give you my word that I will never interfere with your career again."

"Your word?" she spat. "The word of a monster who lurks about in the shadows, who plays absurd tricks—"

"My word as a musician!" He inhaled deeply, and put every nuance of sincerity, truth and conviction into his voice that natural ability and long years of refining had taught him to express. "I swear on Mozart, Beethoven and Stradivari, I will not interfere with you again. Do we have an agreement?"

A long pause, one weighted with years of hostility, insults and threats—but also, perhaps, a previously unimagined thread of connection, of one artist to another, a commonality that still existed between even bitter enemies.

At last she said, "We do."

He was almost surprised. He knew he meant it, but had not truly had high hopes she would believe that. But she was a singer, however much she wasn't one to his own taste or standards. She knew voices. Perhaps she heard something in his.

He let out a slow breath, releasing a tension he hadn't noticed because it was so habitual.

He wasn't sacrificing anything that mattered. All he needed was one night, one performance for Christine to sing the way he knew she could, in front of the right people—and then it wouldn't require a Phantom to drive Carlotta out of the Opera Garnier. The audience, the management, all of Paris would demand to hear Christine Daaé sing.

I was tapping my foot by the time Christine finally emerged from the extra rehearsal Sunday morning; she was the last one out. I still hoped that everything would work out, that we wouldn't leave—but just in case, I wanted to spend the afternoon rambling around Paris with my best friend while I still could.

She hurried up to me outside rehearsal with eyes bright and smile wide. "Meg, I have the most marvelous news! The choir director just told me—you'll never guess what!"

Wonderful news at the special rehearsal? Not so hard to guess. "You've been chosen to sing lead soprano in the gala performance?" I asked, smiling at her enthusiasm, pleased that something nice was happening in this tumultuous world.

Her eyes went wide. "Yes! How did you know?"

I laughed. "Didn't I tell you the Phantom would make it happen?" Because he had time to solve *her* problems. My laughter faded. But that was silly, maybe he *had* solved Mother's problem. Maybe that's why the managers wanted to talk to her Tuesday.

"Do you think it was the Phantom?" Christine asked, tucking her arm through mine as we walked down the corridor. "M. Montagne just said that Carlotta declined to sing, and recommended me as her replacement. It did seem strange…"

"Of course she wouldn't do that on her own," I said with comfortable certainty. "The Phantom must have made it happen." It was exactly the sort of thing he would do. I wondered how he had obtained Carlotta's cooperation; that was a feat even more impressive than the flaming skeleton.

"Perhaps you're right," she agreed, and I would have happily continued analyzing the Phantom's motives, but she hurried on to, "Anyway, I have to go to my dressing room to pick up some sheet music, and then M. Montagne wants to help me prepare this afternoon."

A twinge of disappointment ran through me. "This afternoon?" I repeated.

"Yes, it's very important to make sure everyone is quite ready for the special performance. Why, is something wrong?"

"No," I said, summoning up a smile. "I thought perhaps we could go for beignets this afternoon, or maybe go up to the roof—but that's all right, it doesn't matter." We hadn't been up to the roof for weeks.

She gave my arm a quick squeeze. "Oh, *cherie*, that would have been such fun! But *you* know how demanding art is. And anyway, we'll see each other at the masquerade tonight."

"Of course," I agreed, and that thought did give me a more cheerful outlook as I listened to her chat on about what she would be singing.

When we reached Christine's dressing room she turned up the gas lamp and went over to the enormous mirror to check her hair. I sat down on the low sofa, and glanced towards her vanity table. "Who sent you flowers? Well, *a* flower."

"What's that, *cherie*?" she asked without looking.

"There, on the table." A single large orchid lay on the table, white with vivid red shading at its center.

"I don't know. It wasn't here before." Christine drifted over to the table, picked up the orchid in one hand and with the other lifted an envelope that had been beneath it. The envelope had thick borders of black and I only knew one person with stationary like that. "Here, hold this a minute," Christine said, passing me the orchid so she could open the envelope.

It was a lovely flower, dramatic in its coloring, probably rare. I twirled the stem between my fingertips and watched out of the corner of my eye as Christine pulled a black-edged letter out of the envelope and unfolded it. It probably only *felt* like she was reading slowly.

"You were right about the role in the special performance," Christine said at last. "The Phantom persuaded Carlotta to bow out so I could have the chance to sing. Wasn't that thoughtful of him?"

"Yes." I twirled the orchid again, watched the resulting blur of red and white. Very thoughtful. Well-nigh magical too. It must have required a great deal of time and effort.

"He left a message for you too."

I looked up, fingers tightening on the stem. "He did?" Had my voice sounded too eager?

"Mm-hmm, down here at the end," Christine said, refolding the paper and presenting it to me.

She had folded it so only the bottom bit was visible, a swirling *O.G.* in vivid red and below that a note.

P.S. Incidentally, tell your friend that her mother need not to be concerned, and should make no plans before Wednesday.

I read it three times, but it didn't get any longer or more illuminating on repetition.

Really, it was good. It was something to suggest that the Phantom was going to take care of Mother's job. Even if we were sort of a minor, secondary plot to him. That was better than not being in the opera at all. Wasn't it?

Christine hurried off to her special practice, taking her letter and her orchid with her, and I wandered off in search of beignets. The ballet girls had already scattered for the afternoon, supposing there had been one of them I wanted to invite along with me anyway. Or one who would have come. The roof did not seem as much fun by myself, but my favorite bakery had wonderful beignets and they'd taste just as good alone. It wasn't as though the afternoon would be a complete loss. And I'd need to get ready for the masquerade in a few hours anyway. That, at least, was something exciting to anticipate.

It was really abysmal luck that Meg Giry had happened to come with Christine to her dressing room. The thought would keep reverberating in his head as he paced through the costume room.

He had left the flower and the letter, and then waited on the hidden side of the mirror for a reaction. If it had been a, well, promising reaction, he would have made himself known to Christine and…he didn't have a very clear picture of what he would have done after that, but he had given her the *gala*, that had to count for something!

He was quite sure that the Vicomte de Chagny wouldn't come up with even an orchid. It was more like him to present an enormous, unoriginal armful of roses. The Phantom smiled mirthlessly, running one gloved hand along a hanging expanse of silk and brocade costumes. *Everyone* gave roses. A single orchid was so much more elegant, so much rarer…

But anyway, even if he had had a more coherent plan, he certainly couldn't have put it into effect with Meg Giry sitting there.

He paused, fingering one heavy, embroidered cloak. He also rather regretted the terseness of that post script. He hadn't expected Christine to show the letter to Meg directly. He had assumed that the message would be passed along, and that it would sound less like an after-thought in the passing.

If he was superstitious, he really would have regrets about Carlotta's broken mirrors. However, someone who pretends to be a ghost, who stays alive by playing on the secret fears of the people around him, couldn't afford to be superstitious himself.

He released the cloak with a swish of fabric and walked on towards the next section, the Italian costumes.

What he needed was to decide what to do next. It would be sensible to wait until Monday to seek Christine again, when she would be at the Opera for rehearsals.

But the masquerade was tonight. The annual masquerade, a tightly-packed, riotous mass of people filling up his normally refined Opera. No doubt they'd be disorderly and uncontrolled and prone to all sorts of nonsensical revelry. Not at all the kind of situation he had any interest in becoming involved in.

He stopped in front of the wall of masks, ran his fingertips across a line of grinning, scowling, laughing faces.   Here was every possible identity anyone could want.

Nothing at all was appealing about the drunken, crowded chaos of Mardi Gras. Except. It would be a crowd of people *all wearing masks.*

For one single night, a man in a mask would blend in.   For just once this opportunity existed to be invisible among people.   That was even rarer than an orchid.

Christine would be attending.   She had mentioned it in passing days ago.

He could go to the masquerade. He hadn't quite decided. He still thought it was ill-advised. He was only in the costume room on a sort of whim, he didn't *know* that he would do this. But he could go. Just to see her. Nothing was wrong with that.

He tapped his finger against one mask, one in a row of skull faces.

Attending the masquerade would have nothing at all to do with the probability that the Vicomte de Chagny would be attending too. Just as that fact surely had nothing to do with Christine's decision to attend either.

Chapter Twenty-Five

I lifted my heavy skirts and hurried up the front steps of the Opera Garnier. The evening had finally arrived and the world was ablaze with music and color and life—the opera house lit up before me, the electric lights of the Avenue de l'Opera behind me, and all around the laughing, brightly-hued crowd. It might not be Mardi Gras until Tuesday on the calendar, but tonight it was Mardi Gras at the Opera, the wildest, freest night of the year, when everyone donned a mask and could be anyone they wanted to be. If this was my last party at the Opera, I was going to *enjoy* it.

For a moment I watched from the doorway, heart pounding, happily aware of my shimmering gold dress with its wide skirt and black accents. It was far finer than anything Mother and I could afford, especially to wear for just one night, especially under present circumstances—but I'd begged a loan off the costume director.

I had grown used to the elaborate decorations of the Opera in the years I'd been coming here, but for just tonight the crowd was equally elaborate. With a breath, I plunged into the mad swirl of brocaded skirts, elegant coats, top hats and feathers and shimmering jewels. And everywhere masks—grinning ones and tragic ones, masks covered in swirls and glittering with sparkles, masks that were merely an affectation and masks that covered entire faces.

It was easy to be invisible at the Opera any day, in such crowds of beautiful, talented people. Tonight it was exciting to be invisible by choice, hidden behind my gold mask.

I dodged and twisted and slipped through the crowd, through the chaos of music and laughter and voices, until I won through to the marble stairs. The throng didn't thin here, and I wound my way amidst the crush until I was halfway up. There I stopped, perched against a wide marble railing, an eddy in the swirling crowd making a little space around me as I looked out over the room from my new vantage point.

I hoped to see Christine. Even in disguise, she should be easy to recognize with those dramatic brown curls.

I could see Carlotta on the upper balcony, unmistakable despite the vivid green and purple feathered mask over the bridge of her nose. As usual, she was at the center of her adoring devotees, probably none of whom would tell her that she was wearing far too many feathers; they looked scratchy too.

And with the power of suggestion, the brocade of my mask began to itch. I tried to shift the mask to a more comfortable position, wrinkling my nose as I looked around.

Many of the principal players in the Company were easy enough to identify, even disguised. Some masks were small, other people had a distinctive build or walk. Or in the case of Samuel Richard, the vocal director's assistant, I knew he was the only one who could trip and fall down half a flight of the marble stairs, then bound up and carry on as though he was fine. He was known for that kind of thing.

He didn't crash into me or, fortunately, the managers, who stood near the foot of the stairs. Monsieur Ricard wore an elaborately embroidered costume in peacock blue, while Monsieur Moncharmin was in ordinary evening dress and carrying a mask on a stick. From the way he kept looking around, I doubted he could quite fathom what had happened to the Opera tonight.

My nose still itched, growing more annoying than the prospect of a brief loss of anonymity. Turning my face away from the managers, who I did not want to recognize me, I slipped the mask off to rub the side of my nose.

There was Madame Thibault. She had to be feeling particularly festive tonight; she had traded her black dress for a dark blue one. The Persian made another dark accent to the crowd's brilliant colors. He stood by a balcony railing, in what appeared to be his usual black clothes, a black mask his only concession to the holiday, his perennial red fez his one spot of brightness. I wondered if he had an invitation, or if he had simply come without one. The Company and many of our subscribers were invited of course, but I didn't *think* he was quite either of those...

"Meg!" a voice called, interrupting my thoughts, and a moment later the Vicomte de Chagny had pushed through the masses to stand by me. He wore an ordinary evening jacket and a narrow white domino mask that did nothing at all to hide his identity. "Have you seen Christine?"

As if I was nothing more than a signpost for a more interesting girl. I blinked slowly at him. "Good evening, Monsieur Vicomte, I am very well, thank you. And yourself?"

He waved a hand. "Never mind all that, I'm trying to find Christine. She told me this afternoon to wear a white domino and meet her by the stairs. Have you seen her?"

Why did I think I could expect better from him? "Not so far." I balanced my mask in place and reached behind my head to retie the ribbons. It occurred to me that Christine must have seen him this afternoon, if she was giving directions about meeting when I hadn't delivered any letters.

His eyes scanned the room wildly. "I didn't think it would be this hard to find her! Why does everyone have to be disguised?"

"It's a masquerade," I said, stifling a sigh. Maybe Christine wouldn't need more letters delivered, which would relieve me of a chore—but also a role. And wasn't she worried about the Phantom anymore?

"I know that, but it's inconvenient. I keep going up to the wrong brunettes."

"Best watch that, Monsieur. That's the kind of thing that could get a person in trouble." It was also trouble tying a bow behind one's head. I kept catching strands of hair in the knot. I resolved not to take the mask off again, and to ask Christine about future letter delivery.

He said something like "Mmm," but plainly wasn't listening, neck still craning to look around.

A disturbance on the opposite branch of the marble staircase attracted both our attentions. A man had halted halfway up the stair, confronting several revelers who blocked further progress. The man they'd stopped was wearing an enormous red velvet cloak, and affixed to his back a sign read, *Touch me not—I am Red Death stalking abroad.*

"Won't you dance, Red Death?" a giddy and no doubt tipsy chorus girl called out. I didn't recognize her, but she had to be a chorus girl because she didn't move like a dancer—not even a drunk one. She planted herself in front of Red Death while her friends clustered behind her with laughing encouragement.

I could see the tension in Red Death's shoulders as he looked towards her. I couldn't see his face. Whatever might have been visible at this angle was hidden by a wide-brimmed hat—red, of course, with a curling feather. He slowly extended one gloved hand, and the chorus girl reached out. At the last second she hesitated, looking up at the face I still couldn't see. Then, with her friends pushing her on, she seized his hand.

For just an instant she touched Red Death's fingers, before she shrieked and let go, stumbling backwards into the nearest pair of male arms. "It's like—like lightning!"

Red Death turned suddenly, sending a wave through the crowd behind him as everyone fell back. This new angle revealed an elaborate red and gold suit, topped by a grinning ivory skull. The mask hid every detail of the face behind it. Red Death turned again, and now the crowd in front of him ducked out of his way. He continued his march up the stairs, a circle of empty space moving with him as revelers pulled back, until he was out of sight on the second-level balcony.

"That's a grim costume," Raoul remarked. "Doesn't seem fitting at all. Who dresses up like death at a party?"

I had finally got my ribbons tied, well-enough although my mask tilted a little now, and released the ends. "It's Mardi Gras. Many people dress as Death. And anyway, Red Death is a reference to a story by Monsieur Poe. Mister Poe," I corrected myself. "He's American. Or maybe British. No, I think American."

"I suppose someone has to be," Raoul said, intent once more on his search for the right brunette.

He was still scrutinizing the crowd, and I was wondering how to politely slip away, presuming I cared about being polite, when the cry, "Raoul!" cut across the noise. Christine arrived with a waving arm and a swirl of pale pink skirts, a black domino mask covering very little of her face.

"*There* you are," she said, slipping her arm through Raoul's. "Hello, Meg, that's a splendid dress. You're lucky you can wear *such* bright colors."

I felt an unaccountable pang. That had been a compliment, hadn't it? Yet I suddenly wondered if the dress was *too* bright, too gaudy in its golds and blacks, and if I mightn't have done better to choose something more discreet, more like Christine's pale elegance.

"I've been looking for you everywhere," Raoul informed her, with something just this side of a pout.

"And here I am," she said with a beaming smile for him. "Come on, there's dancing in the Grand Foyer. See you later, Meg!" A wave of fingertips from Christine, and they were off together into the throng.

I smoothed my skirts, adjusted the set of my necklace. The dress *was* a nice color, and I hadn't wanted to spend the evening with the Vicomte de Chagny anyway. I lifted my chin and set off to thread my own way up the stairs towards the Grand Foyer, to find a dance partner myself.

In the Foyer, chandeliers glowed with hundreds of candles, casting light on the swirling crowd below and the dancing murals across the ceiling. Light reflected back from the gold bordering the murals and covering the tall pillars, with Garnier's face the lone spot of silver amidst the blaze of gold. Somewhere musicians were plying their craft, and a dozen singers in one corner were lustily putting on an apparently impromptu performance.

I took only a few steps into the room before a smiling Harlequin caught me. Mask too encompassing for me to identify him, he spun me into the dancing.

If he thought to make me dizzy and have me fall into his arms, he had picked the wrong girl. I wouldn't have got far in ballet if I couldn't keep a steady head. I let him spin me about a few times, because it was that kind of night and I was in that kind of mood, before I slipped out of his hold and onto the next hand reaching for mine.

Plenty of men were willing to smile and whirl off together. If none of them had a smile that made me want to choose a partner and stay, they were still fun for a dance and there were always more to try.

I laughed and danced and traded partners until even I began to grow dizzy and need to catch my breath. I slipped free of my current partner and made my way to the edge of the dancing, to walk more slowly through the crowd and look again at the costumes. It was marginally less crowded out on the balconies overlooking the Grand Staircase.

I wasn't seeking Red Death out. All I did was turn a corner around a pillar and there he was, pursuing his own path right towards me. We both halted abruptly, inches from a collision. His wide hat cast a shadow but didn't hide the grinning death's head skull.

I eased back a step, dipped a slight curtsy. "Monsieur."

He nodded once, and moved to go.

A mischievous impulse seized me. "You know, Monsieur Red Death, putting up a sign forbidding touching is certain to encourage people to do exactly that."

He paused, head swinging to face me—if you could put it that way, when he was so hidden by his mask. He seemed to be looking at me, but I couldn't even see his eyes, lost in the shadows below the ridges of the skull mask. "Then what would you recommend for someone at a party who prefers to be left alone?"

I knew that voice, and below my skirts my knees turned to water.

Red Death was the Opera Ghost.

After all my confidence all these years that I didn't fear the Phantom, suddenly I was afraid. Not the way people fear someone who's dangerous, or who might hurt them—this was a fear about unexpectedly talking to someone who is desperately, vitally important, and having not the slightest idea what to say.

I swallowed, and managed to reply, "Don't go to parties."

He inclined his head to one side in acknowledgment, and stood there looking at me a moment longer. Should I say something else? Should I ask him about Mother? Did he even recognize me? And— what *did* he look like, under that skull mask?

Too many thoughts collided in my mind and nothing coherent came together.

He reached out one hand, and straightened my askew mask with a single gloved finger on the corner. Though I tensed, I felt no lightning, so whatever trick he'd been playing—something with electricity?—he didn't try it on me.

A bow, a swirl of red, and he was gone into the crowd again.

I reached a hand out to the pillar to steady myself. Had the Phantom always come to masquerades and I'd just never known, or was this new?

Once I had my breath back, I returned to the Grand Foyer, where I saw Christine and Raoul dancing together across the hall, and could sometimes spot Red Death along the side of the room. He wasn't always there, but he was easy to find when he was, both for the red hat and the space that inevitably formed around him.

And then just once, I saw Red Death and Christine dancing together. Of course. The Phantom wanted everyone else to leave him alone, but Christine...was special. I wondered suddenly what he would have done if *I* had asked him to dance. Maybe it was better I hadn't tried.

It was hard to keep the Phantom and Christine in sight, as I turned with the music and so did they, but I could see enough to know they moved well together. Christine couldn't dance ballet, but she could waltz.

I may have spent too much of that set looking at the other end of the room; when it was over my partner released me and went off in a huff, after the shallowest bow etiquette would permit. I spared a glance to watch him go, guiltily glad of the mask that hid my identity. Wasn't that the point? No repercussions in the morning.

I stepped out of the throng of dancing, paused by a gilded pillar, and looked for that red hat again.

Red Death was still holding Christine's hand, and seemed to be speaking. I wanted so badly to walk up to them, to ask Christine to introduce me to her dance partner. But he was leaning in towards her, and the invisible walls projecting around him all evening had closed her in now too. Breaking in on their conversation, following the simple dictates of normal convention, felt as impossible as flying from a catwalk.

Christine nodded several times as he spoke, her face turned at an angle frustratingly out of my sight, then slowly drew her hand away. She slipped off through the crowd and I lost sight of her for a few moments, until I spotted her again in the doorway. She was joined now by Raoul, and with one glance around the room, Christine led him away. What had been said, and where was she going? And what would be the response?

I flicked my gaze to Red Death, and saw that he was standing very still where Christine had left him. A few seconds, and then he moved through the crowd, heading the same direction Christine had gone.

As impossible as it felt to approach him, it was equally impossible not to follow. Heart pounding, I pushed through the crowd, maneuvering around clumps of revelers and dodging more hands reaching out for a dance. I felt screamingly slow. I was at the wrong end of the long Grand Foyer, and the crowd that let Red Death through instinctively did not make way for me.

By the time I got out of the Foyer, a red cloak was vanishing up a side stair, and by the time I arrived breathless at the top of those steps, no signs remained of any of the people I was trying to follow.

I wrapped one hand around the banister, looking at the empty hall ahead of me, a half dozen branching corridors in sight. Christine, Raoul and Red Death were all leaving the party, and they could be going anywhere from here.

No indication which way was correct, and I was not willing to go hunting up and down through the hallways. I had too much pride for that—but still struggled to swallow my disappointment. I fingered my necklace, kicked one toe against the bottom of the banister and told myself this was silly and voyeuristic. Surely better things could be done at a party than watching over Christine's business. And maybe she'd tell me about it later. Maybe.

Heavy skirts dragging, I turned to wander slowly back down the stairs. No need to push and rush now. I didn't altogether want to go back to the dancing either, so I continued on down the Grand Stairs, thinking of making a full circuit through the party. Maybe some of the other ballet girls were around.

I was nearing the bottom of the marble staircase when someone called my name, and a moment later I was looking into blue eyes that set off a spark of recognition. They belonged to a man in a silver costume, perfectly tailored and more dignified than I would have expected an entirely silver outfit to appear. Maybe his height helped— from my place two steps above him, my eyes were just on a level with his vivid blue ones.

"You're Christine's friend, aren't you?" he said with a broad smile.

I was growing tired of being identified that way, but in this case it was only fair, since I'd just mentally labeled him as 'Raoul's friend.' It was Léon de Troyes, the one Christine had been so eager for me to meet. The one who had seemed rather pleasant, for the few minutes we had talked. "Monsieur de Troyes, isn't it?" I said, extending a hand.

He brushed a kiss on the back of my fingers and kept his hand clasped around mine, leaning closer to speak over the noise of the crowd. "I was hoping to see you! Raoul didn't know if you would be coming tonight."

Meaning he had asked? "I never miss a masquerade," I said with a smile. "The masks make it so much more exciting than an ordinary party." As I spoke, it occurred to me that, while Léon had been easy to recognize with his mask pushed up to rest on his blond hair, mine was still covering my face. A tingle spread up from the pit of my stomach and Léon rose several notches in my estimation. He might remember me as 'Christine's friend,' but he had known me behind my mask.

"Would you care to dance?" he asked, nodding towards the Foyer.

I tightened my fingers around his. "I'd love to." Dancing sounded more appealing, with an appealing partner. And this was a much better way to spend the evening than thinking about ghosts.

Enough of chasing at the edges of Christine's story. Now was my chance to have my own.

Chapter Twenty-Six

Why hadn't he worn black? He might as well be wearing *bells*, trying to move discreetly in this get-up. At the first opportunity he opened a secret panel, threw Red Death's hat and cape into the compartment and drew out a dark cloak. It would have to be enough to hide the red clothes beneath. He didn't have time for more, if he was going to avoid losing Christine's trail. If she and that fool boy had turned too many corners while he paused…no, he could still hear them up ahead.

The Phantom followed them up out of the occupied parts of the Opera Garnier, far from the noise and the lights and the crowds, up staircases and through corridors, staying back and using his ears more than his eyes to discern their direction. This would be impossible if he didn't know his Opera so well.

He was three flights above the panel where he had obtained the cloak before it occurred to him that he should have traded the skull mask for something a darker shade. Too late now.

He was clearly not thinking straight tonight. Hardly surprising, considering. Moving through the crowds would be unnerving enough (why did people want to approach a man in a skull mask? Really!) but besides that…

Christine had talked about the masquerade, had said how nice it would be to see her friends. Her *friends*. He had believed her—tried to believe her—hadn't quite believed her. He came in a costume he had thought would keep people at a distance, just hoping to see her. And he had found her with the vicomte. The idiot boy she had said wasn't important and she wasn't seeing anymore.

He winced now, remembering the sound of Christine's perfect voice, calling Raoul's name across the crowded stairs. It was as obvious as a lead soprano calling to her preferred tenor at the center of the stage. Erik couldn't have missed it if he'd tried. Then he'd watched, and he'd waited, and finally the boy had gone off for wine or something, and he had contrived to claim her for a dance.

Perhaps it was true, her explanation when he had demanded to know about the vicomte. Perhaps she was planning to tell Raoul good-bye, had been planning that all evening. Still—surely dancing with a man for half the night was taking 'letting him down gently' to an extreme!

Erik leaned against a corner, waiting for Christine to choose a new turn up ahead, and breathed deeply. He didn't want to doubt her. Not Christine. So many betrayals in his life, so much heartbreak and pain— but not from Christine. She wouldn't lie to him. She couldn't. She was too sweet, too innocent. She couldn't hurt anyone. She wouldn't betray him.

So if he believed that, why was he following to make sure?

He should turn around now, let this go.

He didn't. He followed her all the way up to the rooftop, which, lovely though the night air was, seemed like a long way to go to tell someone you couldn't see him anymore.

He couldn't risk the same door that Christine had used; it was too exposed. Fortunately he knew other routes, and came out onto the roof in a patch of deep shadow. He could hear their voices, where they were standing at the roof's edge near one of the corner statues. At home again in darkness, hidden in his black cloak, he slipped behind the winged statue, close enough to overhear the conversation, and tried to ignore the irony of eavesdropping from behind a statuary personification of Harmony.

"Isn't it beautiful up here?" Christine was saying as he settled deeper into the shadows.

"Not as beautiful as you."

The Phantom rolled his eyes. What had she ever seen in that foolish boy? Perhaps he didn't want to think about that...but the point was, she had to see how ridiculous this was! The idiot couldn't even come up with an original compliment, let alone write her a love song.

"Raoul, you shouldn't say things like that."

Because such comments were stupid and unimaginative, and this whole flirtation was about to come to an end.

"Why shouldn't I? I'm on a beautiful rooftop, at a beautiful party, with the most beautiful girl in the world!" Raoul enthused with boyish delight, and then sighed with aggravating contentment. "This is the perfect night, Christine. I wish it would never end. I wish we could dance together forever."

"Oh Raoul," she said softly, "I accept."

The words hung there, inexplicable, utterly disjointed from the sentence that had come before it. He had seen so many operas—perhaps that didn't mean he understood lovers' conversations after all. Or perhaps—perhaps he didn't want to understand, because obviously what he was thinking—no, it didn't mean *that*.

It was the most meager of consolations when Raoul came back with a slightly strangled, equally confused, "What?"

"I accept your proposal."

No. No, she could not mean—she *did not* mean—accepting a proposal of marriage was not *letting him down gently*!

"Oh. I…um…that is, what I meant…well, you see, I—"

All the fury, despair, pain rising up inside of him froze, crystallized, held suspended in a sudden, unexpected uncertainty. It was just possible—Erik clenched his hands into fists, hunched himself deeper into the shadows. Surely even that idiot vicomte couldn't be foolish enough to go back on the offer! He profoundly, deeply, with everything in him *did not want* Raoul to succeed in a proposal—but how dare he refuse her!

And yet, what did it matter what the idiot vicomte did? What was *Christine* doing?

"Before we make any plans," Christine cut in on Raoul's stammers, "there's something very important I have to tell you."

"Yes!" Raoul said all too quickly. "Yes, let's talk before we make any plans."

"I know I've been a bit strange these past few weeks," Christine said, and he strained to hear every nuance in her voice, to interpret the soft uncertainty and diffidence he heard there. "I've been refusing to see you and refusing to explain—but I've been in such trouble and I didn't know what to do! I wanted to see you so much but I was…afraid."

A cold prickle crawled up Erik's spine. Not this. Surely, not this— he had tried so hard, wanted so badly not to frighten her. He sank down from his crouched position to sit behind the statue, drawing his legs up and pressing his palms hard against his knees. When had he ever done anything but frighten people?

Why had he dreamed she was different?

"But what is there to be afraid of?" Raoul said with blithe unconcern. "Why didn't you just tell me—"

"I didn't dare! He knows everything that happens!" It was there now, he could hear it now, that vibration of fear in her voice.

"He…?"

"My singing instructor. The Angel. The *Phantom*."

He'd never heard her say the word like that before. He had grown so accustomed to it as a title, a word that was almost divorced from any meaning it had possessed before he claimed it. Suddenly in her voice he could hear all the background, history and symbolism of this identity he had chosen for himself. All the dark terror of that word.

Raoul seemed to sense none of that weight. Oblivious fool. "You mean that silly superstition the Company has about Box Five? What does that have to do with—"

Christine's voice had turned urgent. "He's not a superstition and he's not a joke, he's real. He's been giving me singing lessons, pretending to be an Angel, and I never dreamed anything was wrong until…until I told him about you. He was so angry, and he disappeared for days, and now I wish…but he came back."

The edges of his kneecaps dug into his palms. She had wished *what*? That he had never returned? Never come back into her life, exacted revenge on Carlotta to avenge her honor, invited her into his most private realm? Her delight, her joy when he had spoken to her in her dressing room after Carlotta's disaster, the glad happiness in her voice as she told him how much she had missed him, rose up in his mind. Tainted, now.

"So you've been talking to a…ghost?" Raoul said slowly.

"Not a ghost, a man!" Christine said, a mere five words containing a world of betrayal. Of secrets preserved for years, revealed in one half-sentence. "A man who lives under the Opera, wearing a mask and writing music and controlling everything that happens above. I know it sounds mad, but it's all *true*. I've been there, to his rooms underground. All those days I was gone, I was with him. He held me prisoner below the Opera for a week."

His stomach roiled and he felt sick. It hadn't been like that…had it? Not exactly. But she had been happy, she had understood! Or he had deluded himself into believing she understood. Into believing that she understood him. That something existed between them that was good and beautiful—not twisted and filled with fear.

"Christine," Raoul said with a new note of horror in his voice, "you don't mean that he—when you were a prisoner—"

"No, no, of course not, it's my voice he cares about. That he's obsessed with. That's why he wouldn't let me go. It was all so…" Her voice broke on a sob. "…*terrifying*, to be trapped underground all those days. And I had to convince him I wasn't afraid, that everything was fine, so that he'd believe me when I promised to come back. That was the only way I could get him to let me leave!"

He would have let her leave without the promise. He would have. Surely he would have.

"But that's terrible." Raoul's voice was rich with concern, the white knight comforting the damsel. "We should go to the police immediately. If you know where he lives, we'll tell the police and—"

"That won't work; he's so clever he'll escape them! And he has a terrible temper. If he knew then he'd come after me—after you—I was hoping…but no, it's too much to ask of you."

"What is? Tell me!"

Her voice dropped to a fervent whisper. "Take me away from here. Promise you'll take me away and protect me—if you love me…"

"Of course I love you, you know I do!" A moment's enthusiasm—then weak uncertainty returned to his tone. "But…but I still think we need to tell the police."

What would he do, if she left? What would be left to him then? They might as well send the police for him. The threat that at any other time would have been horrifying seemed only like a swifter end now.

Her voice grew more distant, less warm. "No, I told you, it's too dangerous."

"But Philippe knows Commissaire Mifroid, I'll talk to him and—"

"Besides," Christine said, "I…I don't want to hurt him."

Should that console him somehow? Was that any comfort?

No. Not really.

"*What?*" Raoul said, half-exclamation, half-demand. "But you said—"

"That I'm afraid of him, and I am!" Soft footsteps as she paced a little away along the roof's edge. "But it's all so…so sad too. If you could hear his music, it's so beautiful. Like nothing I've ever heard. It just haunts me—and he's so devoted to me."

"Christine! You can't mean that you actually *care* about him."

Because that would be so impossible. Even the asinine vicomte knew that was impossible, without knowing half the reasons why.

"No—not the way I care about you."

Erik winced. He had expected her to say it, and it still hurt.

"Except that his beautiful music haunts you!" Raoul said in bitter tones.

"Oh Raoul—if you saw him you'd know how ridiculous jealousy is," Christine said, confident, dismissive.

Erik shut his eyes, hunched his shoulders against what he knew had to be coming next. The only thing that could follow the assertion that caring for him would be *ridiculous*.

"He's not like you," she went quickly on, "he's not like anyone. I saw behind the mask he wears and he's—deformed, twisted, hideous! And that's when I saw his temper too, when I realized how dangerous this all was, that I didn't dare—and now I risked telling you and you don't even understand, you think that I could possibly…" Her voice grew unsteady. "…could possibly ever…be in love with…a *monster*."

The last word didn't echo. It didn't ring out loudly through the night, didn't reverberate and peal and repeat. Except in Erik's head, almost but not quite loud enough to drown out the sounds of Christine's fresh sobs.

"Don't cry," Raoul said with an awkward panic in his voice, "I didn't mean…that is, I…I do understand, really. Don't cry, please. Of course I'll help you—I'll take you away from here, whatever you want."

Her voice was tremulous. "You really mean it? We can go away—be married."

"Yes—yes, if that's what you want. I'll protect you, and if that's the only way—I see that now, you're right, and I'm the only one who can help." His voice was growing stronger, fervent with enthusiasm. "I promise I'll take you far away where he'll never find you."

"We could go abroad," she said, hope audibly rising again. Hope for a happy, blissful life with that stupid boy, who was plainly incapable of protecting her. Incapable of understanding her.

"I'll summon my carriage and we can leave immediately!" Raoul's voice was rising too, sounding all the more boyish. "We could be married by morning!"

"It sounds perfect..." And then her tone, rapturous with delight, changed to uncertainty again. "Oh, but wait—I can't leave tonight. I promised to sing at the gala on Tuesday."

"A silly show isn't important! There's no time to lose."

A *silly* show. Engaged thirty seconds and the boy proved he understood nothing, nothing at all. Why didn't she *see* that?

"But I promised. I promised the vocal director—and I promised *him*. It would be so cruel to leave without letting him hear me sing one more time."

Could *that* be a consolation? A meager degree of consideration for the terrifying monster, a flower to throw to the lonely guard before locking him into the prison of solitude for the rest of eternity.

Not much consolation.

Raoul plainly saw no need for even that much. "We can't risk it, Christine, if he abducts you again—"

"But he won't, not before the gala performance. He wants me to sing in it. And you and I will go away together as soon as the show ends. Don't you see, I can't back out of this—it would be fulfilling Father's dream for me, and then we can go away and be together." Her words grew soft and warm with emotion. "I promise."

Her silhouette leaned in toward his—and he leaned in to meet her—and when the sounds of conversation dissolved into the sounds of kisses, Erik put his hands over his ears. He knew the sound, though he had never experienced such a moment himself, never been an actor in that so simple, so ordinary of human dramas.

In this moment he tried not to hear, not to think, not to *feel*.

Tried, and failed utterly.

The night air was cool on the balcony outside the Grand Foyer, wreathed in shadows against the backdrop of the bright lights on the Avenue de l'Opera. Léon and I had whirled dancing through the crowd until I was breathless and warm, then stepped out to the balcony.

I leaned against the balustrade, looking up at Léon with a half-smile. Just as the shadows seemed deeper against the lit avenue, the silence here seemed somehow more complete, against the distant noise of the music, the talking, the crowd.

"This is a wonderful evening," Léon said, voice soft, somehow not really breaking that silent spell. I couldn't see the blue of his eyes in the dim, but I could tell they were turned intently on my face.

For once in my life I didn't want to talk. "Mm-hmm," I agreed, intoxicated with the night and the magic and the chaos.

Léon reached out one hand, found the edge of my mask and gently lifted it up to rest on my hair, revealing my face. "That's better," he murmured.

Somewhere, in a back corner of my mind, I knew this was an intimate gesture—too intimate for how long I had known this man, for how little else we had shared. Another night, that cautioning voice would have been louder. But this was Mardi Gras. This was the night for sudden intimacies. For concealment but also for revealing. And I might be leaving town anyway. There might never be another night.

He leaned in closer, head tilting slightly, and I knew perfectly well what was happening, what was about to happen.

Some other night I might have backed away.

But this was Mardi Gras.

So of course I let Léon kiss me.

At last Christine and Raoul left the rooftop, returned to the light and life of the Opera below. For a long time the Phantom remained frozen in his shadows, curled into the niche beside the statue, beside the cold stone that had never been forced to feel anything.

Finally, slowly, he emerged from the shadows, crept across the tiles to the roof's edge, where *she* had stood with that boy. The music from the masquerade far below drifted up, a distant merriment that mocked his pain. He turned his back on the city, sliding down to sit against the low wall.

Strike someone enough times and eventually the body goes numb. Why couldn't emotions be the same? Why couldn't he just grow insensible to every new betrayal, every new loss? He had thought he'd stopped caring, all these years at the Opera, until *she* had appeared. The romantic heroine he had been waiting for, with no expectation she would ever appear in his opera.

Perhaps choosing songs from *Carmen* had been unwise after all, that night Christine first came below the Opera, the night he had been so hopeful. The story hadn't ended well. Don Jose had killed Carmen, in the end, when she chose the matador instead. And it seemed clear which part he'd been cast as in this story.

No—no, he could never do that, would never do that.

The boy, though—he could kill that boy. He could have done it while Raoul was standing by the edge of the rooftop—ten flights down to the pavement, it would have been very simple.

But that wouldn't help. That wouldn't appease the pain and rage surging through him. The boy didn't matter, he was an incidental item in the evening's events, little more than a walk-on character in the grander story, in the betrayal that was twisting the Phantom apart.

It was Christine who mattered, who had smiled and laughed and told him how much she needed her Angel, how he was the only one who understood her. It was Christine who had lied.

And it was Christine he still wanted.

He sank down onto the tiles, lay back to stare towards the cold, silent sky. How dare composers through the ages write endless songs about the glories and beauties of love! Love was madness, love was weakness, love ravaged and destroyed and refused to die even when it had nothing left to give but misery. What fool still loved a woman who betrayed him, who feared him, who didn't understand anything?

He had to make her understand. He had to make her see that they belonged together. That stupid boy couldn't protect her from the world, couldn't inspire her voice, could not possibly love her the way *he* did.

But how could he do it? Which mask should he wear, what role could he play? He had tried to be her Angel, had blindly enough believed he was her friend. He had been the Phantom for her, eager to turn the Opera Garnier upside down only to let her sing. He had been a voice, a musician, a guide through the darkness and into the world of music, and none of it was enough. What did she *want*, Don Juan? He didn't know how to play that role, knew that he could never, ever be the handsome nobleman.

And then he realized. She had told him what she expected of him, what she thought he was. She had given him his proper place in this opera, and all he had to do was fulfill it, bringing his tragic love story to its close one way or another.

Very well then. So be it.

If Christine wanted him to be a monster—then a monster he would be.

Chapter Twenty-Seven

Excerpt from the Private Notebook of Jean Mifroid, Commissaire of Police

27 Feb 1881

PDC visited station this morning. V. upset re: RDC and Daaé. Daaé claims to be threatened by Phantom. Have told PDC mere Opera superstition, no basis.

V. worried PDC may do something rash. Ranting about getting Daaé "away from my brother, whatever it takes." Have counseled against action.

Note: attend Opera's performance tomorrow night, in case of disturbance.

It was mid-afternoon on Tuesday before I managed to get to Christine's apartment. She might have already been at the Opera preparing for that night's gala, so I was relieved to find her still in her room. She was getting ready, wrapped in a dressing gown and combing her hair. I perched on her bed, dispensed with the preliminaries as quickly as possible, and said, "So, tell me what happened at the masquerade."

I had been dying to know ever since Monday. Late morning, Monday. I had very thoroughly stopped thinking about Christine, the vicomte, even the Phantom during the masquerade. I had stayed out late dancing, slept later than I had in years, and had not hurried to get out of bed in the morning.

It was only a kiss, of course. But it was a nice kiss. Léon was nice too. Maybe it hadn't been wise, maybe it had been Mardi Gras madness, letting a man I hardly knew take liberties, and maybe I ought to regret it. But I didn't regret it quite the way I probably should have.

I had not told my mother, obviously. I didn't exactly know if I wanted to tell Christine. Finally *I* had a story, and surely she'd be delighted for me—but the thought still made my cheeks pink and it was easier, at least to start, to ask Christine about her evening.

Christine only laughed lightly at my question. "What do you mean, *chérie*? You were at the party."

"Yes, and I saw Carlotta have one too many glasses of champagne and I danced lots of dances with Léon and I saw two violinists get into a fight over some musical question, but what I *want* to know is what happened when you and Raoul went out together." And the Phantom followed, I added silently. Though if she wanted to ask about those dances with Léon—perhaps I wouldn't mind talking about that either.

"Why on earth should anything in particular have happened?"

I was reasonably sure I would have heard about it by now if, say, the Phantom had killed Raoul (not that I thought he would). I was even more sure that something exciting must have happened. We could talk about that, I could satisfy my curiosity—and then I did think I'd tell her about Léon. "Don't play coy with me," I said with a smile, "I don't believe that nothing at *all* happened, when you went off together with a handsome young man." I'd only gone as far as a balcony, and something had happened to me. Something *must* have happened to Christine.

"Well..." She left her comb by the mirror and sat on the bed opposite me, leaning in with a smile. "Do you promise to keep a secret?"

"Of course!" I said, leaning in too, eager for the next chapter of the story.

"*Well...*" she said, took a long, deep breath, and announced, "Raoul and I are going to be married!"

I stared at her, quite blank, not at all sure that I was understanding her sentence. "You're...going to be married? He asked you?" Noblemen didn't marry girls from the Opera. Everyone knew that. It was a fact, like knowing that the Opera opened in 1875.

"Yes, we are! Isn't it exciting?" She reached out and hugged me tightly.

"Yes..." I said, hugging her back with only a momentary delay. I tried to be excited, to be swept along on my best friend's happiness. But somehow it just—it didn't fit together. The excitement wasn't there, too overwhelmed by confusion. "It's only, you always said he was just a friend." And noblemen don't marry chorus girls, I repeated silently. I had no expectations that Léon would marry me. Not that I wanted him to, or had even thought about that very much.

"But you never believed Raoul was just a friend anyway," she laughed.

True. And Raoul might get a romantic notion into his head in the moonlight, and be foolish and impetuous enough to follow through on it. Had he told his brother yet? Somehow it was easier to feel worried about that, than to feel excited by the whole thing.

That must have shown on my face, because Christine pulled back with a little frown. "Aren't you happy for me? I thought you would be."

"Of course I am," I said quickly, trying to smile naturally. "If you're happy." This was so inadequate, and I couldn't tell her what I was really thinking. I flailed for a reason. "I was just thinking...it's a shame you'll have to give up singing." And leave the Opera. Leave me, though I might be going anyway.

An expression I couldn't read flashed through Christine's brown eyes, an instant before a little pout took over her face. "Don't be silly, that won't happen! Raoul knows my singing is very important to me. He'd never make me give that up."

"Mmm," was all I managed in response to that. Noblemen did not marry chorus girls, and they *certainly* did not have wives who sang professionally. Which was too bad, really, because they did have the connections and the money to advance an artist's career—but that was something they did for their mistresses, not for their wives.

This whole pretty idea she'd apparently built up—it was a cloud castle, it couldn't really happen. I was a dreamer, but my mother had taught me *something* about the world. I knew the dreams that were impossible.

"I'll marry Raoul," Christine resumed, "and I'll still keep singing too. So you *can* be happy for me." A little edge had entered her usually sweet voice. "I know so many girls at the Opera will be jealous, but of course *you* wouldn't be."

"About *Raoul?*" I said, unthinkingly, and regretted it as her eyes darkened again. "I mean—you two are so perfect together. Obviously he'd never be interested in anyone else." The more I thought about Raoul, maybe her cloud castle was a little less mad. If ever a nobleman might be persuaded by his wife on, well, any subject at all, Raoul certainly fit the role.

And she was Christine. If anyone deserved everything, if anyone was likely to get it, surely it was beautiful, talented, charming Christine.

"So, tell me how it all happened," I said, trying to put enthusiasm in my voice, trying to feel that enthusiasm. Maybe this would turn out to be a happy love story after all. "Where did you go when you left the masquerade?"

I was expecting that they had gone to a café, or for a walk down the brightly-lit Avenue de l'Opera, or maybe to the Tuileries. I was not expecting her to say, "We went up to the roof of the Opera."

I had almost forgotten the Phantom's role in this story, until this suddenly brought it crashing back, worry twisting in my stomach as my resolution to be enthusiastic faded right away. "The roof," I repeated.

"Of the Opera." I had seen them going upstairs, but had never dreamed they'd *stayed* upstairs, gone all the way to the roof.

"Yes, it's so beautiful in the moonlight, with the lights of the city all spread out…and it was so quiet up there compared to the crowded masquerade. It was really the perfect setting."

I'm sure it was lovely, but that was hardly the point. I laced my fingers together. "What about the Phantom?"

She blinked once. "Goodness, Meg, I know you like to bring him into conversations, but I don't see what he has to do with—"

"He was at the masquerade. Red Death." It was perfectly valid to bring him into this conversation. "I saw you dancing with him, and then I saw him leave when you did." My fingers tightened. If they had left the Opera, they might have easily lost him—he might not have followed at all, I had no idea if he ever left the Opera—but to go up to the *roof*…

Christine looked away. "Oh. I didn't realize you knew…yes, I did see the Phantom at the masquerade. He asked me to dance and I didn't know it was him at first, but then—"

"Didn't you recognize his voice when he asked you to dance?" I interrupted, because how could anyone not? And Christine was a singer, who should know voices.

"I don't know, the party was so loud." She stood, went over to her mirror and picked up her comb again. "But then after we danced—he was very upset that I was dancing with Raoul. Remember I told you he would be? And I tried to explain that it didn't mean anything important, but he wouldn't believe me. It was quite alarming, that's why I thought it would be best if we left."

It made sense so far, mostly. Except she had insisted he wasn't dangerous. It could be awkward, though. So maybe that made sense. Except… "But he followed you out. Didn't you notice?" I had noticed.

Christine sat down at her vanity, didn't look away from the mirror. "It was very crowded."

"With that red hat, how could you possibly miss—"

"I did see something, I wasn't sure—but anyway, that was why I went to the roof, I was sure he wouldn't follow us all the way up there.

He so obviously belongs in the cellars and the darkness, I couldn't imagine him on the roof."

I didn't bother pointing out that the roof at night is in darkness, and went to the more important point. "But he *does* go to the roof. You knew that."

"No, I didn't," Christine said, with a stroke of her comb. "And I don't see how you can either."

She didn't see—how could she *not* see? "But I *told* you—that time I met him—he told me that I should go see the views from the roof." She had her back to me, still looking into the mirror, and I couldn't manage to catch even her reflected eyes. "He couldn't possibly give that kind of advice unless he went up there himself. And that means…" I locked my hands together, one piece of information connecting with another and another, like a line of dancers falling one into another to a final hideous crash. "If he followed you all the way to the roof, and then Raoul proposed and you accepted, and you had told the Phantom you only cared about your career—and you said he's in love with you…"

Christine set her comb down with a click and shivered. "What a horrible idea, Meg! That someone eavesdropped on one of the most important, most private moments of my life."

That pulled me up short. That wasn't one of the disasters I had imagined in my tumbling line. I wouldn't want someone eavesdropping on that kind of conversation. I wouldn't have wanted someone eavesdropping when I was on the balcony Sunday night. Even so, my first thought was how painful it must have been for the eavesdropper, up on that rooftop. And everyone, *everyone* knew that you don't discuss private business at the Opera Garnier if you don't want the Phantom to hear.

"You shouldn't have gone to the roof," I said crisply. "Didn't you expect he would follow?"

"Of course I didn't expect it!" Christine protested, turning to look at me with wide eyes. "I didn't know he went up to the roof—you must not have mentioned that part of the story."

"We were *on the roof* when I told you," I said, hearing my voice rise but not managing to stop it. "I wouldn't have left that part out. And how could you have forgotten it?"

"I don't know, Meg!" Christine cried, waving her hands in a helpless dismissal. "That hardly seems like the important thing right now."

I was at a loss to explain. My story was important—to *me*. If she was my best friend, shouldn't that make it important to her too? Shouldn't she at least bother to remember some of the more relevant details?

Christine turned away again, began playing with the objects on her table, picking up a perfume bottle, setting it down to reach for a ribbon instead. "I suppose the Phantom could have overheard everything. And maybe that's really for the best, if he did."

Was it just me, or was the world not making sense today? "How can that be for the best? That must have been incredibly painful—"

"But now he knows," Christine said with unusual gravity. "It's best to know the truth in the long-run, isn't it?"

In theory, but the actuality felt deeply uncomfortable. "I suppose, but—"

"And while I'm very sorry, of course, you can't expect that I'd give up a life with Raoul to avoid giving the Phantom a little discomfort."

That seemed to minimize it rather—how deeply did the Phantom care for Christine? And it wasn't that I thought she shouldn't marry Raoul, but that she should have handled the matter differently. "No...but—"

"Now, if I'm going to be ready to sing at the gala tonight, I have a million things to do first." She rose to her feet, clearly intent on ushering me towards the door.

I resisted, remaining on the bed, staring at her as I tried to take in this new piece of information. "You're still going to sing tonight?" Even though she was engaged to Raoul? Even though the Phantom knew now that she had chosen the handsome nobleman? What might he do in response? The memory of Buquet flashed into my mind.

Surely he would do nothing like *that*. But Christine had never seemed to take him seriously enough.

"Of course I'm still going to sing," Christine said, innocently matter-of-fact. "It's such a wonderful opportunity, I certainly don't intend to miss it. Raoul understands that it's important to me, and after all, it should make the Phantom happy since he wanted me to have the role. So it's best for everyone."

How could she really believe *that* was what the Phantom found most important? But nothing I said could sway her from that happy delusion, and I couldn't avoid for long being dismissed and shown the door. Outside, I walked slowly down the street, my feet automatically following the route to the Opera. I twisted my necklace and tried to unravel what had just happened.

She should have remembered about the rooftop, about that detail of the most important story I'd ever told. How could she forget that?

But if she didn't forget it, if she remembered and had gone to the roof... No, that didn't make sense either.

In fact, now that I was walking in the clear air and putting it all together, none of it made sense.

If she had been afraid of the Phantom, trying to escape him, why had she left the crowded masquerade and gone off alone with Raoul? I wouldn't put faith in him if it came to a fight. Maybe she would, but why risk it? Why hadn't she simply taken Raoul out the door of the Foyer, down a flight of stairs and straight out into Paris' streets? With Raoul's carriage, they could have gone anywhere.

Instead, she had chosen to go *up* ten flights of stairs, to a deserted rooftop that was still in the Phantom's domain, putting the entirety of the Opera Garnier between her and the street. Perhaps she was upset and wasn't thinking clearly...but who has an instinct to run away upstairs? Who flees along the path of *most* resistance?

Uncomfortably, without intending it, I was remembering what she had said to me once, about how to get rid of an unwanted suitor. Just show a marked preference for another one, and they'll get the message. If she had known the Phantom would follow...if she had known he would be there on the rooftop...then she could have arranged the whole interlude with Raoul to happen in a way that would also get rid of the Phantom.

Once I had put it into words, I was aghast at my own line of reasoning. This wasn't an opera. People did not orchestrate elaborate plots like that, and *of course* Christine wouldn't. She was thoughtful, naïve, kind, innocent. She was my *friend*; I knew she wouldn't set out to hurt the Phantom, or anyone, like that.

I stared at my reflection in a shop window as I passed, noticed the worried pucker of my forehead. Was I really concerned about Christine's secret motivations—or was it easier to think of far-fetched plots than to deal with the reality? I was leaving the Opera, unless something very improbable happened at my mother's meeting with the managers tonight. And my best friend was engaged to a man who couldn't possibly marry her. Everything seemed to be falling apart.

When I reached the Opera, I found that the Company was swirling around in nearly the same circles my mind had been spinning in. About tonight, although they were on about the gala, not the potential outcomes of my mother's conversation with the management. And about Christine and Raoul and a secret engagement that evidently had not managed to stay secret for even forty-eight hours.

It was all over the Opera that Raoul and Philippe had had a shouting fight over breakfast that morning, on the subject of Christine Daaé and matrimony. Apparently one of their maids had told a friend who told a cousin who told one of Carlotta's hairdressers who told Carlotta—who told everyone. The report was that Phillipe had thrown an entire twelve-person tea service against a wall, although since I couldn't imagine two bachelors having a tea service for twelve on the table at breakfast, that seemed likely to be exaggeration.

Although the reaction, emotionally at least, seemed perfectly reasonable. Some things weren't making sense, but apparently my worries about this engagement actually lasting, about Christine not getting hurt in all this, were completely valid.

The Opera was in particular chaos the day of the gala, and the Phantom watched it all with a cold and calculating eye. Chaos was good. He approved of chaos.

He walked above the frantic clamor, metaphorically and sometimes literally in his hidden passages, looking for the right strings to pluck to make the symphony go as he desired.

It was impossible to miss the many conversations about the de Chagnys, and about—her. He couldn't quell an initial stab of pain at hearing his private tragedy bandied about as mere Opera gossip, but he did his best to ignore the feeling. Looking at the matter logically, it was all for the best. It would provide such an effective smoke screen, other directions for the finger of blame to point after the evening's events were done.

He didn't expect *her* to arrive at the Opera until shortly before the performance, and busied himself with other matters. He listened to the managers long enough to confirm that Moncharmin really had 20,000 francs in his carefully-guarded pocket and that their plan was still as it had been.

Commissaire Mifroid arrived and the Phantom listened as the man directed three of his officers to spread out through the Opera and stay alert. He was alert to Mifroid's barely-concealed amusement as he gave the orders, dismissed the policeman as no real threat, and went on to other tasks.

He released a dozen large spiders into the ballet girls' dressing room, and set the gas lights flickering for good measure. That had long been a supposed sign of the Ghost's presence. With a dark thread of amusement, he decided to be a bit flashier for the singers. Such a lot of stage blood was always at hand in an opera house, and the hallway outside the singers' rooms had such elegant, pale green walls, a very effective canvas for mysterious drips from the ceiling. The Phantom had been tempted by the idea many times before, but it had always seemed a bit...much. Tonight, though, this was the night.

Best to keep the superstitious on edge tonight, to set the right tone for what would surely be a very exciting evening at the Opera. He didn't bother waiting around for the shrieks, but went off instead to confirm that the management had not sold Box Five for the evening, reserving it for their laughably ineffective trap instead.

By then the carriages were arriving for the most important guests. He was unsurprised to find that the Vicomte de Chagny's driver insisted on being parked in a spot that would give clear access to a rapid exit, per the vicomte's orders, and refused to have his horses unharnessed. It was more surprising to find that the Comte de Chagny's driver was making the same insistences. Two men planning to leave the Opera Garnier in great haste?

Two men who, upon reflection, both had compelling reasons to feel Christine Daaé should not be at the Opera anymore. How very interesting. And how very easily foiled by slipping a sleeping draught into the flasks both drivers carried—against the cold, of course. If all went according to plan, the drivers and their carriages should be quite irrelevant, but he saw no need to take chances.

Once that was done, it was time to return to the managers' office, for their meeting with Madame Giry. As the Phantom strode along a hidden passage, parallel to the conventional corridor, he recognized the voices in the conversation he was overhearing: Madame Giry and her daughter, confirming that he was precisely on time.

"We've been over this," Madame Giry was saying, "and you know the timing makes it impossible."

"I'll just come for a few minutes. Just long enough to find out what the managers want."

"What you'll do is turn left at the next corner and get to the ballet's dressing room, which is where you already should be."

If he was any judge of the current chaos engulfing that particular room, it was highly unlikely that anyone in the corps de ballet had noted her absence. Idly, Erik wondered if Meg Giry was afraid of spiders.

"Fine, but you'll tell me what they say? Come find me backstage—"

"If I can, I will. In any case, I'll certainly see you after the performance."

A sigh from Meg. "All right, I'm going, see you later…"

He quickened his pace down the narrow passage, was soon hidden with a good view of the managers' office through a peephole. In an opera, no doubt he would have been looking out through the eyes of a portrait, but in life he had found that pinholes in wooden walls were far harder to detect.

He was in place in time to hear the managers usher Madame Giry in.

"We really are so very glad you agreed to meet with us," Ricard said, overflowing with graciousness.

By contrast, Moncharmin's tone was decidedly dour. "Yes, just delighted."

Madame Giry matched his lack of enthusiasm. "Likewise, I'm sure." Clearly she was suspicious of the whole business. Wise woman. The atmospheric music in minor key was all but audible in the air, and would have been actual in an opera at this moment.

"Do have a seat," Ricard urged, then went on to a long, enthusiastic, and rather convoluted not-quite-apology for recent events. Within the first sentence, the Phantom's view was cut-off by Moncharmin, who leaned against the wall during this monologue, pressing his back directly over the peephole.

The Phantom glared through the wood at the unaware manager for a moment, and then had a thought. There was a small sliding panel in this wall, and it was at just the right height. Ricard had his back to Moncharmin, Madame Giry was probably looking at Ricard, and really it was a golden opportunity. It was not according to his original plan, but how could he resist? He slid open the panel, reached out with one gloved hand, and plucked the envelope with the 20,000 francs out of Moncharmin's jacket pocket. It took barely another breath to replace it with the identical envelope he had already prepared, intending to leave it in Box Five later.

Moncharmin never moved, Ricard never interrupted his effusions, and if Madame Giry saw anything, she didn't mention it. That saved him a chore for later.

Ricard finally wound up with, "And so we've decided to go along with this Phantom business, and to show we have no hard feelings, we'd like to have you deliver this month's salary to Box Five."

A long pause followed. Finally Madame Giry said, "I fail to see how my doing a favor for you demonstrates that *you* have no hard feelings towards me."

"Ah. Well…" Ricard stammered for a moment. Was the man actually stupid, or did he just depend too much on other people to be stupid and not ask awkward questions? Hard to say. "We'll pay you!" he said at last, and added, "Ten francs for the delivery," over Moncharmin's outraged cough.

"I think not," Madame Giry said, a rustle of skirts indicating she was rising to her feet.

"And we'll consider reinstatement," Moncharmin said quickly.

A slower rustling as she sat down again. "Very well," she said, though her voice was reluctant. "Give me the envelope and I'll take it to Box Five."

"Excellent," Moncharmin said, stepping away from the wall and pulling the envelope out of his pocket. "It's right here and—wait…"

Erik winced at the crinkling of paper.

"This is—this is—I've been robbed!"

Would it have been so hard for Moncharmin to pass the envelope on unopened? It might have been hours before anyone realized the francs had been replaced with cut-up playbills. So much for efforts to be efficient.

"You! You must have switched the envelopes!"

"That is ridiculous," Madame Giry said sharply. "How could I steal something I didn't know existed until this moment?"

"I don't know!" Moncharmin said, with near-hysteria in his voice. "How does a ghost get a salary to begin with? It's all part of a conspiracy!"

In a way. Was it possible for one man, acting alone, to perpetrate a conspiracy, or did the very name imply confederates?

"Moncharmin, maybe you should sit down," Ricard urged.

"It's *your* fault, you came up with this stupid plan!" A slam as the office door banged open into the opposite wall. "Police! Someone get the police, I—ah, Commissaire!"

A new, much calmer voice joined the discussion. "I was just coming to inform you that my men are patrolling the Opera. Everything should be—"

"Never mind that," Moncharmin interrupted, "I've been robbed!" That last word reached an octave above middle C, an impressive note to hit. "This woman—she stole my money!"

"Moncharmin, be reasonable," Ricard said. "She never got within a meter of you, so how could she steal something in your pocket?"

"And why would I steal something," Madame Giry interjected, "which you were about to hand to me?"

"All right, maybe it wasn't her directly, but it was the Phantom, and she's in on the plot!"

As if he had ever needed help. As if he had ever had anyone who would help.

A sigh from Commissaire Mifroid. "The Phantom is merely a superstition of the Opera Company. In six years no evidence has ever—"

"No evidence?" Moncharmin snapped. "Just a box that's never rented out, at considerable loss of money, and a boxkeeper who claims there's a ghost in it. Not to mention my lead soprano says he vandalized her dressing room, and sent her threatening letters. *And* my twenty-thousand francs is missing!"

"Would Signora Carlotta be able to produce these letters?" Mifroid asked, and the Phantom did not approve of the new interest in his voice.

"Never mind that, what are you going to do about my money?"

"*Our* money, Moncharmin, ten-thousand of it was mine."

"I understand you wish to report a robbery," Mifroid said, accompanied by a rustling of paper. It must be that notebook he carried around. "Who else was aware that you were carrying such a large sum of money?"

"Just the two of us," Ricard answered.

"That's right! *You* knew!"

"Oh come now, Moncharmin, you aren't suggesting—"

"I don't know, nothing makes sense since we came to this blasted opera house. It's this Phantom, he's behind it all."

"If we have established that I did *not* pick your pocket," Madame Giry interjected, "may I leave now?"

"Don't let her go," Moncharmin ordered, "she knows something about this Phantom."

"I do feel you should remain for the time-being, Madame," Mifroid said. "I would like to speak with Christine Daaé as well. She has recently claimed an association with this so-called Phantom."

The so-called Phantom flinched at that. That was not a good connection for the Commissaire of Police to be making. And what did he mean, she'd 'claimed an association?' She hadn't wanted to go to the police—perhaps that idiot boy had done it over her objections. It would be like him.

"Mademoiselle Daaé is singing in the gala performance tonight," Ricard said, then inhaled sharply. "Moncharmin, the performance! It's due to start any moment. We should be out there—"

"Not until we find my money!"

The Phantom moved away from the wall, ran one hand along the rough plaster as he walked silently through the passage. Whatever M. Moncharmin wanted to do, *he* could not afford to wait any longer. Altogether too many men were too interested in Christine this evening. If he could overhear Moncharmin's shouts, someone in the corridor beyond the office would as well. Considering the average speed of gossip, the entire Company would know the whole story within ten minutes. Maybe eight. It was entirely possible one of the Brothers de Chagny would hear something, become spooked and refuse to wait for the end of the performance. That meant the Phantom had to accelerate his plans as well.

Could he do it without attracting the suddenly-alert commissaire's attention...or perhaps that didn't matter. With Carlotta's letters, the managers' and Madame Giry's testimony, it was all but inevitable that Commissaire Mifroid would at last come to believe in the existence of the Opera Ghost.

But what of it? He had nothing left to lose, was already throwing everything away on a wild, hopeless chance at gaining the only thing he cared about.

Tonight, it was time for the monster to stop hiding.

Chapter Twenty-Eight

I could have been later getting to the ballet's dressing room. No one noticed I was missing. No one was noticing anything at all except the spiders.

Girls were flying here, there and everywhere, in a confusion of tulle skirts and bare limbs. Even the ones who weren't normally upset by spiders were being set off by the others, there were shrieks and shouts and frantic demands for someone to do something, and I was not in the mood for the whole business.

"Oh for heaven's sake, they're just *spiders*," I said to the room at large. No one bothered responding. The room was always chaotic, but this was a new level.

"There must be dozens of them!" Francesca moaned near me, her final word almost drowned out by renewed shrieks from two girls as they sprang away from a dressing table, pointing frantically at a black spider on its surface.

I marched that way, picking up a stray scarf as I went, and dodging the two girls leaping past me. I looked down at the table, studying the spider. It was large, maybe the size of a sous, but it had no red markings or other indications it was one of the few venomous varieties. I snatched up an empty glass from the table and clapped it over the spider. It scurried obligingly up the side of the glass, making it easy to pick up and turn over, throw the scarf over the top, and carry the whole thing to the room's one narrow window. I deposited the spider on the sill, watched for a moment as it crawled off across the building wall, then went back for the next.

I let two more spiders out and was trying for a fourth (from the way it was racing about, I was sure it was at least as hysterical as the ballet girls) when Jammes strode up.

"I don't know why you're bothering with all that," she said, and smacked the spider with the heavy toe of a ballet slipper.

I looked hurriedly away from the smashed spider when she lifted the shoe. "You didn't have to do that."

She smirked. "It was a lot faster than your method."

I seriously considered throwing one of my own slippers at her. I might have done it—but Madame Thibault arrived at that moment, to gaze around at the disorder and demand, "Just what is going on here?"

A clamor arose. The clearest voice proclaimed, "The Phantom cursed us with spiders!"

I might have guessed he'd come into it somewhere.

Madame Thibault stared hard at the speaker. "Did he also curse you with stupidity?" She did not wait for a response, turning to snap orders for this girl to get off the table and that one to finish dressing and would you three pin up your hair and had anyone noticed that we were all due on-stage in less than ten minutes?

She got us herded into line and out the door and to our place backstage in reasonably good order, though more than one girl kept twitching and brushing away spiders that weren't there. Once we were backstage I slipped to the edge of the crowd, ostensibly so I'd have more room to stretch my legs and practice my plies, but it also gave me a reasonably good vantage point. I looked around as I lifted into a releve, but saw no sign of Mother yet. I did see Christine across the stage in the opposite wing, wearing a long white dress and looking like the personification of serenity.

She had the only calm face in the crowd. Everyone else I could see appeared particularly anxious tonight. Tension permeated the atmosphere before every performance, but this was something more. Maybe because this one was special.

The ballet girls told anyone who would listen about the invasion of spiders, while a number of singers reported that the corridor outside their dressing room was haunted by a malignant presence who had dripped blood down the walls. Since walls covered with blood came up in the rumors at least monthly, I didn't pay it much attention.

I kept watching for Mother, and instead saw Samuel, the vocal director's assistant, rush in and hurry over to Monsieur Montagne and Madame Thibault. They were standing near enough for me to hear him report, "The managers said we should go ahead and start!"

The vocal director's head reared back and his eyebrows rose to absurd heights. "But the managers are supposed to give an opening speech. It is *their* special event."

Samuel raised his hands in a helpless gesture. "I knocked on the door and M. Moncharmin told me to go away. So I knocked again, and this time he opened it, but when I told him the show was scheduled to start, he told me to go ahead and start then." His voice dropped to a hushed tone that didn't hide his words at all. "And behind him, I saw the *police commissaire*."

That set off a series of whispers and murmurs from everyone else who was also close enough to be eavesdropping. What was Commissaire Mifroid doing with the managers? It couldn't involve Mother, but I worried about the Phantom. I shook my head slightly. Mifroid didn't believe in the Phantom. He'd be fine.

"Then we start the performance," Madame Thibault said, and nodded to the assistant. "Go inform the conductor."

Within moments the orchestra began, the music swelled, and the chorus streamed out onto the stage for the first number, while I wondered about the clearly more exciting things happening elsewhere. If the managers were talking to Commissaire Mifroid, then they must be done talking to Mother. So where was she and what had happened and when would I be able to find out?

I was far too impatient for this whole business to be over to enjoy the chorus' song. It would be the ballet next, then Christine had a duet with the lead tenor, then the ballet again—and maybe I could slip away after that, find out what was happening.

News came to me instead, by way of Sabine, a chorus member who apparently was not assigned in the current scene and had snuck off earlier. She came hurrying back now, with that bright-eyed and pink-cheeked look that meant the most exciting of gossip was at hand.

She plunged into the crowd of dancers, announcing in a loud whisper, "I was just past the managers' office—you'll never believe—the managers have accused Madame Giry of *stealing* from them!"

My stomach dropped away and my limbs felt like ice. Risen on my toes, I thudded back to the soles of my feet without feeling my legs. "They did what?"

My words cut across the excited murmurs and everyone fell suddenly silent, Sabine staring at me with eyes wide in embarrassment. "Oh. Meg. I, um…"

"I have to go," I said, and turned away. I'd go to the managers' office, I'd find out what was happening, I'd *do* something—

Madame Thibault stepped into my path. "Mademoiselle Giry, you are due on stage in barely a minute."

I wove around her. "I *have* to go."

She stepped in front of me again. "The Opera does not look kindly on performers who fail to be in their places."

"So dismiss me," I snapped, glaring at her. "My mother is in trouble and—"

"—and you can do nothing now." She caught me by the upper arms when I moved to go around her again, and leaned in close to murmur in my ear, tone softer than I had ever heard it. "If you go there now, you will increase the confusion, upset the management further, and give them more reason to target your family for disrupting their precious performance. Trust your mother to handle this, Meg, while you fulfill your role in the dance."

I was more taken aback by her tone than her words. I reached for a response, came up with only, "My role's not important anyway." I was a long way from a lead ballerina, an *etoile*.

"Don't be ridiculous," she said, voice returned to its customary sharpness. "*Every* role is important in my ballet. Now go, the other girls are on their way out."

I went. I wasn't satisfied, but saw the logic to her argument—and though I wouldn't have backed down in a confrontation, warmth and understanding from Madame Thibault threw me so completely out of my intended choreography that I found myself heading for the stage before I had my mind back in order.

My thoughts never really lined up, and there were some wobbles in my dancing, some steps out of time, but I managed my role. And not all those missteps were my fault—most of the girls were more anxious, more on edge than usual.

Somehow we got to the end of our dance, and took up positions at the back of the stage to be part of the scenery for the upcoming song, until we were due to dance again. After that dance, I would try again to get away and go to Mother.

Christine and the lead tenor, Gascoigne, came out to center stage for their duet. A polite smattering of applause greeted their arrival, and I noticed a man standing in one of the boxes. He was small from the distance, but the lit chandelier cast enough light for me to be nearly sure it was Raoul.

Gascoigne sang first, launching into a love song in Italian. My gaze drifted over to the wings, thinking about how I could slip past Madame Thibault if she tried to stop me again.

That's when I noticed the disturbance. Two scenechangers were trying to restrain Philippe de Chagny. He had pushed his way to the very edge of the shadows, nearly onto the stage itself, before he consented to halt. He stood there, a scowl darkening his face, glaring at…I followed the direction of his gaze. Christine. Of course.

Then Christine began to sing, voice soaring up clear and haunting. My breath caught in my throat and I felt suddenly as though I might cry—it wasn't even a sad song, but it was *that* beautiful.

In the wings, on the stage, from what I could see of the audience, every head turned towards her. She had sung on this stage before, but now she outshone those previous performances like the sun outshines the moon. Her voice filled the auditorium, and even though all those people had to be breathing, I couldn't hear another sound.

Whatever else he might be, the Phantom was an excellent teacher.

Chapter Twenty-Nine

W hatever else she might be, she was an exquisite singer, with a
voice that nearly made him forget everything else. He had been
right about that much, all those months ago. If he truly was a
disinterested Angel, this would have been a moment of triumph, a
complete and fulfilling satisfaction.

Pity that it had never, ever been that simple.

Even so, it gave him pause. Perhaps he was wrong to interrupt
such a glorious performance. Perhaps it was a mistake to accelerate his
plans instead of waiting for the gala's close.

But a few bars later the tenor joined in, his voice twining with
Christine's, and the Phantom clenched his hands and resolved that there
would be no more waiting. He had created her voice. From now on, she
would sing for *him* alone.

It was too late to go back now. The opening strains had already
sounded, the orchestration was already in play. The gas-man and his
assistants were drugged and unconscious. The proper wires had been cut,
the proper arrangements had been made, and all it needed was to pull one
lever and set the final piece in motion. So he walked across the small
chamber in the ceiling of the auditorium, pulled the lever in question, and
waited for the reaction.

The tenor noticed first. He was looking out towards the audience
and he faltered mid-line, voice dying away while Christine sang on.

High above the audience, the enormous chandelier ponderously swung back and forth, crystals chiming, shadows and lights dancing madly over the seats and their occupants. Some among the crowd began to notice, and a low, uncertain murmur broke the silence that had held sway since Christine's first note.

It needed something more—too many people were still in thrall to Christine's voice, not enough voices were raised in alarm. In all probability, half the audience would believe it was part of the show.

So he interrupted her singing, spoke over her song to fill the auditorium with his voice, as deep and thunderous and majestic as all his considerable skill could make it.

"Behold, she is singing to bring down the chandelier!" And he let his most mocking laughter follow.

Very satisfying shrieks arose at once from the corps de ballet on stage. The audience began rising to their feet, crying out about the chandelier. All it needed then was a few blinks of the gas lights and a full-scale panic reigned at the Opera.

He might not have bothered at all with dropping the heavy canvas scenery at the back of the stage, but why waste the preparations? The crash did speed the exodus up nicely.

He slipped out of his hiding place near the ceiling and clambered down the pillar beside the Imperial box. The occupants had already fled and he paused for just a moment on the balustrade of the box to look at the stage. Most of the performers had abandoned their places and run shrieking away. As usual. He was counting on Christine standing frozen in the center of the stage for just the few seconds he needed, but he'd hunt her out of the rushing crowd if he had to. It wasn't as though seizing a girl off the stage was a discreet plan anyway.

But no, she was still there—and so was Philippe de Chagny, shoving against the flow of the crowd to reach Christine, to grab her by the arm and pull her towards the wing.

There was not the slightest chance that the comte simply had her welfare in mind. Fury coiling in his stomach, the Phantom was almost glad to have such a convenient target. Just another moment to reach the stage—he leaped down from the Imperial Box, cloak trailing him, landing in the shadows of the stalls near the orchestra pit.

And then he halted, suddenly realizing that the movement of the shadows was too wrong, too extreme. He looked up, saw what everyone else in the rapidly emptying auditorium no doubt already knew. The chandelier was still swinging, and the swings were growing wider.

By his calculations, it *should* have been settling by now. Had he misjudged the force, pushed it too far? And wasn't it lower than usual?

With a sickening twist in his stomach, he realized that one of the supports must have broken, setting the chandelier off-balance, sending it swinging back and forth below the domed ceiling, faster than anything that big should ever move. If it kept on like this, the ceiling would crack, more supports would go…

It might not be too late, if he got up there now—his gaze leaped to the stage, to where he had seen Philippe de Chagny dragging Christine away.

Even over the shrieks, the cries, the stampede of footsteps, he could hear the ominous creak of the chandelier. Then a sharp crack as another support gave way, all the crystals in the chandelier chiming and rattling as the giant structure dropped another meter.

In his mind's eye, Philippe's glower and Christine's fear-filled eyes were still vivid.

With a curse and a silent apology to Charles Garnier, Erik sprinted for the stage.

The girls around me went into a panic as soon as they noticed the chandelier swaying. I stared at those swinging lights and held my breath waiting for them to *stop*, because of course it was going to stop, whatever he said about bringing it down this had to be a bluff, he couldn't really mean…I exhaled in something that may have resembled a shriek when the scenery crashed down behind me, dust billowing up around us.

That was enough to send everyone still on stage running for the exits and it was enough for me too. Whatever I thought about the Phantom, I wanted to be somewhere with a nice, low ceiling overhead right now.

But as I headed for the wings, I saw someone going the opposite direction. I turned against the tide of people to watch Philippe de Chagny push through the crowd to Christine, who was still standing in the middle of the stage, still staring out at the audience. He reached Christine and grabbed her by the arm. I felt the ghost of that same hand gripping my arm and winced in sympathy.

I couldn't hear anything they said, but his furious expression and her shrinking away made the situation clear. He started pulling her towards the opposite wings, which in the mass exodus had been left emptier than my own side. I took a deep breath, hoped desperately that everything hanging overhead would *stay* there, and ran across the stage after Christine.

I caught up to them among the curtains of backstage, noticing out of the corners of my awareness that, despite the masses of people only a short distance away, Philippe had managed to find an empty space.

"Let her go!" I grabbed Philippe by the arm, thinking to pry at the fingers wrapped all too tightly around Christine's shoulder.

"Stay out of this, girl," he ordered, shaking me off and jerking the sobbing Christine in the process.

I flung myself at his back. If he'd just loosen his hold enough for Christine to wrench away... Instead, Philippe broke free of me again.

"Ballet rats should remember their place," he growled.

He dealt me a back-hand that sent me stumbling, face stinging. I banged into a prop table that tipped beneath my weight and I fell with a crash into the shadows cast by tall curtains, sprawling among fake swords, masks and all the other detritus of backstage, the end of the curtains whispering over me.

I pushed myself up on one elbow, head reeling, tried to push the curtain away. Philippe didn't even glance at me, continuing to pull Christine along. They had only gone a few steps, and I was still seeking the wits and the strength to get up, when a cloaked figure in a skull mask came up at a run.

"*Let her go.*" His voice echoed and thundered and sounded infinitely more threatening than mine had, saying the same words.

Philippe was less impressed. "I have had enough interference from you Opera people. Get out of my way!"

The Phantom's whole body was tense, voice tight and terrifying. "I told you to let her go. Or I will kill you." The threat held no bravado, no melodrama, only iron certainty. It wasn't even directed at me, and I still felt my heart beat faster.

The comte's face was red with rage, his hand still tight around Christine's arm as she shrank away from him. "How dare you threaten me, you insolent, arrogant *actor*."

"I warned you, Monsieur Comte," the Phantom growled, stalking closer.

He didn't seem to notice me in my shadows, curtains and fallen props. I held my breath and stayed where I was, afraid of what I might see but finding it impossible to look away.

"What is it about Christine Daaé that drives men insane?" Philippe sneered. "You and my brother may be under her spell, but not me. And I will never allow a little tramp to—"

And then the world broke apart in a tumult of sound. The air filled with a screech of horribly overtaxed metal, screams and shrieks mingling with the sound, and a second later a crash, so loud I felt it in my teeth and my bones, felt the vibration through the floor. Everything shook, the curtains swaying and the huge stage itself rattling, amidst the tiny crashes of smaller objects falling and shattering. The Phantom flinched, and that was almost more alarming than the crash itself. I couldn't breathe, ears ringing, unable to cope with what that sound could mean.

The comte and I both looked in the direction of the disaster. The Phantom didn't. Christine moaned and fainted, falling out of Philippe's grip and slumping to the floor.

"What was that?" Philippe demanded, for the first time a tremor of fear beside his anger.

"That, my dear comte, was death." The Phantom's voice was icy, as he jabbed one finger towards the auditorium, out of sight beyond the stage curtains. "That was *Götterdämmerung* and the Last Trumpet and the sun crashing out of the sky. That was the chandelier falling and it is *your* fault. I might have stopped it if I wasn't here dealing with *you*!"

It took me a strange length of time to make sense of his words. The chandelier? Yes, it had been swinging, but that was just smoke and mirrors, like the flaming skeleton. The chandelier could not fall, not the enormous, glittering, multi-ton chandelier. As soon say that Notre Dame's centuries-old towers had gone pitching into the Seine.

"Who are you, to make accusations and—"

"I am the Phantom of the Opera!"

Philippe laughed, but it sounded shaky. "There is no Phantom. That's a story Daaé made up."

"Is it?" The ice had long ago cracked. Now it was flaming, towering rage. "Am I just a story?" He reached up and snatched away the mask hiding his face. "*Am I?*"

For a heartbeat my gaze followed the skull mask in his hand with a kind of eerie fascination. The Phantom wouldn't take his mask off. It was part of him, part of how I had always pictured him, since I was a child. The Phantom without his mask was as impossible a thing as…well, as the chandelier falling.

Out of the corner of my eye I saw Philippe recoil, and my gaze rose to see what he was seeing, to look at the Phantom's face. Even if I felt like I shouldn't be seeing it, I wasn't going to politely avert my glance.

For a second or two, my eyes widening and hand clapping to my mouth, I wished I had. I swallowed, hard. The left side of the Phantom's face was as I remembered it, ordinary, with an arch of eyebrow, a vivid green eye above a strong cheekbone, a faint shadow of cheek and a defined jawline. That side was handsome.

But then the right side…where the lines of the left should have been reflected was warped distortion. A bulging ridge of flesh marked his forehead, spread across the temple and curved under his eye to meet the twisted half of his nose. His right eye, a match to the left, sat in a dark hollow. No eyebrow at all. That side, nearly to the jaw, was marked by reddish patches, not wounds but discolorations, accentuated further by the shadows and lumps of uneven skin. The distortion skirted his lips, and that perfect eye and unmarked mouth emphasized the wrongness of the rest, hinting at the face that should have been there. That was part of the trouble, the eye trying to fill in the echo of the unmarked side.

I took a breath, then another. With my third, air began to come easier. That first, heart-stopping shock faded, and I found myself thinking that it wasn't really *that* bad. I wasn't blind—it was bad—but after the build-up Christine had given, raving about his misshapen, monstrous face, about almost fainting away at the sight, I had been picturing all sorts of horrors. Oozing sores or bared bone. Probably no reality could have compared to what I'd been conjuring up.

The long, suspended moment with the Phantom glaring, Philippe frozen, the unconscious Christine still collapsed on the floor, was broken by the shrill notes of policemen's whistles and barked commands coming from the direction of the auditorium.

"*Merde*," the Phantom muttered. He took two steps forward and slammed the side of one fist against Philippe's jaw. The comte's head snapped to the side, in time to meet the Phantom's other fist, hitting just above his temple. Philippe's eyes rolled back and his body slumped to the floor.

He'd been holding back against Buquet.

The Phantom scooped up the unconscious Christine, flinging her over one shoulder, and ran a few paces to a square of floor that looked exactly like everywhere else. He knelt down, still balancing Christine, and a trapdoor opened at his feet. He slipped through, the door swinging closed behind them.

It all took less than a breath of time.

I blinked twice, staring at the empty space where the Phantom and my best friend had so recently been. Then I climbed slowly out of the fallen costumes and props. My legs consented to take my weight, just, and I crossed unsteadily to where Erik and Christine had vanished. Where I thought it was. Already I wasn't sure precisely which square of floor had opened, and wouldn't have known how to open it even if I knew which it was. I looked at one square and then another, fingering my necklace and trying to think, to reason out what I ought to do now.

Behind me, Philippe groaned, and I looked to see him lifting his head.

It was obvious I couldn't follow Christine and the Phantom, and the thought of dealing with the waking comte made my breath catch and my knees go even shakier. I fled, coming out of the wings and continuing a few steps onto the stage before arriving at a horrified halt.

He had said it was the chandelier, but that hadn't prepared me for the mass of metal and twisted strands of crystals on the floor of the auditorium, seats crushed beneath. Those were the comparatively whole pieces, sitting at the center of a sparkle of shattered glass and dusting of plaster powder sprayed out around the destruction. Instinctively my gaze darted up, as if somehow, against all the evidence, the familiar, perfect chandelier could still be hanging there. Instead, there was a gaping hole, a spiderweb of cracks, a fractured chain. I didn't know how to take in an immutable piece of my world changing so horrifically, how to handle the heavens crashing to earth.

Awful fascination drew my gaze back to the disaster below. Fires from the lit chandelier were flickering out over the seats, darting over the rows of red velvet. More reassuring, the ruined chandelier was surrounded by men, some uniformed, beating at the flames and calling orders for buckets of water.

I felt ill. Who had been sitting in those seats below the chandelier? Had they still been there when the sun fell?

No, I couldn't think about that now, I had to think what to *do*—Mother. I had to find Mother, accused by the managers of theft, back before the world broke apart. I didn't know how to help or even find Christine, so I'd try to help Mother.

Chapter Thirty

H e carried her below the Opera, firmly banishing all thoughts of Hades and Persephone, and finally set her down on one of his couches. He looked at her for a moment, with her eyes closed and hair falling over the pillows, wearing the white dress from the gala. Even now, even after everything that had happened, she still seemed to glow. She still looked like an angel, lit from within, shedding her radiance in his dark life.

He turned away, feeling weary, drained of the passion he had felt above. "You may as well stop pretending to be unconscious."

A few heartbeats slipped by before he heard cloth rustling and pillows shifting as she sat up. "How did you know?"

"Faints don't last that long. And you were too tense." He walked over to the fireplace, snapped his fingers and listened to the crackle of burning wood as the flames flickered into life.

"Why didn't you say something sooner?"

"Carrying you was easier than arguing with you." He turned to face her again, felt a fresh surge of pain when she flinched and looked away. It had been a mad impulse to pull his mask off up above. Not that a skull mask would have reassured her. But then, he was not in the mood for reassurances. That single gesture, that rejection of refusing to even look at him—it was kindling his anger again.

"I don't understand…what's happening?" she asked, voice wavering.

"But you must understand, Christine, you wrote the libretto," he said with a false gaiety, then let his words turn cold. "Didn't you expect the *monster* to do something terrible? What do you imagine your precious Raoul will do about it now that it's happened?"

She looked down, pulled a pillow from the couch onto her lap to hold. "Oh. You know about that."

He ached with fury and betrayal. For days he'd held it all in, and now he could finally express the rage he felt. "Yes, of course I know, I'm an *Angel*, remember? We know everything!"

"I didn't mean to hurt you," she whispered, tightening her fingers on the plush of the pillow.

"Then maybe you should have been *honest!*" He paced a step closer to her, hands in fists at his sides. "Maybe you should have done me the courtesy of telling the truth instead of lying about needing me!"

Her expression crumpled and she turned towards the pillows, hiding her face, shoulders shaking.

He lifted his hands to his head, squeezed his eyes shut in frustration. "Don't *cry*, I can't be angry if you cry." He wanted to be angry. It was so much easier to be angry. But crying set off all his instincts to protect her, confusing the pure, simple flame of fury he'd much rather let consume him.

"It's just—all gone wrong," she sobbed, her beautiful voice catching and breaking. "It wasn't supposed—to go this way."

The flame inside him flickered, fluttered and went out, taking with it the sense of certainty and purpose that had sustained him for two days. He sat down heavily on the opposite couch.

"I didn't want it to go this way either." He thought of the crashed chandelier upstairs, of the screaming crowds, and knew the sounds would haunt him forever. A new sound embedded in his Opera, a painful counterpoint to the music and song. "I never wanted to scare you. That was the last thing I wanted." And the one thing he couldn't seem to avoid doing.

She didn't answer. No reassurance, no renewed accusation. The quiet grew and built, shaped by the faint sound of her breathing. He had dreamed of spending his life listening to that breath, that voice, and instead, somehow, it had come to this madness instead.

"Was it really that bad?" he asked. "That week you spent here?" The question was born of a tiny wisp of…it wasn't even hope, it was just denial. "Didn't you like the music, at least?"

A long pause, finally a sniffle and then, "I got…confused. I didn't know what to think, or feel—the music was so beautiful, and you were so…kind. But you wouldn't let me leave."

"We had an agreement about that." He had thought they understood each other. More or less.

"But you were keeping me here. You wouldn't have let me leave if I'd asked."

"Yes, I would have." He would have argued the idea, but if she had really insisted…he would have let her go. He was nearly sure of that.

A rustle now as she sat up very straight. "Then I want to leave. Right now."

A flicker of the anger reasserted itself. "That's not an option anymore," he said coldly, head held high. "I have to stop you from doing something stupid."

"I promise I won't let marrying Raoul stop me from singing—"

"It's not about your voice! It was never about your voice, you must have known that!" The excuse had been so painfully transparent at the time, she must have seen through it. "I love you," he said, the words an ache in his throat. "He will never love you the way I do."

"Raoul does love me," Christine whispered, pulling the pillow back into her lap, wrapping her arms around it. "I know he does."

"Is that what you want? A boy's love?" He pushed up from the couch, turned away when she flinched. "It has no depth, no true understanding."

"It's innocent."

"It's *passionless!*"

"At least he doesn't *frighten* me!" Christine snapped, sending a jab of pain through him. "At least," she continued, "he doesn't want to own me."

Erik let out a long breath, paced slowly to the fireplace to press one hand against the mantle, his back to the maddening, entrancing girl on his couch. "I don't want to own you, Christine." He rubbed one temple.

"Or maybe I do. I don't know—own, possess, love, belong, connect, they're all just words. They all mean different things to different people. I do know, whatever word you put on what I wanted from you, I also wanted just as much to *give*—my heart, my music, my life, everything I am or ever will be. What will your vicomte give you?"

She didn't even pause, didn't give his words even a moment to linger or sink in, instead announcing with a defiant pride, "Raoul wants to marry me."

The Phantom shrugged. That was so much more and so much less, and not any surprise regardless. "So he'll give you the de Chagny name. Is it so valuable?"

"He loves me—"

"He wants to *own you*," he cut in, turning to face her again. "Because he's a de Chagny. I'll grant that he's charmed enough to forget it for a while, but don't think he won't remember. At least I would have valued what you gave. He'll expect to own you, like any other piece of art, and take it so for granted that he won't even notice he's doing it."

She shook her head, brown curls flying. "You don't understand—"

"No, *you* don't understand." This was a pointless discussion. He was *tired* of the Vicomte de Chagny and all he stood for. "That's why I brought you here. To give you time to understand."

Her voice was faint. "How much time?"

He straightened his back, kept his voice steady. "As much as is necessary."

The Opera was even more frantic beyond the auditorium. All those special guests of the managers had flooded out into the corridors, and no one seemed to know what to do next or even which way to go. It was a mad crowd of shouts and cries and too many voices calling orders or making entreaties that no one else was paying attention to.

I hesitated in the doorway leading from backstage. I didn't feel remotely steady enough to confront that swirling chaos. But I had to, if I was going to find Mother.

I took a deep breath and plunged into the mass, squirming past furious guests demanding explanations and hysterical Company members shrieking about the Phantom. I saw Samuel, the vocal director's assistant, sitting on a side stair and clutching one ankle. How many other people had been injured in this mob—or from the chandelier?

No, still best not to think of that.

I nearly got caught in a cross-current of people being herded into a general evacuation, but managed to squeeze through to an adjoining corridor where the crush was a little less, and from there to the managers' office.

The door stood open, so I smoothed down my rumpled dance costume and walked in. It wasn't an evening for protocol. Opposite the door, against the far wall, the managers were sitting on a low couch. Ricard muttered frantically at the unresponsive Moncharmin, who clutched his hair and looked absolutely gray. Commissaire Mifroid sat behind the desk, conferring with a young man in police uniform. None of them gave me even a glance.

"Meg!"

I turned to my right, saw Mother rising from a chair, and hurried over to hug her. It was such a relief to see her, to see that she was all right and to know I wasn't alone in this madness now. I had to swallow and blink burning eyes, suddenly more overwhelmed by the events of the last few minutes than I had been while they were happening.

"I was so worried," she said into my hair. "They're saying the chandelier fell!"

"I'm fine." It was mostly true. When she leaned back to look at my face, eyes narrowing suspiciously, I tried my best to look calm and repeated it: "Really, I'm fine."

"Then what happened here?" she asked, and touched my cheek.

With everything else, I had almost forgotten about the comte hitting me. "It's not that bad." My eyes darted to the police commissaire. "I'll…tell you about it later."

Mother's stare was fixed on me, boring into me. "If someone—"

"Later, *please*," I said desperately. I couldn't tell her about Philippe without telling her about Christine, and about the Phantom, and should I tell Commissaire Mifroid that the Phantom of the Opera had carried my friend off below the stage? Maybe I should, maybe this was exactly the kind of thing I *should* tell the police—but he'd probably think I was insane. If he took me seriously—what do you do when someone you've been sure is watching out for the Opera for six years may or may not have kidnapped your friend?

I felt the strangest resentment towards Christine. If she hadn't fainted, I might have had a much clearer idea of whether she was in trouble. Was the Phantom being the ghost or the guardian? Abducting her, or simply rescuing her from the comte, from the chaotic crowd?

"But what's going on here?" I asked, trying for a subject change before Mother could continue pursuing the mark on my cheek, before we attracted the attention of the police commissaire. "I heard the most awful story."

"A mere misunderstanding," she said, leveling a glare at the managers. "M. Moncharmin has misplaced some money, and wants someone to blame. If not for this new crisis with the chandelier, I am sure the matter would already be settled."

At that moment, Commissaire Mifroid stood and turned to the managers. He had the calmest expression I'd seen all evening. "Gentlemen, my man here reports that the fire from the chandelier is contained and nearly out already. I sent a runner to the nearest station house some minutes ago for reinforcements to manage the crowd. I believe we can tentatively call the situation under control for the moment."

The idea that the fire might spread had never occurred to me. This was the Opera Garnier—it *couldn't* burn down.

"Chandeliers are expensive," Moncharmin muttered, eyes glassy.

"Were there any, um, injuries?" Ricard asked.

Moncharmin's eyes widened. "Liabilities!"

Mifroid glanced at his notes. "So far we have reports of minor ones only; mostly people shoving each other to get out of the theater.

I'm sure you will be pleased to know that no one was under the chandelier when it fell. Everyone was already fleeing the theater."

I didn't know about the managers, but *I* let out a breath in relief. That shattered destruction in the theater was bad enough; now I didn't have to imagine bodies underneath the twisted metal.

Mifroid turned a page in his little notebook, pencil in hand. "With my men handling the fire and the crowd, I believe our first priority must be to determine if this incident was an accident or deliberate. There may be a connection to the individual who stole your money."

My stomach lurched. Did he mean Mother or the Phantom? I didn't want either one connected with this disaster.

"But we were doing what the Phantom wanted!" Moncharmin burst out, eyes wild. "We were going to pay him, why would he—what did he want us to do that we didn't...that we..." He trailed away, staring at Mother.

"Monsieur Moncharmin?" Mifroid prompted, and when that got no response he followed the direction of the stare to Mother. "Madame Giry. Do you have any knowledge bearing on this incident?"

"I most certainly do not," she said, straightening her back in indignation. "And I remind you that I was in this office, with you, during the entirety of this 'incident,' as you put it."

"Hmm." His gaze scanned to me. "And you are, mademoiselle?"

"Meg Giry," I said, and gripped Mother's hand. "If you care to know, *I* was on stage at the time. The entire corps de ballet can vouch for me." I tried to sound firm and defiant, but wasn't sure I didn't come out defensive. He didn't look away, and after a moment I added, "Madame Thibault can too."

That got a nod, a more affirmative-sounding "hmm," and he turned back to the managers. "This individual who has been writing threatening letters—have any of them referenced the chandelier?"

He could only mean the Phantom—who else would be sending letters? But Mifroid had always believed they were merely a prank. How could he change this years-long stance!

"None mentioned the chandelier," Ricard said, and might have said more if Moncharmin hadn't sprung in with, "Accident! It was an accident. Of course it was an accident."

I studied him, trying to understand this sudden shift. I wanted Mifroid to believe that—*I* believed it—but why would Moncharmin— oh, of course. He expected repercussions from the Phantom for accusing him. It was a wasted effort, as the Phantom was surely not paying any attention right now.

"But Moncharmin—" Ricard began, and Moncharmin hissed at him, "It was an *accident*."

Mifroid sighed. "M. Moncharmin, if you are concerned about the consequences of accusing a blackmailer, the wisest course is full disclosure—"

"No, no, that's not it," Moncharmin protested. "It's a heavy chandelier, chains break, I'm sure it was an accident. Now, if that's all settled, let's go on to *reinstating Madame Giry now.*" His volume rose noticeably on the final words.

My heart leaped into my throat. Maybe, somehow, insanely, this awful disaster could actually solve everything. Or something, at least, an important something. I didn't believe for a moment that the chandelier had fallen because M. Moncharmin hadn't rehired my mother—but if the manager believed it...

Mother stared at him for just a beat, and then, as calm as you please, merely said, "In that case, I'll want a contract with some very definite clauses about termination."

"Of course, of course," Moncharmin agreed, his glance darting up towards the ceiling.

Apparently someone else had the same habit I did, of thinking of the Phantom as lurking somewhere overhead. I found myself glancing up too, even though I knew he wouldn't be there.

"Isn't that right?" Moncharmin said to Ricard, who blinked and said, "Er, yes. If you think so."

My fingers tightened on Mother's hand. "So that means—"

"Let's not make plans until the contract is signed," she interrupted me.

I never bothered arguing with that tone, but it didn't have any effect on the excitement bubbling up through me. If the managers hired Mother back—even if they were doing it for questionable reasons, as long as they hired her back, that was all that really counted. We wouldn't have to leave Paris or the Opera or anything. I'd have to tell Christine—and that thought brought my excitement to an abrupt halt, as the memory of all the other crises of the evening resurged.

Mifroid was staring at Moncharmin very hard. "I suggest we return to this subject later. In the meantime, I want to look at the fastenings of the chandelier, and see if there are any witness reports on the man who yelled something about bringing the chandelier down just before it fell. Someone knew it was going to fall before anyone else did, and I want to know how."

"Maybe he just saw it swinging and guessed," I said without thinking. Because he hadn't known it was going to fall; he had told Philippe it wasn't supposed to.

Now Mifroid turned to stare at me. "You are a member of the ballet. Surely you're going to tell me it was your Phantom? Isn't that the favorite story of the corps de ballet?"

I felt pinned in place where I stood, suddenly trapped, thoughts scattering with no ready response to hand. This might be the first time Mifroid would actually believe a story about the Phantom, and I still didn't know if I wanted him to. "He's not my Phantom," was all I managed to say.

"There is no Phantom," Moncharmin said in a strained voice. "No Phantom. No problems at all."

Mifroid's eyebrows lowered in resignation. "Clearly," he said, to either or both of us, and turned toward the office door. "Now then—"

He broke off at the sudden arrival of Raoul de Chagny, bursting through the doorway with staring eyes and unkempt hair. "She's gone! I've looked everywhere and she's gone! You have to do something!"

I sank down onto the chair behind me, suddenly too tired of it all to stand, resigned to yet more complications. Raoul could not possibly help the situation.

Ricard made an apparently valiant effort to rise to the moment. "Ah, Monsieur Raoul, you seem distressed. Perhaps we could—"

Mifroid cleared his throat. "Considering the state of disorder in the Opera Garnier tonight, I am sure many people are having difficulty finding one another and—"

"You don't understand," Raoul interrupted with a note of hysteria, arms flailing out in emphasis, "Christine is *gone!*"

"Do you mean Christine Daaé?" Mifroid asked, brow wrinkling.

"That lovely little soprano?" Ricard put in.

Raoul stared at them both as though there could be no other Christine in the world. Which was about normal. "Of course!"

Mifroid shook his head, murmured under his breath, "I told the comte this was a bad idea..." He straightened his shoulders, evidently taking control of himself again. "Monsieur Raoul, I regret to inform you that I suspect your brother has abducted Mademoiselle Daaé."

I started. How did Mifroid know that? It was wrong, of course, but I could see why someone might think it—but how did *Mifroid* know enough to think it? I didn't like the idea of the police commissaire actually knowing what went on at the Opera.

Raoul looked completely blank. "Philippe? But why would he..." And then understanding visibly dawned in his eyes, hands drawing in towards his body defensively. "No," he said without conviction. "He wouldn't do that."

I bit my lip. He would—but he hadn't. Was it better if the police were looking for Philippe instead of the Phantom? They wouldn't find Christine, and should they?

Mifroid flipped a page in his notebook, apparently consulting a detail. "The Comte de Chagny was at the police station yesterday making very wild threats. Naturally I counseled against any rash action, but it would appear..." He raised his hands, somehow conveying both innocence and resignation. "I suggest you go to the station and file a report. We will do what we can."

"A *report?*" Raoul repeated, voice rising to a note I was surprised he could reach. "No, you have to help me find her! Immediately!"

"I doubt the girl is in serious danger, and I have a fallen chandelier to examine and potentially a saboteur still at large, so under the circumstances, she cannot be my first priority."

How remarkable. Usually it seemed like Christine was *everyone's* first priority.

I felt bad the moment I thought it. She *was* in the middle of…well, a lot of chaos, at least. And it was good, that so many people wanted to help her. She was alone; she didn't have someone like Mother.

Christine was clearly Raoul's first priority. "If you won't help me, I will find her myself," he declared dramatically and stormed out. It was as good as Carlotta might have done.

"I would not recommend…" Mifroid began saying to Raoul's retreating back, trailed off and shrugged. "How much harm can he do?" he said in a mutter, and turned to the managers. "Now, who can show me to the roof above the chandelier?"

I cast a guilty glance towards the doorway, towards Raoul's direction. Silly as he was, he was genuinely upset about Christine and—maybe being worried myself made me sympathetic. Half regretting it already, I got back to my feet. I felt my mother's hand on my arm. "I'll be right back," I promised, and didn't give her time to object before I slipped out into the corridor.

Maybe I could at least stop him from challenging his brother to a duel. I didn't have to tell him about the Phantom; I could just tell him I knew she wasn't with Philippe.

He hadn't got far down the corridor, and turned when I called his name.

"About Christine," I said carefully. "I don't *think* she's in trouble. It's not quite what you—"

"Oh, what do you know about it?" he snapped, and stormed off around the corner.

I pressed my lips together. Why did I keep trying to be nice to this ridiculous boy? See if I tried it again!

"What *do* you know about it, Mademoiselle Giry?" a new voice asked, soft with an Eastern accent, tone curious.

I whirled to see the Persian, leaning against the wall beyond the managers' office with his arms folded. If he had been caught in the shoving crowd, it wasn't apparent. His black suit was perfectly in place, as was his red fez, and his expression was as serene and remote as ever.

"I don't know anything," I said. How did he fit into the puzzle? What was safe to tell him?

"Really?" He stepped away from the wall, paced closer to me. I held my ground, though it took an effort. "Mademoiselle Giry who is not afraid of spiders and keeps her eyes very open does not know anything about Christine Daaé and…our mutual friend?"

"I don't know who you mean," I said, but it was a feeble resistance. How did he *know*? No one knew! "Anyway," I muttered, "I wouldn't exactly say we're friends."

"Perhaps not. So let us simply say that you are concerned about your friend Christine. As I am concerned this evening about Erik."

My heart jumped into my throat. He knew his *name*. That had to mean something! And he was concerned—was that the Persian's place in the puzzle? Was he really the Phantom's friend? Did he frequent the Opera all these years because of the Phantom? "Christine's with him," I said recklessly. "It was backstage. She fainted when the chandelier fell and he carried her away." It was an unexpected relief to say the words out loud, to *someone*.

He nodded slowly. "I thought as much. I could not imagine he would allow the comte to take her."

"Do you think—is she in trouble?" I asked, desperately afraid of the answer, fingers twisting at my tulle skirts.

He tipped his head slightly to one side, waiting a long moment to respond. "I have never known Erik to harm a woman. I have also never known him to react to anything quite in a manner like…" He paused, made a gesture encompassing the Opera and the entire evening. "…this."

Which was just a long way to say that he didn't know. "I have to tell the police," I said, the words heavy on my tongue. "If Christine could be in danger—they won't listen but I *have* to—"

"They will never find him." His tone settled that possibility once and for all…and pointed to an alternative.

"But you can," I whispered, with a new hope. "You know where he is, don't you? *You* could go after them."

"I am afraid I must." He sighed, looking weary. "I recommend, Mademoiselle, that you think carefully before you ever save someone's life. It can be a heavy responsibility." He nodded to me, and turned to walk briskly down the corridor, in the same direction Raoul had taken.

I didn't know what that second sentence meant, but the first—he was going after the Phantom, he was going to go right into the heart of everything, into the center of tonight's story. "Let me come with you," I called after him.

"Absolutely not," he said without breaking step. "The situation is too dangerous."

It couldn't be that dangerous. He wasn't even certain if Christine was in danger. But I stared at that straight back and steady stride and couldn't argue with them. All I said, probably too softly for him to hear, was, "Maybe I could help."

Maybe I could help Christine. Maybe I could help Erik. Maybe I could find out answers to any of the thousand questions I had, now that I knew someone else who knew the Phantom. Maybe I could actually be *part* of the story, instead of doing nothing but watching it.

Or I could go back into the managers' office and sit quietly while my mother negotiated an excellent new contract.

Chapter Thirty-One

Erik would not have claimed that the evening was going well. But it grew worse when one of his alarm bells rang, a discordant note interrupting his symphony. He lifted his hands from the smooth ivory keys of his pipe organ to frown at the jangling bell.

"What is that?" Christine asked from her seat on the couch, breaking a long silence.

"Think of it as a doorbell." It wasn't altogether unexpected. A person can't send a chandelier crashing to the floor of a theatre and expect to get away without any response. Especially not with a self-appointed conscience hanging about.

"Someone else is here?" Christine whispered, and he tried to ignore her newly hopeful tone.

"So it would appear." He stood up from the pipe organ, crossed the room to pull aside a curtain. It hid a door into what used to be a closet. No need to open it to find out who was here; he knew already. He leaned back against the door, close enough for his voice to carry easily to the room beyond. "Good evening, Daroga. Nice of you to drop in."

The response in Farsi confirmed the visitor's identity, and the string of curses and demand for an explanation was as expected as the visitor.

"You don't like my new entryway?" Erik asked conversationally. "Or did the changing placement of the trapdoor take you by surprise? It's difficult to notice something like that in the dark."

"Let me out of here, Erik!"

This wasn't the worst thing in the world; perhaps the Daroga would even be useful, once he calmed down. He reached for the door handle. But before his fingertips brushed the metal, a second male voice came from beyond the door, this one younger. "Ask him about Christine! I want to know if Christine is all right!"

The Phantom went absolutely still. Very unwillingly, his gaze dragged over to Christine.

Her eyes were wide, cheeks pink. "That's Raoul's voice." Of course she recognized it.

He gritted his teeth. "Yes. I know." He drew his hand away from the door handle. He reached for the nearby control panel instead and flipped switches with abandon, to bring light blazing into the adjoining room.

A new note of alarm was evident in the Daroga's voice. "Erik, this is not funny!"

"It is not meant to be," the Phantom snapped. "I thought you might bring Mifroid, Daroga. I'd have forgiven you for Mifroid. You do what you have to do, I can understand that. But him. You brought *him*?"

"I—encountered him above and we had a—shared concern regarding Mademoiselle Daaé so—"

"Tell us about Christine!" Raoul demanded, accompanied by dull thumps as he pounded the wall. "If you've hurt her, I'll—"

"Oh be *quiet*, Christine is fine and she doesn't need you." He pointed at Christine. "Tell him."

She cleared her throat and called, "I'm fine, Raoul. You shouldn't have come." It sounded more convincing than he might have expected.

Not that it worked on the vicomte anyway. "Of course I had to come. I have to rescue you from *him*!"

She slid off the couch, moved closer to the door. "That's very sweet…"

"Didn't you know I'd come?" Raoul said, with a fervent abandon that would have played well in a romantic opera. "I had to—"

"That is enough," the Phantom interrupted crisply. This was *not* an opera, and who had cast the idiot boy as the hero anyway? "I will not permit a maudlin, sappy declaration about your valiant intentions.

Especially since you're doing very badly so far on accomplishing anything."

"If you unlock this door," Raoul said hotly, with more ineffectual thumping, "and face me like a man—"

"But I'm not, remember?" the Phantom growled. "I'm a *monster*, the rules are different."

Some indistinct noises may have been the Daroga shushing or actually restraining Raoul. "Erik, you don't want to do this," the Daroga said, tone sympathetic and conciliatory.

Erik smiled a twisted smile. "No, I am very sure I do."

The sympathy vanished. "At least put the lights out!"

"Don't overreact, you know they're not lethal in the short-term." He could feel his smile growing ever less pleasant. "It ought to be *hours* before the situation is serious."

"What is he talking about?" Raoul demanded. "I don't understand!"

"What *are* you talking about?" Christine asked in a low voice, brow wrinkling.

He hesitated. But what was there to lose? She already thought he was a monster. Let her see how monstrous he could be. "Beyond this door is a chamber with eight sides, each one covered in mirrors. It creates a remarkable effect, an infinity of reflections in every direction. I built it one day when I grew bored. Did I ever tell you that, Daroga?" he remarked over his shoulder, didn't wait for a response. "I felt that I needed some vistas. Even monsters dislike feeling caged. And as long as it's all rather dim and shadowy, it's quite pleasant. But it's a funny thing about the lights in the ceiling. If you turn them up bright enough—and with all those mirrors reflecting and reflecting them—well, then you have the effect of the Dasht-e Kivar Desert at noon. *All* the effects."

"Erik, enough!" the Daroga said impatiently. "Just open the door."

"But isn't this fun?" Erik said with a wild mirth he didn't feel. "Doesn't it make you feel nostalgic? Remember how much the little Sultana enjoyed my chamber of mirrors, back in the rosy days of Mazandaran? It was her favorite way to execute criminals."

That did it. Christine went pale and Raoul started yelling ineffectual threats. Erik crossed his arms, leaned against the door (starting to feel warm already) and kept his expression blank.

It was probably all over now. No way to salvage this, no way to ever convince her that he wasn't all the worst things she thought he was. But why had he ever thought he could, when he had never convinced himself?

"Please let them out," Christine said faintly.

"No. Your pretty nobleman probably has a gun, and is clearly too unstable to be allowed to roam about."

"So leave him in here," the Daroga suggested, "and let me out to discuss this."

"Hey!" Raoul protested.

Erik shook his head once, though the Daroga couldn't see it, and said briskly, "That's out of the question now. I didn't want to fight you, Daroga, but you chose to be on his side and you can't switch allegiance now. It wouldn't be honorable. And you always were an honorable man. Just like Brutus."

"Spare me your melodramatic opera references—"

"Actually, I was thinking of Shakespeare," Erik murmured.

"—and try to be rational for a few minutes! Just what do you think you're going to achieve here? You can't believe you're going to make that girl love you!"

"That's impossible," Raoul said, with a wealth of indignation and assurance in a mere two words.

And Christine…said nothing. Which hurt much more than the Daroga and Raoul's assessment of the situation. Even if none of it was a surprise.

Erik took a deep breath. "I have not yet decided how the story should end. So perhaps our lovely Christine should choose. There are so many…delightful possibilities."

She looked up at him through her long, dark eyelashes, a question on her face. And was there hope too?

"We could just let them both die," he said harshly, watching the hope retreat again. "They die and you stay, with no promises or expectations. That's the simplest option, we just do nothing. Or we could have a more dramatic ending, something truly operatic." He spread his hands to encompass all around them, lowered his voice to a harder note. "Everyone dies."

"Those aren't *choices*," Christine said, hands clenched at her sides. "Either way they die and I just get to decide whether you strangle me like Buquet?"

He might have backed away from the idea, if she hadn't brought up Buquet. So she blamed him for that too? Why not, everyone else did, even if the police had marked it a suicide. He kept his gaze locked on her face, his voice steady and hard. "No, I said something *dramatic*. Did you know they stored gun powder in the opera house during the Siege of Paris? Many, many barrels are still down here. And I know how to light them."

Furious protests arose from Raoul and the Daroga both, but his attention was on Christine's pale face.

"I rather like that option," the Phantom said, tone musing. "It's all just over, for all of us. The hideous villain sends the great marble edifice of the Opera Garnier tumbling to pieces, because the fair maiden wouldn't love him. Nothing could be more operatic than that."

She looked away. "I don't believe you. You love the Opera too much to do that."

"Do not test me." He did love the Opera. But he loved her more, couldn't she see that? If it took destroying the Opera to prove it...

And yet, he thought of the Opera, of his Opera.

He thought of the great dome with shining Apollo at the top, of the marble stairs and the golden pillars and the intricate detail everywhere the eye might land. And the music, the years of music embedded in every stone, hidden in every crevice, the gossamer wisps and invisible wraiths of past symphonies, operas, arias. Surely if he blew the whole place to pieces, all that music would be set free, free to come crashing down around him, and he'd die smothered, drowning, consumed in music.

No, that was only an airy fantasy, a fairy tale, and he knew too much of the world to believe in fairy tales. If he set off the gunpowder, the stones would crumble, the tunnels would collapse, and everyone in the Opera would be crushed, not by music but by hard, merciless masonry. It would be bloody and painful, swift only for the very lucky. There would be bleeding ballet girls, mutilated singers, devastated musicians destroyed together with their instruments. Mighty Apollo would come tumbling down into the street and there would be no music for any of them, ever again.

Could he do that? Really do that? Or was it just a mad threat, just a ridiculous bid to convince her of...of what? The seriousness of the situation? The intensity of his feelings? Or maybe he was still trying to be the monster, to play to perfection the only role she would permit him.

And if she would cast him only in that role, well, that meant the third option he intended to offer was an impossibility—but why not play the farce out to its end?

"One more option left," he said, calmly, coldly, without looking quite into her face. "I let them go. Your vicomte and his new friend leave together, free and unharmed. You stay. As my wife."

Not how he had once dreamed of proposing marriage to her—but a monster must take his chance as it comes.

Predictably enough, Raoul started shouting threats again, but he was irrelevant, what he thought didn't matter.

What mattered was what Christine thought, and the only clues, as he dared to look for them, were her white face and wide eyes, gaze darting about the room as though still looking for another answer.

"Well?" the Phantom said, voice harsh. "Those are the choices. Which one do you prefer?"

"I don't...I don't know, I can't...this wasn't supposed to happen!" Christine burst out, throwing her hands to either side, a desperate note in her voice he'd never heard there before. "This isn't how it was supposed to go. I didn't think that you would—and I never *dreamed* Raoul would—and this is all so...*wrong*, I don't understand it! I just wanted to sing and now...now I don't know what to do." She sank down into the armchair, lowered her head into her hands, brown curls falling forward to hide her face.

"Do you think this is how I wanted it to go?" Erik asked, feeling hollow, empty. "You were supposed to...see me. *Really* see me, past the mask, past the face. But perhaps that was my mistake. I wanted you to see something better in me—when there's nothing better to see."

Christine didn't answer, didn't lift her head.

He took a deep breath, drew himself up and straightened his slumped shoulders. "Very well. I can wait. They can't," he said with a nod towards the chamber of mirrors, "but I can, so by all means, take your time deciding who lives and who dies. Perhaps a little music while you think? I aim only to please, you know."

He crossed over to his pipe organ, almost entirely at the opposite end of the room from Christine in the armchair. A love song might have helped his cause now, but the only music tingling in his fingertips tonight were crashing discords in minor key.

Chapter Thirty-Two

I t should have been easy to negotiate a contract with a management that was suddenly willing to capitulate on every possible point, but somehow it still took ages for Mother and the managers to settle. When I paid attention, it sounded like Mother was being very careful about exactly how everything was worded—and everything was to be in writing. Ricard wrote; Moncharmin nodded a lot. Mifroid had long since left, off to investigate, off to do something that mattered.

I didn't pay much attention. I passed the time sitting on the edge of one of the managers' chairs, trying not to listen for gunshots or screams or falling light fixtures.

I took deep breaths and worked to convince myself that the Persian would take care of Christine, if she was even in trouble—and if Raoul challenged Philippe to a duel, I couldn't imagine Raoul killing anyone—and Philippe surely wouldn't be hot-headed enough to kill his younger brother—so everything would be fine.

I wished I could think of something I could do, but my wildest ideas of running off below the Opera, or trying to chase down Raoul, or…or…it was no good, I couldn't manage to choreograph a single step that made any kind of sense. I couldn't even think of a way to get any answers about what was happening.

I should have run after the Persian while I had the chance. *He* knew where to go; I didn't. Maybe in the morning I could find Raoul, or the Persian, or Christine herself if she went home again. I'd get answers somehow, but tonight, tonight while it was all happening, I could think of nothing to do but just sit here. Barely an audience member, not even a supporting character.

I *hated* that.

Finally Mother seemed satisfied with the new contract, she and the managers signed it, handshakes went all around, and we left the office.

"One could almost believe in a silver lining to every storm cloud," Mother remarked, slipping the folded contract into her bag as we walked down the emptied hallway. This was an extraordinarily rosy view, coming from her, and at any other time I might have teased, or pointed out that she must have wanted to stay as much as I did.

I couldn't concentrate well enough for teasing. "Mm-hmm. I have to get my cloak from the changing room and then we can leave." If I wasn't going to *do* anything, I just wanted to go home—preferably without even stopping, but I couldn't leave the Opera in only my dance costume. All I wanted was to get my cloak and *leave*, to not hang about, painfully conscious of doing nothing.

Mother stopped walking, looking into my face with a hand warm on my shoulder. "I thought you'd be pleased. This means we don't have to leave Paris."

"I know." I hurriedly put on a smile and hoped it looked real. "And I am pleased. Really. I'm glad."

Her expression softened into a more sympathetic concern. "Are you worried about Christine? The Comte de Chagny is not a pleasant man but I don't think he would be foolish enough to—"

"No, that's not—I mean…yes, I'm sure you're right." I started walking again, quickly, as though that would prevent her from noticing what a muddled non-answer that had been.

Mother only walked enough to catch up to me, to put her hand on my arm again and stop me. "What happened to your face?" she asked, with a weight to the words that told me she'd had them in the back of her mind all this time.

My stomach sank. I had hoped to avoid this longer. I might have said someone had bumped me accidentally, while everyone was fleeing the stage, only Mother always knew when I was lying. "The comte tried to drag Christine away from the stage. I tried to stop him. And..." I gestured towards my cheek.

Her eyes narrowed and her mouth set into a grim line. "The police commissaire must still be in the building. We will find him and—"

"Mother, no!" I cried, catching her arm when she started walking again, faster now, no doubt to seek out Mifroid at once. "It's not that serious—I'm *fine*." I was glad she couldn't see the bruise that was surely on my hip from falling into the prop table. She was reacting badly enough already.

"We will not just ignore this. We will report it to—"

"But he's the *Comte de Chagny*," I protested, pointing out the obvious, knowing she must be truly upset to ignore the practicalities herself. "He's rich and powerful and—"

"It wouldn't matter if he was Louis XIV!" Mother said, louder than I had ever heard her before.

"But it will matter to the commissaire," I insisted, heart pounding, head spinning with all the trouble this would cause. "And to the management and—you know what will happen. Mifroid will give the comte some fine that'll be barely pocket money for him, and I'll get fired from the Opera for attacking a subscriber. That's what will *happen*, even if the management is scared of the Phantom now."

Her mouth grew even tighter. "He cannot simply shrug off abducting Christine. Even a comte can't do that. If we report both to the commissaire, he has to take the matter seriously, and so will the management."

I exhaled, blowing my bangs upward. "But he *didn't* abduct Christine. The Phantom stopped him."

Her eyebrows rose. "I see," she said, voice going carefully neutral. "You saw this?"

"Yes," I said faintly, knowing she wanted more, wanting so much not to say anything else.

"Then why are you so worried? And why is Christine missing?"

I squirmed inwardly. How could I say this? "The Phantom... carried her away." That sounded every bit as bad as I had not wanted it to sound.

Her voice continued with its careful precision. "And why would he do that?"

I had thought of telling her about the Angel of Music weeks ago. But so much had been going on—and the story had grown bigger and bigger—and I'd never known how to explain any of it. "Do you remember that Christine had this story her father used to tell her about an Angel of Music?"

Mother's intent, deliberately calm expression didn't change. "Not really, no. But I think you'd better tell me what it has to do with anything."

We had continued walking and were outside the ballet's changing room by now. I pushed open the door, found the inside still lit by gas lamps but deserted of all its occupants, only a scattering of tired-looking costumes left lying about. "I'll just find my bag and my cloak, and when we get home I'll explain."

"No, we are not putting this off." Mother took my arm and led me firmly to the nearest chair. "By the time we reach home you'll have decided you don't want to talk about this tonight."

"I already don't want to talk about it tonight," I muttered, but sank into the chair. I might be tired and frustrated and sick of the whole business, but when Mother got *that* look, it was no good arguing.

The only reason good enough to argue in spite of it all, the possibility that the Phantom could be lurking nearby so we had better not discuss his business here—well, that just didn't seem like a genuine concern right now. Whatever he was doing tonight, he wasn't listening to me.

He didn't track how much time passed. It might have been five minutes, was probably more like an hour, but wasn't long enough for him to feel significantly calmer or even resigned. No telling how this time might have stretched on, but as it was, he was interrupted again by a jangling bell.

"Does that mean someone else is outside?" Christine asked, her first words since he had resumed playing music.

"Don't grow too excited, a bell in that note means someone is by the lake." Too far away to signify any immediate threat. He rose from the pipe organ, moved closer to the mirrored chamber's door. "Daroga, I have an intruder at the lake. Did you tell Mifroid how to get here?"

"Yes," the Daroga said instantly. "That must be him so you had better go see."

"Do you know you talk faster when you're lying?" Erik asked in conversational tones.

"I am not, it really—anyway, *someone* must be out there, your own alarms are telling you that."

"Yes, but that particular alarm has an irritating tendency to go off when an overweight rat runs over the wrong stone." He shrugged. Maybe it was a rat, maybe it was a human, but he couldn't bring himself to care either way. "You'll pardon me if I disregard it for the moment, considering the circumstances. Although I don't know what you think you're going to do if I leave the room, Daroga. If you had found the hidden mechanism to open the door from the inside, you would have used it by now. You are looking for it, aren't you?"

A growl. "Yes."

"Very good, I'd be disappointed in you if you didn't try." He really would be, he realized. He had always thought well of the Daroga. Unlike how he felt about some other people. "How is our fine nobleman handling the situation?"

"I'm dying, you demon," Raoul said, voice hoarse and strained, "but it's worth it for Christine!"

"And I thought opera people were dramatic!" Erik said with a roll of his eyes. "I'm sure you're uncomfortable, but you won't be *dying* for hours. Of course, it's not up to me whether you stay there for hours more or not." He turned to Christine. "Are you ready to make a decision, my dear?   Bring the whole sorry tale to a close one way or another?"

She straightened in the chair, raised her chin and clasped her hands in her lap. "I'm ready to talk about it."

Immediately his guard went up. "I see nothing to discuss." No new options remained, no new storylines to consider.

"But neither of us wanted things to be like this," Christine said, a note of pleading entering her voice. "Why can't we try to find another way?"

"We are past that." Once, perhaps—but all his hopes had died that night on the roof.

"But you were wrong, what you said before," she whispered, rising to her feet and taking a step towards him. "I do see you."

Instinctively he took a step back. "Yes, I found out on the rooftop exactly how you see me."

She twisted her hands together, mouth pulling into a grieved expression. "I didn't mean for you to hear—and I may have spoken a bit...strongly."

"*A bit strongly?*" He barked a laugh. "Would you like direct quotes? I have an excellent memory!"

"I was upset! You were angry with me at the masquerade. And all I was trying to do was find a way to not hurt you or Raoul."

It was obvious who had been the priority. "That worked out *so* well."

"And I was confused," she continued.   "By what I feel for Raoul...and what I feel for you."

His mouth was dry. She didn't—he *knew* she didn't... "You said— I heard you, you said you could never love a *monster.*"

She tipped her head to one side, blinked those wide brown eyes at him. "That's what I told Raoul. And myself. But..."

"Don't *lie* to me!" he ordered, raising one hand, clenching it into a fist when he saw that it was shaking. If he believed her—and it wasn't true—

"Let Raoul go," she said softly, walking closer, "and I'll stay here, and you can be my Angel again."

"No," he said, didn't know if the word meant that that wasn't enough or that he didn't believe her. Both. He backed away a few more steps, bumping into the back of his couch. He steadied himself against it, one hand desperately gripping the cushion.

"I'll be your student again." She paced closer. "Your protégé."

"*No*," he said, retreating along the length of the couch.

"And maybe, eventually, we could try to be...something else to each other." She stopped within arms-length, smiled a sweet and hopeful smile. "Someday."

It was a half promise that he couldn't risk believing. And that he couldn't resist wanting. "You don't mean that," he managed, even as his heart hammered and leaped in his chest, as he tried to crush down the surging thoughts that maybe, after all, this opera wasn't over yet, maybe he didn't understand the libretto after all, maybe he hadn't been entirely wrong before when he had thought that just maybe...

"I do." She reached out, placed her hands on his shoulders, and his every muscle went tense at her touch. "I really do."

She moved closer, lifted her face, he closed his eyes with an instinct he didn't know he had and then her lips were on his, warm and soft. Her body pressed against him, her arms wrapped around his neck. Slowly, cautiously, he dared to put shaking arms around her and wasn't rebuffed.

It was so much more than even the most romantic opera had led him to imagine.

Symphonies rolled out within him, melodies shaped not of notes but of dreams previously unhoped for, of joys thought unattainable. He had thought she didn't feel as he did, that at best she could half-promise him someday—but surely this changed everything, she had to feel this too, how their bodies fit together, how their hearts beat in tune and souls met in perfect union.

After an eternity yet still too soon, she broke away, leaned back, not so far that he had to release her. He wanted to hold her forever.

"Will you let Raoul go now?"

Erik opened his eyes.

In Christine's face he read—nothing. Nothing more meaningful than a cheerful hope, nothing to show any change from a moment before. None of the joy he had felt. And no love.

The symphony he had dared to believe in ended with a sudden, discordant shriek of pain.

He let her go, backed away a step, then another and another until he was around the end of the couch. He sank down to sit on the cushions, held his head in his hands. There was no music now, only an ashen, empty silence.

She didn't love him. And she never would. Not if that glorious, shining moment had meant nothing to her.

She must love that boy very much, to make such a sacrifice for him.

"It is a better option, isn't it?" she said urgently. "You will let Raoul leave?"

"Yes," Erik said into his hands. How could he not, now?

"Good," she breathed. "And then it will be just the two of us, and everything will be all right, just like it used to be, and we'll sing together…"

He couldn't listen to this. He lurched to his feet, moved to the mantle and braced himself against it. What was she saying now? Still something about singing.

He was never going to sing again.

He found the switch hidden in the mantle's molding, and turned off the lights in the mirrored chamber with a click. A second switch and the door snicked open behind him, a rush of hot air against his back. He heard Raoul stumble out, heard the Daroga's soft tread, heard Raoul rasp, "Christine!"

Did Raoul have a gun? Perhaps the nobleman would prove to have some use after all, would give him an exit from the stage and save him from the wrenching, clawing pain of continuing the tragedy of living.

He didn't turn around.

But no bullet came and Raoul wasn't a patient man. Just a useless one.

Perhaps Christine would grab Raoul's hand and run, spare him the necessity of further conversation. No, instead she had to say with a sweet resolution, "I promised I would stay."

Through cold lips where he could still feel her kiss, he pushed out the word, "Go."

He heard blank amazement in her voice. "But I promised—"

"I release you. You love him. Go with him." How many times would she force him to say it? If she protested again, he wasn't sure he had the strength to tell her another time. No—the patter of footsteps, the rustle of cloth, and he knew without looking that she was embracing that wretched boy. Was she kissing him? Probably. Perhaps *that* would mean something to her.

He gripped the mantelpiece so tightly that the carvings pressed grooves into his fingertips. With an exertion of will he lifted his head, turned to face the room, straightened his waistcoat with one tug.

His attention found the Daroga first, standing by the open chamber door. His uneven breathing, already starting to steady, was the only indication of what he had just been through inside.

Erik lifted one shoulder, a 'sorry, but what could I do?' shrug.

The Daroga sighed faintly, and with a rustle of cloth gave a similar shrug.

That was all. It was enough. Another song in a complicated collection, and they weren't going to hate each other over this. Maybe someday that would be a comfort, in the unlikely event that the anguish ever faded enough to make space for other feelings.

Then he couldn't avoid it anymore, he had to look at Christine, as she held Raoul's hand, their gazes locked on each other's faces.

Erik cleared his throat. "Don't forget…to work on the lower end of your range. See that you find a teacher who won't neglect it."

Christine pulled her attention away from Raoul, met his gaze and nodded.

"And…keep in mind our discussion about that aria from Saint-Saens, you were making excellent progress on that one."

"I'll remember, Erik," Christine whispered, and his name was like a stab as it came from her lips.

He clenched his jaw, managed to nod, and had to turn away again, leaning his arm against the mantle, forehead pressed to his sleeve. He listened to the footsteps—the boy's heavy and decisive, hers light and quick, retreating, departing, moving towards the door.

At the last possible moment he whispered, "Christine."

The footsteps halted, hers a step before his.

He cleared his throat once more, feeling as though he would never speak easily again. "Try to remember me…as the angel, not the monster."

A long, long pause, then finally a breath, a murmur: "I'll try."

Footsteps. And she was gone.

He listened to his own heartbeat, loud in his ears. How could it go on beating? One beat. Two beats. Surely it was going to stop, any moment, no one could survive this. Seven beats. Eleven.

Another footstep brought a different rhythm to the world, drew his attention outward again. He didn't delude himself; not even for an instant did he mistake who that was. It reminded him of something he should say. "You had better go after them, Daroga." He was surprised by how steady his voice sounded. "They don't know the way out."

Suddenly this seemed hilariously, hysterically funny, the farce that broke the tension of the tragedy. His shoulders shook, his body convulsed with laughter, until he sank down to sit with his back against the post of the fireplace, until tears of laughter became just tears and he drew up his legs and covered his face with his hands.

Footsteps. Not leaving, approaching.

"Please go," he said, fighting to swallow sobs. "They really don't know the way out. Please, Daroga…"

A hand on his shoulder, a sympathetic press. The hand lifted, there was a glide of footsteps, and he was alone.

Chapter Thirty-Three

Excerpt from the Private Notebook of Jean Mifroid, Commissaire of Police

1 Mar 1881

I am a fool. Opera Ghost stories seemed like nonsense for so many years, I did no investigation. Pieces all in front of me, and I was blind until now.

Why was no one at Opera ever <u>clear</u> instead of <u>melodramatic</u>??

Have opened new case re: trespasser and saboteur at Opera Garnier. Must also investigate disappearance of C. Daaé. My deep hope is PDC not involved.

Erik stood on the edge of the Opera's roof, acutely aware of the pavement thirty meters below. He had somehow survived the long hours of night, locked in unrelenting darkness. As though the heavens had aligned to curse him, even the moon hadn't shown. The hours had ticked relentlessly by, and dawn would break soon. But not for him. Never for him.

The rooftop was where it had all fallen apart. Not the ending—the preceding night, the final scene, had unfolded scores of meters down from where he now stood. But here had been the beginning of the last act, of the hideous unraveling of everything he had been fool enough to hope for. Here *they* had acted out their adorable little love scene. Here he had learned what she really thought of him. It didn't matter that she had tried to prevaricate later. He knew the truth.

If she could kiss him and leave him, she could not possibly care for him.

He walked along the edge, atop the narrow wall lining the roof. It was a stone wall less than two feet wide, the roof to his right, the open air and the wide sweep of the city to his left. Paris was quiet in the pre-dawn. The only sounds were a faint rustling of the wind making music among the trees, the distant clatter of one early cart providing a steady if unmelodic rhythm.

When the sun rose it would be the first day of a new world, a world without her. It would be a world he didn't know how to live in.

He stopped at the front of the building, just in the center, and turned to face the Avenue de l'Opera. This would be madness at another time of day, but now no one stood in the boulevard to see the monster looming above the Opera.

Here was where the ending had begun. Here he could make the final ending. Would she be sad? Would she be relieved? Perhaps she wouldn't even care. Their duet had already come to a close. She was off to explore new melodies, while he lingered here in a lurching, solitary strain. All it needed was one final note, one plagal cadence to bring the whole sad symphony to an end. He did not have to live in this new world.

He ran the toe of one boot along the outer edge of the wall, tipped his foot forward towards the emptiness beyond.

It was a deeply tempting completion, to let go, to soar out into space.

What had the devil said to Christ? "Throw yourself down from the parapet of the Temple, see if your Father sends angels to rescue you."

No angels would be coming for him if he leaped from his temple. He was sure of that much. It would be a leap, a fall, a crash. Pain? Or perhaps it would be too instantaneous for pain.

And after that, after the end?

Maybe a void, a dissolution, an absolute, final end with nothing after.

Something inside him recoiled. He hated his life, hated his very self, and yet some deep instinct rebelled against a ceasing. Something still clung to existence in some form.

He didn't believe it would be a void anyway. Man, in his capacity for love and hate, for ecstasy and agony, for cruelty and compassion, all the depths he could sink to and the heights he could reach for, had to have some grander existence than this brief crawl from cradle to coffin.

So what came after? The Church was clear on the fate of suicides. He wasn't certain he believed that either—though a deliverance from one torture to be handed into eternal torment was exactly the kind of trick life had always liked to play on him. Why should death be any less cruel? And however a suicide weighed in the balance of judgment, already too much in his life tipped him in the wrong direction.

If he could be sure it would make her happy, then he could do it as the ultimate sacrifice. If he could be sure it would make her sad, then he could do it as a way to claim just one corner of her heart, even if it was only in grief. But when he couldn't know which it would be, couldn't know if it would be either, and with the void or eternal damnation whirling before him…

With a sigh, he shifted his weight backwards, bringing his heel down to rest on the stone wall, toes this side of the void.

"And in that sleep of death, what dreams may come?" he said softly. "Thus conscience doth make cowards of us all."

He didn't want to live. But he couldn't bring himself to die by his own hand. So it had always been, or he would have ended things long ago, on other lonely, empty days. Maybe it would have been better if he had.

The breeze blew through his hair and his cloak, wafting with it the scent of baking from the Café de la Paix across the wide plaza. A harbinger of that new day beginning. A warning to the creatures of darkness that it was time to hide away before the light exposed them to the eyes of the curious throng. Time to descend from the roof back into the shadows.

No man lived forever and some day he would have his last note. But not today.

In the morning I went early to Christine's apartment, eager to hear what would no doubt be a thrilling story. I had slipped out, leaving a note for Mother, somewhat uncomfortably—because after all the revelations of yesterday, I knew she wouldn't take well to my wanting to go out. But I *had* to find out what had happened—and then she could lock me up for a week if she wanted to.

The day had dawned gray and I wrapped my cloak around me as I walked along the quiet boulevard, but at least it was light. Everything always seems better in the morning.

I could even smile a little as I walked. It seemed obvious that of course the Phantom wouldn't hurt Christine, of course the Persian would go check and make sure everything was fine, of course Raoul and Philippe would both calm down long before they inflicted any real damage on each other or anyone else.

I had exaggerated the danger, been foolish to worry so much. Foolish also to feel so left out of things?

Well…maybe not foolish about that.

I shook my head, focused on everything I was about to learn from Christine. Perhaps she had even been able to restore her friendship with the Phantom. If that had happened, I would *insist* that she introduce us. Surely a best friend could presume for that much.

I felt a little guilty as I passed the turn to the Place de la Madeleine. I was supposed to attend morning service for Ash Wednesday. I'd go later. Even with all my daylight-induced optimism, I still couldn't face an hour of references to dust and ashes and death, not before I found out for *sure* what had happened to Christine.

I reached Christine's home and knocked briskly at the door. Madame Valérius answered and I said, "Good morning, is Christine here?" as though it were an ordinary day.

Madame Valérius smiled dreamily. "No, my dear, I haven't seen her since yesterday. I think she may have gone away with her angel. Would you like to come in for coffee?"

A weight sunk in my stomach as all my worries came flooding back, multiplied from yesterday. That was over twelve hours now that she'd been gone, since the Phantom had carried her away. If Christine hadn't come home, if she wasn't here, then where could she be? I knew she had stayed away for a week before, but this was so different! The situation was so much more fraught, with a crashed chandelier above, the Phantom so angry, Raoul and perhaps the police looking for her—and the Persian, he had gone to find her. What had he *done*, if he hadn't brought her back?

I declined the offer of coffee and walked away again, not wasting time discussing the situation with Madame Valérius. The woman had always been utterly useless. Nice, but useless.

I wandered slowly down the boulevard, beginning to fill as the day wore on. I was just aware enough not to bump into anyone, trying to think rationally amidst the worried spin my thoughts kept taking. I could not go on doing nothing, there had to be some action possible, at least some way to find something out. I twisted my necklace, wishing for an ally, wishing for someone to talk to about all of this.

If only I knew where the Persian lived. *He* would know what had happened. But I hadn't the slightest idea where in all of Paris he had lodgings, no idea who could know, and the Opera was closed for Ash Wednesday so I couldn't hope to find him there.

I could have gone home, talked to Mother, but I already knew what she would say. She had been adamant enough the night before, and she already wouldn't be happy that I'd slipped out. She had insisted nothing could be done and of course Christine would be fine. I had tried to be truthful when I told her the story, but she hadn't seen the Phantom with the Comte de Chagny, had never quite understood the fascination Christine could inspire. Somehow I didn't think she understood the seriousness of the situation, as though she thought it a harmless flirtation complicated by an innocent prank.

Part of me suspected that she *did* understand, and that's why she concluded her advice by saying that I should stay well out of the whole business. Even at the time I noticed that her gaze kept hovering around my bruised cheek. Clearly whether she believed what she said or not, her chief concern was to keep me out of any more trouble involving angry comtes or the police. It was such a mothering view, and so entirely unhelpful when I desperately wanted to *do* something.

Finally, as a last resort, I went to the home of the de Chagnys. The odds were long that Raoul would have any answers, if he would even see me, but at least I knew where he lived. A bad option was still the best one when I couldn't find any others.

The house was a looming edifice that thoroughly intimidated me. I gazed at its marble expanse for a moment, and took a deep breath. Then I plucked up my courage, reminded myself that the Opera Garnier was far grander, and marched boldly around to the back door. No amount of fabricated courage would get me to that front door. Besides, I wanted to see Raoul, but didn't want to accidentally bump into the comte in the entrance hall. Somehow it seemed like it would be easier to avoid him by going around the back.

At my knock the back door was opened by a housekeeper, a gray-haired woman who looked me over with an appraising eye and did not appear to like what she saw. I had put powder over my bruised cheek so it wasn't that, and I had worn my blue striped dress today, nicer and neater than my lavender one. But some people seemed to *know* when they were looking at a dancer, and not all of them felt the Opera Garnier lent any respectability to the profession. She informed me frostily that the family was not at home.

I dug my fingernails into my palms. Maybe it was just what the servants had been told to say? "Please, Madame, it's *very* important that I speak to the vicomte, just for a moment—"

"It's Monsieur Raoul you're looking for?" she said, eyebrows rising. "We get girls desperate to see the comte now and then, but I hadn't thought—well, men will be men, I suppose."

It suddenly came clear to me why she thought I was here, and my cheeks flamed very hot. "Oh no, it's nothing like that!" Though wasn't it, sort of? One step removed. "It's my friend…"

"Mm-hmm," she said, as though she'd heard all this before too.

I pushed on. "My friend Christine, she—"

"Christine?" For the first time I had caught her interest. "You're Christine Daaé's friend?"

Somehow it didn't seem surprising at all that she knew about Christine. Christine was like that. "Yes!" I said eagerly. "I've been trying to find her—please, if you know anything…"

She pursed her lips tightly. "It's not my place to say, but…Monsieur Raoul and a young woman who did not give her name came in very early this morning. *Very* early. And everyone knows Monsieur Raoul has been making a fool of himself over a Mademoiselle Daaé. A brunette, is she, with big brown eyes?"

"That must have been Christine!" If she had been here with Raoul, then she was all right—and she wasn't with the Phantom—and perhaps I could talk to her! "Are they here?"

She shook her head. "Collected a few items, were out by dawn. Monsieur Raoul told us to inform the comte that they were leaving the country. Beyond that, I really don't know." She smiled, perhaps seeing on my face the suddenly stricken feeling I had, and reached out to squeeze my hand. "I wouldn't worry about your friend. Monsieur Raoul has always been a good sort, and she didn't seem unhappy."

I managed some kind of thanks, which would have been sincere if I had been thinking clearly, and got away with the minimum of courtesy. I walked slowly out towards the gates, trying to get a hold of that relief and cheer I'd felt just a moment before. This was *good* news. Christine wasn't in trouble; she was with Raoul and I wasn't worried about her with him.

It was only…leaving the country?

I slipped out through the iron gate, leaned against one of the stone pillars supporting it, and wrapped my fingers around my necklace. I stared without seeing at the oblivious procession in the boulevard beyond. It was as though a key support pillar of my life had suddenly vanished, and now everything else was crashing down around it. I had known Christine for less than six months, yet somehow she'd become so integral so quickly, other bits of my life falling away as she became more important. Now I didn't know what to do without her there.

I tried to tell myself it could be a short trip and they'd be back within a week—but back to face Philippe, to face the Phantom? Not likely.

Just a day ago I had thought I was leaving Paris—but I had never expected things to end like this, even if I was the one going. With all the mystery and excitement and unanswered questions of the last few days, the last few months...how could it just end with no answers, no explanations, no resolutions? Not even a good-bye. Just my best friend vanished out of my life without a word, even swifter than a fever might take a little sister.

I swallowed hard, blinked, stared out at the endless stream of life in the boulevard, carrying on as though nothing in the world had changed.

I had been fine before I met Christine. Yet now I felt horribly alone.

Chapter Thirty-Four

E rik did not bother to rise from his armchair when there was a knock at his door. It was not her. It would never be her.

The knock was renewed, louder this time. Erik went on staring at the grinning gargoyle to the right of the door. The ones outside were ominous; inside, grinning. Why had that seemed like a good idea? Why had he wanted cheerful gargoyles? Wasn't it an impossibility, really? What did a gargoyle have to be cheerful about? Lonely, misshapen, rejected…

A creak as the door swung abruptly open and spilled the Daroga into the room with stumbling footsteps. "Your door wasn't locked!" he announced, sounding personally offended on the subject.

"No," Erik agreed without moving. "Apparently not."

"You always lock your doors. You even lock your secret doors!"

"Yes. Usually. I had this strange idea I wanted to stay alive." And what good had years of caution, of struggle to survive, done for him?

The Daroga's tone softened. "So it is as bad as that, then?"

Erik sighed, rubbed a hand across his eyes. It was only as his fingers touched ivory that he observed he had put his mask on. Habit alone. "Why are you here, Daroga?"

"To see how you are." A scrape as he pulled the bench from the piano closer.

"I am terrible," Erik said. "You may leave now."

The Daroga inhaled, a faint breath, and his voice was too kind and placating. "We have both had experience surviving terrible things. Surely—"

"My life has been nothing but a long series of terrible things." The Daroga didn't understand, he had no conception of the magnitude of this. Of the emptiness she had left. "I thought, finally, maybe it was all going to make sense, it all brought me to *her*—and then I lost her too. I am *tired*, Daroga. I am tired of fighting, tired of losing, tired of going on when there's no point to it all." He groaned, shifted in his chair and rubbed his forehead. "Why can't people *really* die of a broken heart? It would be so much easier. In the operas it happens all the time."

"Sometimes it happens," the Daroga said. "Even in life."

"How?" Erik asked, though he had no real hope. "How do they do it?"

"Well…they just stop eating, I suppose," the Daroga said, voice unusually uncertain. Perhaps the topic bothered him. He never did like talking about death.

Erik sighed and shook his head. "No, that's no good, I thought of that already. Deliberately not eating when I'm not physically ill, that's merely a slow suicide. I don't want to *kill* myself, Daroga, I just want to stop living, have it happen out of my hands somehow."

The Daroga sounded oddly relieved. "You see, you know that isn't an answer. People who waste away—they're not thinking, and you are far too aware to let something like that happen."

"To not think," Erik said, drearily and a little dreamily. "What must that be like? I never stop thinking, Daroga. Never. Almost never— sometimes when the music is especially exquisite and it reaches into my soul and it lifts me up to new heights—then sometimes I come to the final note and realize I haven't been thinking at all for the whole piece, just listening. Or playing, if it's my own."

"That's your answer, Erik," the Daroga said, voice growing absurdly lightened, as though everything was going to be solved in this one brief conversation. "That's what's left to you, a reason to go on. Your music, your genius for composing, for playing. You still have that."

"No." He stared at the ceiling, listened to the thousand nuanced tones of silence in these gloomy vaults. Once they had seemed filled with melody. "It's gone. She took it away and I have no music left. It's dead, as dead as I am." He curled his hand into a fist, pressed it to his forehead. "Dead—and I have to keep breathing!"

"You are being melodramatic," the Daroga said sharply. "Life is not an opera, and it does no good pretending it is. You cannot disappear from the stage at the closing curtain, so what you must do is carry on living. A woman left you, fine. It happens. That is no reason—"

"Not *a* woman," Erik said, hearing a dangerous edge enter his voice, feeling a dangerous fury start to stir inside him. "*The* woman. The only woman."

"I grant she is very beautiful, but Christine Daaé is hardly—"

"Don't say her name!" Erik was standing before he noticed getting up, looming over the Daroga. "Don't say her name," he repeated, turning away. "And don't tell me she doesn't matter, that she wasn't important. Don't ever tell me that."

"Erik, this is—"

"Wouldn't it be more convenient for you anyway, if I died?" He stalked towards the piano, ran one hand over the keys without depressing any enough to sound. "If I died nicely and quietly down here, you could stop worrying about that pension still coming to you from Persia. I've always known that's why you never wanted the Ghost to be caught. A sensational news story splashed across the papers—someone back in Persia might start wondering about that prisoner you assured them was dead. The musical one with the misshapen face—oh yes, they might put that together, mightn't they, and you'd have rather a problem."

He could hear the suppressed anger in the Daroga's voice and welcomed it. "Erik, that is hardly the only reason—"

He whirled, jabbing out with one finger. "But it is a reason! You admit that it *is* a reason."

It was a long moment before the Daroga spoke again. "I do not know what you hope to accomplish with this."

Erik sagged. "Nothing. I do not hope to ever accomplish anything ever again." He crossed heavily to the armchair, sank into it again and put one hand over his eyes. "I did not invite you today. Get out."

"I came here to try to help you, and—"

"Like you helped me by bringing that wretched boy?" Never mind that it didn't really matter, that the fault was all his own, that it never, never could have worked. He couldn't ignore all that for long, but for a brief space—yes, it would be so easy, so comfortable, to blame someone else for just a short while. He lifted his hand, stared hard at the Daroga. "I forgave you for that in the moment, true, but I suggest you get out before I start dwelling for too long on that particular plot twist of our little opera."

The Daroga must have read something in his face. Even with a mask on, it could be terrible. He rose in a faint rustle of cloth. "I see I won't be accomplishing anything today," he said, with admirable control in his voice. "Until next time, then."

Next time? What next time, he was throwing him out under oblique threat of death. That allowed for no next time. The Daroga got all the way to the door before that suddenly seemed just a touch appalling.

"Fezzes aren't even Persian, you know," Erik said abruptly, an odd, hostile-sounding peace offering.

The Daroga's voice lightened, just a fraction, as he said for what was at least the fifth time they'd had this conversation, "I know that and you know that, but I will keep wearing it until anyone else at the Opera realizes it."

"They won't." The East was all one amorphous mass to the Company. Unsophisticated, incurious, blind fools, unable to look past the narrow stage and the empty tales they played out upon it.

"Perhaps. Perhaps not," the Daroga said, as he always did, and stepped out the door.

Silence and solitude, once again.

The Daroga hadn't put the piano bench back into place. Erik contemplated it for a moment without moving, then turned his head and resumed staring at his gargoyle.

I had a letter Monday afternoon. I stared at the envelope in our letterbox, recognizing the handwriting at once.

For nearly a week, since the disaster of the previous Tuesday, I had been able to learn nothing. No word from Christine, no sign of the Phantom or the Persian, not even any rumors at the Opera when rehearsals resumed—well, rumors aplenty, but nothing with the slightest ring of truth. And now, a letter.

I dropped my bag onto the paving stones and slid a fingernail below the flap of the envelope, tearing it open with anxious eagerness—not too quickly to not notice that the envelope was very thin. Still, a letter was a letter, and in all the worried flutters I'd been having, I hadn't dared hope for even that much.

I fumbled the envelope open at last and pulled out a single sheet of paper.

My dear Meg, just a note to tell you that I am safe and well and leaving Paris with Raoul to be married. I do not know when or if we shall return, but until we see each other again, know that I will always remember you as my true friend.

Christine

I sat slowly down on the shaded doorstep and read through the note a second and a third time, as if it might tell me more on repeated viewings. She was well and she was leaving and that was all.

I told myself that she must have written in a hurry, that she couldn't give me an address to write back to because she didn't know where she'd be yet, that surely she'd write again soon when she and Raoul were more settled.

This couldn't really be it, because surely a friend deserved something more than a two-sentence good-bye.

Excerpt from the Private Notebook of Jean Mifroid, Commissaire of Police

7 Mar 1881

Attempted call on PDC today. Housekeeper reports PDC and RDC not home since Thu, did not think to contact police. Idiot woman. No one has seen PDC since just before chandelier fell. <u>Connection?</u>

Wednesday morning, I walked towards the Opera with the firm determination that I was simply not going to think about Christine, or ghosts, or chandeliers. I thought very hard about dancing, Venice and macaroons, all the way until I turned the corner onto the Boulevard des Capucines and the news stand confronted me.

Blazing headlines proclaimed, **Tragedy at the Opera: Wealthy Patrons and Beautiful Soprano Vanish Without a Trace!!!**

The chandelier had warranted a headline too, but while that article had been an excitable report, it had also been an accurate one that was at least trying for responsible journalism. This was clearly a different situation entirely.

I read the headline three times in a kind of numb disbelief. It was so surreal, part of my life appearing in a newspaper, especially looking like this. I handed over a sou, took the paper, and found the first empty space to lean against a wall and scan the article below the headline. I told myself I wasn't being voyeuristic, that I was a concerned friend genuinely searching for information.

I already knew that Christine and Raoul had disappeared. Philippe had never crossed my mind. I couldn't feel any anxiety about his reported disappearance now, though I wondered what it meant.

And then I did feel anxious as a new thought struck me. Surely my mother wouldn't—the way she reacted to Philippe hitting me, she might have—no, of course she didn't. That was just nonsense. His disappearance didn't mean that.

I was also sure it did *not* mean what the newspaper thought. Unidentified "witnesses" had seen Philippe with Christine on stage, sources "close to the family" reported that Christine and Raoul were romantically involved, and the subsequent disappearance of two brothers and a beautiful woman prompted some very lurid theories.

I winced and hurried past that paragraph. The rest of the article was full of details I knew for a fact were false, or could at least dismiss on the grounds of wild improbability. The journalist did not seem to know that Christine and Raoul had been seen at the de Chagny residence very early in the morning after their disappearance at the Opera, so either he hadn't spoken to the housekeeper or she hadn't shared that.

My heart beat even faster when I found one sentence about a man in a black cloak who had been seen approaching Philippe and Christine on stage. Nothing suggested that he might be connected to the Opera Ghost, or even that this was important; considering the chandelier had fallen at nearly the same moment, one man in a cloak hadn't made much of an impression. I tried to be comforted by the brevity, since surely that was best for the Phantom. My presence at that moment wasn't mentioned.

The article also quoted Jean Mifroid, Commissaire of Police, with the statement, "I wish to assure the good people of Paris that we are taking this matter very seriously, and will be making this the highest priority. I have known the Comte de Chagny personally for many years, and intend to put all powers at my disposal towards investigating the disappearance of the comte, his brother and Mademoiselle Daaé."

I'd never heard Mifroid take *anything* about the opera house that seriously.

I refolded the newspaper, and resumed a slow walk down the boulevard. Apart from the news of Philippe's disappearance, the article had mostly just confirmed that no one else knew more than I did.

I discarded the paper before I reached the Opera Garnier, in some vague attempt to avoid having to talk about the matter. That was thoroughly pointless. I saw six other copies, clutched in other hands,

between the entryway and ballet practice. In the practice room a knot
of girls broke apart at once, rushed over and re-formed around me.

"You were Christine's friend, right?" Liliane said, eyes bright
and voice eager. "What do you think happened?"

"Do you think she really ran off with Philippe and Raoul?"
Francesca squeaked. "Do you think she *would*?"

"Yes, *do* tell us your theory," Jammes drawled in bored tones.
She was not in the cluster around me, standing just far enough away to
project disinterest, while close enough to interject a comment.

"Yes, do!" two other girls said, without a trace of Jammes'
sarcasm.

"I don't have a theory," I managed, shrinking in a little. I liked
these girls, for the most part, but just now they were all staring at me
with the hungry eyes of the gossip-seeker. In the press of people I
couldn't formulate any reasonable answer, some way to defuse this or
to help Christine or the Phantom or just myself by banishing the idea
that I might know anything.

Madame Thibault saved me for that moment, by loudly clearing
her throat and asking if we had come to gossip or to dance.

Obviously we were here to gossip, but we all found places at the
barre to warm-up anyway, and the rest of class was remarkably
ordinary, considering.

I should have fled the Opera as soon as the practice was over. I
did flee from the ballet girls, managing to extricate myself from their
further questions. With a kind of morbid fascination, I couldn't tear
myself away from the Opera entirely. I wandered around the building
with relative anonymity once I was out from among the dancers, and it
took no effort at all to find relevant conversations to eavesdrop on.
Only one topic held sway at the Opera Garnier right now.

Here, everyone was talking about Christine. She was one of our
own, even if the newspaper thought noblemen more important. And
the Opera Ghost kept being mentioned too. The relatively bland "man
in a cloak" of the newspaper story was reported here as a walking
skeleton, which was slightly less mad than it could have been. He *had*
been wearing a skull mask. More than one rumor suggested that the
Phantom must be responsible for Christine's disappearance; after all,

hadn't he been trying to help her career? Clearly he was deeply interested in her, and who wouldn't be, as beautiful as she was?

I walked aimlessly onto the Grand Staircase and down to the landing where the two stairs met before I noticed Commissaire Mifroid at the bottom. One of the boxkeepers was speaking to him, her shrill voice carrying easily. She was telling a variation on the walking skeleton story. Mifroid had that infernal notebook out, and the usual sly amusement at the corner of his mouth was entirely missing.

I did flee the Opera then. I was in no state of mind for an interview with the Commissaire of Police.

He walked along the edge of the underground lake and tried not to admit that it was not very different from walking along the edge of the Opera's roof. At least the cold air over the water was less inviting than the light breeze beyond the roof's borders.

The walls and the silence of his rooms had felt all too enclosing, both too small and too empty without *her* there, without any hope of her ever coming again. Her voice haunted his home, echoes of those few precious hours when they had sung together.

So he had gone out, out into the shadows and the cold and the faint murmur of a nearly-still lake, to walk among the arches stretched over the expanse of black water. Only a narrow ledge along the side provided a path, with deep, chilled water just beyond, reminding him that choices could be changed. He still didn't want to kill himself, and yet...

An obstruction to his path interrupted these morbid thoughts, as he approached a humped shape breaking the even line of the ledge. He frowned, knelt next to it and put out one hand. Water-soaked wood. A small boat, upside-down and half-submerged. A boat normally resided at the Opera end of the lake, used for infrequent inspection tours.

He had considered borrowing the boat when he took *her* below, but the symbolism of Charon and the River Styx felt too pointed. Wasn't that just his fate, to be Keeper of the Underworld, when all he really wanted was to be Orpheus. Not that it ended well for Orpheus either. Why did everyone always *look*? Still, Orpheus had been loved, however briefly it had lasted...

Had she looked back, as she walked away from him? He hadn't been able to bear watching.

He started to push the boat back into the water, out of his path, but as his palms pressed against the hull, he wondered. If a rope had frayed and the boat had floated out here on its own, it should be upright. Nothing on an empty lake could tip it over.

Unless someone had been in it. He recalled with a detached regret that his alarm bell had gone off, *that* night, warning about movement by the lake. The alarm bell he had ignored.

He listened to the faint ripple of the water against the stone, against the wooden boat. Someone who didn't know what he was doing could have capsized easily enough.

The boat had drifted here. The occupant... No one had shown up dripping on his doorstep. Someone might have made it back to the Opera side of the lake; never mind that the boat had wound up much closer to the far side. Or the occupant had never climbed out of the lake at all.

Not wanting to live next to stagnant water, he had made sure the Opera's original construction included a slow but steady flow between the lake and the Seine. After a week, anything sunk in the lake was gone by now.

More ghosts to haunt his domain. It had been much simpler when he was the only one, when wretched memories weren't taking up so much space.

Perhaps he should go up to the Opera and learn if anyone was missing.

The chandelier falling, and a disappearing soprano and vicomte were surely creating even more of a stir up there than Buquet's death had done. The Opera would be alert. Perhaps Commissaire Mifroid was investigating. It was probably a terribly dangerous time for a Ghost to be abroad.

He thought of the deep water, of the open air, and thought that yes, perhaps he would go up to the Opera.

Chapter Thirty-Five

W e were open again for shows Wednesday evening. I could
only guess this was the influence of Monsieur Moncharmin,
who no doubt had been having fits over the revenue lost while we
weren't performing. Men had been at work in the auditorium around
the clock, patching up the damage from the fallen chandelier. It wasn't
exactly back to how it had been, but it was more presentable by now,
even with the chandelier absent.

As the final curtain closed on Wednesday's performance, I
picked up my bag, prepared to hurry back to the changing room, get
dressed and *go* before I could be cornered yet again by someone with a
new idea about Christine. I hadn't told them about my letter from her.
It seemed so—inadequate.

If I had thought it would quell the rumors maybe I would have,
but I doubted its effectiveness for that. They were too excited by the
whole salacious situation, and I was so sick of listening to everyone
talk in excited tones about what terrible things must have happened to
Christine. What horrible things the Phantom must have done to her.

I couldn't decide which were worse—the ones who fell suddenly,
guiltily silent when they saw me, and then stared at me like I might
manifest something supernatural, or the ones who desperately wanted
my opinion on their pet theories about what had gone on.

Either way, I was even more 'Christine's friend' now than when she'd actually been here.

I felt a sudden yearning for Leclair. At least I was *me* there, among people who had never even met Christine.

I made two steps towards the nearest exit from the theater before Madame Thibault came in through my intended doorway, Commissaire Mifroid beside her.

My stomach turned over at the sight of him. I wanted to see him even less than I wanted to see anyone else—but it quickly became clear he wanted to interview the corps de ballet, and while I might have dodged him, I knew I couldn't dodge Madame Thibault. She herded us all together, and he looked us over with a stern gaze. His usual wry amusement was still alarmingly absent.

I sat down on a spare chest near the back, tried to be invisible amidst the crowd of mostly standing girls, and hoped this wouldn't take long.

"As you no doubt know," the commissaire announced, looking us over, "I am investigating the recent disappearance of the Comte de Chagny, his brother Raoul, and Mademoiselle Christine Daaé, as well as any possible connection to the fall of the chandelier. I am seeking anyone with information pertaining to these events."

At once a babble of voices arose. Usually the girls were reluctant about speaking to the police, but not tonight. Tonight the gossip was too good. I ducked my head a little lower, forearms on my knees, and gritted my teeth. It was bad enough that my best friend had left the country, without having to listen to practically everyone else I knew go on about her violent death.

"One at a time, please," Mifroid requested, with no discernible effect on the tumult. Then Madame Thibault glared at us, and everyone fell silent.

I dug my fingernails into my palms and listened to three girls give stories about how Christine and Raoul were *clearly* having an affair, *everyone* knew it, and the comte was *so* upset, and it wasn't a bit surprising that something had happened to Christine, the way she had been carrying on.

I had known, long before all of this, that Christine wasn't exactly popular with the other girls. She was too popular with the men whose attention they were all trying to attract. But I had thought everyone else agreed that she was innocent, likable, sweet. I hadn't expected all this viciousness.

What would they have said if it was *me* that had disappeared?

Through it all, Mifroid kept up an expression of studious interest and nodded frequently, but I watched his pencil and it didn't move much.

"That's all very helpful," the police commissaire said, cutting off Francesca, the fourth girl trying to get her two centimes in, "now can you tell me anything about a man in a black cloak who was seen on stage just before the chandelier fell?"

My stomach, already tight with nerves, clenched harder. I had so hoped that Mifroid hadn't attached any significance to that part of the story. I hated hearing everyone talk about Christine, but at least the stories couldn't hurt her. If the Opera Company started telling the police about the Phantom...

"Everyone knows the man in the cloak was the Phantom," Francesca put in quickly, pushing forward a step in her eagerness. "He probably killed Christine and Raoul in a jealous rage!"

"When last seen, Mademoiselle Daaé was with the comte, not the vicomte," Mifroid pointed out.

"Yes, but of course Raoul went to find them later," Francesca said with a roll of her eyes. "Or why would he have disappeared too?"

That theory actually made some sense to me. Christine had left the auditorium with the Phantom, but then she had left the country with Raoul, so they must have met somewhere. I had been spinning possibilities in my head ever since I got Christine's letter. Maybe Christine left the Opera and found Raoul. Or maybe the Persian, who had refused to take me with him below to the Phantom's apartment, had decided to take the Vicomte de Chagny instead. They had both walked away in the same direction, at the crucial moment.

I felt sure I would have been of more use.

All around me, the whole crowd was off and running again with their murder theories and their hideous ideas about what must have happened to Christine, to Raoul, what the Phantom must have done. Of course he had dropped the chandelier, of course he had killed Raoul, and Christine, and Philippe, of course this, of course that, blood and death and horrible ideas such as only a lot of girls with overactive imaginations who had seen too many operas could come up with.

Still sitting small and tight in my place, I wished desperately that Mifroid would stop all this chatter. Then I stopped thinking about him, too appalled by the depth and detail of the stories, by the cheerful attitude towards the most hideous notions. It was as if they had forgotten that they were talking, not about characters, but about *people*.

Finally I couldn't stand it anymore, and without thinking I burst out, "None of that's true! None of that could have happened— Christine and Raoul aren't even dead!"

I was angry and defiant and not prepared for how many faces turned towards me when I spoke, their owners falling quiet and expectant. My shoulders tightened in the sudden scrutiny as girls drew back to either side, leaving me in plain view of the commissaire. I wasn't entirely sure when I had stood up.

"You sound certain they're alive," Commissaire Mifroid said, pacing closer. Was this why he was interviewing us like this, hadn't asked Madame Thibault to stop the babbling crowd? Not that he had expected me to speak, but that he had thought someone would, someone who knew something real and would contradict the wild stories. He peered at me closely, pencil ready above his notebook. "Do you have evidence to share?"

I stared up at him, my heartbeat loud in the heavy silence. I automatically thought of denying everything—or of claiming I'd had an angelic visitation telling me they were alive. But what was I even trying to hide? Wouldn't it be better if he wasn't hunting the Phantom for their murders? "Christine wrote to me," I said, hearing an intake of breaths around me. "After she and Raoul disappeared."

"Do you still have this letter?" Mifroid asked, voice tense, gaze locked on my face.

Of course he would ask that. I hadn't shown the letter to anyone except Mother. Not because it was personal—but because it wasn't. No way to avoid it now, so I reached into the bag slung over my shoulder and dug out the envelope I had stuck in there. I handed it to Mifroid, hoping he would read it silently and give it back.

He read it aloud, all two inadequate sentences of it: she was leaving with Raoul, she didn't know when she was returning, I was such a good friend. I could hear whispers all around me, and didn't want to know what they were saying.

The commissaire looked at me over the top edge of the note and asked, "Did this arrive by post or messenger?"

"By post. You can see the stamp on the envelope."

"Mm. So you have not spoken with Mademoiselle Daaé directly since her disappearance?"

"No," I said, throat tight. Would it have been *so* hard for her to say good-bye in person? And what did he think was the significance of that? Not to mention all the girls listening.

"You are prepared to swear that this is Mademoiselle Daaé's handwriting?"

"Yes." I'd carried enough letters from her to Raoul to be sure of that.

"Do you have anything else to share?"

I might have admitted that I had spoken to the de Chagny's housekeeper, but I didn't want any more attention from the police than I was already getting. I carefully kept my gaze on the commissaire's face and said, "Nothing else."

"I see." He folded the letter and put it away in his inside jacket pocket. "You understand of course I will need to keep this as evidence."

"Of course," I echoed, feeling bereft of a note that, up until now, had been distinguished by its lack of meaning. But short as it was, it was the last thing I had from my best friend.

Mifroid nodded once. "Thank you, mademoiselle, you have been most helpful." Unlike the time I told him about the glowing skeleton, he seemed to mean it. "I will be in touch if I have further questions."

The commissaire closed up his notebook and soon went on his way. He was barely gone before Jammes started.

"My, that was such a *personal* letter, wasn't it?" she purred, moving towards me through the crowd with her hips swaying.

"I'm sure she wrote it in a hurry," I said, trying to smile as though I was entirely sincere and unconcerned.

"Do let us know when she writes again. I'd just love to hear more about dear Christine." Jammes exchanged a glance with the girls nearest her. Most of the crowd had already begun to drift away, leaving perhaps half a dozen girls still watching this new drama.

"You might have told us about the letter before," Francesca put in, sounding offended. "We *asked* you."

"It wasn't very much information," I said, a weak excuse and I knew it.

"Oh, of course Meg will tell us next time," Jammes put in smoothly, a rescue I didn't want. "*If* Christine writes again."

"I'm sure I'll hear from her soon." I didn't want to be polite, I wanted something that would wipe the smirk from her face—but I could never think of the right scathing things to say to Jammes until it was too late. I'd be walking down the staircase later and *then* think of the perfect biting comment.

Jammes smiled sweetly at me, ready with a biting comment of her own. "I suppose it's not too surprising really. Christine was always more interested in the Phantom than she was in anyone else."

I just wanted to walk away. To get out from among the staring, murmuring girls, to go home. But that confused me. "Christine didn't intend to get involved with the Phantom. She was never even interested in him." The Phantom was my interest, not Christine's. At least, until he started playing an angel.

Jammes' eyebrows rose. "Oh? Well, perhaps I was wrong. I just remember talking to her the first day she was here. I was with Signora Carlotta in the Singers Foyer, and Christine seemed quite intrigued by the Phantom. She had all sorts of questions about his salary and his influence on productions. And then of course, I assumed she must be talking to you about the Phantom too."

I stared at her, caught on her words about the Phantom's salary, confusion only growing. Because I was sure that Christine and I had talked about the Phantom's salary, in our very first conversation. She had made that mistake thinking that the 20,000 francs was annual, not per month. That was after she'd been at the Opera a few days, and if

Jammes had spoken to her on her first day, then she should have already known that. *And* known that she was in the wrong Foyer.

But of course Jammes had her dates wrong. That was obvious.

Or Christine had pretended to know less, so that I would tell her more.

"Why, Meg dear, you look quite shaken," Jammes said in tones of concern that I didn't believe in the slightest.

I tightened my lips and lifted my chin. Letting them *see* I was upset made it so much worse. "I'd rather not discuss Christine, thank you," I managed, and walked away with whatever dignity I could still muster.

I walked steadily enough, but my thoughts were whirling. I was just being silly. And yet…it made a kind of sense, that someone who wanted to know more about the Phantom would choose the daughter of the Phantom's boxkeeper for a friend. What else was there about me to set me apart from all the rest of the pretty, talented corps de ballet?

Christine hadn't really sought me out for a friend at all, come to think of it, we had literally bumped into each other…directly outside of Box Five. And again in the Dance Foyer, where Christine wasn't even supposed to be, right after she could have easily overheard my mother telling me to go there.

No, this was nonsense—why would she want to know more about the Phantom? Unless she was thinking that someone with an annual salary of a quarter of a million francs and a keen interest in the Opera was the kind of person an aspiring prima donna ought to know.

I toyed with my necklace, stared at a grinning satyr in the gold decorations overhead. I *knew* this was mere paranoia. Christine was my friend, I knew who she was, and none of this made sense. Just like that trip she took up to the roof at the masquerade had never made any sense.

I needed space, somewhere to think. I stopped at a crossing of corridors, both busy with members of the Company rushing about in the aftermath of the performance. I couldn't leave the Opera in my dance costume, but I also couldn't face the changing room and its crowd of girls at this moment. No quiet could be found backstage, the auditorium was still busy with guests, and people were all over the nearby rooms, the Foyers, the Grand Staircase. Nowhere was empty of people—except one place.

No one was ever in Box Five.

Chapter Thirty-Six

M other found me an hour later, curled into my blue cloak and a red velvet seat in the Phantom's box. She fell back a step as I lifted my head above the seat's back, then exhaled when I pulled my hood down to reveal my face and hair. "Goodness, Meg, you startled me. What are you doing in here?"

"Thinking." I hadn't got anywhere. I knew it was ridiculous to question that Christine and I had been friends, to assign complicated ulterior motives to her actions—and I would have felt entirely confident about that, if she hadn't abandoned me with nothing but a two-sentence letter. But putting it like that was telling the story as though it was all about me, when obviously it wasn't and never had been.

"Couldn't you find a less gloomy place to think?" She strode across the box to the small shelf at the front. I saw the tiniest pause before she reached to pick up the program. An untouched program. No envelope from the Phantom.

"He didn't come," I said, which was only what we were both thinking said aloud. I hadn't thought he would be here after the performance ended, or I never would have come—but it had given me a new pang when I entered to see that he hadn't been here at all.

"That is not unusual." Mother swept the program into her bag with her typical efficiency. "Under the circumstances, it's only to be expected."

"Maybe he'll be back for the next performance." Maybe then, despite Christine being gone, the world might start to feel more normal again—though even I could see how strange it was to deem ghostly visitations a sign of normalcy.

"Or maybe he's left the Opera," Mother said. Her face looked reluctant but stoic, as though voicing an unpleasant truth that duty demands.

It was not a truth I was prepared to face. "Maybe for a while." Not forever. What would the Opera be, without the Phantom? And how could he exist anywhere else? I had never imagined the Phantom outside the Opera Garnier, even before I knew that his distorted face might be keeping him here. It didn't matter—this was where he *belonged*.

Mother sat down in the seat next to me, looked me in the face. "You must realize there's another possibility as well."

I widened my eyes. "I don't know what you mean." But I did.

She tightened her lips, said with careful calm, "It is possible the Phantom is dead."

"Don't say that," I said instantly, something inside me curling away from that possibility. That idea was harder to think of than of him leaving, and even that seemed impossible.

She went on, inexorable. "We know Christine and Raoul left together; how do you imagine that came about?"

We had talked about this already, in the intervening week, and I had had to reluctantly admit that, whatever had happened, the Phantom couldn't have been happy and eager to let Christine leave with Raoul. "Maybe the Persian brought Christine back to the surface—maybe she talked to the Phantom, made him understand she wanted to leave—"

"Maybe Raoul went to rescue Christine and killed the Phantom."

I laughed shortly. "Do you really believe *Raoul* could kill the Phantom of the Opera?" Impossible. Not that cloaked man who leapt from catwalks and rescued the Opera's girls from threats.

Mother didn't even blink. "With his bare hands? No. But with a gun? Yes. No man is immortal."

I shook my head. Flashes of gunfire and masks passed through my mind, and I wanted to run, to hide, to shove that possibility as far away as it could go. "No. You're wrong." A wild note entered my voice. "He is *not* dead. I don't believe it."

She reached for my hand. "We both know it's a very real possibility that—"

"*Don't say that!*" I snatched my hand away, heart pounding.

Mother stared at me, face creased in concern. "Why is this so important to you? You talked to him *once,* six years ago."

"You just—don't understand!" I flung in desperation, pushed out of the chair and fled Box Five, ignoring Mother when she called after me.

I couldn't explain it myself, not fully. But the Phantom was my proof that the impossible was possible, that strange and extraordinary and wonderful things could happen. If he was gone or dead, then everything magical had gone with him. The story would be over, and how could it be over when I had never had a chance to really be part of it?

Gabi was gone, Christine was gone and if the Phantom was gone too, the world would be too lonely to bear. We might just as well go to Bordeaux after all.

I prowled the Opera, avoiding eye contact and paying little attention to where I was going. The building gradually grew quieter. Many people left, and those that stayed were grouped in the Foyers or the dressing rooms.

Finally I found myself back in the auditorium. By now it was deserted and most of the lights had been turned down, leaving the enormous room shadowy and still. I came in from the back, and walked slowly down the center aisle towards the stage, between rows and rows of crimson seats.

I stopped in the middle of the auditorium, directly below where the chandelier had hung. The seats and the carpet had been replaced, while the ceiling didn't bear looking at, the chandelier still absent. I turned slowly in place, looking at the great empty spaces around me, the golden decorations shining even in the fainter lights left burning now that the performance was over. Everything was quiet and serene while my stomach was in knots and my whole life felt as echoing and empty as the auditorium.

Part of me wanted to scream and scream. When I opened my mouth, though, what came out was, "Erik?"

I had no reason to think he was here. He hadn't been at the performance, why should he be here now? Though maybe now, with the auditorium deserted and dim, maybe now, after all, was the perfect time for him to be here.

"I just wanted to say…" I had no idea what I wanted to say. "…I'm sorry. About how everything turned out. And I don't believe that you meant—I mean, I don't think it was all your fault, or that you did all sorts of horrible things, the way everyone else thinks." I grimaced. That was awful, reminding him that everyone else was hostile. "I just thought you might want to know, that someone didn't believe all of it." Though why should he care about my opinion? The truth was, *I* wanted him to know, with no idea whether he cared about knowing.

I clenched a fold of my skirt between my fingers, looked around the silent theater with my heart pounding. No movement, no sound. "And if you ever wanted, I don't know, to talk to someone…I'm at the Opera practically all the time, so…" I shrugged, hoping by now that he really wasn't there, because he'd be sure to think I was a complete idiot.

I shook my head and gave up, turning my back to the stage and beginning the long walk up the aisle to the exit.

"Wait."

His voice was low and cold, identity unmistakable even in that single syllable.

I froze, heart jumping to a faster tempo. I *knew* he couldn't be dead.

I turned slowly back around, to see him exactly where I had expected he would be, standing at the balustrade of Box Five. The black was unrelenting today, from the long cloak to the mask that covered all of his face, except for his eyes and a squared-off notch revealing his mouth and chin.

"How do you know my name?" he asked, cold as marble, and I couldn't tell if his voice seemed to fill the room because of the silence or because he was deliberately projecting it.

I was so occupied listening to the tone that I nearly missed the content. "I...saw it on a letter. One that Christine had."

He flinched when I said her name, eyes momentarily closing. He opened them again and nodded curtly. "I see."

He stared at me for a long, long moment. I could see almost nothing of his expression behind this mask, only the flat line of his mouth, supplemented by the tense set of his shoulders. I was suddenly conscious for the first time in an hour that I was still wearing my dance outfit, with only my blue cloak over it—the cloak that, oddly enough, he had paid for, out of those extra francs left in Box Five just after Buquet's death. I wanted to twitch the cloak farther closed but that would just draw more attention and—and what a ridiculous thing to be thinking of, I should think of something to *say* but my mind was so full of things that I couldn't find anything coherent at all, could only stare back at him as he stared at me.

He too was silent, and we stood like that for so long that I was beginning to think this was all there was going to be, that he was going to fade back into the shadows without another word, when finally he asked, "Do you have a habit of talking to ghosts?"

My tumult of thoughts steadied with something to focus on, and I even dared the smallest of smiles. "You're the only ghost I know." Though it could hardly be said that I knew him. Even if I felt like I did.

He didn't comment on that. Instead he pressed his palms against the balustrade in front of him, pushed up to stand for an instant on the railing, then leaped down to land silently on his feet on the auditorium floor three meters below. The ease and efficiency of it all made it clear he gave no thought to a jump I certainly wouldn't have risked, even with all my experience of leaps in ballet.

I was too impressed to be alarmed. He didn't carry himself like a dancer, and yet there was a fluid grace to his movements that I had rarely seen outside the ballet. I didn't even think about whether I ought to retreat until he had strode along a row of seats and was pacing up the central aisle towards me. By then it felt too late to run—and I was too curious, too eager for this conversation, to want to leave.

He halted a few meters away. No eagerness sounded in his voice when he asked, "Why do you want to talk to me?" Just a flat, direct query.

The answer involved a hundred reasons across multiple years, tangled up with feelings and ideas and instincts that I couldn't even explain to myself. I took refuge in a shorter explanation. "It's just, now that Christine's gone—we were friends—"

"I know."

"—and so now that she's gone…it's lonely." I hadn't admitted that to anyone, not even Mother, but somehow—he wasn't someone to lie to.

His cloak moved as his shoulders shifted in something not quite a shrug, too controlled for that. "Surely you can find some ballet girl to gossip with."

I looked down at my toes, damp palms pressing against my skirts. I didn't want to talk to the ballet girls right now, with all their murder theories. I wanted to talk to *him*. And part of me had hoped that, maybe, he'd want to talk to me. "I thought you might be lonely too," I said softly.

His voice had been cold; now it was like the crack of ice breaking. "I am not interested in your charity."

My hopes cracked too at the harshness in those words, my fingers curling around the folds of my skirts. I was all too sure that what he really meant was that he wasn't interested in *me*. He had learned why I knew his name, and did not care to learn anything more.

If that was the case, why bother pretending? Releasing my skirts, I tightened my hands into fists, lifted my head and snapped, "I wasn't being charitable, I was being friendly. If you are not interested in *that*, then I am sorry to have wasted your time, which is undoubtedly very occupied." I turned and marched towards the door. If he had so little interest in me, I wasn't going to force my company on him.

I heard no footsteps but my own, yet somehow he passed me in the wide aisle as easily as a shadow moving in a spotlight, to stand solid and silent between me and the exit. Apparently he did not consider this obviously-concluded conversation to be over.

I looked at that cloaked figure in my path and swallowed. For the first time my stomach flipped with a different kind of nerves. I could be in a great deal of trouble here.

I reminded myself that he had rescued Marie from Buquet, and that Christine was 'safe and well' according to her own letter, and that after all, I'd never believed that nonsense about blood on the walls anyway. I looked him dead in the eyes, and from this closer range I could see how green they were. I wouldn't stand for nonsense like this from anyone else, so why should he be an exception? "I know ten other ways out of this room."

"I know fourteen."

"Congratulations." I turned to cut through a row of seats towards another door.

"You are not frightened of me," he said with a faint confusion in his voice. "Everyone else is. Why aren't you?"

Lucky he didn't know how shivery my legs felt. But no, I wasn't afraid of him the way everyone else was. And while his tone still wasn't friendly, there was a genuine curiosity to the question. So he was a *little* interested, and that made me want to stop, look back and answer. "You're not frightening."

He made an exasperated sound and I hastened to add, "I've been here for years and I've kept my eyes open and...I just don't believe you're as dangerous as you try to make people think. You never did hurt Christine—"

"Stop repeating her name." The razor edges were back in those words.

"Sorry," I said automatically. I should have known; I'd seen him flinch before. "Anyway, you didn't, and most of the stories about you are—well, it's obvious they're just stories."

"Are they?" He crossed his arms, black sleeves almost invisible amongst the black folds of his cloak. "And what makes you so sure that you shouldn't believe the stories? Everyone else does."

I could have just kept walking but—maybe something was at stake in this conversation after all. I frowned, twisted a bit of my skirt as I tried to think how to explain. "I suppose it's because, when I was small, I met someone who…everyone else said he was frightening and dangerous, but when I met him, he wasn't like that at all. I haven't put much faith in what 'everyone' says since then. I'd rather figure things out from what I see myself."

Another long moment in silence as he studied me, and I tried not to visibly do the same. Finally he just nodded curtly. "Kindly don't spread your theory about me around. It will ruin my reputation."

At that I stopped pretending not to scrutinize him, but he still seemed perfectly impassive, no change in his stance or what little I could see of his expression. I couldn't convince myself that the sentence was a hint of anything meaningful, that he was remembering saying something very similar to me, very long ago.

I could have just reminded him that I had met him once before, that the anonymous 'someone' I had mentioned was no real mystery.

I didn't say it. I was afraid that I would mention it and find out he'd forgotten the incident entirely; I didn't expect it had been as important to him as it had been to me, but it would hurt to have that confirmed. And on the other side, if he did remember it, I didn't want to be tied entirely in his eyes to that long ago memory. I didn't want to always be that crying little girl.

I lifted my chin and straightened my shoulders. "If you really wanted to keep up a fearsome reputation, you shouldn't have been so polite to my mother all these years."

"Evidently that was an oversight." He walked past my row of seats, down the aisle towards the stage. He was up to the third row, nearly to the orchestra pit, before he stopped again. "It may interest you to know," he said without turning around, "I am occasionally in Box Five for some time after performances. I expect I will be on Saturday."

Which seemed to imply an invitation to speak to him then. If a rather ungracious invitation. "It's mildly interesting," I said cautiously, a warm excitement in my chest building despite my best efforts to not invest too much in this. But surely he wouldn't have offered if he wasn't willing to see me.

He looked back over his shoulder at me, and I wished so much that I could see his face, for whatever hint his expression might have given me. No clues revealed themselves in his perfectly calm voice as he said, "You realize, of course, that I'm the villain in this story."

I couldn't tell if I should take that as funny or tragic, so I half-smiled and said, "I won't hold it against you." Then I shrugged, and the same impulse that had made me confess loneliness led me to add, "If you don't hold it against me that I'm only a supporting character."

He didn't agree or argue, merely turned away. He continued his silent walk a few more paces, until he could leap down into the shadows of the orchestra pit—and was gone. I didn't know of an exit from that spot, but I was sure there was no point in going to the edge to see if he was still there.

I sank breathless into the closest seat.

He was not *nearly* as charming as I remembered. But he was just as fascinating. It still felt as though wherever he stood became center stage, still felt as though anything at all might be possible when he was there.

And after all, even if he was off-putting and unfriendly today, he *had* been the charming man who showed me the way to ballet practice—and Marie's rescuer—and the owner of that breath-taking voice that sang to Christine—and even the man who gave my mother the best tips of any subscriber at the Opera. Today had plainly not been his best side and possibly not his worst side either, but it was only common sense to expect that a man who lived under an opera house pretending to be a ghost would be…complicated.

I had been waiting for six years to talk to him. Now that I finally had, I wasn't exactly sure that I liked him. But I was intrigued.

The saga continues in

Accompaniment

The Guardian of the Opera, Book Two

Also by the Author

The Wanderers
A wandering adventurer, a witch's daughter, and a talking cat – what could go wrong? With damsels to rescue, monsters to fight and Good Fairies to avoid at all costs, you'll recognize elements of a number of fairy tales as Jasper, Julie and Tom set off down the road.

The Storyteller and Her Sisters
A retelling of the Brothers Grimm story, "The Shoes That Were Danced to Pieces," the twelve princesses tell their own story here–about defying their father, who hopes to marry them off to successful champions or behead the ones who fail, in order to rescue twelve cursed princes.

The People the Fairies Forget
Let Tarragon, an unusual fairy, lead you through some familiar fairy tales–and introduce you to some characters you may not have noticed. Like the servants who fall asleep in the castle when Sleeping Beauty pricks her finger, or the young woman who fits into Cinderella's slipper but doesn't want to marry the prince.

The Lioness and the Spellspinners
A brooding heroine with a dark past finds herself trapped on an island where she finds the locals suspiciously friendly–and their talk of magical knitting doesn't reassure her.

Find out more on Cheryl's blog, Tales of the Marvelous.
http://marveloustales.com/NovelNews

Acknowledgements

My love affair with this story began when I was eighteen years old –
thank you, Cate and Panda, for introducing me to the madman in a
mask. And thank you, Meaghan, who has been waiting ever since then
for this book to finally be published.

Thank you to all the people who let me wax on about the Phantom and
this story over the…six? seven? years I've been writing this trilogy—if
you remember any conversations like that, I mean you! Thank you to
the Stonehenge Writing Group for all the scenes you read and the
encouragement you gave that, yes, even for some of you who had never
met the Phantom, you liked this story and this character. Erik and I are
grateful—Meg too, but she'd be less surprised.

Thank you especially to Karen, Ruth, Kelly, Jackie, Dennis, and
Meaghan, for your beta-reading and invaluable feedback.

I am indebted, of course, to Gaston Leroux, who began it all, and to
Andrew Lloyd Webber and Susan Kay, who carried it forward so
beautifully. I am grateful to all the men who have portrayed this
complicated character in so many ways: first and particularly, Michael
Crawford, who will always be the voice of my Phantom; Lon Chaney,
Claude Rains, David Staller, Charles Dance, Earl Carpenter, and too
many more Webber Phantoms to name. I am grateful too to Terry
Pratchett, whose *Maskerade* is the funniest book I have ever read, and
whose Christine is surprisingly closer to mine than any other I've seen.

And thank you to Charlies Garnier, for all the inspiration of your
gorgeous opera house, and apologies for making you share the credit
with a masked Phantom. Erik and I both recognize your genius.

About the Author

Cheryl Mahoney lives in California and dreams of other worlds. She has been blogging since 2010 at Tales of the Marvelous (http://marveloustales.com). Her weekly Writing Wednesday posts provide updates about her current writing, including excerpts and updates on books that are coming soon. She also posts regularly with book and movie reviews, and reflections on reading. She has been a member of Stonehenge Writers since 2012, and has completed NaNoWriMo seven times.

Cheryl has looked for faeries in Kensington Gardens in London and for the Phantom at the Opera Garnier in Paris. She considers Tamora Pierce's Song of the Lioness Quartet to be life-changing and Terry Pratchett books to be the best cure for gloomy days.

A Note on Research

This trilogy has been the undertaking of many years, and has involved extensive research into the Phantom of the Opera, classical music, ballet, the Opera Garnier, and France of the late 1800s, as well as two trips to the Opera Garnier itself. For those wanting to seek out more information for themselves, here are some of the sources that were most useful in this adventure.

Burrows, John, editor. *The Complete Classical Music Guide*

Fenby, Jonathan. *France: A Modern History from the Revolution to the War with Terror*

Gill, Miranda. *Eccentricity and the Cultural Imagination in 19th-Century Paris*

Guest, Ivor Forbes. *The Paris Opera Ballet*

Hall, Ann C. *The Adaptations of Gaston Leroux's* Phantom of the Opera, *1925 to the Present*

Hart, Charles, Richard Stilgoe and Andrew Lloyd Webber. *The Phantom of the Opera.* Really Useful Group, 1986.

Kay, Susan. *Phantom*

Leroux, Gaston. *The Phantom of the Opera.* Leonard Wolf, Editor

Lofts, Norah and Margery Weiner. *Eternal France*

Meyer, Carolyn. *Marie, Dancing*

Meyer, Nicholas. *The Canary Trainer*

Moatti, Jacques. *The Paris Opera, photos*

Perry, George. *The Complete Phantom of the Opera*

The Phantom of the Opera. Directed by Rupert Julian. Performance by Lon Chaney. Universal Studios, 1925.

Phantom of the Opera. Directed by Arthur Lubin. Performance by Claude Rains. Universal Studios, 1943.

The Phantom of the Opera. Directed by Tony Richardson. Performance
    by Charles Dance. Hexatel, 1990.

The Phantom of the Opera. Directed by Darwin Knight. Performance
    by David Staller. Hirschfield Films, 1991.

Siciliano, Sam. *The Angel of the Opera*

Schlor, Joachim. *Nights in the Big City: Paris, Berlin, London, 1840-*
    1930

Made in the USA
Monee, IL
13 July 2022

99573877R00197